THE GIFT CHILD

Also by ELAINE McCLUSKEY

Rafael Has Pretty Eyes

The Most Heartless Town in Canada

Hello, Sweetheart

Valery the Great

Going Fast

The Watermelon Social

The
GIFT CHILD

ELAINE McCLUSKEY

GOOSE LANE

Edited by Bethany Gibson.
Copy edited by Paula Sarson.
Cover and page design by Julie Scriver.
Cover image: Mali Tzitrinboim, *Birds on the Bike*, 2022, acrylic on canvas, 22.9 × 30.5 cm. etsy.com/il-en/shop/MaliArtwork.
Printed in Canada by Marquis.
10 9 8 7 6 5 4 3 2 1

Library and Archives Canada Cataloguing in Publication

Title: The gift child / Elaine McCluskey.
Names: McCluskey, Elaine, 1955- author.
Identifiers: Canadiana (print) 20230533442 | Canadiana (ebook) 20230533450 | ISBN 9781773103242 (softcover) | ISBN 9781773103259 (EPUB)
Subjects: LCGFT: Novels.
Classification: LCC PS8625.C59 G54 2024 | DDC C813/.6—dc23

Goose Lane Editions acknowledges the generous support of the Government of Canada, the Canada Council for the Arts, and the Government of New Brunswick.

Goose Lane Editions is located on the unceded territory of the Wəlastəkwiyik whose ancestors along with the Mi'kmaq and Peskotomuhkati Nations signed Peace and Friendship Treaties with the British Crown in the 1700s.

Goose Lane Editions
500 Beaverbrook Court, Suite 330
Fredericton, New Brunswick
CANADA E3B 5X4
gooselane.com

MIX
Paper from
responsible sources
FSC® C103567

To Poppy and Sage

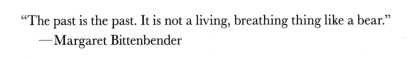

"The past is the past. It is not a living, breathing thing like a bear."
—Margaret Bittenbender

Truth

Most of this book I wrote from memory. Aided by notes and observations. I wrote as truthfully as I could, knowing that my memory is as imperfect I am, a mess of bad clothes and bad decisions and men I should never have trusted. Other parts wrote themselves, and they may be true. They may be life correcting itself. You can decide. Lying runs in my family, and I try not to lie. But truth is complicated. Your truth. My truth. The best truth.

When I was writing this memoir — wondering how many choices I had left, and who I could blame for my existential crisis — I asked myself: *How could any of us survive if there was only one truth? An absolute truth that does not allow for karma, mercy, or redemption? A truth that denies us a guardian angel?* At the centre of this family memoir is my celebrated father, Stan Swim, whom you may have heard of. I started this book with a true scene involving my cousin, the unlikeliest of anti-heroes, and I ended, as I must, with me.

— Harriett Swim

What Happened According to Witnesses

A tuna head. A silvery-grey head with two dull eyes. As big as a forty-dollar *piñata*, as dead as yesterday's dreams. In the basket of Graham's bicycle. Wrapped in a clear plastic bag, a great disembodied reminder that some days were better than others, some days were worth getting out of bed for.

Graham had ridden a Schwinn delivery bicycle onto the wharf in Pollock Passage, population three hundred. Two tuna, word was. Worth a small fortune in New York or Japan. The bite of the morning had given way to excitement — an excitement that could not be marred by worry or the Captain Morgan shakes.

Graham waited until they unloaded the two four-hundred-pound tuna. He waited until they cut off the conical heads. He waited until they hung the muscular fish so that the blood drained the way it was supposed to, not pooling and tainting the taste.

The dead head, the one that ended up in Graham's basket, had been cut clean off at an angle behind the gill plates. It had a large mouth and a pineal window for navigation.

"So, tell me," a man asked on an iPhone video from the morning, "why they give it to you."

"Because Jesus H. Christ was busy."

"Okay, Graham, I was only asking."

"And I was only telling."

Graham was wearing a faded green T-shirt with white iron-on lettering, *Graham* on the back. And on the front:

Fast Cars
Hot Women

That is the last image anyone has of Graham before he was swallowed up by the fog. Vanishing as mysteriously as the UFO that crashed into the mendacious waters of nearby Shag Harbour, leaving a ripple of backward glances for over fifty years. Graham with a tuna head. Gulls circling.

People at the wharf described the scene in detail after Graham was reported missing. While trying out a new iPhone, a deckhand had shot a four-minute video. It captured Graham's flip exchange and his departure with the tuna head. "It put me in mind of *ET*," the deckhand told the investigating Mountie, an officer named Ostapchuk. "When buddy had that alien fella on the front of his bike."

That is how I wrote this scene, from others' recollections. The air would have smelled like kelp. And hard-earned money. There would have been boats all around, tied up so tight that you could hop across them. Cape Islanders painted billiard-ball colours with whimsical names like *Stairway to Heaven*.

If you were a city person like me—a person who did not know that you should never watch a loved one's boat steam from sight, a person who strays off the path when no one is looking—you might occupy yourself by noting names and pondering their meanings. *Aquahaulic. Margarita 2.* Three *A*s in a name is lucky, they say.

You might get lost in their imagined stories.

Pollock Passage is a three-hour drive from Halifax—look for the roadside sign that says *Christ Died for Our Sins*. And the house selling miniature lighthouses.

I cannot tell you if the man who questioned Graham in the video was the resident troublemaker, the local menace who stole dogs, aggravated people, and accidentally set himself on fire until someone stabbed him at a party. Every village has one. Dead or alive. I cannot tell you what Graham intended to do with his prize. I'd like to, but I can't.

In 1979, a man from my hometown of Dartmouth landed a blue-fin that weighed 1,496 pounds. And wrote a book about it. The landing of a tuna of any size is an event. Known for their strength and speed—they have been clocked at eighty-eight kilometres an hour—the bluefin is a formidable opponent with a mystique rich enough to have lured the notable and the notorious to these shores. Ernest Hemingway. Al Capone. Habs icon Jean Beliveau was photographed with a 790-pounder.

Maybe giving the tuna head to Graham was a sacrifice, a ritualistic gesture. I don't know.

All I have is this scene, constructed with equal degrees of truth and probability.

Maybe in a kinder world, a more forgiving world, Graham's days might have played out differently. He might not have vanished.

It was foggy. That I know. And when the fog rolls in, the kind of fog that dampens your hair and reduces your world to square metres, some feel beaten. Others feel free. Free from the need to paint the shed. Free to not appear preternaturally happy. Free to trudge through the half-light the way they want to, knowing we are all one unnumbered heartbeat away from the end. Fog puts things in perspective—the inevitable, the Instagram illusions—and sometimes, fog lets evil creep in like a plague.

RCMP is asking for public's help to locate 60-year-old Graham Swim. Swim was last seen three days ago in Pollock Passage driving a red delivery bicycle with a tuna head in the basket.

His family and police are concerned for his well-being.

Swim is white, 6 foot 2, and 136 pounds. He has short black hair. He was wearing a green T-shirt. He may be wearing a black-and-gold Boston Bruins ball cap.

When someone goes missing, it has deep and far-reaching impacts for the person and those that know them. We ask that people spread the word through social media respectfully.

Anyone with information on the whereabouts of Swim is asked to contact Barrington District RCMP at 902-400-XXXX. Should you wish to remain anonymous, call Nova Scotia Crime Stoppers toll free at 1-800-222-XXXX, submit a secure web tip at www.crimestoppers.ns.ca, or use the P3 Tips app.

—September 16, 2018

What Should Have Happened

Graham rode up a lazy hill from the wharf to the main road. One of his legs did not work properly, but he had learned to manage. A polar bear folding pocket knife was in his pants, picked up at a yard sale for twelve dollars — it was stainless steel with bear graphics and a metal gift tin. Graham stopped a half kilometre down the road in front of a house the colour of wild blueberries. He checked his pocket knife. The fog tasted salty on his tongue. Two vehicles were approaching: a Ram 2500 with a lobster sticker on the back window followed by a Chevy Malibu sedan. Both black. The Ram 2500 pulled over, and the driver squinted. It was so foggy that he and Graham could have been in a Montréal steam bath.

"You look as awkward as a crow on an icy rock," the driver charged. "Let's throw that thing in the back."

Despite his bad leg, Graham moved in a peppy fashion. He moved as though he had been at a poker table of hard drinkers and one drunk had insulted another's girlfriend; he moved like he had to get out of there. After Graham clambered into the cab, the driver noted that the tuna head looked a good size. "Yep," replied Graham, "good enough for me."

The driver said his father had caught many a tuna back in the day when he worked on a swordfish boat. He was one of the best strikers in the fleet. "You had to have a strong arm like my old man, and you had to have a fucken good aim."

Graham said, "Well ain't that right down lovely." And off they went.

1

Nobody knew why my father stole Graham. But, one day, there he was. In Stan's living room in Dartmouth, as thin as a dying birch tree, as coarse as a pair of old wool pants. It was nine months before Graham's disappearance, which Pollock Passage talked about for as long as it talked about the last blue lobster. Then rarely, if at all.

"Hey!" Graham barked by way of greeting when he saw me.

"Hello, Graham."

It was clear, from his clothes and his demeanour, that Graham was not from The City. It was clear that all this—whatever it was—was a bad idea.

"Happy birthday," Graham said.

It was my brother Peter's birthday, not mine. December 12. Peter and I had agreed to stop by our father's house for cake. Just me and him, we had thought.

Peter and I had arrived at the same time, climbing the front steps and entering the house our parents purchased when I was two. A suburban split with three bedrooms, a den, and a basement Peter had once turned into a gym. Out front, our mother had planted a hydrangea, which blushed pink in September, the blooms ending up in a vase.

After removing our boots in the hallway, we sat across from Graham. Uneasy. If you knew my father the way I do, you would understand why. With Stan, you never knew what movie you were in. Was this *Network* or *Willy Wonka*? Our father was occupied in the kitchen. Graham was seated on the floral sofa, directly under a $4,000 watercolour of a shaggy Sable Island pony. He had left a pair of lined green rubber boots in the hallway. There was a hole in the heel of one of his grey work socks.

I had not seen Graham in over twenty years. He was, it later emerged, not exactly who he appeared to be on this day. He was a person who easily acquired questionable friends and questionable nicknames. Slick. Damien the Devil Child. The Missing Link. He was complicated.

Since our mother's death, the house smelled different—it smelled like cooking oil and ennui. Stale stories. On the dining-room table, where Mother had once set her all-white bone china, was a stack of papers. On a hutch was a photo of our parents on their fiftieth anniversary, Stan's arm draped around Mother too possessively, too demonstrably, as though he was proving something. Next to them a photo of a monkey in a straw hat with a chin strap.

I hated that monkey.

Before Peter and I had time to dwell on our cousin's presence, our father, a once-famed broadcaster and personality whose face had graced billboards, entered the room. Bypassing normal conversation, he took the floor.

"I remember this day fifty-five years ago," Stan announced, looking vaguely in Peter's direction as though Peter may or may not have been there. "It was stormy as hell. I was interviewing Hank Snow in the old studio. I got the call that your mother was in the hospital, but there were no cabs." When Stan had an audience, he extended some words, he artfully clipped others for effect.

"Ahhh, yes," muttered Peter.

"By the time I got there, one ear was frozen." Stan was using his on-air voice, the one with the built-in large-diaphragm microphone, wiped clean of a childhood Pollock Passage accent. "The cold, I tell you. Not like today."

Actually, it was just "like today." Cold. But no one bothered to correct Stan who told the same story every year, with him, not Peter, in the starring role. Peter was a bit player, a catalyst. Some years, my father told the story of how baby Peter fell out a window, fracturing his skull in two places, and Stan raced to save him. But not today.

Peter half smiled the way he was supposed to. Graham stared spookily at my brother.

Our cousin was in the wrong seat. Visitors sat in the white velveteen wingback by the bay window. Through the sheers you could see the house where a Mister Shrum, once the cause of a momentous Stan meltdown, lived before the paramedics took him away in an ambulance. As Shrum was being stretchered, my father stood outside and clapped. Shrum's son, an actor who had starred in a morose biopic about a child TV star, showed up late, high, and wearing a checked *gamucha*. When Shrum failed to return from the hospital, Stan scoffed, "I thought that man was too lazy to die."

My father left the room to get the cake. A radio was blaring in the kitchen.

A family is not a liver. It cannot regenerate if a piece is removed. It cannot replicate its cells and reform the extracellular matrix. It will always be altered; it will always be less. We had become a sad little nucleus of three. Stan widowed. Me divorced and underemployed. Peter married with his wife Suzanne up North on a nursing contract. Their son Luke, our family's golden child, was decamped in a place without emotional fault lines. What were we supposed to do with Graham?

There was an insistent buzz around our cousin, and I heard myself saying, to drown out the buzz, "I'm off work tonight."

"How's work been?" inquired Peter.

"Power outage last night and *that* was a gong show."

"It's always out, isn't it?"

"No, that's my condo. I live on the Street of Eternal Darkness."

Silence.

Graham had that old-man-living-alone scent. I could not pin it down to a habit, a condition, or a food, but it was there: as fusty as a barn that had been left to collapse, a wreck of shingles and hay infused with the prints of animals. His face reminded me of Harry Dean Stanton's when the cult actor was old and nothing but hollow cheeks and haunted eyes, skin the hue of a suede leather hat. The personification of sadness.

Stan returned. The Superstore cake was fine. Our father also had a party tray of cold cuts. Graham did not eat anything, not surprising given how thin he was. Graham's plaid shirt was tucked into green work pants tethered to his fleeting frame with a belt. He had a black brush cut—the texture of low-pile velveteen—in our family of dirty blonds. And he sat on the edge of his seat as though he could spring off at any time.

"Are you living in The City now?" Peter inquired, unable to ignore Graham's staring any longer. The City being the generic term for Halifax, which included Dartmouth.

Graham had *heterochromia iridis*—one eye was brown and the other gecko-green. Peter found it unsettling. I found it interesting.

"Yep," Graham yelled, "a cat's jump from here." He yelled so loudly that he could have been at the end of a wharf.

"Is Rick still fishing?" asked Peter, not knowing what else to say.

"Yep, he's still at it. Got himself a new boat. She's all black."

Graham and Rick were the sons of Stan's late brother Maynard, who died young. Until his move to Dartmouth, fully planned and orchestrated, it turned out, by my father, Graham had lived with Rick in Pollock Passage. Before that with his now-departed mother, occupying himself with odd jobs. The arrangement seemed to suit everyone. Our cousin had a "condition" that had, among other things, left one leg weakened. The details were as vague as he was.

"Graham has an apartment at 14 Cavalier Drive," announced my father, who rolled the word "Cavalier" on his tongue as though it was Chivas Regal.

"Is that the building where they had the lobby fire?" Peter asked.

"Yes," allowed Stan, "but they caught her, the woman who was setting the fires. Three different buildings, not just Graham's."

"Ahh," muttered Peter, unconvinced, "that's good, I guess."

"She set her hair on fire, too."

"Wasn't there a drive-by shooting?" asked Peter. My brother was wearing a blue shirt and a pained expression, which was, under the circumstances, past and present, reasonable.

Stan ignored Peter's question. "Being in town is more convenient for Graham's appointments," my father said, making the word "appointments" sound lofty.

Graham continued to stare at Peter.

After our cousin vanished, someone asked if he was my father's biological son. Or his down-low boyfriend. One of the regulars at my job posed the theory that Graham had stumbled across an international coke-smuggling ring on the shore. Did he have a drone? I admitted that I did not know him well enough to have an answer. All I knew about Graham then was that he loved the Boston Bruins and Giant Tiger, which sold *Jimi Hendrix Experience* T-shirts, hunter orange, and all things plaid.

"Too many coyotes on the shore," my father added. "A pack of them grabbed a deckhand from his front yard. One of the Comeaus. All they found was a rubber boot —"

The first time you hear your parent tell a brazen lie in public — one you know is a complete fabrication — and they do it with total ease, total poise, you feel a paralyzing chill. And then you backtrack. It is as though you are writing a novel and four years in, you realize that your protagonist is a boor full of petty grievances, and the plot, the one you had slaved over, is garbage.

"— covered with saliva."

My father, then a two-pack-a-day smoker, once told his listeners that he was training for the Boston Marathon.

He announced that he was going to Russia with international jewel thief Aksel Andersson to recover a stash of hidden gems.

He claimed he owned a Siberian husky named Baba.

He said Mikey, the straw-hatted monkey, was being sent into space.

Graham barely moved. His stillness felt like performance art—he could have been a live mannequin in an alternative store that modish people frequent. The only time he budged was when Stan forced a baggie of leftover cold cuts—mainly mock chicken—on him. "These will last you all week."

And then as we were about to leave, our obligatory visit over, Graham followed me and Peter into the hall and did the most random thing. He kidney-punched Peter. My brother was bent over and putting on his winter boots, and Graham punched him from behind. Hard. Hard enough to hurt. Peter, of course, never saw it coming because it was such a stupid thing to do. And my brother, who was fifty pounds heavier than our cousin, had no idea how he was supposed to react.

"What," demanded Peter on the outside step, "the fuck was that?"

*

My father's theft of Graham, followed by our cousin's disappearance, were the events that sent me on a quest to figure out who We were. And what was wrong with Us. Because there *was* something wrong with Us. These events were the impetus for this memoir. The idea was conceived at a writing workshop where I pitched ideas, and my instructor, after gently dismissing them all, said, "You are Stan Swim's daughter?"

"Yes."

"There must be a story there. Correct me if I am wrong but those people, people like your father, exude a messianic energy, don't they?"

They do. And I would, I decided, write about Us, which included Graham, whose relationship with my father helped explain *Us*. The idea sounded better than some. A fantasy set in an underground world of stick people, a vengeance novel that spanned three generations of Irish longshoremen. Our story, I told myself, could help others on a similar "journey." That is the old chestnut that journalists feed reluctant sources who do not want to air their dirty laundry: Your story may help others. If a reporter tells you that, you are being conned.

I was one of them, a photojournalist, back when newspapers still employed them. Before reporters were armed with iPhones and editors were lifting your photos from Facebook. Before the *Scotia Standard* laid off all six of its photographers, including me, who mainly shot courts and crime scenes, forcing one colleague into "boudoir photography" and another into dog-walking "problem dogs."

In the span of three years, I had lost my mother, lost my husband, lost my job. But I felt safe in the workshop, a judgment-free zone of hopes and quiet obsessions.

"You *could* show it to your father when you are finished," Pamela assured me. "You don't *have* to, but it might make you feel more at ease."

"I don't care. He won't care."

Pamela was an established author who had written seven novels and was attempting to get the eight of us, all novices, on track. She was as patient as the moon.

"There could be surprises in your research," she warned. And then, "One can't write a memoir and float through life on a pouf of blithe indifference."

Pamela had frizzy hair and fine, worn-down features. Years ago, she had thrown herself into her art, choosing passion over prosperity. She wore outsized scarves to hide her disappointment, and she guided us with a sincerity that was equal parts sad and admirable. I had the feeling that Pamela understood important things like tragedy deep enough to change your molecular structure. She recognized the people who stood outside life, tapping on the window of happiness, too scorched or broken to enter. She was also relieved to send me on a mission that seemed, unlike some, half feasible.

"I'm good," I said. "I don't mind surprises."

I had no problem throwing my father under the literary bus because Stan lived his life on the double line. He liked it there. That is where he felt alive. Besides, it is not like he would read my book. He would, if it were published, place it on his mahogany coffee table as proof that I had done something noteworthy. He would position it as prominently as one of his old BBM ratings books by the bowl of wrapped liqueur chocolates, but he would *not* read it.

"Can it be about more than Stan?" I asked.

People already *knew* about Stan, or *thought* they knew. Or knew what they *wanted* to know.

"It can," she promised, "be anything you want."

When you have a job like my current job, working nights at a casino populated by pensioners, you do not take it home on a jump drive. Your time is yours to muddle through a book that might start as one thing and end up as another.

When I started this memoir, I did not know that my research would take me to a minor place warped by the weight of superlatives. *Canada's greatest. The world's most investigated.* Where I would meet a woman who did not know who she was anymore, and a man who may have been lying about everything.

The hardest part of this memoir was, it turned out, the part about Graham. I was good with Stan—I knew what I wanted and needed to say—but it proved difficult, for me, a first-time writer, to find an appropriate tone for someone who just vanished. Someone not like me. Someone I would nonetheless follow down a rabbit hole of lies and family secrets.

2

Days after Graham was reported missing, Stan and I found ourselves at the Halifax cop shop. This I know because I wrote it down. That is one of the things I try to do to stay on track with this memoir. I write things down before my brain alters or deletes them.

When we arrived, teens were being given a tour of the station. They were members of a boxing club, the tour intended to keep them on the right side of the law. All were wearing track suits, one with a Canada flag. And then there was a burst of noise when a cop slapped handcuffs on their coach, and the coach, a senior with a nose broken more times than my heart, exclaimed, "You got me, copper."

The boxers folded in two from laughter.

And the coach added, "A nice gold medal for the copper."

I wondered if the teens had ever seen a James Cagney movie, Cagney who had specialized in sardonic gangsters, but also played a hard-luck boxer who lost his sight. As well as Tom Richards, the fictitious newspaperman who quit the business to become a vagabond. There are days when I try to remember why we all thought it was so important—the news business—more important than sleep disorders or anniversaries. I try to remember what it was like to be that invested in a job one rung below vagabond.

In the waiting room were wickets manned by commissionaires

dealing with people questioning parking tickets or reporting fender benders. One man was wearing, instead of a hat, the liner from a construction helmet.

The boxers moved to another room, taking the levity with them. We were seated next to a man who looked as if he had been on a two-week bender, a ruin of a man reeking of piss and rum, a man who decided to unload his life's philosophy on Stan.

"If I could be born again, I'd be twenty per cent smarter or twenty per cent stupider," he slurred to Stan, whom he recognized. "I am in a fucken no man's land. I'm not smart enough to become a crypto billionaire—I don't even know what the fuck it is. Do you? Does anyone in this fucken room know what crypto is? Okay. Nobody. Thought so. And I am not stupid enough to enjoy the things people like him enjoy." He pointed at a desk sergeant, who was biting a pen like it was corn on the cob.

"Well," said Stan enigmatically, "don't sell yourself short."

"Thank you, Stan," he slurred too sincerely, and then, like most drunks, would not let it go: "You see what I'm sayin', doncha?"

"Of course," agreed Stan, who was wearing his Order of Canada pin.

Leaning forward, the drunk forced his eyes to focus. "I mean, look at him!" Pointing again at the sergeant. Stan turned his head ever so slightly to look.

Stan had been invited to the station because he was the person who reported Graham missing. He had filed the report after Graham did not answer his land line at 14 Cavalier for three days straight. Stan then phoned Rick, who said Graham had been in Pollock Passage but they had not seen each other. Graham did not own a cellphone.

Two days after he filed the report, Stan received a call from a surprisingly forthcoming Mountie named Ostapchuk, who recounted in surprising detail Graham's last-known sighting in Pollock Passage. The Mountie seemed pleased with the thoroughness of his report, which included the weather, Graham's last words, and the weight of the landed tuna. Ostapchuk talked about the iPhone video the deckhand had shot. Stan put the call on speaker for me. I heard the officer report that the red Schwinn bicycle had an extra-large basket to accommodate parcels. Ostapchuk painted the scene so clearly that I could see it. I could depict it at the start of this memoir. A gaunt man on a worn-out work bike that could have once delivered groceries.

*
*

An uninformed officer arrived for me and Stan. He escorted us to a room with a tile floor and furniture in shades of queasy green. It was the green you might find in a rancid bus station where lonely people with red GoodLife bags wait. He barely spoke. He left and closed the door behind him.

I am always guarded around cops. I covered enough trials to know that your fate, the next twenty-five years of your rotten life, can be decided by the twelve people who were too lazy to get out of jury duty. People willing to show up for forty dollars a day. To endure all sorts of trauma. People who, in many provinces, cannot be police officers, firefighters, Members of Parliament, senators, lawyers, law students, soldiers, sailors, physicians, dentists, veterinarians, priests, clergyman, probation officers, or members of a religious order who have vowed to live in a convent. Leaving exactly whom?

Cops have a tough job. But cops are as sneaky as reporters. They are as sneaky as that half-hearted promise to yourself—you think you know where this is going and then *boom*. I tried to stay grounded by studying a calendar featuring police dogs. This month's dog was a German shepherd named Radar.

After Graham moved to The City, my father took him to lunch. He drove him to doctors' appointments. He gave him leftover hockey-night pizza. In return, Graham was expected to follow a set of arbitrary rules that Stan had unilaterally imposed: no smoking, no drinking, no VLTS, no online gambling, all in contrast with how Stan had lived his own life. The parts I knew about anyway. Graham was obliged to answer his home phone before the second ring. This had been the drill for nearly a year.

"Do they know who gave him that foolish tuna head?" demanded Stan, already bored in the little green room. "Who in hell?"

"They wouldn't tell us even if they knew," I whispered.

"They wouldn't tell us if there was a meteorite heading for Earth, a meteorite as big as goddamn Prince Edward Island!"

"*Shh.* Don't swear in here. There are cameras."

"And I would care why?"

The interviewing officer arrived, closing the door behind her.

"Ahhh, hello."

"How are you today? I am Constable Frederickson."

She was a pretty officer who had once ridden a horse. Everyone in Halifax knew her because she was the pretty blond cop on the police horse. Too pretty to be a cop.

I was a pretty blond once. I was, for a time, that girl who got by on her looks. I lived on a carousel of excitement where I stole men who weren't mine and kept them or lost them. There are people who cannot give that up—the one thing they found easy—but I could, and I did. And then I got old, and it did not matter anymore.

"Is that Norwegian?" asked Stan.

"Hmm, maybe."

Not this again.

People who have done questionable things in life often enjoy reliving those things, so they find ways of dancing around them in conversations. They mention a person who got arrested for pornography because they are titillated by pornography. They talk about fires because they like to set them. Stan, as often as he could, brought up Norway.

"I had a producer named Eva from Oslo."

There it was. Eva from Norway.

"Has Mister Swim gone missing before?" the constable asked, getting down to business, and not caring the least about Eva. "For a short time or a prolonged time?"

At this point, Stan and I believed, based on what we knew and what we *imagined*, that Graham was hiding somewhere. A far-fetched theory, but we wanted to accept it.

"No," replied Stan, switching to his on-air voice. "Never."

A lie.

"Not really," I interjected.

"Well, he went to Cape Breton with his friend Slim, but he wasn't missing."

"He was at first," I noted.

"*Until* I found out about Slim."

"But that wasn't until you went to his building, and they told you. Remember you talked to that woman who let you in."

"Mary the Superstore cake decorator. She knew me, of course." This recollection pleased Stan. "Slim works at the shipyard. His wife died. He has three brothers, Hughie the Twin, Kenny the Twin, and Corky, who is a bastard."

Pause.

"Probably good with a can of kerosene," Stan added, "Corky."

"Did you meet Corky?" the officer asked.

"Well, no. Hardly my type."

Sigh.

At first, my father had been miffed because Constable Frederickson did not know him. Over the years, he had interviewed several chiefs. Besides, everyone knew Stan: at the farmers' market, in the tavern where he went for clams and chips on Friday, in Graham's building where tenants opened the door for him and a serial arsonist. Any time my father attended a funeral, he said the same thing: "They were so happy to see me." The family may have been reeling from a suicide or a double murder, riven by grief, and my father's takeaway was, "they were so happy to see me." Stan had an insatiable need to be loved by strangers.

"So how did Graham get down there?" Frederickson asked. "To Pollock Passage?"

"Well, he hitchhiked, I guess," said Stan. "His friend Slim took him another time. Slim's family owns a farm. Organic, I believe."

"Not exactly," I said.

Slim was not from The City *or* Pollock Passage. He was from one of those frayed, faded towns that was trying to hang on, to iron out the wrinkles and darn the holes. A town of ramshackle houses with satellite dishes. Pick-ups with homemade wooden sides. In the downtown was a storefront for the Injured Workers Association, and around the corner a church that put on a ten-dollar spaghetti dinner. A town you could unkindly call a dump.

"Do you know any of Graham's other *associates*?" Frederickson asked. "That could be helpful."

Such a strange word to use about Graham.

"Graham doesn't have *associates*," said Stan, emphasizing the word. "He has me and one friend named Slim, who lives in his building." And then a pause. "Slim is a pipefitter, Red Seal. They all get steady work even though they all have terrible tempers."

Stan had just made all of that up.

"The heat probably."

"Slim is a nickname," I volunteered awkwardly because I had been at the cop shop before, and that had been awkward. "I think his real name is Augustus."

Constable Frederickson nodded. They never give anything away, cops. Not even the pretty ones. Whether they believe you or not. Whether they are on your side or planning to frame you for murder. They listen, they nod, and before you know it you are in The Hole in Renous penitentiary "for your own safety."

When my Audi was stolen and used for two break and enters,

the cops did not tell me that they knew who did it. I did not know until I received a letter informing me that Korey St. Clair Scudder was appearing in court, and I could file a claim for restitution and a victim impact statement. Korey, who parked my car in his driveway, one block from Graham's building. I did—because I was curious—creep Korey's Facebook page. I saw him, goose-necked and greasy, in knock-off Eckō gear, flashing hand signs and posting "Stick my dick in your ear and fuck what you hear." Korey had migrated to Dartmouth from Nowhere, Nova Scotia. His display photo was a selfie in a motel bathroom—he was wearing a ball cap, a white singlet, and, in a pose popular on gangster dating sites, holding an open fan of twenty-dollar bills.

"And you, sir," Frederickson asked Stan, "do you have any *associates*? Anyone we might need to talk to, anyone we might know?"

That word again.

"I don't know who you know, but everyone knows *me*."

"People who could be connected to this case."

My father told Constable Frederickson that Graham had a modest pension that covered his North End rent. He said Graham stayed at his house on nights when they watched NHL games on TV, sleeping in Peter's old bedroom. The West Coast games were especially late. Stan did not drive at night. Some of that was true.

The officer did not tell us if they knew where Graham had been staying in Pollock Passage. Or who owned the red Schwinn delivery bike. Or why they were interested in anyone's "associates."

When we left the cop shop, unsure if we were considered victims or perps, we saw the boxers on the outside steps. Five boys, one girl. I liked the way they looked, loose and tight at the same time, as though they had a long game, and they did not care if you liked it. Because they knew—everyone knew—that boxer George Dixon[1] had come

---

1   George Dixon was born in 1870 in Africville. He was the first Black world champion in boxing and the first Canadian to win a world championship in any sport. There is a recreation centre in Halifax named after him and a mural in what was once Africville.

from these streets, and he was the best in the whole wide world. And how often can you say that about anyone: that they were the best in the whole wide world?

Instead of rushing by, Stan and I paused. The lone girl had the magical glow of youth. She looked like she could leap across a pond or catch a falling star, and when she laughed, she hid her mouth with her hand, as though she had been caught doing something silly.

What Could Have Happened

Stan and I were taken to a cozy room with soft chairs that enveloped us. On the way we passed a runaway wearing a fanny pack large enough to contain a kitten. Her mom was coming to get her. When Constable Frederickson arrived, she knew Stan—she greeted him as though they were old friends.

"Would you like a chocolate biscuit with your coffee? No? A shortbread cookie? We have a lead on this," she confided, "and I need you to trust me on that. Do you think you can do that?"

This is so much better than the last time I was here, I thought. *The time my previous car was stolen. The Acura TSX.* That time I was directed to an officer with scary eyes. Scary Eyes was angry at me for coming in uninvited. Apparently, I had violated protocol I did not know existed. And so, in a shameless show of victim shaming, he attempted to pin the blame on me.

"Did you do anything to anyone?" he demanded.

Like what?

"Did you photograph someone you should not have been photographing?"

Someone stole my car and torched it because I took their picture?

He twiddled a tube of lip balm between his fingers as though it was my life, and I knew there was something there. An unkind childhood. A trauma that had warped his views. An absent father and a neglectful alcoholic mother who had staggered into traffic and been run over by a bus. When I touched my iPhone, Scary Eyes snapped, "Are you recording me?"

This is so much better.

Frederickson gave me an empathetic smile. She knew why I was there. Stan and I left the building happy. Outside, we saw the boxers and their coach on the steps. Stan had a peculiar way of classifying people. He had two categories: people "who had done something in life" and those who had not. If you had gone to war, won a boxing title, or scraped your way up from nothing, you had done something. If you had not, you fell into the miserable group that included his old neighbour Shrum.

We were almost past the boxers when I heard their coach shout with the confidence of a man who had paid his life's dues in ten-rounders: "When are you going back on TV, Mister Swim? I miss your stories."

Stan recognized the coach. He recognized him as a man who had trained fighters for fifty years, a man who had one hundred twenty fights himself, as far away as the Dutch West Indies. And so, Stan replied, as he did when he was dealing with someone who had "done something" in life: "Hard to say, Mister Paris, hard to say. I'm old and feeble, not like you."

And Mister Paris, who enjoyed a good joke, laughed.

The whole business with Graham started three years ago, after my mother died. My father determined that he and Graham shared a passion for the Boston Bruins. The Black and Gold. The Big Bad Bruins.

At first, it seemed harmless—Peter was a Canadiens fan, and I did not follow hockey even when I lived blocks from the Montréal Forum. Graham gave my father a compatriot to celebrate or commiserate with. Stan had a phone plan with unlimited minutes. Every time Zdeno Chára had an exceptional shift, my father phoned Graham, then living in Pollock Passage with Rick, who had promised their mother on her deathbed that he would look out for Graham. As he did.

"Did you see that fight? Did you?" Stan would demand.

"Yeah," Graham would chuckle. "Big Zee flipped him like a mackerel."

"He knocked on the Big Man's door and Zee answered."

And then Stan, who was in the habit of ending calls abruptly, would be gone.

The Bruins were a new obsession of Stan's. For as long as I could remember, Stan had only been a casual hockey follower. This he would deny if you asked him. He was, he would tell you, the Bruins'

Greatest Fan. When one of his former viewers learned of his (fake) lifelong passion for the NHL team, she mailed him a stuffed Bruins bear.

Both Graham and my father were in love with Zdeno Chára, Boston's then-captain, the stern-faced father figure, a man who took a puck to the face and played three games with his jaw held together with metal plates and titanium screws. And shrugged it off as business. At age forty-two. Chára, the six-foot-nine defenceman from Trenčín, Slovakia, known for his incredible strength and dexterity with headlocks. Chára, who could have played a wild-eyed James Bond villain.

Graham's fascination with Chára was self-explanatory. Chára was strong, while he was not. Chára could speak seven languages and Graham barely one. Chára's father, a Greco-Roman wrestler, had instilled in him a rigid work ethic, while Graham had no work ethic to speak of.

I considered lying here. At this point in my memoir, I considered saying that Stan and Graham loved a prettier player, one with better hair. I could have gone to an internet list—hottest players in the NHL—adding the spell of beauty to these pages,[2] but I stuck to the truth. I could have said they loved Sidney Crosby, who is from here and has a nice smile, but I didn't.

All this would have been fine—this aberrant Zdeno Chára worship—if Stan had just left Graham in Pollock Passage. Graham had his own room at Rick's, I later discovered. His own TV (with cable) that he could watch when he pleased. A family dog named Chief that he walked along an abandoned railway track.

It is hard to make Graham's move to The City sound logical, but it happened. As Gore Vidal quipped: "A narcissist is someone better-looking than you are," which is only partly true. Stan simply

---

2 According to people in the know, the only correct answer is Henrik Lundqvist, the (now-retired) Swedish-born goaltender and New York Rangers icon. Proving that life is not fair, Lundqvist has an identical twin who is equally handsome.

believed that everything was about him. Even when he was being helpful. Stan could not imagine that anyone could be taller, sicker or healthier, luckier or unluckier, more renowned or more blessed with the common touch.

And so, in a series of events that no one could explain — no one could tell you when it started or more importantly why — my father, the Swim who had made it, the celebrity who had interviewed astronauts and prime ministers, the only relative with two honorary degrees, a Gemini, a Queen Elizabeth II Golden Jubilee Award, two Hall of Fame inductions, an RTDNA Lifetime Achievement Award, an Order of Nova Scotia, and an Order of Canada, decided Graham "would be better off in The City."

"Why?" Peter asked Stan, days after the kidney punch.

"There is nothing for him down there."

Peter got stuck on stuff, right and wrong, sensible and irrational, while I was more flexible.

"He lived his whole life there," said Peter. "He likes it."

"You try living down there. You try it and see how you like it."

"I probably *would* like it."

"You'd like living in the sticks?"

"Yes, I would. I'd go fly-fishing. I would enjoy the sunrises and have a perfectly peaceful and normal existence." *Normal* being a concept important to Peter.

A snort from Stan. "Well, you and I are different."

My father was used to people not questioning his whims and wishes. My father was accustomed to having a degree of turmoil, a vortex of weirdness and disorder in his life, and when he needed a hit of post-retirement dopamine, he stole Graham. At first, I wondered if he did it just to be disruptive. Stan had always been disruptive. That was part of his job. Or maybe Graham reminded him of Maynard, the family's problematic ghost. Did Stan have unfinished business with Maynard, the sibling he had once shared a bed with? Was Graham payback or penance?

Or maybe Stan just did stupid things that hurt people. Over and over again.

"He could get murdered in the North End," Peter insisted.

"Don't be so foolish," snapped Stan.

As though that never happened.

You cannot blame Zdeno Chára—from all accounts an honourable if forceful man—for Graham's predicament, any more than I can blame Stan for the poor decisions I have made. There have been many. Like convincing myself that my husband, Jack, and I were good when we were not. Like then dating Dante, a stand-up comic who was—justifiably, it turned out—accused of stealing gift cards from a wedding table. His parents were degenerates who gave Dante's nephew a carton of illegal smokes when he graduated high school. When their house in Lower Squirreltown burned down in an early-morning grease fire, they moved into the basement. And *liked* it. That's on me, isn't it? In the same way that Graham is on Stan.

If you think you have heard my father's name before, you have. A personality and a *provocateur*, he was on the air, in one form or another, for over fifty years. The public came to believe it knew Stan—his life story, his pets. The way he wore his hair and his favourite type of cake: fruitcake.

In the nascent days of his fêted broadcasting career, my father was known as Stu Shark, Stan Ralph, and Stan the Man. At one time in private radio, forty per cent of on-air personalities employed aliases, all meant to be memorable or marketable. There was a Doctor Joe, a Captain Billy, and at least one Randy the Fat Butcher.

Occupations can change people, and those changed people glide through life on a Segway of denial or ambition. They wait for the crowd to part. They create their own truth, pliable or bold. As evidence of how familiar Stan's name is, every person in my writing workshop knew it. All eight. Even a woman who was new to the country, a woman who said she had a vivid dream each night and remembered them all, which made everyone envious until she recounted one and it was horrific.

My workshop met for ten consecutive Thursdays. We talked about plots. We talked about settings. Life. Differentiating scene from exposition. The efficacy of opening old wounds and creating new ones. People shared personal stories—it was similar to AA, except we were not trying to talk anyone out of that next 750 ml bottle of Brights fortified sherry.

"I always thought Stan Swim was funny. I remember that time he agreed to be hypnotized for a piece on forensic hypnosis," said Ingolf. Pause. "But not too funny."

Ingolf was a retired Dalhousie University organic chemistry professor attempting his first novel, which was laced with obtuse chemistry jokes no one understood. It takes a rare skill, I suggest, to make biomolecules hilarious.

"I always wanted to know," offered a romance writer, "who did his makeup and if his hair was real."

"It is," I confirmed.

"Okay. I wondered because it looked kind of fake."

"Consider," posited Ingolf, "if you will be contravening any number of popular assumptions about your father."

"I will."

"Ingolf," asked the romance writer, who never missed a chance to ask the professor a science question, "is it true that depressed people remember the negative better than the positive?"

"That is not an organic chemistry question, but yes."

"In one of my dreams," the dream woman recalled, "I was crushed by an elephant. I thought he was lonely. And so, I tried to touch him, and he crushed me."

Have you ever had a dream so brilliant, so healing, so transformative that you wake up happy? And night after night you will yourself to have that dream—you close your eyes, you pray for it—because someone owes you that much, don't they? I had that dream once. A fairy tale of a dream that absolved me of guilt, a dream that convinced me that people I had once known, innocent people ambushed by tragedy, were now okay.

✻

When someone disappears, you remember the last time you saw them. The first time. You wonder—and, of course this is self-indulgent—if they liked you. Or not. You may not have cared a whit before, but suddenly it seems important, their opinion now irreversible. After Graham disappeared, Stan embellished him to make the story more newsworthy. Suddenly, Graham was a renowned axe-thrower (a lie), a dog whisperer (a lie). He had been recognized by the lieutenant-governor for his charity work with injured seabirds (another lie).

Stan and Graham looked nothing alike—their colouring, the way they dressed—so people were confused about how they were connected. When Stan took Graham places, he led him about as though he were a pet poodle.

In old age, Stan had developed a habit of infantilizing people. He tried it with me and Peter. He spoke as though Peter's son, Luke, in his twenties, was permanently twelve and "too busy for girls." Stan talked to Graham as though he was a sullen teen and not a six-foot-two man who had survived for decades without him. If Stan could fool you, through largesse and false proprietorship, into becoming dependent on him, then he had you, or so he believed. You would surrender your free will. You became a poodle on a retractable leash.

Families normalize behaviours that are, in hindsight, not normal. At what age do the adult children figure it out? Twenty? Fifty-two? *Oh! Not everyone has a special "Uncle" Gerry who visits when Dad is at sea? Not everyone has a wrestling ring in the attic? Not everyone has a celebrity father who thinks he is a puppet master.*

Do you have to be facing an existential crisis to see it? After it came to me—the realization that Stan was not right, and nothing had ever been normal in our home—I worried about myself. I worried that I was not right. And genetically doomed.

My father is five-foot-ten but appeared taller on TV. He looked like a soap opera doctor from the eighties. I believe that some people are born with a face or a voice that dictates their job—I cannot imagine Stan doing anything else. Stan's voice was deep but not excessive. It was not that sonorous bass that could only report on military coups or killer cyclones. It was relatable, but you knew it was him.

Stan knew what clothes suited him. Except for a short flirtation with a handlebar moustache, he never fell for trends: textured polyester safari suits with white turtlenecks. And so, he never seemed out of date in the public eye. Just older.

Today I would say that my father was an attractive man. Not handsome—attractive. I don't feel odd saying that because he would tell you that himself. And he did. He would not say the words "I am attractive." But he would label individuals "ugly" or "Jo-Jo the Dog-faced Boy," or "Cement Head," the inference being he was none of the above. When a parent is that critical of blameless strangers, it distorts your thinking. You find yourself joining in, you start doing the same, and then one day you wake up and say, "This is madness."

I remember the first time I contemplated that my father, a celebrity by Canadian standards, may not have been handsome in the pure sense. In the way scientists measure handsomeness, using symmetry and the space between your eyes. Averageness, which humans like because it is familiar. Or in the way my mother was beautiful.

"Your father isn't *that* good-looking," my comic date Dante informed me. "You and your brother look like your mother in her pictures."

When I graduated from photo school, the first school I genuinely enjoyed, I was the tall blond in a field of men. And yes, I *did* resemble my mother, which worked for me. But still I felt defensive about Stan. At that moment, I felt like slagging Dante's family—they looked like basement-dwelling rodents in cheap velour bathrobes with burn holes—but I did not. Dante's comment was, I now concede, innocuous. But I had been programmed to believe that my father was The Best. That was the foundation upon which our family was built. That was our narrative.

"His eyes are squinty," Dante continued. "Gilbert Gottfried squinty."

"It's his *head*," I replied too firmly. "You need a large head for television. Lollipop people, they call them."

"Didn't know that. Should have, I guess."

"Surprised that you didn't."

"Surprised that peanuts are used to make dynamite." Dante pulled a stupid face.

"Stan wears a size 8 hat, which you can only get online," I replied. "In the navy, the biggest regulation hat is 7¾, which tells you something, doesn't it? If you lived in a big city, New York or even Montréal, you could probably find them everywhere, oversized hats."

"I just meant that your mother was pretty."

"Yes, she was."

I sounded snippy.

By the time Graham disappeared with a tuna head, my father was a weary-looking octogenarian. He had caterpillars under his eyes, puffy beige caterpillars. His hair was the pure white of a giant marshmallow, not the jaundiced white of nicotine-stained fingers. He had a pacemaker and a pot belly. He had had his squinty eyes "done" years back in Toronto—he claimed that "the abjectly small-minded brass" made him do it. That may have been a lie.

Stan looked too tired to have lured Graham to The City on a whim. Or as part of a late-in-life childhood reckoning. He looked too worn out to deal with the eventual fallout. But my father could still trick you, and you were a fool if you told yourself that those days, his tricky days, were over.

4

The Halifax police called Stan one day after our visit to the cop shop. Officers were going to Graham's apartment in the North End. Not Constable Frederickson but different cops. We could join them, they said. I was surprised by the offer—it seemed irregular—but I went anyway.

On the way there, I stopped at a McDonald's. A multitude of things in this memoir transpired at McDonald's. None of it was planned. It just happened. At the counter was a bald man with an elaborate tattoo on the back of his head. He was wearing a hoodie under a leather biker vest with lace-up sides, and he was accompanied by a glum boy who appeared to be his son. The man was talking into his Bluetooth. The boy seemed used to being ignored. The man's eyes darted in my direction, as though it was his job to catch me watching him, as though catching me was proof that he was dangerous or thrilling.

I do not care about you, I wanted to reply. *I have seen people die, so I do **not** care about you.*

Just because you love someone does not mean they cannot lie to you, they cannot trick you, they cannot lead you down a garden path of false hope. They can. And they will. I felt like telling that to the boy, but he already knew it.

‡

I had never been to Graham's building before, although Stan had. He had, in fact, found the apartment without telling Rick, who would have objected to the secretly planned move. The building was two kilometres from Stan's house but across a conspicuous social divide, a Berlin Wall of economic demarcation. You went from a neighbourhood of ordinary homes to an area of iffy rentals. There *were* houses, built in the fifties and not unlike Stan's—some even had lake frontage—but they were outnumbered by apartment buildings with flags in place of curtains.

On Graham's street, two overflowing dumpsters gave off a foul smell. A store advertised *Prepaid Cellular*. I saw a magnetic-grey Sentra with one blue door. I saw a Chevy Malibu with darkened windows—it slunk away when the unmarked cop car, a red Ford Taurus, pulled up.

"You won't need to talk," Stan informed me. "I'll handle Starsky and Hutch."

The young cops were plainclothes detectives with badges on their belts. They recognized Stan, and this made him happy. The tall one—his name was Nightingale—had played university basketball. Stan's station had covered his team in the playoffs. Nightingale had the confidence of a man whose jump shot had brought face-painted fans to their feet, fans he towered over and fist bumped when they tried to touch him.

"Do you happen to know a retired sergeant named Crowell?" asked Stan of Nightingale.

"No."

"Ahhhhhhh," said Stan, as though he did not quite believe him. "Surprised you don't." Pause. "One bad eye? You could never tell where he was looking."

"No."

Stan, as often as he could, brought up the Crowells.

Overnight, there had been a stabbing on the street. Police had secured a section of sidewalk. Inside the yellow tape, a trail of blood had turned as dark as a shadow. The four of us, me, Stan, and the cops, walked past the crime scene. The white forensics ghosts had come and gone.

I may have forgotten portions of the visit—I forget things when I am uncomfortable. The event speeds up and compresses. Parts disappear. My trauma-impacted brain works differently than yours. It did seem odd that the cops were putting so much manpower into Graham's case.

Stan believed it was because of Him. Because Graham was his nephew, and he was a man of influence. "The chief probably straightened out Frederickson."

Fourteen Cavalier was a classic four-storey brick building. Most of the tenants were from somewhere else: towns that had lost their mills and mines, the engines of survival. Graham's neighbours came to The City to find work, and the ones with a trade or luck, like Mary the Superstore cake decorator, made out just fine. The others did not. In time, they found drugs and trouble; they got shot or shot someone else.

When I was at the *Standard*, we covered the funerals for towns like theirs. And then, when not looking, found ourselves in the same story: a purposeless cohort, adrift and redundant, one step removed from stealing copper wire from construction sites. Driving a Ford Taurus Wagon with twenty-one Rust Check stickers on the side window. The next low: pilfering catalytic converters.

The super met us in the lobby. He was wearing plaid pyjama pants and ignoring the empty pizza box on the floor. The super gave the cops a rundown of the building—he kept looking at Stan to see how he was doing. Stan gave him a discreet nod. More than anything, the super struck me as lazy. A man content to spend his day in a pleather recliner watching bootlegged porn, as the building looked after itself. Trying to offset that impression, he was "over" engaging.

"I never had no trouble with Slick," offered the super, who called

Graham Slick. The cops had not suggested Graham was "trouble," so his comment was needless. And then the super added, "If they'd been causing trouble, I'd have straightened them both up, Slick and Slim."

I had the feeling that the super had been around cops before. He said that before Slick (Graham) disappeared, one of Slim's brothers had been hanging around. Hughie the Twin lived in a converted cop car, a white Ford Crown Victoria. He had been arrested, the super said, for stunting halfway to New Brunswick. "You can look that up. That would be in your files." On the trunk lid of Hughie the Twin's car was an emblem, *Police Interceptor*.

For a lazy man, the super had a wealth of superfluous details. Hughie started work at three a.m. at a company that made breakfasts for food trucks. At night he side hustled as a prostitute. He used cardboard to block out his car's windows. He had a trial gym membership that he used to shower twice a week.

"I was never overly fond of him."

The detectives did not react at the word "prostitute," ensuring that the super continued to talk. Stan was also good at not registering surprise, a useful skill when an interviewee has started to spill his guts.

As the super was talking, a man in a black Puma track suit came to the door, saw the cops, and left. Detective Constable Nightingale was new enough to the force to not yet understand that this was his reality, I decided. All of it. He still had one size 14 foot in his glorious past. He could still see himself in that skinny kid at the Boys and Girls Club shooting hoops after dark. If you were a homeless person, Nightingale was the cop you wanted to see when you were high and belligerent, not the cop who broke an old man's nose outside a homeless shelter. Not Scary Eyes.

I never did meet Hughie the Twin. But I did see his "police car" parked in a Walmart parking lot and it *did* have cardboard in the windows. I did meet Slim. But I cannot tell you if his wife was dead or if he worked at the shipyard where the pay is good. It may have all been lies. I *do* know that Slim had two stock expressions: "I just needs some time to clear my thinking material," and "go fuck a duck."

Stan had been angry when he first found out about Slim. He thought Graham should have no friends or associates other than him, while he could have as many as he pleased. Stan had a habit of forming intense and unlikely friendships—a Romanian stowaway he interviewed, a radical preacher who performed exorcisms—and then abruptly terminating them.

The only thing Stan demanded of his "associates" was blind, unquestioning worship. Beyond that, the person could be a thief, a liar, or even—and this is more than a rumour—an individual with an unhealthy affinity for the Boy Scouts. Like Robert, who visited Stan to tell him how much he missed him on-air. Robert was five-foot-six and worked at a recycling depot. He drove an electric bicycle and wore a full-face helmet. He was obsessed with Facebook quizzes, the ones that relay your personal information to Russia after you upload your photo.

What Job Were You Born For?

(Insert name and photo) Robert Dooley
Gang Leader. You are a natural born leader that your gang both fear and respect. No one dare challenge you or else.
Can we guess your profession based on your profile picture?
(Insert name and photo) Robert Dooley
Mattress Tester

"I find Robert creepy," I told Stan one day. "He is a little old to be dyeing his hair purple, isn't he? And he will never look me in the eye."

"Are you foolish?" Stan demanded. "Robert has been involved with the Boy Scouts for twenty years."

"*That* is my point."

I probably should not have brought up Robert here, but I am new at this. And, as you may have guessed, I don't really care for Robert.

We proceeded to Graham's apartment on the first floor. When Nightingale opened the door, the space felt like a wasted life, smoke-stained and empty. Stan said there had been a twin bed. A shrine to the Boston Bruins that consisted of a knee-high cement Bruins gnome, a felt Bruins pennant, a Bruins beer mug, a Bruins snow globe, and an eight-by-ten photo of Zdeno Chára, once branded the Scariest Man in Hockey.

"Hmm," muttered Stan. "The gnome didn't walk out on his own."

On the kitchen counter were two objects that told me nothing I did not already know. An empty pack of Pall Mall XL and a brochure from the Jehovah's Witnesses.

What Hope is there for the Dead? asked the brochure. *Death touches every one of us. But does death end it all? Read what the Bible has to say about death.*

Outside, sirens were screaming in the distance.

How was Graham's apartment empty if he had hitchhiked to Pollock Passage? Where were his belongings?

After the cops finished in Graham's apartment, we took the stairs to the second floor. The cops were ahead of us, and Stan was talking — it was rapid panic talking, as though he had to fill the halls with noise, or the walls would see right through him. His volubility a smokescreen.

"I think the Mounties were thrown by the bicycle business."

"What do you mean?" I asked.

"I interviewed a con man who told me he drove a bicycle to disarm people, to appear virtuous. He said you could put Jack the

Ripper on a bicycle these days, armed with a butcher's knife and chloroform, and people would say, 'Oh look at Jack, he's on that bicycle every night!'"

"I don't think Graham is Jack the Ripper."

"Who knows who anyone really is?"

"Well, you said you knew him when you brought him to town."

"*IIIIIIIIIIIII*" — he stretched out the word for emphasis — "brought Graham to town?"

The level of faux outrage was impressive.

"Yes."

Nightingale ducked under a hanging light in the hallway, the way he had been ducking under objects for years. Both cops were doing a good job of ignoring Stan. The shorter cop seemed bored. He had the comical walk of a short man in a long coat.

"You are being foolish," Stan told me. "You sound like your brother, Peter, Lead Officer of the Blame Brigade, 'Constable Peter reporting for duty. Hand over your phones and personal diaries.'"

"Peter hasn't said a thing about this," I whispered.

"Not yet!"

After dragging Peter into something he had no part of, Stan paused long enough to change course. "The Jehovah's Witnesses could have stolen Graham's gnome after they left the death brochure. And that super could be in on it. That man is as shady as late afternoon."

"But why?"

"Why does anyone do anything irrational? That is the whole point of irrational."

There may have been a modicum of merit to that. I stole Jack from a woman named Isabelle. It seemed rational at the time, as rational as anything I have done. We were so besotted, so taken with each other, that we never thought about how others perceived us. We were as oblivious as a pair of Jehovah's Witnesses at your door.

Someone wrote that love at first sight is borne out of need—the need to be nurtured, the need to be taken care of—but that wasn't the case with Jack. I was drawn to Jack in the same way you might be drawn to a lightning storm or a moonlit beach or the most poignant piece of music you have ever heard being played around a corner by a street artist too pure for this world. And was that love or was that desire, and what difference does it make?

The police used the lazy super's key to enter Slim's second-floor apartment. They acted like they did this all the time. Stan and I waited in the hallway, which smelled like sour milk. There was a window on the far wall, and I wandered over. Outside, I saw a man with a pit bull straining on its leash. I could feel something off in the building, an energy that did not seem right. I had once felt the same low charge, the same subliminal stimuli, in a bank that was robbed two minutes after I left. All over the news it was. A man with an air pistol painted black.

Stan was pretending to be supervising the cops. Fooling no one. My father was not as sharp as he used to be. This, I now believe—his failure to pick up signals and his belief that he was still the cleverest man in the room—proved problematic. Stan thought he was two steps ahead of the cops when he was not.

When the detectives emerged, Nightingale said, "We are done here. You have a good day now." When he said it, he smiled at me. I like to think he knew how uncomfortable this was for me. I like to think he knew that I, like him, had once associated with finer individuals. That I had a decent husband and a decent job. That people *liked* me.

"Thank you," I replied.

That, it seemed, was too much for Stan, who sniped, as soon as the detectives were out of earshot, "I have a bad feeling about old Officer Mockingbird and his sidekick Pigeon."

Bad feeling? That is a lie. You are angry because the officer spoke to me, not you.

"It is Nightingale," I corrected him.

"Nightingale. Hummingbird. Chickenhawk. Maybe next time send Sergeant Ring-Necked Pheasant and his deputy Downy Woodpecker. Then we might get somewhere."

5

If you live in Dartmouth — most parts of it anyway, not the part where Stan relocated Graham — you know someone who is friends with musicians Joel Plaskett or Matt Mays.

You know someone who claims — even if no one believes them — that they went to junior prom with Sidney Crosby, the Pittsburgh Penguins captain, #87, the hockey superstar next door. Or Nathan MacKinnon,[3] his sidekick in those Tim Hortons ads in which the two NHL stars freak out customers by working the drive-thru, cracking up when one man butchers the word "jalapeño."

You might be familiar with Pat Stay, the late KOTD[4] rap star who rubbed shoulders with Eminem. Pat, the "Sucka-Free Boss straight out of Scotia."

And you know someone who competes in paddling. The Eurocentric sprint version that can take you places you might otherwise not go, places with medieval castles, cathedrals, and after-parties with an early Club Med vibe. If you walk by Lake Banook, you will

---

3 Nathan MacKinnon is the second most famous person from the Dartmouth suburb of Cole Harbour after Sidney Crosby, aka Sid the Kid or Crybaby Sid. MacKinnon won the Stanley Cup in 2022.

4 Pat Stay was murdered on September 4, 2022. He was stabbed, allegedly by a man with a long history of violent crimes.

see them: the multicoloured boats made in Portugal and Poland, trailed by motorboats and coaches. At times, the lake resembles a video game of remote-controlled characters. You will see paddlers in authentic CANADA gear. Not the knock-off stuff from The Bay. Buff tanned paddlers, who race in Poznań and Duisburg and have a Danish friend named Caspar, who has red roses custom-painted on his boat. On the water or running the circumference of the lake. As proof they have been places, they may wear a singlet from another country. And like the boxers at the cop shop, they are part of something with potential, something with international scope.

Some days you will also see an old Black man jogging around Lake Banook in long johns, shorts, and work boots, punching an imaginary speed bag. *Bam. Bam. Bam.* He has nothing to do with paddling. He will tell you, if you give him a chance, that he was once a sparring partner for the great Muhammad Ali, and that he was driven to a hidden training camp in the desert in a black Cadillac. His ring name was Bobcat. Some of that is true.

This is the wholesome side of Dartmouth, the fresh-faced side. This is the side you want to show in real estate ads — throw in a stand-up paddleboard and a dragon boat for good measure, maybe the iconic white geese. This is *not* where Graham lived.

That was four bus stops and one 911 call away.

✻

Dartmouth used to be its own city with its own parade and its own mayor, but then came amalgamation.[5] There are people who are still mad about the change. They put up old Dartmouth flags. They vandalize signs that say **HALIFAX**. That is them, not me.

---

5   In 1996, the government amalgamated roughly two hundred places within Halifax County to create HRM, later shortened to Halifax. One of these communities, the sparsely populated Ecum Secum, is a two-hour drive from the city and has nothing in common with Halifax proper.

The unofficial Dartmouth separatist movement tried to enlist Stan. It deployed the aforementioned Robert, an enthusiastic foot soldier. "If you have a sheet cake in a room," Robert told Stan, "you have a party."

Being from Pollock Passage, Stan was hardly interested in their saccharine sheet cakes and old Miss Dartmouth beauty pageants, but he played along. Stan had made a good career out of playing along.

"Robert," Stan later told Graham, "is as subtle as a ball-peen hammer."

And Graham, before he vanished like an entire city, laughed.

Dartmouth is called the City of Lakes — there are twenty-three — but Banook is the alpha. Its name comes from the Mi'kmaq phrase for "first lake." There are three canoe/kayak clubs on Lake Banook, plus a national training centre. Rowers. A 1,000-metre racecourse that hosted senior paddling worlds and 1989 junior worlds, the latter made more newsworthy by several Eastern Bloc defections.

Nova Scotians — and you may not know this — are fascinated by people from faraway places. Moldova. Romania. They are, to them, like rare birds blown off course. Or orphans. Exotic creatures with a backstory more exciting or tragic than their own.

Paddling legends such as Maksim Morozov (Olympic multi-medallist and Russian National Team Coach Training Athletes for World Championships and Olympic Games, according to his LinkedIn) have added international dazzle to Lake Banook over the years. Morozov, who famously raced with a broken hand taped to his paddle and was awarded the Order of the Red Banner of Labour. Morozov, who unknowingly played a bit part in our story. Morozov, who was in the Soviet habit of towel changing on public wharves.

As late as December and as early as March, you will see the paddlers in toques and pogies. Gingerly lowering their carbon fibre boats into the water from a wharf slick with frost. Forming flotillas that start and stop through openings in the ice.

My brother Peter was one of them. When the boats were made of wood.

It may have been the first time in Peter's life that he escaped our father's shadow. Peter lived in a sub-world that was thrilling and heartbreaking, generous and cruel, and I vicariously lived there with him. A sub-world so all-consuming that it left no room for the everyday horrors that are Life. A sub-world with subplots I will, at some point, explain.

Peter had training and race results that defined him. I had "friends," and "friends" when listed as your main interest in the high school yearbook, means beach parties and boys and things your parents do not know about. Neither of us had any interest in rural cousins or a village named Pollock Passage. I had more romantic locales in mind, locales with delis, boutiques, and dangerously handsome men.

I *did* eventually meet them, the dangerously handsome men.

I hung around paddling for the fun parts: the dances, the regattas. Peter did not mind me being there. My brother looked different then — resolute, with white-blond hair that he kept out of his eyes with a terrycloth sweatband. He wore training singlets that showed off his muscular arms. Cotton shorts and Adidas sneakers. Girls watched him from afar. I saw them.

You can see dreams in the air. They look like lucent white lights. You can smell them; they smell like the musty whiff that comes off a lake at five a.m. You can taste them; they taste like Côtes du Rhône. There are the fleeting dreams that fizzle, and you almost forget that they existed, and there are the big dreams that crash and take part of you with them. I dreamed of growing old in an art-filled stone townhouse with a tiny, framed handprint on one wall. Peter dreamed of going to the Olympics. My mother dreamed that we would both be happy. Stan dreamed of being Stan Swim. It wasn't more complicated than that.

*

There was a time when I could not tell you what Stan was up to from month to month. I could not have picked Graham out of a police lineup. I left home early. I went to college. I got work. I found the things that were mine: my joy, my men, my troubles. I associated with people who spoke of esoteric concepts such as "the enamel" on your heart, and then I returned, skid marks on my soul.

Only my mother truly missed me, I am now convinced. In those years when I was at photo school, and then in Montréal living above a grocer that sold fresh baklava. In Montréal, I did street photography for me. I imagined I was Elliott Erwitt, who captured the ironic and the absurd. I carried a Leica, small and unobtrusive, with a leather strap. I shot skateboarders and fashionistas checking their makeup in store windows. Against a backdrop of patched brick buildings with iron railings and metal fire escapes that clambered up, down, and sideways. Some of my black-and-white prints I framed, some I mailed to my mother. She liked them.

If you have a parent like Stan who lives for his public, you are an accessory that only works with select outfits. Most times you are not needed. On occasion you add a splash of colour, an accent of domesticity—you are a human pocket square.

One month before Graham disappeared, Stan insisted I join him and Graham for lunch. As soon as we were seated, Stan spotted someone more important across the room—the owner of a car dealership—and abandoned us. Graham and I talked about dogs—he said chocolate Labs can be "buggers" to train—and then said nothing.

For years, my father had waited for the Senate call. And then it failed to happen. Billy Bow Tie—my father refused to speak his name—got the nod instead. ("A delightful-looking hamster.")

After that, my father became a reckless critic of the Power Elite he had hoped to join. If my father had a defining flaw, it was this: he believed that he could do whatever he pleased, and the fallout would never wash up on someone else's shore. That was false. If you don't believe me, ask Peter.

When Stan retired, he was offered a position as a citizenship court judge, which he declined. "You are not a real judge," he said. "You are pretending to be a judge." Stan was invited to charity events, and after a while, the offers dropped off. He became bored and bitter.

When a person's dream collapses, they go through stages. The first is withdrawal: they hide their shame, they hide their disappointment, and they hide their broken heart because it cannot take any more scrutiny.

When a person's dream collapses, you can hear the relief around them. It sounds like the vacuous laughter of a mean girl. It sounds like bros picking up growlers at a drive-thru. It sounds like a couple opening their Florida condo in December and congratulating themselves on the view. Relief sounds smug among people who do easy things, people who, unburdened by a curious mind or a keen intellect, pose such a minuscule threat that society says, "Ahh, just let him have it."

Peter recovered after his paddling dream crashed on a cataclysmic day. He became an engineer and built bridges. He married Suzanne. They put Luke in paddling, and it started all over again. When Peter was in their sub-world—when the time controls were going their way, when there was no nasty crosswind or current, when the semi-finals were not rigged, or the criteria as crooked as a Central Park shell game—he was happy.

Peter and Suzanne drove Luke to trials in Montréal and Georgia. They bought him one $5,000 NELO kayak after another—the last one had a blue shark painted on the bow. They went to dinner at Olive Garden with Luke's girlfriend, who paddled for Sweden and wore white Oakley sunglasses and tank tops. It was all exciting for a while. Peter was back in his sub-world, the one without Stan's shadow. And then he wasn't.

Jack and I packed a U-Haul and left Montréal when our dream crashed. Iggy Pop was singing "Lust for Life" on the stereo. We had the windows wound down.

6

I was alone in my condo when I heard a knock. There was no Jack in my life anymore. No Iggy Pop. I slowly pulled open my door and said, with exaggerated confidence, "Yes?" Nobody likes to see an unannounced man at their door. Is it ever good news? I cannot give you the precise date of this, because I did not write it down. I can say it was weeks before Graham went missing.

The man was a florid-faced commissionaire. He reminded me of a *Standard* editor who now had a job delivering flowers. The last time I saw the editor he was carrying the all-white Eternal Friendship funeral spray, and he seemed befuddled. One of those men of a certain age who had become both hesitant and slow-moving, one step behind. In his eyes was a look of shock, as though he knew what was happening but could not stop it.

"I like what I'm doing," the editor had said, convincing himself as much as me. "Who doesn't like to see the flower guy?"

"No one."

"Anyway, I'm doing better than most. Getting on with my life."

"Yeah, me too. Miss the old crowd, but me, too."

His tone changed. And he stared at me with an intensity that was not right.

"Have you seen the paper lately? Looks like garbage. The front page on Saturday—the *main* story—was a story about a dog that needed a home. The dog had been named after Alan Doyle of Great Big Sea—the dog's name was *actually* Alan Doyle—so the paper phoned Alan Doyle and asked him if he thought someone should adopt the dog, and he said, 'Yes, b'ye. That would be wicked.' Like what the hell is he going to say? 'No. Kill Alan Doyle the dog.'"

"Sad."

"Page one above the fold with a handout picture of Alan Doyle." And then, for emphasis, "The *singer.* Not the dog."

Tragic. All of it.

But it was *not* the old editor I had seen delivering flowers to a neighbour. This florid-faced man was here on official business. *Had I been caught speeding again and not received the ticket?* I wondered. *Radared at 140 on an open stretch?*

The commissionaire was relaxed. "So, you got the stolen Audi A4." He made it into a question.

Ahhh. It was not a speeding ticket.

"Hmm, yes." Cautious. "It's a 2011, dent on one door. Beige metallic."

It was about my stolen car.

"Police found him pretty easy, since he parked your car in his driveway. You are lucky. The cars are usually torched when they find them."

I did not feel particularly lucky, but I agreed anyway.

It is a disorienting feeling when you walk outside, keys in hand, and your car is gone. You look around, uncertain. How, you ask yourself, could something that substantial vanish? Were you drunk last night? Were you so plastered that you forgot you left your car outside that wine bar with the exposed pipes and the urban industrial vibe and took a cab home?

"Yes," I said, "that's what happened last time. The last time my car was stolen, they torched it."

And then the commissionaire handed me a subpoena.

Her Majesty The Queen/Sa Majesté la Reine

v./c.

Korey St. Clair Scudder

*Subpoena/*Assignation
*(to a witness/*à un témoin*)*
(Sec./Art. 699 CC)

I ORDER YOU to attend court September 24, 2018
JE VOUS ORDONNE
de comparaître devant la cour le 24 septembre 2018

According to the subpoena, I was obligated to give "evidence concerning the charge." *Why now?* The cops had caught Korey red-handed. *Why did they need me?* The surveillance camera at the Ultramar had captured him stealing gas in my Audi. Timestamped 3:20 a.m. At one point, he cleaned out my trunk, taking an anorak, a tripod, and a Canon lens worth $8,000 new, all reported, all still missing.

When my car was returned, it looked like a skeet party. Up front were Cool Blue Gatorade bottles and a hoodie used as a carryall. Stolen binoculars. An empty bag of roast chicken potato chips. The smell of bad decisions. The glove box had been cleaned of overdue bills I had neglected to open.

I don't do social media. But I do have a fake Facebook account, which I used to creep Korey St. Clair Scudder. I did not want him to know what I looked like, I decided. I did not want him waiting for me when I got off work at two a.m.

I had no idea that Korey would turn out to be a carrier pigeon of hard truths and revelations. Truths important to my story. I thought he was just a skid.

*
*

September 24, the date on the subpoena, I dutifully went to the Dartmouth courthouse as instructed. At this point, Graham was gone.

There had been a slight lead in his case. The RCMP had received a call from a woman who remembered seeing a bicycle pass her Pollock Passage house the day Graham went missing. "He had something in the basket," she said, "but it was foggy." The witness had also seen an unfamiliar black Chevy Malibu. "I couldn't tell you the year. My husband could, but not me. He's the one that's good with cars."

The Dartmouth courthouse is across the street from a hospital. Peter went to the ER there once after he fell off a ladder. I don't know why Peter has a history of falling, but he does. When Peter was being processed, an employee asked, because there is no such thing as patient confidentiality, "Any relation to Stan?" (Who hated hospitals, calling them "a great place to die.") Yes. "Well, you must be proud of him!" Aggressively. Some people have a stable childhood — orderly days and predictable nights — but that was not our experience, mine and Peter's. We lived with the chaos of Stan. When Peter smiled vaguely, the woman doubled down. "Not everyone has a father like that." And then she glared at Peter as though she had taught him a lesson.

The courthouse is a bland semi-modern building. It looks like a place where you would see a podiatrist. In this humdrum setting it is hard to evoke gravity. It is hard to envision a fire-and-brimstone judge booming, "Mister Scudder, the road to redemption is long and arduous, and you will spend the rest of your life walking it unless you change your sinful ways."

I saw a family scurry to the entrance, followed by a lawyer carrying an immense black briefcase. I believe the briefcases are intentional props — the bigger the briefcase the less likely you will be mistaken for a criminal or his wretched family.

It was raining, and a woman, the mother of a perp, had a coat over her head. I have an unspoken agreement with people in complicated situations: I will not judge them, and they will not judge me. The mother had a face changed by life, altered by a constant state of readiness, an inability to relax, because she did relax once. She did, for an evening, not worry. She dropped her guard, and then what happened?

And so, she reverted to a tight, hard knot of fear.

If you have been there—outside a locked washroom stall or a-by-the-hour motel or an ER where people die waiting to be seen—you know.

There are things that can break your heart. A hospital ID bracelet. A tattoo. Someone else's baby.

But you probably already know that.

*
*

When I was new to the newspaper business, two sheriffs in body armour brought in a killer. Described in his parole review "as a violent individual with a high risk for lethality," he had been caught with a .32 calibre pistol with five rounds in the clip. He was dressed in a grey Roots sweatsuit with a beaver emblem. The sheriffs loaded him onto the elevator and walked him up a flight of stairs. They had taken the cuffs off, per protocol, at the bottom of the stairs. I was leaning over the railing to get a frame when a fist came out of nowhere and clocked me. *Boom.*

What does a murderer look like? Most times, they look exactly like my assailant minus the beaver emblem. Their crime the product of a rapid and predictable escalation. You can smell evil, you know. It smells like ethanol. It smells like the blood-splattered side of a highway. Occasionally, they look like Volunteer of the Year. The med student or the accountant.

Today, the sheriff's van was parked out front. It would not be carrying Korey. He would come in on his own. He would not be in shackles, because he was a petty car thief who smelled like roast chicken potato chips. He was not the young offender convicted of killing, while high on weed and Fireball whisky, a young woman just off a bus. Three months past his sixteenth birthday, having completed grade 9 and part of grade 10, he killed her on a path near Graham's apartment, on a night when he had originally planned to start a bonfire in the woods.

If I had been shooting Korey St. Clair Scudder, an unlikely scenario given his low standing as a newsmaker and a criminal, I would get the frame when he cleared screening. I would use my 70-200 zoom without a flash. It is more surreptitious that way, the shots grittier. If I was lucky, he would lift his head. The *really* bad men stare at you as though they are recording your face.

A sign said: *All cases have been moved to Courtroom 3.* I went there and a sheriff growled, "We are not open to the public yet." When I told him why I was there, he said, in the voice he uses on everyday felons, "Go to the prosecutor's office."

I am not a criminal, I wanted to say, but I didn't. Nobody cares. Nobody.

Courthouses have a travelling-circus vibe. You never know if, inside the big top of justice, you are about to witness someone clichéd like Korey St. Clair Scudder or someone truly chilling: a hitman for an El Salvador drug cartel. And often the players look the same. And the families look the same. On both sides. Occasionally there is a whiff of glamour, like the day that jewel thief Aksel Andersson appeared, and a star-struck sheriff gushed, "They will make a movie about you one day." Andersson, who had a wine collection of two hundred rare bottles in his cedar wine cellar and owned a dacha in the middle of a magical pine forest. Andersson, who had been dubbed the Danish Prince of Thieves by a breathless Toronto news magazine, which called him, without restraint, "spectacularly handsome."

While I was waiting for the elevator, two women were grumbling. They were there to support an unspectacular dealer up on multiple charges, including human trafficking, and they both looked as rough as a dirt road in April.

"I don't know why I'm with this loser," one griped.

The oldest question in history.

"Well, it ain't like there was a lineup."

They shot me that *what-you-looking-at-bitch?* look.

I do not care about you, I wanted to reply, because this is my mantra. *I have seen people die, strangers and a very close friend, so I do **not** care about you.*

Then, in the next five minutes, it all came to an abrupt end. The front desk employee in the public prosecutor's office informed me, after a search of records, Korey had been in court on another matter weeks earlier. He had pled guilty.

"Ah, sorry. You should have received a call." She did not look up.

"Okay. I've seen St. Clair spelled a couple of ways."

"No," she stated. "It is him."

Sigh.

"It's the second time I've had a car stolen."

She shrugged as though she was tired of dealing with losers. "I had kidney cancer."

I had no comeback.

I took the elevator to the ground floor. In the lobby, I spotted the *Standard*'s court reporter, who had a workspace in the building. The reporter made a point of not going into the paper's main office, operating on the up-to-now valid belief that he would not be laid off if management never saw him.

Layoffs are by nature clandestine and cruel. You *must* be caught off guard. You *must* be subjected to the humiliation of sitting there when the shock hits, as you involuntarily cry or get angry. And if you do get angry, Security is there to remove you. When I was laid off, I was told to gather up my belongings and leave. *Now.* Cut loose at an inconvenient age: too young to retire, too old to learn a useful trade like mortician.

The court reporter knew the sheriffs, the lawyers, and the drill. He knew a tattooed undercover cop who bought cocaine from a hang-around member of the Hells Angels Nomads chapter. He had been assaulted by both criminals and their families. But he liked it here.

When the reporter did see someone from the other side, he could not shut up.

"What are you doing here?" he asked me. Followed by, "Oops, sorry."

"It's okay." I showed him the subpoena. "Witness."

He read it and said straight-faced, "Korey St. Clair Scudder, yeah, I know him. He's just back from a gap year in Tanzania."

We laughed out of habit.

The only gap year Korey would ever take would be in prison.

Before I left home, I had checked Korey's Facebook page. He seemed like a man with a flawed life plan:

> I drink my beer and smoke my weed
> but my good friends is all I need

"I didn't cover him. I only do the big stuff."

Courts are easy to cover. There is always a story. You don't have to think too hard. You can't over-organize or procrastinate. You just show up on time.

"Of course."

"I had a murder trial that day. The victim tried to stop a fight outside the Seaview Bar. The Crown had amazing video. I don't know why it was such high quality. You can *actually* see the knife. You can see the eight-ball tattoo on the killer's hand. So, buddy was screwed. He pled out on manslaughter, which means he will be out in seven. Anyway, your case should be online eventually."

"Okay, thanks."

I started to leave, but he was still talking.

"So, you're related to the missing guy with the tuna head. Right? Heard your father on the radio."

"Yes. He is still missing."

"Have you heard from Dicky? He keeps calling and trying to go for lunch."

*

Can I tell you a story? A story that has nothing to do with Graham or Stan? Because that wasn't always my life, you know. I wasn't always this invested in immediate family, living and breathing the Swims. My last name was Flower — Harriett Flower — and I had a life of my own, a life with Jack. Jack was a painter. And when we lived in Montréal, we lived in a bubble of art. *Our* sub-world. All around us art was free for the taking. Graffiti and fountains, light shows and sculptures, where you did not expect to see them. A street violinist playing Tchaikovsky on cobblestones. In a sub-world, your existence is grander and smaller, heightened and less real.

Jack and I had a friend named Didier who was sad-eyed and romantic. Didier, who had been born in Haiti, was so fluid, so smooth in his movements, that he reminded me of a raindrop. A six-foot-tall human raindrop. Didier was free in the manner of someone who had grown up with nothing. Jack was free in the manner of someone who had grown up with everything. Jack thought they were the same.

Didier loved the dark movie *Trainspotting*, and that edgy soundtrack became his soundtrack. Some days, while Jack was painting, Didier would visit, and they would play it. They would sit in Jack's light-drenched studio with the north-facing windows, and they would play "Lust for Life," and it was proof that things could be that much more out of control. They could be Ewan McGregor aka Renton shooting up smack. They could be doomed to a life of crime and betrayal in a squalid shit hole named Edinburgh, but they weren't.

Didier had a girlfriend named Camille, and she knew about things I did not know about. Like velvet. Ciselé velvet, crushed velvet, transparent velvet, and velvet that is hammered or embossed. I was in awe of the things she knew and how important they seemed. Camille, who made dresses and capes from velvet, told me that her mother had died when she was ten. And that tragedy had altered her molecular structure. "I think that we are all born with a protective coating on our heart, an enamel," she explained, "and in some people the enamel is thicker, so it lasts longer. That is why you will see old people going to the theatre, looking as free as the day they turned eighteen. You know they have the same suffered losses that you have. And you think: *Aren't they lucky?*"

At the time, I did feel lucky. One of the lucky ones.

*

I spotted Dicky as soon as I entered the sports bar. Dicky Doiron looked like that over-the-hill rugby player who drops dead in a rowdy pub while watching darts. He was wearing his all-season uniform of khaki shorts and a golf shirt crested with the name of a sports event he had covered.

Dicky and I had worked together at the *Standard* for years. He became friends with Jack because they had both played serious baseball, and Jack loved baseball as much as Dicky loved to talk about it. Jack and Dicky could talk baseball for hours.

The bar had #87 hockey sweaters on the walls. A pair of goal lights. Photos of famous athletes, most of whom Dicky claimed to have discovered. I knew how the next two hours would unfold. All our lunches followed a template—they started with the *Standard*, moved on to Dicky's sports discoveries, and ended with Jack.

Dicky's table was under a long north-facing window that let in light, the kind of light Jack liked to paint by. Dicky wasted no time on formalities. As soon as I sat down, he brought up the *Standard*'s former Sports editor, a man who carried a first aid kit on assignment after witnessing a bleed-out on a field.

"Can you believe Oakley and the wife opened a B & B?" Dicky asked, as though he and I were doing so much better. "My idea of Hell. I can't even stay in one let alone run one. The owner is always creeping around, counting every bar of soap, sneaking into your room to turn down the heat, or touch your underwear."

"Yeah, I hate that," I allowed.

The last time I saw Oakley his eyes had the hollowness of a man who had survived a three-person fatal car crash that was probably his fault. They were blank and at the same time terrified.

"I heard that Oakley fainted when he saw Chucky coming for him," I told Dicky.

"Amazing."

Chucky was the moniker staff had given the paper's executioner, its chief financial officer, whose lone skill seemed to be terminating people. Chucky got her nickname because her LinkedIn profile picture was so ridiculously Photoshopped that it made her look like a porcelain doll. An evil killer doll.

Executioner is a tough job, but Chucky liked it.

"Carmichael from Business is a tour-bus announcer," Dicky said. "*To the left you will see the* Titanic *graveyard, the final resting place of one hundred and twenty-one victims.* Only Carmichael could make an epic disaster boring."

The paper's long-haired cartoonist was now a crossing guard—he says it gives him time to think—and a member of a medieval fighting group. A photographer had moved out West and become a rodeo photographer — he got gored by a bull. A copy editor had morphed into a full-time Twitter vigilante. "He doxed a stranger he saw walking his chihuahua on ice without booties," said Dicky. "He posted a photo, and the mob went mad. He is also angry about the US college admissions scandal because, you know, Harvard was really on his horizon. Either Harvard or a new Nintendo."

"Amazing," I said.

Dicky and I laughed to lighten the load, to set it adrift in a plume of quips and glib recollections. But it was there, wasn't it? The slow death of a business that had consumed us. Then burned us. And we were surrounded by casualties. And they had formed a club of sorts, populated by laid-off journalists who did not know why they were so inconsolably, inherently sad.

Ten minutes later, our food arrived, and Dicky tackled his with his usual vigour. Dicky was not shy around food. When we worked at the *Standard*, he possessed the takeout menu of every pizza, Thai, donair, and Chinese restaurant within delivery distance. He enthusiastically participated in the employee Wine and Cheese Club. I packed a lunch.

I have an odd relationship with food. I go through phases during which I eat the same thing over and over. For a while, it was samosas, and then chicken liver pâté — I would eat pâté with a baguette and a glass of red wine every night. And then orange juleps — I would go an entire day in Montréal on orange juleps. I don't even know what that says about me. I am just trying to be honest.

"So how about Ellie Black?"[6] asked Dicky. "Going places, eh? Yeah, she's a world-class gymnast, but she has that *other* factor, that likeability factor, which I noticed the first time I saw her."

"You called it," I said.

As proof, Dicky pulled out his phone and showed me a photo of himself with the photogenic Olympian.

---

6   Gymnast Ellie Black placed fifth in the all-around competition at the Olympic Games in 2016. She is, from all reports, not only talented but personable.

"Great face. Smiles with her eyes."

Dicky nodded and then carried on. "It's like when Sid was coming up," he said, his eyes getting that wild, overexcited look that some people get at an all-you-can-eat dessert bar. "Do you remember what I wrote? I said: 'Sid is like Domino's, the way he delivers. Sid comes with a sixty-minute guarantee.'" We laughed.

And then I told Dicky with as much sincerity as I could muster, "You called that one, too." Discovering Sid the Kid, nicknamed The Next One, a prodigy marked for superstardom at the age of eight, at a rink in nearby Cole Harbour was like discovering the Empire State Building or the Taj Mahal. It was like discovering grass.[7]

Dicky and I took a trip down memory lane. I let him talk about the things he could not talk about with other people, and he did the same for me. The desert. The dark-haired woman with the face of an indie actress. The time he went missing for four days on assignment with the company car. Jack.

"How is your brother's boy doing?" Dicky asked. "The paddler."

"Fine, I guess. He's in BC."

Luke had moved to BC after he lost a sketchy sports arbitration that ended his Olympic dream, and now, for him, defined paddling. He wanted nothing to do with "the bullshit sport" or "the losers" in it, which unfortunately included Peter. The whole thing was a sorry mess. For everyone. Do you remember the first time that something horribly unfair happened to you? I do. Other people get that out of the way early: poor people, oppressed people, or unlucky people.

"When I hung up the cleats, I was lost for a year," said Dicky. "I went to Vegas and met a rodeo rider named Sally, a barrel racer. I don't think I ever met a woman with forearms that strong. It's from hanging on to the horses. She took me for a drive on the desert."

A couple sat at the table next to us. I saw Dicky glance at the

---

7   Sidney Crosby was the Number 1 NHL draft pick in 2005. Crosby has too many records to list here. Henrik Lundqvist, aka King Henrik, aka the handsomest man in hockey, was once fined $5,000 for squirting Crosby with his water bottle.

woman, who was striking, with dark eyes and slicked-back, wet-looking hair. Her mouth was half open, as though she might, in a moment of passion or anger, bite you. She wore bold red lipstick and eye makeup exhausted from the night before. A dress with a plunging neckline. Everything about her was uncomplicatedly her — her mood, her eyes, her clothes — and she was young. As young as we all had been.

If I were still doing street photography, I would shoot her with the soft light coming through the window.

"So," Dicky said, almost through his lunch, "how is the job?"

Dicky said "the job" as though he could not bring himself to name the place where I was employed, the Lucky Lady Casino. I alternate between the floor and the payout wicket. Dicky thought this was beneath me. And by extension beneath him. The Lucky Lady made Dicky as nervous as footsteps behind him in a parking garage at midnight.

"Good," I said. "Frees up my days. I am trying to do some writing."

The Lucky Lady is on the outskirts of Dartmouth. It is a jazzy operation with a real Lucky Lady who twice a night taps a gambler with a wand, says, "This is your lucky day," and gives them fifty dollars in free playing money. The human Lucky Lady wears a floor-length white gown with sequins — it looks like a Disney costume. She is always pretty. When people realize she is standing behind them, they sometimes lose their breath.

At the Lucky Lady, there is flashing neon everywhere, and who does not like neon? There are big-screen TVs. A bar. But the best thing is the demographic. The hip people do *not* go there — the men in short-legged suits tight at the ankles, the women with undercuts — they don't go there. You can never be too old or too uncool at the Lucky Lady, every aisle an obstacle course of wheelchairs and walkers. A buffet lineup as long as the Great Depression. No one who matters will ever see you.

I see working at the Lucky Lady as a test of character, a reminder that none of us is better than the other, vanity is a vice, and there is nothing wrong with honest work. Some of that is true.

"Did they ever find that cousin of yours?" asked Dicky, eager to change the subject.

"No. You know how those things go."

"Heard your father on the radio."

"Yeah," I said, and we left it at that.

Stan had been on the radio because he had received a phone call, he claimed, from a psychic who had a vision of where Graham could be found. The psychic—her name was Magda—had seen a rusted-out car and a barn. A rippling stream in the background.

"Why did she phone *you*?" I had asked, suspicious.

"Why wouldn't she?"

By now, I was looking at the woman at the next table. I was thinking about when you pass *that* age, when you are no longer the pretty girl no matter how you paint your eyes. Someone is always younger, and she could be tall or short, fair or dark. She could have chartreuse hair and a nose ring. She could look fetching in a cotton dress and canvas Keds. A sleeve tattoo.

When I was young and living in Montréal, I knew the photo playboys and the players. Some were handsome, some were fun in the same way that sky diving is fun. Some had been to hot spots where they collected press passes and women. It is not that hard, is it, to invent yourself as an amalgam of bon vivant and outlaw if you want to. If you are okay with that. And what became of them when the business collapsed? After years of parlaying his charisma into a porn tape of adventures, one shooter made a radical turn. At sixty, he moved to a filthy shack in a mountainside village in Serbia, where he skinned wild animals, drank foul drinks, and rarely bathed, a repudiation, it seemed, of his prior existence. A grotesque mockery of his previous self and his previous conquests. You can't get caught up in all that, I told myself back in the day. That updraft of untrustworthy men.

Dicky finished his beer, and I asked, "Any news workwise?" We had both been other people once, me and Dicky, before we had lost a part of ourselves. We knew that.

Dicky had started a sports blog—it was called *DD's Plays*—and was making pocket change by participating in university studies. A "side hustle," he called it. Dicky had taken part in a study on ticks. "I only got bitten twice," he said. And another study for men with low sexual desire. "At my age, define low."

"I keep waiting for *Das Experiment*," he continued. "Did you see that film? German, of course. Saw it with Pierre at the NFB. In the film, the hard-up journalist joins a scientific experiment, which descends into madness. Some of the participants play prisoners and some play guards. The journalist suffocates to death. And, of course, people do things they never thought they were capable of."

"What aren't we capable of?"

"I am not capable of finding a decent job, apparently, or I wouldn't be doing this shit."

Dicky was claiming to be two people, himself, and his husband Pierre, in an online study of multi-partner couples. "I am answering for both of us," he said.

Pierre was a lawyer and Dicky's financial safety net. While Dicky had covered sports for thirty years, Pierre had risen to partner in a firm that Dicky privately called Beavis and Butt-Head. Pierre had been grey since his twenties. He had a mean pinched mouth, which he deliberately made meaner. Pierre wore extreme eyeglasses that became more extreme each year. He was also, in a word, smug. Smug in the way that people who do not recognize their good fortune are smug, people who believe that it all comes down to "personal choices," never allowing for systemic poverty, mental illness, or bad fucking luck.

The couple at the next table left. It was easy to tell that *he* was infatuated: those eyes, that décolletage. It was hard to tell if she cared. The waiter was back, asking if we wanted anything else. No. Dicky showed me the study on his phone. We were lingering.

"You get one hundred forty dollars in Amazon gift cards, seventy dollars each," Dicky explained. "I'll keep it all since I am doing the whole study myself. Both parts."

"Excellent."

"Of course, it will all be lies. At *some* point, *some* people should not be talking about their sex lives because the mental image of them engaged in anything while naked is frightening. I put myself squarely in that category. So, yes, it will be lies."

"Amazing."

Dicky caught his breath, which seemed like a struggle. Dicky was showing his age. Maybe that came from being out of work or maybe he was onto something. No matter how hard you resist, your hair will become as drab as an old newspaper, your face will get disconcerting age spots, your nose *and* waistline will expand. You will feign a passion for blues pioneer Robert Johnson in an attempt to appear old-person cool, and that is life. If you only focus on your losses, each day will be a disappointment.

"It sounds like you have it all figured out," I offered.

"Jack used to say that half the stories I wrote were lies."

"Ahhh, yes," I scoffed, "Jack is an expert on lies."

And then Dicky asked, before we got up from the table, "Did you get your driver's licence back?"

"Oh yeah, I got that covered."

It was nice of him to ask.

If I were writing a novel, I then decided, I would not make my protagonist a fifty-two-year-old woman who dates Dante and drives too fast. Such an inexact age. A fifty-two-year-old woman is in a no man's land of hockey moms who still take their kids to the rink

and early retirees from the federal government. Mournful widows.
I would make her the woman from lunch. The red-lipped woman
who had created an aura about her, an aura of autonomy and allure,
while being exactly who she wanted to be. If you were not paying
attention, you might not notice her allure at first, but then she would
laugh, and her face would be transformed into an astounding out-
burst of joy and teeth and abandon — the kind of abandon that you
live for. Men waited for that to happen, I could tell. I would create
a woman like her, a woman who still had choices. And I would give
her clothes that I would never buy. I would give her black open-toed
pumps imprinted with tiny flowers, red, green, and blue, and the
heels would unapologetically click when she crossed a room.

1

When I worked with Dicky at the *Standard*, I shot a spy trial. It made me think about how people — and that includes all of us — can take *that* step, the one that seemed like a good idea at the time, the one there is no coming back from. Jeffrey Delisle,[8] an anodyne Canadian naval intelligence officer, got snared working for the Russians. It started when he contacted the GRU in Ottawa. He was nearly caught returning from a meeting with his handler in Brazil, carrying the universal accessory of spies and blinged-out crack dealers everywhere: prepaid credit cards. In Halifax, Delisle had access to a data bank of classified secrets shared by the Five Eyes community: Canada, the United States, the United Kingdom, Australia, and New Zealand.

There was nothing ominous or seductive about Delisle. He did not look like a Hollywood spy, distractingly handsome or seditiously cold. He looked ordinary.

I photographed Delisle twice in 2013. On both occasions, he was doing all he could to make himself smaller. A human hedgehog. Hunched over in a hoodie, chin tucked, climbing into a sheriff's van. When he saw the hungry media horde, he raised a paperback

---

8   In 2019, convicted spy Jeffrey Delisle was granted full parole after serving one-third of an eighteen-year, five-month prison sentence.

to his face. And this is the curious part, the part I could not make up: he had a different paperback each time, and each time it was a spy novel. One by Tom Clancy and the other *The Far Side of the World*.

Delisle's case was a novel take on the theme of betrayal. Delisle was motivated, he said, not by money, not by ideology, not by seductive Russian escorts, but by the discovery of his wife's affair. Not surprisingly, they divorced.

Delisle was not the first or last spy in Halifax, which is strategically located on the Atlantic with submarines, jetties, and a sprawling shipyard that builds warships. A history of girls who foolishly pin their dreams on American sailors in sparkling whites. The home of the Canadian Navy, Halifax was the marshalling point for massive Allied convoys during World War Two. I doubt if there is a great need for navy spies in Winnipeg, but what do I know?

I *do* know that my parents had a neighbour who had worked stateside for the CIA, and when he died, US military brass and dark suits came to his funeral, the message being he was still one of them. He looked like that guy who buys drinks for everyone at a wedding. His name was Buck. I assumed it was a nickname, but when his obituary appeared, it gave his proper name as Buck. Buck, who was dead by the time Stan stole Graham.

"Buck's son didn't respect the spy life," Stan then informed me. "At Buck's funeral, he showed up in a Scottish piper outfit he made himself. He had the little Glengarry hat and a lightweight kilt, and it looked so *cheap*."

"Okay."

"At a funeral with important people. I was embarrassed for him." Stan, who prided himself on his funeral attire, shook his head. "He runs a used record store now with a Sinatra section at the front. Wears the Glengarry hat from time to time. So cheap. Two of Buck's friends couldn't make it to the funeral, which was just as well. Former CIA, working in Qatar. Did I tell you they hired a man to pose as a photojournalist to keep tabs on their subjects in Qatar?" Stan raised his brows at "photojournalist" as though this had anything to do with me.

"No."

"Great money, but you had to accept the downside: the heat and the fact that you might mysteriously disappear."

"I see."

I never knew what to believe with Stan.

"Did I mention that the CIA men were identical twins who performed the old switcheroo? Triplets actually, but the third one went into parimutuels."

"No."

*
*

My parents met when Stan was twenty-two, my mother twenty-one. In old photos, Mother looks like Ingrid Bergman with dark-blond hair pinned to one side. My mother—her name was Kathleen, but she went by Kaye—had taken a secretarial course and was working for a family doctor. Stan proposed on the second date. Broke, they were married by a justice of the peace, Mother in a borrowed blue dress.

My mother had a quick laugh, and people liked that about her, and that made Stan jealous. When Mother laughed, Stan visibly panicked. Mother, whose parents died young, was raised by her grandparents. Their last name was Hatt. There was no need for me to investigate Mother's family because they were, unlike the rest of us, normal. If there was a bad gene or a history of poor decisions, it came, I believed, from the Swim side, Stan's people.

My mother loved movies and later in life, for reasons known only to her, became obsessed with *The Godfather* trilogy. She owned the boxed set on VCR. She thought that Al Pacino, then achingly young and sensitive, was the most beautiful man in Hollywood. It broke her heart when Michael Corleone (played by Al) ordered his brother Fredo (played by John Cazale) killed.

Beauty makes some people, like my mother, kind, and others as cruel as a Mafia don. Here is the thing about beauty: it will not ennoble you, save you, or spare you. You may still suffer indignities; you may still be betrayed. One of the most pitiful sentences you will ever hear in this lifetime is, "I thought we had an understanding."

My father got his start at CKBW on the South Shore. CKBW is the radio station where Donald Sutherland worked as a teen, a talking point when my father met the actor, who had by then starred in *M*A*S*H*. Stan interviewed the star when he blew through town in a fedora. When you are in the company of someone that charming, that large, Stan explained, you wait. Soon you will be pulled into the updraft of timing and wit, and the interview will be, as it ought to be, perfect. "You are along for the ride. You are that dog in the Ford pickup with his head out the window." And then, in case you got the wrong impression, "Donald said the interview was smashing."

Stan cut his teeth on phone-in shows, radio newscasts, and play-by-play sports announcing. Working for peanuts. He made it to Halifax, switched to television, made it to Toronto and back again. The early years toughened Stan. They made him seek out exciting people, provocative people. He developed an appetite for the outlandish. He had no taste for the boring. If Stan did not think you were worth his time, he would leave the room mid-sentence, or his eyes would glaze over.

One day I listened to a trivia show like the one he hosted in his early years. It was a test of how much psychological torment the host could endure. Regulars phoned in, and it was astounding the things that they did not know. Under the format, the host read them a "trivia" question about Canada. The caller could request another question. He could use a helpline.

Host: "What is the last word in the title of this Gordon Lightfoot song 'If You Could Read My...'?"

Dead silence.

Host: "What is the last word in the title of this Gordon Lightfoot song, 'If You Could Read My...'?"

Pause.

Host: "Here is a clue: the song was covered by Johnny Cash and Glen Campbell. 'If You Could Read My...'?"

More silence.

Caller: "I'll take another question."

Host: "Here is your new question, Trent: What is the only Maritime province that is an island? The only *Maritime* province."

Caller: "An island, you say?"

Host: "*Yes*" (emphatically).

Caller: "Ahhhhhhh..."

Host: "What is the only Maritime province that is an island (a more emphatic tone)?"

Caller: "Can I have a lifeline?"

Host: "Okay, Trent, your lifeline says her answer is Prince Edward Island. Do you accept that answer?"

Caller: (large exhale of anxiety) "I was thinking Cape Breton, but I'll go with that."

After that, Stan took any opportunity that came his way, and who could blame him? For a while, my mother, Peter, and I stayed in Dartmouth, where my parents had purchased their house. Stan came home when he could. The house had been a risk, more than they could afford at the time. But then Stan landed the TV job in Halifax that defined him, the one that made him a Name. With that came a wardrobe, a hairstylist, and memberships on boards and charity committees. The billboards. The Air Force made him an honorary colonel.

Not everyone could do what Stan did—the road to obscurity is littered with forced pauses and a singsong delivery. Stan was better than that. He was quick. He had a signature style. He could be dry as vermouth.

Stan's retirement was preceded by a month-long countdown. At the top of each newscast, the station displayed the number of days remaining. Stan indulged himself with oddball interviewees like the woman whose "life mission" was to have annuals banned. The flowers were "an environmental liability," she said, and more importantly cruel. It was cruel to give life to an object knowing it would die.

When The Day finally did arrive, there was a cake. (Stan threw up his arms in mock surprise.) A gift for Baba, who did not exist. Tears from the crew. Stan's replacement would not be named for two weeks, keeping the spotlight solely on Stan. A local magazine ran a story calling my father "the personification of poise and professionalism." It compiled a sidebar of Stan Swim quotes over the decades, including:

> "If you can't ask the hard questions, get into another
> line of work. Become a dog groomer or a senator.
> Either one. I personally would choose dog groomer
> because I never had a dog lie to my face."

> "Liars. Con men. Sociopaths. I interviewed them all,
> and I worked for a few as well."

> "The viewers mean everything to me. If it weren't for
> my loyal and devoted viewers, I would be nothing.
> Beatrice, Andy, Georgina, the whole gang. You know
> who you are. You are family."

Stan's most devoted viewers were the people the bourgeoisie democracy counts on to never question anything. They owned a Cabbage Patch clown with squeaking shoes that they believed was priceless. They spoke only in clichés ("Not all heroes wear capes."), and they loved all the things people like them are programmed to love. Their local anchor. Free slab cake on Canada Day.

The station gave my father a highlight reel, which I, his *actual* family, watched. Missing are the interviews that went famously south. Most notably the godawful ParticipACTION piece that descended into a mad riff about Vikings, the Dark Lord, and Lilith. The improper fetishizing of Scandinavia, which included mention of the Old Milwaukee beer Swedish Bikini Team, which only pretended to be Swedish. Stan later claimed that Graham watched the reel and "could not get enough of it."

The reel *did* contain nostalgic shots: Stan behind the wheel of a stock car, Stan hypnotized. Stan interviewing a famed madam whose face was concealed.

In one of the lighter segments, he is interviewing a plastic surgeon, who was making a killing fixing "Grandpa ears." The doctor worked in a clinic where he played Sade and performed the surgery under local anaesthetic, trimming the earlobes that mysteriously, incrementally grew with age. The story ran under a banner: *Grandpa Ears the Next Big Thing.*

"It is incredible, isn't it," Stan marvelled on-air, "how big people's ears become. They could be a type of tree fungi."

When Stan was being clever, he allowed himself poetic leeway.

"I am not sure I like the fungi analogy," the doctor huffed.

"I'm not sure you have a franchise on plant pathogens."

"But —"

The doctor looked as smug as his tan suit and loafers.

"Play along, doc, play along."

*
*

The walls of Stan's den today are proof of who he was. Stan with the Pope. Stan with Anne Murray. Publicity stills and bronze-coloured plaques. At the apex of Stan's career, there were awards. Honours. There were group shots with precious people like the Toronto producer who boasted of being an *off-piste* skier before that business no one talked about anymore: someone underage somewhere.

There was an awkward bronze sculpture of Stan's head, made by one of his viewers. It looked nothing like my father. It looked like Lucille Ball.

Pamela, our workshop instructor, asked me if there were photos I could use in the book. If so, that could help get it published. I assured her that Stan had professional stills: black and white and colour. None, I said, of Graham.

"Any of Stan with famous people? Recognizable people?"

"Hmm, yes, Gorbachev and Bill Clinton."

"I like Bill," one would-be writer said. "I know he did bad things, but I remember him at funerals, the way he could cry and make the families feel better."

"I think that's a Southern thing," noted another.

"He's from Arkansas."

"Oh, that explains it."

Some of the lesser people in the photos—not Bill Clinton and Mikhail Gorbachev—had been to our house. One of Stan's old bosses was considered a "pioneer" in the business. My parents invited him and his wife for dinner, and when they were eating cheese fondue, the boss began interrogating his wife, asking her if their adult son, the massage therapist, was coming to dinner on Sunday. His wife told him yes. He continued to question her.

"Is he still seeing that woman?" he demanded. "You know, what is her name: Crystal or Chrysanthemum or Chemise?"

"You *know* that it is Crystal."

"Did he find her on the Home Shopping Network?"

And then she said, in front of everyone, "Oh, shut the fuck up."

My mother was gracious when Stan entertained colleagues, even the louche lushes, who bickered. For a time, she worked in a bank with normal people. Only once did I hear Mother complain about Stan's job—she complained about the hours. She complained about him staying overnight in an apartment the station kept in Halifax.

"Would you rather be married to a navy clearance diver who dismantles bombs and booby traps?" Stan nonsensically replied. Even if my mother were alive, she would have been unable to stop Stan from stealing Graham. She could not stop him from doing anything. Pamela told us that our main character should be sympathetic, likeable, or powerful. It helps if they had saved a cat or were in jeopardy. I could cheat and make up a backstory of Swim family altruism, but I won't. "Your character," she said, "should be very good at something." Stan was very good at broadcasting, and I was good at street photography. Graham had a talent for something I learned about later. He was musical.

Pamela explained that there is a writing device known as the "unreliable narrator." The story the narrator is telling might not be accurate, it *might* be distorted, because the narrator might not be in his right mind. Or he might be hiding something. And when that becomes apparent, it adds a giant twist.

"I can't," said Ingolf, the organic chemist, "see that working."

The initial theory was that was that Graham had been hit by a truck and knocked into a ditch. There was talk of a mystery truck going too fast. One witness described it as a black Kenworth 18-wheeler with gold cursive on the sleeper cab that said:

Burt Reynolds
1938–2018

Nobody knew who owned the mystery truck or where it was from, only that the owner must have been a *Smokey and the Bandit* fan. Bandit, played by Burt Reynolds, in those hit movies that made trucker life seem glamorous, with Jackie Gleason as Smokey the Texas sheriff chasing him as though he had nothing better to do.

There was an organized search for Graham in September. Volunteers and the RCMP covered main roads and beaches. A command post was set up in a converted school bus. Inside were topographical maps and pots of coffee. Some searchers drove thirty minutes from Yarmouth, a port town of 6,800, substantial enough for a Walmart and grand Victorian houses from the seafaring Golden Age.

There was, of course, the possibility that someone had murdered Graham.

But who would want to murder someone as minor as my cousin? In 2018, Nova Scotia had eleven homicides, a slow year compared to others. If you really want to get murdered, move to Ontario, where there were 266 in 2018. If you really don't, move to PEI, where there were none.

Most murder victims in Canada know their killer. According to Statistics Canada, "the majority of homicides in Canada are committed by an acquaintance (34%), a family member (33%), a stranger (19%), or someone with whom the victim had a current or former intimate relationship—non-spousal (6%). In 2018, 8% of victims were killed by someone with whom they had a criminal relationship."

Searches of the ditches showed nothing. No body. No bike. No tuna head. It was as though Graham's red bicycle had miraculously lifted into the sky to escape the bad guys. Passing by the moon like Elliott with ET, the extraterrestrial, draped in a blanket of love. The nearest hospital came up empty. Graham did not own a credit card. He did not have a driver's licence. People at the wharf said he was in fine spirits when he left with the tuna head. And then—poof—vanished. Nothing, the police said, "of evidentiary value thus far located."

Rick, the family liaison, had been at the command post. He did not, he told the media, believe that the Burt Reynolds truck was involved. "It's just my gut feeling. That's all I've got to go on—my gut."

*
*

While the search was under way, I drove by Graham's North End building. I don't know what I expected to see. The Burt Reynolds truck looking guilty?

I passed a used car lot that charged twenty-two per cent interest. An unlicensed body shop. A gym owned by a 10th-degree black belt, who grew up on Sipekne'katik First Nation and made his name in the US free fighting. On a curb, I saw a pair of wooden candle holders and a Naugahyde sofa filled with holes.

I did not spot Hughie the Twin's cop car. But I *did* see the same Chevy Malibu, black with darkened windows. It was a 2013 with twenty-inch chrome wheels worth half as much as the car. A bulky man with a top bun was unlocking the door. He was wearing two gold statement chains, one plain and one with a cross on the end. A star tattoo on his cheek. I thought I recognized him from court, but I was not sure. I get my murderers mixed up.

Graham's neighbourhood was built on a precarious sinkhole of potential danger, and if you lived there, one day it could be your turn. Maybe you were a single dad with a call-centre job, or maybe you were that lonely senior who fed the pigeons, and it would not matter. It would be your turn. There had been a murder two days earlier. A man up on kidnapping and rape charges was gunned down, and rumours ensued. He was a police informant, he owed drug money, he was a liability.

The *Standard* ran a story about the search for Graham while it was happening. The headline read:

Pollock Passage Man Vanishes with Valuable Tuna Head
Searcher Says Case Is "Fishy"

The story contained a photo of the searchers in fluorescent vests and a stock shot of a tuna. The piece was twice as long as it needed to be. With a gutted staff, the *Standard* had space to fill and most of its stringers were underpaid. The paper had room for free contributed opinion pieces advocating family nudity, pit bulls, and Prince Philip, the misunderstood Royal. The paper reduced its page count, increased its font size, and had taken to running fuzzy half-page photos. The *Standard*, the joke went, had no standards.

This story also contained a paragraph on tuna heads. Clearly copied from a Japanese website.

> The Tuna Head is separated into the flesh of the upper head, the cheek, the jaw and the eyes. Kabutoyaki, a stunning dish, is a bluefin tuna head cooked as a whole. The flesh from the top of the head is called kashiraniku. Kamatoro refers to the gill flesh, and there are only two pieces that can be cut from each tuna. Kamatoro is made into sashimi and sushi. It is also used as an ingredient in shabu-shabu.

The story then quoted an RCMP officer who talked about the efforts to find Graham. "Searchers have covered a lot of ground. We haven't been able to recover anything linked to Mister Swim, but we're pleased with the progress."

"The searchers had ruled out one hunting camp deep in the woods," he said. "Missing people are sometimes found in places like this," the Mountie explained. "Some are disoriented. Some are lost. Some are hiding because they feel in danger, real or imagined."

If you drive through Pollock Passage, you will see the ditches and the ocean. If you live there, you know there is more: the inscrutable inland beyond that where people have camps used for hunting or drinking. Where there are side roads paved with chip seal that gives way to gravel and blackflies. Where I *imagined* Graham was hiding.

"When somebody goes missing, it's considered an open investigation until a body is found," the Mountie explained in the story posted online.

A reader wrote in the online comments: "The Mounties down here couldn't find their own dicks."

"Our big fear is of losing someone in the woods," stated the Mountie in the story.

"My big fear," the same reader wrote, "is that the Mountie gets caught behind No Frills with his pants down."

Another person added, "Looking for his dick."

And a third: "If you don't want the Mounties on your ass, stop selling crack."

It was too soon to determine when the case would be downgraded from active to missing person, the Mountie elaborated.

Graham was already a statistic: one of the seventy-thousand-plus Canadians reported missing to police each year, most found within seven days, some within hours. And then there are the others. The unfound, whose stuck-in-time, faint-hope photos appear in airports.

The *Standard* quoted an official with Lands and Forests who confirmed there were coyotes in the area. Yes, they killed cats and chickens. "If you see them, do not run." And yes, there were bears. "Also dangerous."

The rambling story had room for Rick's wife, Rhonda. "I want to thank everyone for helping in the search. It's what you'd expect down here, but thanks." Graham had not been living with them, she said, or he might not have gone missing. "Everybody knows that is a whole other story." Rhonda said it was hard, for sure, especially because Rick's father, Maynard, had vanished in 1967 while fishing. "You keep thinking of that."

The police *do* find missing persons deceased. And when that happens, they may know who you are. Or they may post disturbing still lifes of the clothes you were wearing, a Metallica T-shirt and a pair of muddy Dunlop thermo work boots size 12. They may ask the public for a name.

After the *Standard* story appeared, I thought about a day when I had seen Stan and Graham grocery shopping. It was at the No Frills in Dartmouth. Graham had just moved to The City. He was pushing a shopping cart, Stan at his side. My father bristled. He resented the fact that Graham was visibly taller than he was, as though that was Graham's fault. In the cart was a bone-in ham. I was surprised that Graham cooked when, of course, he must have. He could not live on the leftover pizza that Stan sent home after hockey night.

"There is a great sale on hams," Stan told me with conviction. "This will last Graham all week." I do not know when it broke down, when Graham started to chafe at the puppeteer's strings, when he missed bumming rides on four-wheelers or taking a boat to an island. In hindsight, the arrangement did not seem sustainable. Graham had a mind of his own.

*
*

Weeks after the *Standard* story, Stan's TV station ran a report. The search had gone cold, the reporter explained. "Is Graham Swim doomed to become an unsolved mystery? The man with the tuna head."

The reporter interviewed Rick, whom I had not seen for decades. Rick was wearing a camouflage ball cap with a Mustang Survival logo. As much as Graham looked fleeting, Rick looked stable. He looked like a man who knew what he was doing. Rick answered the reporter's questions, and then he said, "Graham had things good down here. He didn't need to go haywire. He had a quad, and I took it from him as he was driving drunk on the wharf. Everyone knows that."

Stan had never mentioned a quad or drinking. Maybe because Stan himself used to drink a lot, back when the city had a press club aglow with brass. When the station sent a driver to pick him up before his broadcast and return him at night. Stan only drank beer from a station mug now, pretending it was coffee.

The TV report infuriated my father. Stan was irrationally livid that Rick had been interviewed by his old station. And not him. "What the hell does he know? He's never done anything in his life." Rick who had been a captain for over twenty years. Stan had a plan.

He was going to go see Slim, Graham's friend from 14 Cavalier. He was going to solve the case *and* discredit Rick who had the temerity to tell the public that Graham drove a quad on a wharf while drunk, Graham, who in Stan's mind, was twelve.

It was not clear to me what had transpired between Graham and Rick. I do not know if the seized quad was behind Graham's move. It may have been. Graham mentioned his brother from time to time. "The last time I was Home" — Graham said Home as though Pollock Passage had been replaced on Google maps with Home — "he was out on his wheeler."

"Oh, those bloody wheelers," sniffed Stan. "They are so foolish."

I had reason to balk at Stan's plan. I had not liked the feeling in Graham's building, which was in the news again. I had not liked the smell. Using an online site, three losers had lured another loser to 14 Cavalier for sex. The female in the trio took the stooge into the bedroom, relieved him of three hundred dollars, and told him to remove his clothes. Her accomplices burst in with a machete. I believe there must be a good online business somewhere for machetes because they show up in the hands of an inordinate number of losers with PayPal accounts.

"You'll be coming with me." Stan made it an order.

"Why do you need me if you are talking to Slim?"

"In case he tries to pull something tricky."

Oh, those tricky people.

"I am sure you can handle Slim."

"How do you know? He could have that bastard Corky with him."

"Does Corky even exist?"

"Why would I lie about that?"

Hmm. Because you are a liar.

When you are a child, you believe everything your parent tells you. As an adult it is difficult to process the fact that they may be wrong — about important things and minor things — because if they were wrong about those things then maybe they were wrong about you. *They*, the people who loved you.

To my relief, Slim did not want Stan coming to 14 Cavalier, which I considered a microcosm of bad choices. Slim wanted to meet behind a North End arena with a parking lot that filled with hockey cars on the weekends. In the back, he told Stan, by the playground. There is a swing set. Meet there.

*
*

It was eleven a.m. We parked and walked to a scruffy playground with a direct view of the arena's refrigeration system. There was one bench and we sat on it. A teenager who should have been in school was taking runs on a half-hearted skateboard ramp. No one else was in sight.

I spotted Slim approaching, and he was as thin as Graham. He was wearing a jacket with Dale Earnhardt's #3 on the sleeve. He could have been the floor installer from Kijiji — the guy who drives a Vibe with a Bic lighter on the seat. He illegally parks, he has his second Red Bull of the morning in his hand and barely enough tools for the job.

Stan met him midway. Slim did not seem in a particularly friendly mood. Maybe it was because someone had shot up a pizza delivery car the night before. Maybe not.

"I took Graham down Home," Slim stated after the greetings. "He seen stuff. He enjoyed himself. At least I done that for him."

"Yes, you did," Stan replied, not sure if he had been insulted.

"He was always tight of money."

Uncomfortable silence.

My father had no innate understanding of money. It was the one part of his habitus he had not outgrown. He gave money away. He worked for less than he was worth. He assumed college educations and orthodontic braces were free. People assumed we had stuff when we didn't. Stan operated as though he was wealthier than he was and, at the same time, above money, all the while impressed by people, even the deplorable ones, who had it.

Stan could move in any social circle. However, as someone who grew up poor, he had his tells. He drove an old cream-coloured Cadillac. He loved paper towelling so much that he panicked if he ran low. Paper towels, overpriced shoes, and party trays of cold cuts his obsessions. He kept empty shoe boxes. Money, on the other hand, slipped through his fingers, which were not accustomed to the feel of wealth. It never occurred to him that Graham was broke.

Slim broke the silence with a sniff. I think Slim felt he had been unfairly outnumbered—with me as the potential third man in—and that was making him defensive.

My father started to ask Slim if he knew where Graham had been staying in Pollock Passage, but before Stan could finish, Slim interrupted with an exaggerated frown of concern. "Is there something wrong with your foot?" It was clearly a stab in the dark by Slim, because Stan's foot looked, to a casual observer, just fine.

Slim pointed at Stan's right foot, which was wearing a brown Hartt shoe.

"Why no," said Stan, taken aback.

"Well, you look like there is something wrong with your foot. I'd get that looked after if I was you." The story came out rapidly, pausing to gain conviction, and then continuing like a man who has decided he can drive home drunk. "I knew a man down home and he let it go and he lost the whole thing. He went to one of them clinics, and they put the run to him, the dirty bastards. I knew another fella that done lost both feet, but he had the sugar diabetes like my shit-face brother Corky."

"Ahh, that is too bad."

"If that's what you want to call it."

Slim was stonewalling Stan, which did not happen. People told Stan the most outrageous stories and confessions. That was *his thing*.

Stan made cautious people feel safe, reckless people in danger. He was that stranger you sat next to on an airplane, the one you would never see again, the one you decided, after the third glass of in-flight Chardonnay, to confide in because we were all one mechanical failure away from our Maker, weren't we?

"So, you don't know where Graham was staying?" Stan pressed.

"If I knowed that, I'd be one of the Psychic Twins."

Stan tried for the follow-up question, but Slim was contrary.

"Make sure you get that foot looked at. I can tell you right now, as God is my witness, it is no walk in the park when you has no fucken feet. You think you got problems now."

And then it happened, the way it usually did. Stan gave Slim's story ten seconds to take a bow before he changed his tone. Before he erased the distance between him and Slim until they were sitting in a fishing camp in stained undershirts into their fifth warm beer.

"Do you think you can help Us *at all* with Graham?" The way Stan said "us" felt personal. He sounded like an old friend. This was my father's gift, the one that Peter believed was false and dangerous.

Slim softened. He nodded at the arena. "Graham went inside and watched his share of games." I could tell that Stan did not know this. "He heard that Marchand played here when he was with the Subways,[9] so he decided the hockey must be good. He loves The Rat. King Rat, he calls him."

"We all do."

King Rat was Boston forward Brad Marchand. Marchand who stood a mere five-foot-nine and grew up around here. Number 63, who scored a short-handed clutch goal for Canada in the final moments of the 2016 World Cup, leaping into the air like Baryshnikov on a pair of Bauer skates. Marchand, the anti-hero, the face licker, the slew footer, the last player in the NHL you were supposed to love but unapologetically, passionately did.

---

9   Brad Marchand played with the Dartmouth Subways before entering the QMJHL and being drafted by Boston. After starting as a fourth-liner with the Bruins, the Rat became a bona fide star.

"Graham had other friends, ya know," said Slim. "Associates."
Slim seemed relaxed now. Or sly. Possibly both.

"Hughie the Twin?"

"No," Slim shook his head, "Hughie the Twin had nothing to
do with this. Did that lyin' super say somethin' about Hughie? That
jailbird."

"No," Stan lied.

"Because if he did…"

The threat was out there.

"Okay," said Stan soothingly, "but can you help Us?"

"I just needs some time to clear my thinking material."

And then it happened.

Slim blinked, and he blinked again, as though he was clearing his
head of something, a doubt, a reservation that stood between him
and the truth, or maybe he was conjuring a spell, or maybe Stan had
put a spell on him, because Slim blurted out the only clue he had:
"Follow the gnome. That's all I can tell ya. Follow the gnome. If you
do that, you'll figure her out."

*

An orange cat had been hanging around Stan's house, appearing at
the porch door and then, when Stan went to feed him, scooting. I
saw him several times. One day he pressed his face against the glass
and gave me a withering get-a-life look.

I was not at Stan's as often as the orange cat implied. All the incidents in this story were spread out over months. The street where I
live suffers from power outages, and I went to Stan's when my power
was out. Nobody knows why the power goes out at the hint of a
breeze, the rumour of rain, and nobody cares to do anything about
it. I took my Mac, and I went downstairs. From there, I could, if Stan
had a visitor, eavesdrop on the stairs, which I do not recommend.

My one-bedroom condo is spartan at best, an impulse purchase.
I bought it after Jack because it felt safe and easy. I paid $150,000. I

did not know about the power outages. I did not know that it was on an escape route that thieves like Korey St. Clair Scudder used on nights of crime, returning to their North End lairs filled with milk crates, white undershirts, and keyboard cleaner.

One day I will decorate.

There are twelve units in my building, and everyone who inhabits them is guarded. It is as though they are hiding from the results of an AncestryDNA test. They drop their eyes. They search for keys—there is no chance to chat about the weather or who stole my car from the parking lot. No chance they will know me.

Some nights, when I have trouble sleeping in my unadorned condo, I try to recall the name of every man I kissed. I count them on both hands. Then again. It is my version of counting sheep. Sometimes, I cheat. I skip someone I should never have kissed. I linger longer than I should at another. *Who*, I wondered, *would have made life exciting? Who would have been awful?* One list is short, the other stupidly long.

Maybe you have one.

The best part of my condo is that it is near Lake Banook, where Peter and Luke raced. I can, with a short walk, see people chasing their dreams. I can hear the loudspeakers on regatta day calling paddlers to the line. I can feel the excitement. I can hear the accented English of a paddler from Quebec City, who was, you could convince yourself, if you were young and foolish, in love with you.

*

There were other rumours about Graham. There always are. Most missing person's stories follow a pattern. And then there are the radical exceptions that upend everything you thought you knew about life and chance and the human psyche. Like the middle-aged woman in New Brunswick who vanished after her shift at a tax kiosk. Grabbed, as it turned out, at knifepoint by a sadistic stranger. Held prisoner in a filthy basement where she was assaulted for twenty-six days. Her husband had not killed her as those stories often go. She had not run away. She had, in fact, found the will to escape by thinking constantly of her family. Her case was not the scenario anyone envisaged.

As shocking as her story was, it gave hope to other families. The ones who never stop looking. Who print flyers and post rewards. Who form their own search parties. Who hire helicopters, psychics, drones, and dogs long after the official odds are against them.

I was at Stan's during his last conversation with Graham. Stan was in a foul mood. He had misplaced six hundred dollars he had taken out of the bank to pay an electrician under the table. Stan liked the feel of cash. He liked pulling out a roll of fifty- and one-hundred-dollar bills. The six hundred dollars was for pot lights downstairs, and pot lights seemed important at the time—a sign of being with it—in the same way that shag carpet had once seemed important.

I had come upstairs to make a coffee. Graham was in the white visitors' chair. His body was hunched. He looked like there was a pair of invisible hands holding him in place, to keep him from springing off. I was in the hallway, where neither Stan nor Graham could see me, but I could see them.

Graham was wearing his prized Bruins ball cap. It had a high crown. On the front was an embroidered Boston logo. On the bill, the years the Bruins had won the Stanley Cup. Chára's #33 was on both sides. Stan never wore ball caps—they looked ridiculous on his lollipop head—but Graham looked like he'd been born in one.

I was at Stan's when Graham first produced his Chára hat. The excitement was palpable.

"I near took a fright when I seen it," Graham said.

"No wonder," said Stan. "It looks good, and it's the right size."

"Nothing rides my ass the wrong way like a hat that don't fit."

Finding the hat was a sign, they had agreed: an omen for the

Bruins. It was not that hard to stumble across Leafs' castoffs in a second-hand store — "Who wants that garbage?" asked Graham — but a genuine Chára hat, *and* one that fit — that was like finding a one-hundred-dollar bill on the sidewalk.

"I think Big Zee mighta wore it his self," Graham said. "There is writing on the label that looks like a Z." As though Chára, who made $8.5 million one year, had to write his name on his belongings like a preschooler.

"It's possible," suggested Stan. "Totally possible. For a man his size, almost seven feet on skates, he *could* have a small head. Heads are funny things."

Unlike Graham, I cannot get enamoured with public figures: professional athletes, movie stars, or politicians. To me they are just people I used to photograph. Many are pleasant, some are not. There are groupie journalists who sleep with premiers, and journalists who confuse the importance of their subject with their own importance. That is not me.

In Canada, there is a cohort of intelligent, razor-sharp people, some with law degrees, who will stop at nothing to advance their agenda. You can't get tangled up with them because they will out-talk you, they will out-sue you, they will out-trick you. They will go to dark and sinful places you could never conceive of, and many of them work for good causes, and many of them work for bad causes, but they are not like me or you. They are wicked.

Over the years, Stan interviewed enough of them to fill a prison: strategists, pundits, mandarins, pollsters, and activists. He found them far less fascinating than the seven-foot (on skates) Chára, less nuanced than the more common criminal.

On this day, the missing six-hundred-dollar day, Stan turned on Graham. He told Graham — with absolutely no evidence — that Graham's Zee hat, the one they had gushed over, was contaminated by bedbugs. Bedbugs were, he declared, on the city buses (untrue) and in a coffee shop (untrue) and in the used clothing store where Graham had bought his Chára hat (undetermined). "Those things will eat you alive."

I thought it was cruel for Stan to suggest that Graham's prized possession was garbage, but Stan was like that. He could go low, and he did, which made him a fair match, I suppose, for the wicked people.

Stan was being mean to Graham because he had discovered that Graham had taken a bus to the Halifax casino—I do not know who ratted him out—and this was in violation of Stan's arbitrary rules.

"Whoever tole you that," replied Graham, indignant, "he is a liar."

"I am starting to think that you are a liar."

"I am starting to think that you needs your ears cleaned out."

This was the only time I had witnessed Graham challenge Stan. Usually, Stan asked annoying questions of me or Peter, and Graham laughed on cue. Graham left Stan's house, and I never saw him there again. If you eavesdrop enough times, you are bound to hear something you do not want to hear. I told myself that I would not do it again, but I did.

After Graham left, I made myself seen. Stan was still wound up. "I told Graham," my father griped, "that if he brings a bedbug here, he can hit the road. I wouldn't go on one of those buses if you paid me."

"Well, what if you *need* to get to work?" I asked.

"You *need* to get bedbugs?"

Sigh.

And then Stan turned angry. "After all I did for him."

Graham did not tell Stan many things, I later discovered. Graham did not tell Stan that he regularly took a bus to a Giant Tiger, where he bought cheap smokes. Or that one of his buddies, a man he chummed around with in the North End, came home one day and found his dog dead. And that dog was the only thing in the world he had. And he cried and cried and cried. And the animal rescue people told him the dog had died of rat poison. And he cried some more. And that was a zillion times worse than bedbugs.

What Could Have Happened

Stan and Graham were sitting in Stan's living room, and they were fired up. So fired up that they did not notice I was in the doorway, near the spot where Peter had once been kidney-punched.

Graham claimed that he actually encountered Brad Marchand that day. The Bruins winger was in town for a family wedding. King Rat was wearing casual rat wear, Graham said, barely able to contain his excitement, and driving a rented BMW, when he stopped for gas.

"Are you sure it was him?" asked Stan, who was trained to recognize important people.

"Oh, yes. I yelled, 'Hey, Marchy,' and he turned."

"Hmm," murmured Stan.

"He seen my hat with Chára's number, and he said, 'Were they sold out of the good numbers? Sixty-three?'"

"That sounds like Marchy."

Stan was in his zone. Like most in the media, he was fascinated by superlatives. The first. The greatest. The biggest. Marchy was, according to some unofficial polls, the league's most hated player. And the least boring. Chára was, according to Stan—and I have no authority to challenge this—at one point, the NHL's tallest, oldest, and in possession of the league's hardest shot, a hockey trifecta.

"Some snot-nosed kid run up to him at the pump and said Crosby's team was going to win the Cup this year," Graham explained. "Marchy told him he looked too young to be day drunk."

Stan laughed.

"I'd like to see Marchy punch crybaby Sid in the face," Graham said after a moment of silence. The way he said it, dead serious and malevolent, should have told me something about my cousin. About who he was and where all this was going. "That would teach him to shut his crybaby mouth."

"They train together in the summers," replied Stan, "him and Crosby. I think they get along."

Silence.

And then Graham stated, as he did whenever anyone questioned Marchand's motives or methodology, "Marchy don't care."

Just then an electrician showed up at Stan's front door, and my father got up and let him in.

*
*

This was temporary, I told myself, all of it. This lamentable life I was living. I would write a book to prove that I had the discipline to stay with an extended task. Someone would find Graham. I would get a better job. I would buy a condo where the power did not go out, and I would stop wasting my time on losers like Dante. Have you ever dated someone, and you cannot, in retrospect, explain why? You cannot come up with a single good reason.

I met Dante at the Lucky Lady — he was performing in the Show Room on Comedy Night. Dante flashed a bogus smile. The smile you get when a dog owner has let her two Italian mastiffs run off leash. She knows it is against the rules, but she does it anyway. And when the mastiffs charge your legs, she hits you with that smile. It is a ruse to convince you there are no dogs at your legs. And if there are, you should be happy about it. And if you aren't, you are a nasty old bitch.

That was Dante's first and only appearance in the Show Room. In his publicity photo, he had both thumbs hooked in the front pockets of his jeans. He opened his act with a joke about the signs posted throughout the casino (as mandated by law.)

"I'm sure you have read the signs," Dante told the audience of seniors. "*Dooooo* you have a problem with gambling?" He pulled a face. "*Why else* would you be here? You probably drive a car with a front plate that says, *Born in Cape Breton, Living in Exile.* You are probably wearing an adult diaper. You were probably reported missing two days ago. *Of course*, you have a problem."

On my birthday, Dante took me to dinner at a high-end restaurant. He ordered a rib-eye steak and a baked potato, and then proceeded to cut all the food on his plate into small pieces before he took a bite. It took forever. At one point, his face looked pained. He paid for dinner with a gift card that I later discovered he had stolen from the wedding we had attended with his degenerate parents. It was tragic. I get that.

Some people who have turned their lives around say they had to reach rock bottom first. Caught with a $100K unauthorized charge on Grandma's VISA. At rock bottom, people find their footing— they are no longer floundering in a nebulous middle ground of failure. Was that what I was trying to do? To see what it was like down there?

9

I impulsively decided to drive to Pollock Passage that October. It had been years since I was there, and I kept the trip a secret. It was not until months later that I visited Rick, Rick who had been no match for Stan in the turf war over Graham, lacking the strategic advantages of celebrity and surprise.

I have an unspoken agreement with impulsive people. I will not judge them on what foolish, intemperate, and at times, irrational choices they might make, and they will not judge me. The people who buy a Ducati Monster they immediately crash or enter amateur Fight Night in Thailand and get wrecked.

I just drove into town.

Impulse decisions don't feel like impulse decisions at the time; they don't feel like anything. You are just doing something without judgment or expectations, yours or anyone else's, and there is a purity to that, isn't there? The act of doing. When I was in high school, a friend and I hitchhiked to PEI where there were, we'd been told, beach parties and cool lifeguards. We went without a tent, and no one knew where we were.

No one knew I was in Pollock Passage, but I had an excuse to be there, didn't I? Graham. Maybe, I told myself to keep the trip pleasant, Graham was enjoying himself at a fishing camp. Maybe there was a dog. Someone had found a blood-stained pair of jeans in a ditch outside Pollock Passage, but they were not Graham's, it was quickly determined. They were size 38.

Not every impulse decision is bad, I would argue. I knew a man who bought a racehorse, and it turned out okay. I was flat broke when I walked into a Montréal camera store and bought my Leica on layaway. The store let me hold it whenever I made a payment. I took it out of the red cardboard box: 560 grams of chromium-plated brass and vulcanite. The black rubberized material felt solid in my hands.

Chilean photo legend Sergio Larrain, who collaborated with Nobel laureate Pablo Neruda, bought a Leica when he was a student. "Not because I wanted to do photos, but because it was the most beautiful object I could buy," the *New York Times* quoted him as saying. That, for Larrain, was the start of it. The enduring images he made roaming streets until his eye found truth or beauty. There are magical objects that, in the right hands, possess prodigious power, the power to transform you and your surroundings, and my Leica was, for a time, that thing.

I need to tell you what Pollock Passage feels like before I go further, so that you can process why I was pulled in, why I became involved in something that you, if you are not an impulsive person, may have trouble understanding.

Pollock Passage is both raw and purpose-driven. It looks like the fishing village you used to see in old government travel brochures, when tourists strapped wooden lobster pots on the roofs of Oldsmobile station wagons. Its inhabitants know who they are and what they are supposed to be doing—there is a freedom and an inertia in that. In Pollock Passage, the danger of the sea has not been painted over with a palette of heritage colours. There are no five-star restaurants serving mackerel stuffed with scallops. No Carhartt work jackets worn as fashion statements. The lone restaurant closes at seven p.m. because the day starts at four a.m.

Imagine that there had been a tsunami, and when the first wave retreated it left a smattering of white wooden houses, a working-class Atlantis. Some dropped on the shoreline, some further inland. And then when the subsequent wave — the one no one expected — hit, it deposited a church, a government wharf, and a fish plant. And everywhere, in splashes of colour, boats. It feels like *that*.

I could picture Graham here. He would be part of the landscape, like the massive rusted-out anchor dropped on a lawn as décor. Every time I saw Graham in Dartmouth, he looked temporary. He looked like someone who had been driven in to The City to see a cardiologist. After the appointment, Graham and his driver treated themselves to a meal, and Graham tried to give the driver twenty dollars in gas money. He looked like that.

When Stan said there was nothing for Graham down here, he was wrong. There was space, there was the volatility of the ocean. Days and nights that made sense.

*
*

In Pollock Passage, there was a hint of fog that day. If you like fog as I do — if you are not in the business of shipping or flying or war — you would like it there. You can hide in the fog: who you are and what it was that wounded you. I am not going to romanticize fog because people die in fog — boats run aground and planes crash — but if you can get past that, fog makes you feel as though you are viewing life through a white chiffon scarf. Fog makes you believe you are in *Casablanca*. Fog blocks out context. None of your bad decisions seem important in fog. None of them feel lasting.

I expected to feel a twinge of recognition, a genetic memory of an earlier era, but I did not. I had naively believed it would wash over me, enlighten me. The resilience, the hard times that made us who we were. Images of an earlier life.

Before I left Dartmouth, there had been a development, and Stan had phoned to inform me.

"They found the gnome," he said.

"Okay, where?"

There was no need to specify *which* gnome.

"At the pawn shop with the foolish name. They are certain it is his. Graham's gnome was holding a puck. Some don't have the puck. They have a stick. Anyway, it looks like his. And here is the bad part —there is a chip out of one foot."

"Did they find anything besides the gnome?"

"Just a minute, will you." Then gone. Stan thought nothing of putting me on hold. Just a minute, he would say, acting annoyed but actually excited at the thought of a more important person calling. Five minutes later, back. Who was that? I would ask. And the answer could be the premier or it could be a member of the Dartmouth separatist society with new evidence about a failed 1746 French invasion fleet that had sought refuge in Halifax Harbour.

With Stan back on the line, I repeated my question: "Did they find anything besides the gnome?"

Slim had clearly oversold his clue.

"Not that they are telling me."

"Okay," I said. "Keep me posted."

"They wouldn't tell me if they found the Oak Island treasure." *Click.*

It was typical of Stan to end a call without a goodbye. *Click.*

I knew the pawnshop. It was a variation on the classic model. It was run, not by a grizzled tough guy with biker connections, but by two hipsters in hairbands who wanted to make everything ironic. They had coyly named it One Man's Junk. They gave out shots of craft beer, until someone reported them and they were ordered to stop. Most merchandise was standard, bicycles and watches—the valuable pieces inside a locked case—but occasionally something like the gnome to convince themselves it was all a lark. A dusty stuffed weasel.

Stan was interested in Graham's disappearance, but not

emotionally invested. Stan was like that. His heart came with the thickest-grade enamel. He could attend the grimmest of funerals, hear the most tragic of tales, and not be wounded.

My mother was a different story. If Peter or I were upstairs, heart-broken, my mother could not watch TV because she could feel our pain—it was sitting across from her in a pair of flannel pyjama bottoms with tears streaming down its face.

I drove to the wharf where Graham received the tuna head. I sat in my car processing the scene. I saw forklifts and numbered wooden fish boxes. A Ram 2500 with a Browning sticker on the back window, the ride of one of the two fishermen engaged in conversation.

One day, I overheard Graham and Stan talking about this wharf, the Pollock Passage epicentre, with Graham claiming, his voice too shouty, "I never went near there at night when them jackasses was getting their rocks tumbled."

"That is good, Graham," Stan replied. "I am glad you have more sense than that." Stan frequently commended Graham for his good sense, believing this positive reinforcement would influence Graham's decisions—it would keep him from gambling, drinking Golden Wedding whisky, or having sex on a public wharf—when it had no influence at all.

I shot the fifty or so boats tied up, all the colour of billiard balls with white wheelhouses. I wrote down their names. Someone analyzed the names of Nova Scotia inshore boats and found that the greatest percentage are in honour of daughters or granddaughters (*Jeannie & Jen*). After that are wives and girlfriends. In descending numbers again are names with marine references (*Whitecap II*), names related to birds (*Golden Eagle*), geographical locations (*Atlantic Amigo*), or names that show humour (*Almost Paid For*). One boat this day was named *High Roller*, another *Lobstermania*.

There are other catches down here, but lobster is the king. The catch that makes or breaks the economy in a six-month season.

Unlike vague industries like tourism, you can touch and smell lobster, which turns, when cooked, the red of prosperity. If you combine this fishing district, number 34, with the adjacent one, number 33, you have an industry worth hundreds of millions a year. You have over five thousand fishermen spread over sixteen hundred licences and dozens of ports. Filling cargo jets destined for the main markets of the US and, in recent years, China.

I sat listening to the low rumble of a refrigeration truck. Finally, I decided, since I had made the trip, to approach the two men in plaid work jackets. It wasn't much of a gamble. I am good with strangers. I just don't like them at my door.

"Nice day," I said.

"Yep," one of the men replied. "Could be dirty weather coming, though."

The men seemed like they had been waiting all day for a stranger to meander up and ask how things were going. Their ball caps and boots a uniform for thirty years.

"How's the mackerel running?" I asked.

There was enough wind to carry the smell of bait.

"Good, real good. Last year weren't so good but they're back."

They did not seem to care why I was talking to them. I could have been a tourist or a summer-home buyer. Clearly, I was not a fisheries officer. People never feel threatened by me — it made my work as a news photographer easier. It was always that way, not only when I became old. Some journalists come across as too eager. Or sneaky. People fear they will be tricked — they will be shot at a low, unflattering angle with Grandpa's collection of Winchester hunting rifles in the frame. That was not me.

"How long have you fished out of here?" I asked.

Warmed up, they started to banter back and forth, the way they had for years. One of them had lost his two front teeth.

"This fella used to be quite the ladies' man," the one with all his teeth joked. "People mistook him for George Clooney."

The toothless Clooney played along. He said, "Now the ladies call me Fang." Fang did not seem concerned about his appearance, as though he had earned it. They both seemed ready to take the piss out of someone, and I could not tell when they were putting me on. Or not.

We chatted, me asking about their boats, and then I mentioned Graham.

Fang said, "The Missing Link."

I decided not to volunteer that I knew him, but they were, I suspect, on to me. "So, you know him?" I asked.

"Hard not to," said Fang.

"They say he was last seen on this wharf."

"That's what they say."

"With a tuna head."

"Yes, they give him that, and he had a bicycle one of his friends give him. They used it to pick up empties. Buddy had it all on the video. The whole shebang."

"Some people think he might be hiding," I suggested.

"Some people think the moon is made of green cheese."

We went quiet.

And then Fang took in a breath, as though he needed it. "One thing I will say about Graham is: he had no shortage of friends. I'll give him that. Most of them was fine, and some of them was more trouble than a raccoon in your attic."

"*Fancy Pants*," muttered the second man.

"Yes, *Fancy Pants*." Fang shook his head. "My wife likes to say, 'I don't know how he combs his hair so the horns don't show.' His mother used to call it 'mischief,' the stuff he got into. The poor soul, she don't know the half of it."

"Or don't want to."

I thought about asking what he meant—who was *Fancy Pants* and what did he have to do with Graham, whom they had just called the Missing Link?—but I did not get a chance. Fang decided to get us back on firmer ground lest I think they were nosy bags with nothing good to say about anyone, including a missing man who might be dead.

"Another thing I'll say about Graham," Fang volunteered, "is that he could play the harmonica like the devil, he could. I'll give him that, too. He could play any song he wanted. One night I heard him play 'Amazing Grace' and 'Tom Dooley' at a party, and he had me near in tears."

Harmonica? None of us had entertained the idea that Graham was good at anything. None of us were the slight bit musical.

"That's how he got his self mixed up with *Fancy Pants*. That fool thought he could play the guitar, which he could *not*. He can't do nothing 'cept set fires."

"Some say that's where Graham might have been staying last off, over with the Fancys," offered the second man.

Who were the Fancys?

"Graham, he always lived with Rick, his brother," said Fang. "Always. Rick, he is steady as they come. If you want a good captain to go fishing with, that would be Rick. His boat is out right now." He pointed at the ocean. "Rick kept an eye on things."

"You *had* to with Graham."

"It was nice talking to you," I said after a silence.

"I hope we didn't run on too long," said Fang.

"Oh no," I said.

And, as our conversation ended, Fang, the former ladies' man, gave me a wink, as though we were in on something together.

*

It was fall. This was the first version of Pollock Passage I witnessed. The one before the start of the lobster season, when the air was thick with expectations. Captains were on edge about the cost of bait and fuel. Boarding houses were taking in out-of-town crew. Unattached hands were posting messages looking for a site:

Anyone need a man lobstering 34 give me a message. Splice.
Do gear. Have my svop Small Vessel Operator Proficiency
(SFTY 1125). Can run a boat under 15 ton. ill never miss
a day and i work hard. Got references. My number is *******

38 years experience. Got my own transportation. Don't drink
or do dope. Won't complain if a trip don't make nothing. My
number is *******

I would eventually see two other versions of Pollock Passages, one at the height of the lobster season, which runs from November through May. And another in the sweet lull called summer. I would come to know their moods.

Pollock Passage is a village within the Municipality of the District of Barrington, total population 6,600. Barrington Passage is the hub—it has the truck dealerships, the furniture store, the fast-food outlets, and the sign that boasts *Lobster Capital of Canada*. The smaller communities run together along the coast.

Just after you leave Pollock Passage you slide into Shag Harbour, a village of four hundred. Half a century before Oumuamua, long before *The X-Files* and Agent Mulder, there was Shag Harbour. Where on October 4, 1967, a clear still night, an unidentified flying object flashed across the sky like a psychedelic dream and disappeared into infamy with a *whoosh*.[10] I would eventually go there, but not this day.

I located the Pollock Passage house where Stan and Maynard grew up. I took a picture. The old Swim house wore a coat of weary white shingles that may have sighed. There were blue lobster traps in the yard, telling me a fisherman lived there, and on the clothesline work shirts that flapped and fluttered like hope.

---

10 The Shag Harbour UFO incident is featured on a collector's coin released by the Royal Canadian Mint. There is also an official Canada Post Shag Harbour cancellation stamp.

"Do you remember," Peter had asked long after our grandparents died, "the smell of the kerosene heater? That's what I remember, that and biscuits."

"No," I had told him, "I don't."

The house was smaller than the one in my memory, a storey and a half with two bedrooms. Fortified with layers of linoleum, it was built in the 1800s, when families kept bins of potatoes, turnips, and carrots buried in tubs of sand in their cellar, the foundation banked with eel grass. I tried to remember what it had felt like inside. *Had it felt poor? The kind of poor that corrodes your gut with worry.* When Stan was "rich" enough to own more than one pair of dress socks at a time, he bought five identical pairs. He believed that no one had ever had this idea before—it was his alone and brilliant.

Across the road, an entrepreneur had set up a self-serve stand. *MINNOWS $1.00 a DOZEN* over a red cooler and an honour box. Stark and lifeless, the unvarnished scene reminded me of a Robert Frank photo from his seminal trip across America. *What if I was related to the entrepreneur? Maybe he knew Graham or Fancy Pants.*

The first day, Pollock Passage, all of it, seemed organic, except for an ultra-modern $1 million-plus statement house. Extreme enough to be featured in a magazine, it was stuck on galvanized stilts over a rocky cliff. Wood and steel and glass, it looked nothing like the other houses. It looked like it was daring people to say something. I wondered who lived there. They had to have money. Dicky had a saying: "I am impressed by rich people if they are giving me money. At *that* precise moment, I am impressed. Otherwise, no."

When you enter a town as a journalist, you look for the telling details—the ones that make it look appealing or ugly, thriving or down on its luck. If you already have the story written in your head, you see what you need to see: the community garden or the burnt-out loser cruiser. I went into Pollock Passage with an open mind.

I *did* see Rick's house—I looked him up on Facebook. Two storeys, it was substantial compared to the old Swim house. Prepared for anything with heat pumps, new windows, and vinyl siding. I had seen photos of Rick's wife, daughter, and two grandchildren online, but I did not stop in. I probably should have. I should have told him that I was sorry about Graham, but I didn't.

We were, I admit, a family of secrets. I had mine: what happened that night in Montréal. Peter had his. Graham, it later emerged, was a walking, talking secret with a Hohner harmonica in his pocket. And Stan, well, it was impossible to know how many secrets he had. There were secrets he kept from his public — he only had nine toes. The big toe was missing on the right foot, which he did his best to keep covered. The foot that Slim had needled him about. *Had Graham told Slim about the toe, or was Slim, for once in his life, just lucky?*

There were secrets Stan kept from us. When you live for the public's adulation, you cultivate an image, you create a persona. You associate, in shady corners, with deal makers and deal breakers you keep private.

One day I saw Stan having coffee with a man who could have been in disguise. His large nose looked fake, his black moustache looked fake, his *trust me I won't sell you a bill of goods* half smile looked fake. He looked like the last person in the world you would trust, and he was Stan's Member of Parliament.

On another day, I saw Stan climb out of a green vintage Austin-Healey. It took him a while. He walked over to the driver's window, as though an afterthought had come to him. Behind the wheel was a lean man in a ball cap and aviators. I could not see his full face, but I was convinced that I knew him. He was, I believed, Aksel Andersson.

"Did you see anyone today?" I later asked Stan.

"Well, the furnace man was here. I thought the furnace was shot, but he changed a filter, and I am good. Otherwise, never left the house."

A lie. With my long lens, I had taken a picture of the stranger and his car.

Does it seem odd that a secretive person from a secretive family would be writing a family story? And yet it seemed logical when Pamela proposed it, revealing my family's paradox: the need to be seen and not seen at the same time.

＊
＊

I saw the wooden church where Uncle Maynard's funeral was held. It had a graveyard on two sides. The church is central down here, where work is hard and hazardous. People believe that when a person goes to sea — after you see them off with extra socks and a case of water — the only guaranteed reunion is in the afterlife. The afterlife, because nothing in this mean, shitty world makes sense without it.

For a person who loved attention, Stan was conspicuously short on stories from his childhood. He only had two: one about the time he found a washed-up circus trunk on a beach and another about a captain named Ruff Comeau. Others his age were brimming with charming recollections or hard-luck tales about taking a boat to school. Stan had nothing. It was as though his life — the one that mattered — did not start until he became someone else. A Name.

Stan's story about Ruff Comeau went like this: "Ruff Comeau made a good living, and he took care of business. My father — Lark, they called him, although his name was Clarence — was too worried about the small stuff. So, they cheated him on weight, they stole from his traps. Nobody stole from Comeau. One guy tried it and he shot him. Comeau also took care of LeRoy, the village pervert who could not be trusted around children. LeRoy came from a long line of island lighthouse keepers — imagine what went on out there during a game of hide-and-seek. So, Ruff Comeau shot him, too."

Stan told the Ruff Comeau story many times. I did not know if the captain existed or if Stan had invented him as a prototype of how a man should live. I did not know if Ruff shot two men. I do know that when Stan concocted other lies—such as the one about the deckhand "stolen" by a coyote—he used the name Comeau.

Here is the thing with liars. The worst lies are the ones you never hear, the lies of omission about where they have been and who they have been seeing. The lies you cannot weigh. Lies of omission are worse than the instant blurted lie. They continue for months or years, and when you discover the truth—unbelievable as it always is—you think of all the conversations, all the plans and dreams, all the trust you had invested in someone who had, day after day, deceived you. The open lies are easier. You have, with luck, a chance of seeing through them. It was obvious that there was no dog named Baba. Never had been. I had my doubts about Ruff Comeau.

Not much has changed in Pollock Passage since lobsters sold for twenty-five cents a pound. And fishermen went into the woods and harvested spruce trees to bend into traps. The new traps are plasticized wire now. Although old-timers will tell you that the wooden pots came out of the water easier. They will also tell you that a fisherman saw a fanged sea monster, fifty to sixty feet long, covered with barnacles and coral, and it was terrifying.

What exactly was I doing here? In a place of half memories and myths. At some point in life, your choices are limited. They are limited by age and place and the tragedies that have upended your life. They are limited by who you have allowed yourself to be. I wanted to believe I still had choices.

Do you believe in omens? Forerunners? One day, in Montréal, a dead mouse dropped from the sky and landed on my head. At first, I thought it was an acorn that had fallen from a tree, but it was a mouse. Dead on the sidewalk after it bounced off my hair. Maybe, Jack later speculated, a bird had dropped it. Maybe, I allowed. I took a photo of the dirty-looking little rodent—part of one ear was missing—and I made a print, and maybe I should not have made that choice, maybe I should have kept on walking, because nothing good happened after that in Montréal. Nothing good at all.

✱

I returned to the wharf. Fang and his friend were gone. Two new boats were in, and one was not like the others. Solid black, the eight ball on the table. A monochromatic Jedi warrior of a boat named *Second Chance*. It was Rick's new boat. I had seen it on Facebook. I pondered the name's meaning, and I remembered that men, young and old, fathers and brothers, died on boats like this.

In Nova Scotia your chance of dying while fishing is nineteen times higher than at any other job. Most deaths are caused by crew falling overboard, a third by "the stability of the vessel," according to the Workers' Compensation Board, which notes that most fatalities occur in fisheries that use traps, like lobster and crab. In addition to the fatalities are the lost limbs and catastrophic injuries.

In 2013, Rick almost died on his old boat, *Rosie & Rhonda*. The *Standard* ran a story. He was caught in what they call a pot smasher, a storm bad enough to smash lobster pots. He held steady, and then the monster wave hit. Rick's forty-five-foot yellow boat cracked up, the cables broke, and he had as much control as a bale of hay in a tornado. The call went out over marine VHF radio, and all went quiet, as quiet as death, as quiet as a bad decision. It was quiet for forty dire minutes.

Sergeant Thomas Laybolt, a Search and Rescue technician for twenty years, was awarded a bravery medal for hoisting Rick and his crew to a hovering chopper. These days, you can find something bad to say about anyone, but I defy you to say something bad about a person who willingly drops into Hell on a rope.

When you have well over a million dollars tied up in a boat, gear, and a licence, there are risks you take. Good and bad. And then there is the unexplainable. A following sea. A mechanical breakdown with cascading consequences. In December 2020, a scallop dragger sank in the Bay of Fundy, claiming a crew of six. There was no killer storm. No once-in-a decade wave. There were years and years of experience on that boat, rough and rugged men who would not have panicked. And yet, they perished.

When the truly tragic happens, it can alter your brain in one of two ways—you may become hypervigilant, fearful, convinced that the next blow is cocked, or you may become numb. Flat and untouchable. The worst has already happened, so life can go fuck itself. Jack was one, and I was the other. Otherwise, I might have been more freaked out about Graham. I might have seemed, in the telling of this story, sadder.

*
*

Before a dead mouse fell from the sky, another peculiar thing happened in Montréal. And maybe it was an omen as well. Maybe there were many warnings and we could not see them, living, as we were, in our sub-world. Our friend Didier was a performance artist. He was obsessed with geodes, ordinary-looking rocks that, when cut open, contain dazzling colourful crystals. They represented, he said when he was high on peyote, the potential of mankind. They represented the beauty and mystery within us.

One day, Didier made a cloth facsimile of a toddler in overalls and a blue wool sweater. He propped it against a drugstore wall. The stuffed "child" looked about three and you could not see its face. The idea was to elicit a reaction from passersby. Most people stared, then smiled; some were alarmed and then relieved when they figured it out. And then a homeless man wearing a plastic see-through poncho kicked the stuffed child so hard that it went into traffic where it was run over by a BMW. The car kept driving.

＊

One night our writing workshop discussed inspiration. "What inspired you to create your main character?" Pamela asked. And everyone had a story.

Dorothy, who had lost her husband five years earlier, said she had worked for a woman who stayed on her mind. The woman was a fitness fanatic, explained Dorothy who herself was plump and white-haired. The woman had been a plain teen made to feel that her looks were not enough, and so she developed an obsession with her body. She starved it, she tested it, she punished it. She ran ultra-marathons. She suffered through a ten-day cycling event that damaged her kidneys. She became hysterically phobic of pesticides and dairy. She was sixty years old when Dorothy last saw her—*sixty*—and still not convinced she was good enough.

The woman had a boyfriend, Dorothy said. Another fitness adult, an Australian who smelled like old socks. Together they ran, they cycled, they took canoe trips. When the couple went to a wilderness site on an island, he made her carry all their gear. He loaded her up like a pack mule, front and back. He put a fifty-five-pound canoe on her head. He posted photos of her online, and she went along with it to prove that she was "strong."

"And that," said Dorothy, "was one of the saddest things I have ever seen."

"Ahhh," said someone.

"I had a lovely husband, you know. We had a lovely life."

Didn't we all?

10

After I started this story, I went to the provincial archives in Halifax to view old newspapers. When you enter, you place your belongings in a locker. You must use a pencil to take notes, leading me to believe that someone must have done something bad there once.

Later, in another archives, a smaller, less secured one, I would discover things that threatened my entire narrative, but that was not this day. This day was ordinary. There were two other visitors on my floor, and they did not look like the type to poke holes in old documents. One was a Dalhousie professor whose arms were covered with a graphic novel of tattoos. The other was a well-to-do retiree in a pink cotton shirt. Both were silently busy.

Halifax always had a rich South End and a poor North End, even though gentrification has blurred the physical borders. If you were from the South End, you wore certain clothes, drove certain cars, had certain hobbies, used certain words, went to certain schools, and married certain people, although I would be at a loss to tell you what those things were. You had to be in the club to know.

The class line in Dartmouth is vaguer. Sometimes you can explain who people are by who they are not. We, for better or for worse, were not the Dandos. When Peter and I were children, the Dandos lived on our street. The family carried an aura of implicit shame. They seemed to be descended from a long line of mole people, people dipped in smoke and coal dust, people who lived on a diet of canned peas and margarine they had neglected to colour.

I think of that margarine when I think of the Dandos. Why would someone not add that packet of colouring, the one that came with it? Why was that so hard? Our family was not like that. We could be bright and shiny and fresh as butter; we could look like we were, all of us, trying. We could look like we had no genetic memory of poverty or tuberculosis. We could seem special.

One night, one of the Dandos came into the Lucky Lady. I knew him at first glance. His looks had not changed except that his hair was grey. The family had only one nose among them. It was as though that was all they could afford on the father's butcher salary. A droopy nose that gave them all a melancholy presence.

"Great to see you," I said.

After high school, Danny had, it turns out, gone to work at a brewery where he was employed for thirty years until he retired with a pension and a lifetime allowance of beer. He wintered in a Florida trailer. He and his wife developed an aptitude for bridge, which they played three nights a week. He was wearing a Hawaiian shirt.

The Dandos, I must note, never hurt a single soul.

They joined the navy cadets, they attended vocational school, they had paper routes. The Dandos, despite their downtrodden demeanour and weak infrastructure, never hurt anyone, which I never understood the importance of until I was older.

"Is your dad still in the house?" he asked.

"Oh, yes," I replied.

"Well, tell him Danny Dando says hello, Danny with the hand grenade."

"Okay."

"Me and your father, we had some fun with that."

"I remember," I said.

*
*

I was having trouble loading a reel of microfiche, and the professor assisted me. The room returned to its unnatural quiet, so as not to disturb the genealogical ghosts. I was there to research 1967, the year that Maynard disappeared, the year of Canada's centennial celebrations and the Shag Harbour UFO. The *Scotia Standard* only started in 1975, so I was looking for older papers.

People write family stories, Pamela had told our group, for a myriad of reasons: (a) self-discovery, (b) aggrandizement, (c) catharsis, (d) revenge, or (e) simply because they have a good story to tell. My reason, I told myself until I believed it, was *e*. Revenge sounded too obvious.

The people in my workshop were beginners, but that did not matter to Pamela, who lived on a higher plane. All she wanted from us was The Truth — cold, naked, chilling, or maudlin. If it was Your Truth, the one that shaped you, damaged you, or empowered you, then it was valid. Pamela wanted us to bundle up all of our pain, our epiphanies, our fantasies, into something that made sense, when life rarely made sense, particularly in the hands of beginners.

I thought about truth and versions of the truth as I pored through old newspapers in the archives. I found no mention of Maynard's 1967 disappearance, which was not surprising. I did see stories about the Shag Harbour UFO. One story said a four-man diving team from the HMCS *Granby* would be assisted by divers from Halifax. Another story contained a bizarre quote from Search and Rescue: "Something definitely went into the water...it could be anything from a grasshopper to another planet."

A week later, the *Halifax Chronicle-Herald* ran its most startling story, the one that quoted an officer from a shadowy Ottawa department "for the investigation of Unidentified Flying Objects" as saying this could be that rare case of "something concrete." Meaning aliens. Intergalactic news.

An older woman arrived, clutching a notebook. She was wearing grey socks in Birkenstock sandals. She looked like that woman who would always, no matter where she ate, say she "hadn't really enjoyed" the meal. She nodded at an employee and took a seat. On the cover of her notebook, in block letters, was **The Rottmanns**. The woman wasted no time in getting down to business, storming the stacks.

What are you looking for? I thought. *Validation, elevation, proof that your forebears were remarkable?*

The woman cleared her throat as though she had heard me.

Do you want to discover a Rottmann horse thief or a wealthy landowner who lost it all? Would that explain who you are?

She cleared her throat again.

Or do you want to catch someone in a lie? Do you want to find an extra branch in the family tree or roots in illegitimate soil?

And then I asked myself, *What do you want? Epigenetic clues?*

One day, I told Peter that I had seen Danny Dando at the Lucky Lady, and he had mentioned the hand grenade.

"Oh yeah," said Peter. "He and his brother found it at a dump. Their parents didn't care."

"Why not?" I asked.

"You know the Dandos," he replied. Peter had been inside the Dando house. He told me the children, who were nice enough, got their aura of shame from their mother. Her father had run off with another woman when she was a child, and she wore that transgression like an electronic ankle monitor for the rest of her life. Even when she could have been happy in her own home with her own children, she refused, in a state of self-imposed ignominy and self-pity, to get over it. She refused to colour the margarine, and that, Peter and I agreed, was not our story. Neither Stan nor my mother felt diminished by their humble beginnings, and if there were dark family secrets, they stayed secret.

✳

I do not remember Uncle Maynard's funeral. I was only a baby. But I am told I went. One morning, Maynard was sitting by his stove with a cup of tea, and then he was gone. No one recovered his body, Stan told us. The seas were eerily calm that day — the calm of a saint waiting to die, the calm of a sniper, the story went. It was 1967, and I am told I went.

When you are poor, you live in a wind tunnel of anguish, and you cannot stop pushing, you cannot stop resisting, or you and your loved ones will be blown away. That changes you. When you are rich, the air is still and easy. You can wear pink shirts or fey floppy hats. After Jack and I moved East, I bought things and I hid them. Vintage photos on real fibre-based paper. Black-and-white street scenes from Paris and the Bronx. A hard-cover copy of *Workers* by Sebastião Salgado. Sometimes I kept my purchases in a closet because Jack never looked there, but none of that was the cause of anything important. Jack didn't care about money because his family had always had it.

Maynard was two years older than Stan. A stubborn man who suffered difficulties I did not know about until I went to Pollock Passage. Maynard was known to fish hard in mean weather. Once while fishing alone, Maynard caught nine thousand pounds of pollock and dressed them himself. He went into the woods and did not come out for eighteen days.

When I looked at the *Chronicle-Herald*, I saw Personals from another time, and they sounded old-fashioned.

> Bachelor, 33, with new car and good job wishes to correspond with lady 25-32. Please include phone number. Box 807.

> Lady will correspond with a respectable gentleman aged 35 to 50.

I saw ads for used cars.

a 1966 Volkswagen for $1,495, and a '66 Buick four-door hardtop with power steering and 12,000 miles for $3,095.

I read an Associated Press story about a dead horse in Alamosa, Colorado. The story stated that an autopsy had been performed on the now-legendary Appaloosa named Lady whose owners believed she was killed by the "inhabitants of a flying saucer." Aliens, it seemed, were everywhere in 1967, much like the Beatles.

The genealogy woman cleared her throat again; it seemed like a tic. Back in the stacks, I located a newspaper from Yarmouth. As I reached page six, the genealogy woman made a noise—*ruff ruff*—and I thought she was clearing her throat. She did it again—*ruff ruff*—and again and again, and it soon became clear that it was a bark, and it was not going to stop. Both men acted as though nothing had happened.

When you have lived a life like mine, you believe that we are all flawed, haunted, and to a degree, doomed. You allow for tics and peccadilloes. You allow for human blunders, but you draw the line at deliberate cruelty. And murder, of course.

The Yarmouth paper contained photos of the Irish moss industry. An ox pull. In a nod to the times and the outside world, there was a story with the lurid headline:

Toronto's Yorkville Village, a World of LSD, Drugs, and Sex

When I lived in Montréal in the days before Jack, a man stopped his motorcycle and offered me a ride. I said, "Oui." We drove through traffic, me with my Leica tucked to my side. Past delis and bagel shops, I held on to a strange man I would never see again. He dropped me at my apartment, and that was that. There was nothing else. Just a random interaction on a random day.

*

If you look at old pictures — my father has a sepia one of him and Maynard outside a fish shed — the brothers look alike but different. Maynard's hair was darker. Stan was smiling, wanting people to like him, while Maynard wore a scowl. My mother told me that Maynard was their father's favourite because he was eager to do chores like whittling lobster pegs. Stan was closer to their mother.

In fairness to my father, he must have been a worker to make it from Pollock Passage to Toronto, where people applied his makeup and adjusted his mic, where he sat on a pedestal of privilege. He could not have been lazy. "I'm not sure how long our father went to school," Stan once said. "Probably grade 4. My mother said he took correspondence classes. I doubt that."

I only met Stan's parents a few times. We went to their home after Christmas, and I remember there was an outhouse out back and a wood stove in the kitchen. A kerosene heater in the front room. My grandmother was wearing a cotton housedress under a sweater, and my grandfather a work shirt and suspenders. At least that is how I remember them.

They spoke as though their words were rationed. "She looks like her mother," Stan's father said about me. "And the boy here, you say he is smart?" And both of those things seemed important.

I do not recall much else: if Stan looked like his mother or his father. In my memory, they are vague older people who gave me and Peter each a silver dollar.

*

I went to Stan's days after my visit to the archives. Stan had replaced a china swan with a photo of my mother. And after that, each time I returned, there were more photos of Mother, her presence growing. Mother with Peter on her lap, Mother with her head back laughing, Mother in her wheelchair. It was futile — with Mother gone, the walls would always be darker, the windows squintier, the air as stale as leftover pizza.

At some point in their lives, people try to determine what got them Here. Was it genes? An unhappy childhood? Fate? I thought about the woman at the archives. Had she found something that made sense to her? Would I?

There is a danger when you go snooping. You may find something that is hidden for a reason. Because it is too destructive to take a place at the Christmas dinner table with ordinary people doing their best to lead ordinary lives. It is the drunken Rottmann uncle who kicks over the Christmas tree. Or you find something you believe is huge — he is not really your uncle — and everyone already knows it.

It had been a trying night at the Lucky Lady. A British aircraft carrier with a crew of one thousand was in port. There were bar fights. Police were called. Some crew took a cab to the Lucky Lady, where they did not fight but did require watching, with one sailor professing his love for the human Lucky Lady.

"C'mon, love, you'd be happier with me."

Have you ever worked at a job you think is beneath you? At first, you feel proud that you are so open-minded, and you secretly expect your co-workers to be impressed by your largesse, but they are, you soon discover, not. Some of them are better at the job than you are. Some of them are stealing.

The casino job was fine, not good, as I implied to Dicky, but fine. There were no photography jobs left. No news business as I had known it. Most real news coverage had been overwritten by Twitter propaganda and one-source stories quoting people who should never be quoted because they had no idea what they were talking about.

Man enjoys going barefoot all year even in 42°C.

As though that was a good idea.

Spryfield man says painting he bought at Value Village for $5 is an original Van Gogh.

As if.

Grandmother encourages others to think about adopting a bear.

Why not?

The *Scotia Standard*, which had seen me to the curb, was on a steep slide. I felt sorry for the real journalists still at the business, trying to do their best. One Saturday the main story was about a carrot that allegedly looked exactly like Justin Trudeau.

> GRANVILLE FERRY—Norman Adams and his son Fred made an amazing find in their Granville Ferry garden on Sunday. Norman told this newspaper's reporter that he had never seen anything like this in sixty years. The carrot has a distinct bump where a forehead would go and a nose that resembles the prime minister in profile, he explained, posing for a photo with the rare root vegetable.
>
> "We are deciding what to do with it," Norman said. "My wife is a Liberal and I am a Conservative so we don't know if the carrot will make it to dinner or not."
>
> "Imagine," his son joked, having "the prime minister for dinner."
>
> "Never thought," his father replied that "it would happen in my lifetime."

On and on it went for a full twenty inches with two iPhone photos taken by Norman himself with the headline:

Couple Conflicted Over Trudeau Look-alike
One-of-a-Kind Veggie

‡

Stan and I removed some items from the downstairs. After that, Stan decided to put on his highlight reel, and I, too tired to protest, agreed to watch. We sat on opposite ends of the couch. Stan was by an end table, where he had, until he quit smoking, kept a marble ash-tray. If you were a stranger who had wandered into this scene, you might think I was someone who had run out of choices, reduced, like Graham, to the status of pet poodle. You might think I had made a series of very bad choices.

I had not, in case you are wondering, told Stan that I was writing a book. I don't think he would have believed me. Or he would have lied and said *he* was writing a book, and it was a guaranteed bestseller.

Graham's gnome, Stan's "proof" that he cared more about Graham than anyone else did, was staring at me, his left foot chipped. The captive gnome looked as temporary as Graham had. He looked like he wanted to get out of there.

"Graham loved that gnome," stated Stan, daring me to challenge him. "He *did*."

"Sure," I said because there was nothing else to say. "Sure."

"I couldn't leave it there. Some people would, but not me." He waited, hoping I would comment, but I did not.

Earlier that day, I had bumped into a former reporter from the *Standard*, and she was pushing a stroller. The infant inside was round and pink, the embodiment of contentment. So perfect that she could have been a doll.

"How old?" I asked.

"Four months," the mother replied.

"So sweet."

The reporter talked about the news business. The *Standard* had run a story on a man who kept a record of how many bags of potato chips he had given out on Halloween over twenty years. That was it. The entire story. Plus, a photo of him beaming madly at the camera. The reporter said she should have become a librarian, not a journalist. Better hours, less drama.

"It's not too late for you, is it?" I offered. I think the people who are the most upset about the business shrinking are the ones who *could* have done something else. *What*, I wondered, *could I have done? With my life?*

Stan had the highlight reel playing. In one interview, he is talking to a palliative care nurse who had written a book. It contained stories of people in their final hours, and "how forgiveness made their final journey softer." It was an interesting topic for Stan — forgiveness — as he never entertained the possibility that he needed forgiveness for anything, a sentiment that Peter, lead officer of the Blame Brigade, would dispute.

One day Stan declared, "I don't regret a single thing I did in my life." It felt like a slap in the face.

Peter had his own issues with forgiveness — he was not very good at it. He held grudges against Stan that were not getting him anywhere; he was caught in a ruminative loop of justifiable outrage. Peter needed to move away from Stan or move on. Forgiveness comes easier, I suppose, if you have a history of screwing up — you build it into your plan. I know I did.

Stan decided that we should watch his interview with Aksel Andersson, the infamous thief born in Halifax to Danish parents. Andersson whom I had, I believed, seen with my father recently.

"It was an exclusive," boasted Stan. "I was retired but they brought me back because Aksel wanted *me*."

Of course he did.

Andersson was tall and blond with an elegant nose you might find at a Copenhagen tennis club. He had fine lines at the corners of his eyes, as though he had been squinting into the sun. The Danish Prince of Thieves looked weary when he sat down with Stan. He touched his vintage gold Rolex to assure himself it was there after four years in prison.

For decades Andersson had eluded Interpol and the FBI. He lived for a time in Paris and for a longer time on the east side of Moscow. All this, ordinary Nova Scotians — not to mention the Toronto news magazine — found exotic.

Some of the Andersson story was already known. He stole a Fabergé egg from the Hermitage Museum in St. Petersburg. He lifted rubies from a Paris safe, a commission job for the Russian mob. When the police swooped in on Andersson's lakefront home, a home more opulent than any they would ever enjoy, they found treasures so remarkable that they staged them and invited the media, which took pictures.

Some of the story was new. Andersson told Stan he had received a $50,000 advance for the Paris job, which was to be returned, minus expenses, if he could not deliver the goods to Moscow. If he botched a job within Russia, the mob had the connections to bail him out until he could flee the country. If he was caught outside Russia, it would be complicated. All this, he said — this life of rarefied crime — was behind him.

"The station was excited about the interview." Stan put the tape on pause to explain. "It was risqué. We were . . . *shocked voice* . . . interviewing a Criminal. Not one of the classic ones from Ottawa, but one who hid in ceilings. Aksel had that whole Cary Grant cat burglar persona. And he came bearing a gift, as one would do in Russia: a box of chocolate truffles."

"He is a thief," I noted.

"And you," Stan countered, "are Nelson Mandela?"

Stan restarted the Andersson piece. The thief was wearing a blue suit that hung perfectly on his tennis-lean frame. His prison weariness made him look more romantic. Andersson's obsession with stolen jewels had caught up with him — a jealous girlfriend his undoing — but had done little to dim his celebrity.

I shot Andersson at court once, and he *was* romantic compared to the generic criminals. The jealous girlfriend — the one who turned him in — was there. She tried to catch his eye, but he ignored her. Later I heard that she visited him so often in prison and caused so many problems with guards that he got thrown into The Hole.

Silly woman.

As the interview continued, Andersson recalled his heists with more pride than one might expect for someone who had gone straight. He outlined the history of the Fabergé eggs—the important ones were crafted for the royal Romanovs, murdered in one of most horrific murders in modern history, gunned down and bayoneted at Yekaterinburg in 1918 by Communist revolutionaries.

"It was savage," Andersson said, "all those little children."

I had known men like Andersson: reckless and alluring. Characters as old as heartbreak. Andersson flew his own plane, a Cessna. He was university educated.

If Andersson did not look like your idea of a criminal, Stan told me, you can blame the system, the one that regularly ignores the crimes that people who look like *him* regularly commit. Money laundering. Conflict of interest. Bribery. "In Canada, we go after the truly dangerous element like the eighty-nine-year-old pacifist who refused to fill out the census. Thank God, we got her off the streets."

Aksel's grandest thefts, Stan alleged, were never reported because most of the world's historically significant treasures—the jewels and artifacts guileless tourists pay to look at—were looted in the first place. A convenient rationale. "The cops got the steel safe," Stan scoffed, "but what was hidden in the walls? What was buried in the yard? Ha!" He huffed, as though he had made a spectacular point.

"How," I replied, "would I know?"

It was clear to me that Stan enjoyed the scope of Andersson's crimes. He enjoyed the foreign locales. He enjoyed Andersson's stories about working with his then-wife Svetlana, the stunning decoy. There was a third member of their team, an expert in computer hacking and alarm systems, skills learned in the intelligence branch of the Soviet army.

Aksel kept the team together for fifteen years, performing heists throughout Europe, North and South America, Africa, and the Middle East. He and Svetlana were separated, but still, Stan said, in love. It was a love letter from Svetlana, in fact, that precipitated his jealous girlfriend's betrayal.

Stan enjoyed it all. He enjoyed it as much as he enjoyed a mixed tray of cold cuts with palate-cleansing pickles in the middle. Most of all, Stan liked the anti-hero, the flawed character who defies social norms and is, in certain circles, ennobled. Stan found all of them, not just Andersson, electrifying. He envied their defiance, even when patently self-destructive.

"Aksel and his team drove to the Russian frontier village of Kyakhta and illegally crossed over into Mongolia. I suspect we will be getting into more of that when we go to Russia." He paused for a direct look at me after the taped interview ended.

"Russia?"

A lie. They were not going anywhere.

"Of course, Russia is top secret. You can't breathe a word or Interpol will be all over us."

"Of course."

"I am not joking about that, you know."

"Do I look like I am laughing?"

*

Before I went to work at the Lucky Lady, I briefly had a job with the government shooting and archiving stock photos. It was dull, but I thought I had landed on my feet. I had called in every favour I had to get the job, including one that someone owed Stan. For a while it seemed okay, and then my supervisor died.

The supervisor—everyone agreed that she was "a lovely woman who never complained"—was found one Monday morning, having spent the weekend both dead and at her desk. Her phone was on the floor next to a box of Girl Guide cookies. It was, from all reports, awful, and in that state of awfulness, management promoted Mackenzie, whose go-to when anyone did anything positive was: "Do you want a hero cookie?" Mackenzie—her last name was

Butts—moved with the grudging dilatory speed of a woman who lived for statutory holidays and smoke breaks. Who said "good morning" *only* when in the mood.

I am sure that somewhere in the universe there is someone less suited to their job than Mackenzie—someone more surly, more dense—I just haven't met them. Everyone in the office dressed like it was casual Friday at a tow-truck business. I was okay with that. The department employed a receptionist, an older woman who went out of her way to clean up after parties and keep the coffee maker filled. Mackenzie could not pass Judy's desk without making a "joke" about hot flashes. "Need a fan over here, Judy? Maybe we can move you by an open window." Mackenzie asked Judy to "sensitivity read" a brochure called *Loneliness and Seniors: When the Lights Get Dim* when sensitivity reading was not in Judy's job description.[11]

At the time, I wished Mackenzie was a beauty, a ravishing, spoiled beauty who trampled over people with the immunity that the beautiful possess. That might make sense. But Mackenzie was thick-waisted with the unnatural hairline of a Lego mini-figurine. She could have been born without ears. I could imagine Mackenzie, at the end of the day, removing the orange hair accessory and climbing into a plastic Lego bed. Alone and earless.

It is not that I *could not* deal with Mackenzie and her petty streak. I'd worked with misogynists, drug addicts, an angry witch who practised alchemy, and a photo boss who threw a laptop from a third-floor window, yelling, "Merry Christmas, motherfuckers." I just didn't *want* to.

---

11 When I stated that Mackenzie Butts bullied a co-worker because that woman was old, that worker was, in fact, me. I was not forthright. I lied. That I attribute to vanity. I could not admit that I had been bested by a woman with Lego hair and a horrible disposition. And yet it happened. This probably requires more than an end note.

11

How many times did I go to Pollock Passage that fall? I don't even know.

At first it felt as though I was stealing something from Stan: his place, his people. And I liked that. I liked the fact that all I could smell was the ocean, all I could hear were pick-ups or seabirds. It was Different, in the same way that Montréal had been Different. Sometimes, when I thought I had seen it all, I saw something new: a man driving a forklift with a wood stove on the forks. A schooner moored in a cove.

When you live on the ocean, the unknown is a constant. Anyone can appear on the horizon at any time. A cocaine smuggler, one hundred seventy-four Sikh refugees,[12] or a too-perfect family sailing around the world and home-schooling two sun-baked children, who never, one was led to believe, got bored.

When I was on the highway, I often turned on the radio for that timeless social experiment: the open-line show, a free-for-all Stan

---

12 On July 12, 1987, one hundred seventy-three men and one woman waded ashore in Charlesville, NS, thirteen kilometres from Shag Harbour, after being dropped off by a freighter. They were all Sikh refugees. Not knowing the geography of the area, one man asked for a taxi to Toronto.

once hosted. It was confirmation that the world was unapologetically, undeniably mad.

The host's name was Kurt. No one normal ever phoned in.

There were the regulars. Meryl, the Trump lover — "He is a great man. I don't care what you say, Kurt."

Floyd, the conspiracy theorist — "If the system were any more rigged, she'd be the *Bluenose*." Floyd was ninety-six and still able to get under Kurt's skin. If Kurt challenged one of Floyd's conspiracy theories with a fact, Floyd would respond: "Well, I don't know nothin' about that."

Until one day, Kurt lost it and shouted at a ninety-six-year-old man calling in from a nursing home: "I don't know nothin' about elephants, Floyd, but I know they can't fly."

It was all too much.

The open-line show had a doctor on answering medical queries once a week. On this day, a woman was phoning from the hospital where her husband was receiving treatment. If they were at the hospital, I wondered, why did she need to phone an open-line show for advice? Her husband had, she said, a urinary tract infection. He was on antibiotics, but he had developed a severe pain in his penis.

"Could it be kidney stones?" suggested the host, jumping in.

"If we have kidney stones in a penis, Kurt," said the doctor, "we are taking this show on the road."

On this day, the sun was as bright as the lights you see in a baseball stadium at night. It was so bright that the asphalt, damp from rain the night before, turned iridescent white. On one side of the road, the water sparkled. And it was the most exquisite thing — that water — you could lose yourself in it; you could, without the slightest compunction, lose all of your worries, all of your fears, in those dancing shimmering lights.

When you are a photographer, you think about light: high overcast, first light, or backlight. Light changes everything. Clarity. Emotions.

I was so invigorated by the light that I impulsively decided to stay, to check into the only accommodations I could locate — a Barrington Passage motel that smelled like last winter.

"One night?" the man at the front desk asked, not giving me a look. He must have had a second job because he was wearing grease-stained coveralls.

"Yes," I said, pleased with my decision.

My room had two beds and a mini fridge. I was used to checking into discount motels when I was journalist armed with gear, but this felt exciting. Unplanned. What exactly was I doing there? Who did the front desk worker think I was?

"Harriett is a people person like Stan," my mother told a neighbour long ago. "They get very involved with people, and they have vivid imaginations."

Was it ever a good thing to be compared to Stan?

"Does she make up stories?" the neighbour asked.

"Yes," Mother replied, "but not like Stan. When Harriett makes up a story, she believes it."

Did I? How did Mother know?

I am not good at many things, but I am, I humbly allow, good at some. I never ask strangers difficult questions such as "How much do you earn?" or "Why does your baby not look like you?" That may sound like a superfluous boast unless you have encountered, as I have, individuals who *will* ask, "Why do you think he left you?" or "Did you try to have children?" Those people *do* exist, and maybe, you might argue, should not, but they do. You cannot kill them for being odious.

At the time I overheard Mother, I wondered, *Am I really a people person?* I *was* that child who would drift off with strangers. The child who, when walking home from a friend's house, accepted an invitation to go inside a Bible chapel to watch a movie about lambs and Jesus and was considered missing for two hours.

When I was older, I did employ my purported "people" skills as I carved out a career as a news photographer—first in Montréal and then in Halifax. I did have the ability, like Stan, to make people comfortable, although my father, I concede, was the master. With me, people never sensed that I was looking for something from them, something they needed to protect. I was trustworthy, at least on the job.

*

When I lived alone above a grocery store in Montréal, I slipped downstairs each day. I liked it there. It felt European, and I had been to Europe. The low-ceilinged store was cramped, the aisles as dimly lit as a seedy bar, and I liked that, too. At the back were the fresh pastries. One day while I was buying baklava, in an evanescent moment, I saw a man behind me. He was beautiful and wearing a grey wool sweater that I knew would feel rough on my fingers. And so, I came back. Twice a day until I happened to come around a corner and bump into him, *startled*. We started to talk. He wanted to walk me down the street, and I told him I lived upstairs, and so, we talked upstairs. He did not tell me that he had a girlfriend, but I knew that because I had followed him before. I had taken his photo. I had followed him to a shabby chic pub where Isabelle was waiting, and I saw him peck her cheek and I did not care. On that stage of checkered tablecloths and hockey memorabilia, Jack was his most beautiful. He had long brown hair and a glorious Andy Samberg mouth, before I knew about Andy Samberg. So, I stole him.

In the grocery, Jack had noticed the yellow stains on my fingers. They signalled that I was part of a club, photographers who wanted to feel their prints come alive in the developer without gloves, their bare skin adding heat and friction. He liked that. Jack had specks of paint on both his hands, which meant he was a painter, and I liked that too.

If Jack was so easy to steal, an acquaintance suggested, maybe he was easy to lose. But that wasn't the story. That wasn't the story at all.

(139)

✳

That night in a Barrington Passage motel filled with people who had not been dealt Life's perfect hand, I willed myself to have the Dream, the one that someone owed me. But it did not happen. I slept with the window open, my consolation dream scored by a bass line of trucks.

Before I went to sleep, I thought about Jack. Graham. How do you steal a person? When Stan stole Graham, our cousin could have been a lawn ornament, a miniature jockey with no will of his own. That is how Stan viewed him. When I stole Jack, I knew he was a person with his own free will. But I sensed that he was spoiled. I sensed that he was reckless. I sensed that Jack was willing to go along with the thing that made him feel the happiest, the most alive, on any particular day. And that thing, for a while, was me.

The next morning, I was pleased with myself because wide-legged pants seemed to be back in style. I had bought a pair that week, and wide-legged pants looked good on me. Or so I believed. I am not a clothes person. I am not good with clothes. I once bought a poncho in Spain, and I looked so awkward that someone asked if there was a costume party. These pants covered the toes of my boots, and when I walked, I felt as though I was gliding.

I drove to the McDonald's for breakfast. As I stood in line, happy, in my wide-legged pants, two counter workers were shooting the breeze.

"There is a shark down at the causeway eating seals."

"Yeah?"

"It's on Facebook," the worker added. "Buddy was fishing for mackerel when he saw it come right out of the water. The whole thing—it was out. He shot it with his phone."

I looked out the window in the direction of the causeway, which connects to Cape Sable Island. There is a sign saying that it opened on August 5, 1949. If you cross over to the island, as I later did, you will see other signs such as *The Bait Man* or *Ducky's Bird Carvings*.

You might, if you are lucky, see rare birds and a ghost in a trailing white dress.

At the drive-thru was a Ram 3500 pulling a side-by-side quad.

"Billy Joe's being greasy at the drive-thru again," the female worker said.

"Tell him you'll tell his wife," suggested the male worker.

"I told him that last time."

"Okay, I'll tell him."

And then I heard him say into the microphone, "Billy Joe, smarten up, or I'm calling your wife."

The customer ahead of me had a real raccoon tail attached to her purse the way people attach Ty Beanie Boos lions or unicorns. I wondered if she owned the car in the lot, the one with the *Sexy Bitch* plate. If so, I admired her confidence.

*

If you want to see the fishery in high gear, if you want to feel the buzz of commerce, cross the causeway to Cape Sable Island. Over the centuries, the island has survived wars, hurricanes, the Acadian Expulsion, and American privateers. Sociologists use words like "utilitarian individualism" to define the ideology of the small-boat fisherman. Add to that the island mentality. As well as raw beauty, there is a wildness to Cape Sable Island, a ferocity that tells men to go to sea when others won't — it tells them to drive mossy-green camouflaged ATVs, hunt deer, and not give a fuck what city folk say.

Halifax — and you may not know this — can do whatever it wants, and rural Nova Scotia never gets a say. It can raze the entire Black community of Africville. It can block the harbour view with office towers. But as soon as someone in Eel Bay wants to build a driving range, Halifax is all over it. I had the impression that CSI, as I like to call it, did not care what city people with soft jobs and itchy wool statement hats thought.

If you go to Cape Sable Island on dumping day, the opening of lobster season, you will understand. You will feel the intensity. The danger. Dumping day is like the start of an IndyCar race, that large, that expectant. Boats laden with traps and buoys steam from port. People on shore wave flashlights. Children hold up signs: *GOOD LUCK. BE SAFE.* I went there once to see for myself.

When you go to a new place, any new place, it takes time to get your bearings—to figure out what makes people happy, what makes them scared. Down here, it is the ocean, the constant that runs through villages and graveyards. Vacillating between benevolence and rage. The ocean is what feeds families; it is what breaks mothers' hearts. You can pretend that it does not matter so much—you can pretend that it is not bad luck to be followed by a shark, that dope and booze do not give you courage, but they do.

In the McDonald's parking lot was a pearl-white Range Rover. The driver was crossing the parking lot as I was. We were going in opposite directions, me with my Canon on one shoulder. He was wearing an ultralight down jacket. He was clearly not a fisherman or a birder. The latter are odd creatures weighted down by binoculars and floppy hats, people who last year, on their Christmas Day count, recorded, along with the usual suspects, twenty-one turkey vultures.

He said, "It is a fine day to be taking photos by the ocean," which surprised me.

Nova Scotians will nod at a stranger, they will hold open the door, but they will *not* stare a stranger straight in the face and say, "It is a fine day to be taking photos by the ocean." Not normally. Or maybe the comment surprised me because of his eyes—they were green and direct. They made the greeting seem more personal than it should have, more than a cordial interaction.

The man looked like a former managing editor of mine, I thought. And then I realized that everyone reminds me of someone from the paper. It is as though the world was populated by changelings who took over the bodies of my redundant colleagues.

The M.E. was six-foot-one, lean, with a full head of hair. He looked like William Hurt before Hurt started playing bad guys. He was one of those people who got things because he looked the part. People assumed there must be more there, when there wasn't. He spent his entire life hiding the fact that he was devoid of vision, depth, or for that matter, good judgment. He made enough bad decisions to fill an Airstream motorhome, but he looked like The Man for the Job.

The stranger reminded me of the M.E. If the M.E. had *those* eyes. If the M.E. had been a come-from-away. If the M.E. had not landed a plum job in the premier's office, where he tightens his mouth and pretends that he knows what is going on, when he does not.

I kept thinking about the strange man longer than I should have on the drive home. I thought about the fact that I liked his bold green eyes. I liked the way he walked. I wondered if he was going to Cape Sable Island, which seemed to have a magnetic pull.

If I were photographing the man, I would shoot him with an extremely shallow depth of field. With nothing else in focus. The past, the future.

I was still thinking about his eyes that night. We were not known for our eyes, my family. We had straight noses and Colgate smiles, but our eyes were unremarkable. The stranger had exceptional eyes, and I think—no, I am certain—that he knew it.

*
*

When I was at the paper, I shot portraits for a "Top 25 Nova Scotians Under 25" series. The series, a doomed attempt to draw in millennial readers, ran over a week. In addition to the predictable young overachievers was a mechanic who was skilled with superchargers.

The mechanic—his name was Jordan—was wearing bib coveralls and a red plaid shirt when I shot him. His face was ruddy, permanently flushed. He lived outside the city and had a waiting list of customers. In his garage, we talked cars—I drove an

Audi, he drove a Mustang GT. He also owned a red 1969 Ford
Ranchero — and then he asked me if I had been to Florida.
"Yes," I replied, "a couple of times. It's okay."
"That's my dream," said Jordan, "to go to Florida. They got a
place down there where they keep all the monkeys from the movies.
They got dozens of them, some from *Planet of the Apes*, Michael
Jackson's chimpanzee Bubbles. And that's my dream, to go there.
They say they won't let you into the place, but I am pretty sure I
could get in." He paused to let the dream establish itself. "They've
got the twins, Jacob and Jonah, from the Tim Burton movie. They
got the Clint Eastwood orangutan." Pause. "This is something I
know I would be good at, dealing with monkeys." He looked at me
with the unfettered optimism of youth. "I could make it work." He
smiled, and I believed him. "I make things work."
"And what about your baby?" I asked because he had one. The
baby was sitting in a car seat in the garage. And he was dressed
exactly like his father, in bib coveralls and a plaid shirt. Only miniature. He was not wearing shoes, just white socks.
"I'll take him with me."
"Okay."
I thought about Jordan and his miniature matching self. I thought
about how people may not be what they appear. How they may be
moving in a direction you cannot see, getting all their ducks lined
up under your nose like Jack did.
Did the stranger with the bold eyes have a life that might surprise
me? Two wives who did not know about each other? A catamaran?
Was he capable of loyalty or deception? I thought about him for a
while — where he was from, or what he might do for a living.
Around this time, I was losing confidence in my memoir. What
if it turned out worse than Ingolf's chemistry novel? Boring. While I
was in the city, thinking about what I was doing with this story and
my life, two things happened. One of them changed everything I
thought I knew about Graham.

✳

I was in my condo when I saw an online police release. It was late November. A man had gone on a "crime spree" in North End Dartmouth when he was supposed to be serving weekends. The "spree"—not an expression you use in the news business because it makes crime sound frivolous—occurred the first weekend that he was scheduled to turn himself in to the Central Nova Scotia Correctional Facility. Also known as the Burnside jail aka Hell aka a Hazardous Shit Hole, where you might be beaten unconscious while ten prisoners form a circle around you. Instead of reporting to Hell, where no one with any survival instincts would voluntarily go, he had committed more crimes. All this was close to Graham's building. And the recidivist was Korey St. Clair Scudder, the skid who stole my car.

Police release

Police charged a Dartmouth man for robbery and two other incidents that occurred in Dartmouth.

On November 26, at approximately 3:00 p.m. police received a report of a vehicle that had been taken from a residence.

Later that night police received a report from the Central Nova Scotia Correctional Facility of a man who had failed to attend for his court-ordered intermittent sentence. It was the same man.

On November 27, at approximately 1:45 p.m., police received a report of a robbery at a residence in the 200 block of White Street in Dartmouth. A man was assaulted as he entered his residence. The suspect demanded money and fled the area. The suspect was identified as the same man from the two previous incidents, both times wearing black skeleton gloves. He wore one black sneaker and one white one.

On November 28, the suspect was arrested without incident at approximately 11:45 p.m. in the 0-100 block of Cavalier Drive in Dartmouth. Twenty-four-year-old Korey St. Clair Scudder of Dartmouth is scheduled to appear in Dartmouth Provincial Court to face the following charges:

Unlawfully at large contrary to section 145(1)(b) of the *Criminal Code*
Robbery, contrary to section 344 of the *Criminal Code*
Assault, contrary to section 266 of the *Criminal Code*
Breach of probation, contrary to section 733.1(1)(a) of the *Criminal Code*
Taking a motor vehicle without consent, contrary to section 335(1) of the *Criminal Code*
Theft Under $5000.00, contrary to section 334(b) of the *Criminal Code.*

This is annoying, I thought. What if he had returned to my building? What if he had decided to attack me because the Crown subpoenaed me? Why didn't someone keep track of him? How hard was that?

✱

I forgot to mention something of note from my time in Barrington Passage. At the McDonald's, I saw a Missing Person poster for Graham on a bulletin board by the entrance. Graham was bare-headed in the photo. He looked fuzzy, as though he had been cropped out of a group shot and blown up. I could see the collar of a white dress shirt, and if I had to guess, I would speculate that he was at a wedding. Graham was glancing sideways—his velveteen hair almost shimmered—and he looked, despite his hollow cheeks and haunted Harry Dean Stanton eyes, happy. He looked like he belonged.

MISSING
HAVE YOU SEEN GRAHAM SWIM?

Last seen on September 13, 2018, in Pollock Passage wearing a green T-shirt and a black-and-gold Bruins ball cap.

I should have mentioned it earlier, but I hadn't wanted to think about it—it made his disappearance too visceral, too real—or maybe I was preoccupied by the man with the bold green eyes. Maybe that is the truth.

*

Still killing time on my computer, I went to an online group for photographers. Coastal Images is peopled by marginal pros and amateurs with day jobs. One Hasselblad-wielding man wears a vintage 1930s Japanese military coat and a dog fur hat. It is a mindless place to go. Members post photos of sunsets and dishevelled fox cubs; they debate lenses. When my lens was stolen, I warned members against buying it.

My message light came on. A DM from a photographer named Marshall, who was in real life a firefighter.

Hey. I saw your post about the Canon 300 2.8 lens.

Okay. I replied. *That was a while back.*

The timing seemed suspicious, the same day as the police report about Korey.

I can get it back to you.

You can?

Yes.

I am interested. Let's talk.

The stolen lens was worth $8,000, and I had not yet collected the insurance payout. I could have ignored Marshall's message and let my claim go through, but it would be more honest to get the lens back, and my rates might not go up.

After establishing that Marshall was not a serial killer or an overzealous insurance adjuster, I arranged to meet him at a Tim

Hortons, the safe zone for Kijiji sales, blind dates, and job interviews for commission-only positions. I had, by then, checked Marshall's Facebook. I saw photos of him at the fire station and photos of his girlfriend. He seemed legit.

*
*

The coffee shop Hortons was empty, except for three old men seated at a table. They had two boxed sets of VHS movies in front of them as though they were selling or exchanging them. One set was "Wars That Changed the World," the other was "Mister Bean," and during the entire time I was there, the movies never moved.

Marshall arrived, looking like a millennial firefighter might. He looked like he spent time at a gym and owned a photogenic dog, possibly a blue heeler named Sloan. Marshall was wearing a micro beanie and an olive-green North Face jacket. He seemed to be doing okay.

Fashionably stubbled, he sat across from me. "Hey, how is it going?" Marshall was a low close talker. "It's good to meet you. You used to shoot for the paper, a lot of court stuff, right? That must get intense. My girlfriend's uncle worked at the paper in advertising." He mentioned a name.

"Yeah, I know him. Good guy. Had a heart attack, I think."

"That is right. He was a runner, too."

"You never know."

We shrugged at the uncertainty of life.

"My girlfriend is a Jungian analyst," said Marshall, still low talking. "She took social work at Dalhousie and then studied at a Jungian institute." Marshall was one of those men who felt compelled to tell you he was off the market, even though I was there at *his* request. It is annoying. And it happens.

"Ahhh, that's cool."

"It is. She helps people. She is leading a course now on mindful origami." He took a sip of his coffee, letting the image sink in. "The idea is to be creative and mindful as you make something from paper. You have to stay in the moment. At every fold, you have to be aware of the paper: the feel, the sound."

"I see," I said. "Never tried it."

There are attractive people who create a sexual charge when they are in your company—they make you feel both bothered and indecent—and Marshall seemed to think he was one of them, when he wasn't. Marshall was trying to keep his imagined superpower under control by being extra boring. Otherwise, he seemed to believe, he would have been too much for a sad old woman like me.

"Well, if you do, do *not* judge yourself. Maybe your hands were stiff, or the air was humid. Maybe the paper was not compliant."

Marshall had managed to slow everything down, the conversation, my breathing. He had even slowed down the three men at the other table, lulled into an origami stupor. Marshall should not have been worried about me. I had known the playboys. Men who were up for anything—yet nothing—at the very same time. Men far more dangerous than he. The true playboys have no off switch, I could have told Marshall. They are enchanted by all women, including old ones, or maybe they are enchanted by themselves—it feels the same.

"Do you do it, the origami?" I asked. Because this is where I was. Sitting in a Tim Hortons with a blabbermouth carrying stolen goods. One day you look in the mirror and you look fifty, the next day seventy-five. Your jawline has weakened. The crinkles around your eyes are no longer crinkles—they are crevasses. I was not there *yet*, I told myself. Strangers might still stare me straight in the face because I seemed interesting.

"I've done the easy ones, the tulip," Marshall said.

One of the old men closed his eyes, as if to say, *This is too much.*

"You can use paper that is coloured on one side and then the head will be a different colour..." On and on he went.

Finally, I asked, because I *had* come there for a reason, "What can you tell me about the lens?"

The lens, Marshall said, was in his Jeep.

Before we moved on to the purpose of our meeting — exchanging the lens — Marshall felt a need to tell me the story of how he came to possess my property, a story that was half-believable. He frequented a pawnshop, he said. "You never know what you'll find." Marshall named the shop — it was the one with Graham's gnome, the pawnshop run by the hair-banded hipsters, who wanted to make the business ironic, *One Man's Junk*, the jejune hipsters who did not have the necessary biker connections.

"I once picked up an Elinchrom light kit someone dropped off."

"Cool."

When Marshall was in the shop, two characters showed up. "It's not that big of a place." The young guy sent the older dude to the counter with the lens, Marshall recalled. He stayed by the entrance, looking just strung out enough to be a problem. A customer was buying an engagement ring from the locked case. Marshall waited until he was gone.

"I wanted to de-escalate the situation."

"Sure, I get that," I lied.

"I don't know what I was thinking."

Marshall said the younger guy looked like part of a gang of meat thieves that frequented North End grocery stores. We had both seen them. They show up mid-day in ball caps and hoodies. They are always strung out. They overload shopping carts with roasts, forty-dollar turkeys, and T-bone steaks, and they *actually* believe they are going to make it out the door. Ensuring that does not happen are two detectives, easily made by their hands-folded detective stances. The strung-out thieves are so strung out that they think they are fooling the detectives with their commentary: "Mom is really going to like this ham." And then comes the takedown. The young guy looked like that.

"So, I told the owner to take the lens, and I'd buy it from him. Just to get rid of them."

"Makes sense," I said, when it did not.

Soon it became clear why Marshall needed to return my lens. Because he was a photographer, it could be established that he knew the lens was worth more than the $100 he paid. That meant he could be charged with possession of stolen goods over $5,000, an indictable offence that could get him up to ten years.

If I have one piece of advice based on my years of covering courts, it is this: do *not*, if you can in any way avoid it, get mixed up with the law. The *Standard*'s court reporter estimates that if you do, there is a *seventy per cent* chance they will get it right. Once you build in the conscripted jurors, the racial profiling, the lying jailhouse snitch, the angry judge with the benzo addiction, the political operative, and the slick-willy lawyer from Toronto with the Charter loophole in his pocket. Are those odds good enough for you?

If you have been in court when a bad decision comes down, when a rapist walks or an innocent man goes to prison, you will have seen families at their most primordial. It is both dark and discordant. You try not to feel guilty when you photograph them. You show relatives in a group hug, faces obscured. You zoom in on a baby photo of the victim that someone is holding. You try to be kind.

"I believe in law and order," I said, "but I'm not fanatical about it."

Marshall nodded as though we were on the same page. Marshall was acutely aware of how much trouble he could be in. He liked his job with the fire department—last year he made $120K. The photo business was a sideline that got him access to concerts. He liked the house he shared with the Jungian analyst who made osso buco.

"I don't know what I was thinking," he sighed.

The line sounded even less sincere the second time.

I knew what Marshall wanted me to say. "I can tell the insurance company that someone found it in a dumpster. They'll be happy."

"Really? That is great," said Marshall. "The store's cameras weren't working, so we're all good there."

We?

"I just wanted them out of there before anyone got hurt."

Marshall and I talked about the photo business — he said he was starting to shoot raw. He was experimenting with large-format print-making. "Mindfulness helps," he added, "for me."

Marshall went to the washroom. The three old men had come out of their origami stupor and were talking politics. There had been a debate on TV, and one man said: I'd rather vote for the dog next door. Another said: I'seen two-year-olds in mud better behaved than that. And then the third said: That Diefenbaker was a character, wasn't he?

When Marshall returned, one man gave me a nod of sympathy.

"It is really good that you are doing this," Marshall said.

"Sure," I shrugged. "It is a win-win."

"I am pretty sure they had bear spray."

I offered to reimburse Marshall his hundred dollars, but he declined. We walked to Marshall's Jeep, parked out of range of the surveillance cameras. A worker in short sleeves was putting garbage in a dumpster, and we waited until he finished. It was an unusually mild fall. When Marshall handed me the lens, I did a quick check — it seemed intact.

Was I doing the right thing? I could have collected the insurance money.

"My girlfriend will be happy."

This again.

"Do you know who they were?" I asked as Marshall climbed in the Jeep. "Was one of them named Korey?"

"Dunno. The young guy was wearing skeleton gloves and different colour shoes."

"That's him, the guy who stole my car."

"The old guy — I've seen him around the bus stop, tall, skinny, always smoking. I think he fences the goods because they don't care if he gets nabbed."

"How so?"

"He's disposable. He wears a Bruins ball cap, which I noticed because I am a Habs fan." Marshall was searching for details.

I paused. I did not want to ask the next question. I did not want to ask in the same way that you do not want to open that statement from the tax man, in the same way that Marshall did not want me to think too hard about his half-believable story.

"Was there a number on his hat?"

"Yeah, thirty-three."

"Thirty-three?"

"Yeah, the Big Zee."

While I tried to keep a poker face, Marshall got a confused look on *his* face, as though he was attempting one of the hard origami patterns.

"He did the weirdest thing. The old dude. When the owner bent down to pick up a speaker, the dude punched him from behind. And then he laughed." Even the stubble on Marshall's face looked confused. "I don't know why he did it."

There it was. Graham was a serial kidney-puncher and a fence. And Stan had elected to move him into a building near Korey's lair. Next door to an unlicensed barber shop run by an ex-con. Graham's meeting Korey was as illogical as it was logical. And we were dealing with that sector, weren't we? The one that believes, "If the system is fucked why not fuck the system?"

"It was the short owner," noted Marshall, as though that made a difference.

I tried to put the dates together in my head: my Audi theft, Graham's disappearance. I told myself that this was good. It was humbling (as though I needed more humbling), to learn that I had an actual criminal within my family after years of covering actual criminals. What kind of people did Graham deal with? Were the Swims lower than the Dandos?

✳

"Are people born evil?" a would-be writer asked Ingolf one night. "Are they born criminals?"

"Well," the professor replied, as he had before, "that is not an organic chemistry question, but yes. Criminogenic traits *have* been traced to both biology and genetics. Studies of identical twins have proven the gene factor, while researchers have established environment. By which we mean not only immediate family but neighbourhood."

Ingolf was not a terribly talented writer, but he tried to contribute to the group by answering any and all science questions.

"I don't know if you are aware of the Dutch Hunger Winter in World War Two," he said. "Scientists studied children born in the famine. When those children reached middle age, many had higher cholesterol levels. They suffered from obesity, diabetes, cardiovascular disease, and schizophrenia."

Ingolf added ballast to our tippy boat, captained by Pamela, who was startled by sudden noises, throwing up her hands when a car backfired outside. Pamela, who read a section from one of her novels to us, and it was so beautiful that Dorothy cried.

"I kind of wondered," the first writer said, "because I have someone evil in my book."

"Ahh, good to know," said someone.

"The character is based on my ex."

"Ahhh."

"When he visited me in hospital after our son was born, he brought flowers that he stole from a graveyard."

"Ahhh."

Pamela, who was wearing an enormous tie-dye scarf, flinched as though she had touched a hot stove.

*
*

I finally found Korey St. Clair Scudder in the court decisions. Not for the latest offences, but for an old one. Korey had been charged with operating a motor vehicle while impaired, contrary to section 253(1)(a) of the *Criminal Code*. A witness saw him huffing a $9.93 Emzone Air Duster in a Walmart parking lot. Korey passed out six times, the witness said, for up to twenty seconds before driving away in a Hyundai Santa Fe. The witness called 911. By the time the cops caught Korey, he had grazed a school bus. Korey, whose depraved world was colliding with mine.

"Mister Scudder has a history of abusing cocaine, mushrooms, ecstasy, marijuana, and alcohol," the decision wrote. "During his pre-sentence report interview he also stated that he has taken the prescription medications of others. These included Percocet and Tylenol with codeine. He does not believe he has a drug problem and has never sought help."

12

Peter was at Stan's to fix a door a week after I met Marshall. It was Stan's birthday, but he was ignoring it. He steadfastly ignored all of his birthdays, although he felt compelled to "celebrate" ours out of respect to Mother. For years, to not feel like a bad person, I had given Stan birthday presents and never saw them again. Stan disliked his birthdays as much as he disliked hospitals and the birthday gifts people gave him.

"Have the police spoken to you at all about Graham?" asked Peter, who was holding a screwdriver.

"They wouldn't tell me anything," Stan scoffed.

"Clearly, they would tell you if they discovered something. Like why his apartment was empty..."

"Shows how well *you* know the police."

Twitch. When Peter was with our father, his left eye twitched. There it was: the involuntary twitch that started decades earlier. All it would have taken from Stan, at any point, was a quiet apology to make things better, a modest show of remorse, but Stan was incapable of either. He did not have the vocabulary to admit he had ever done anything wrong.

If something did not go the way Stan had planned, he would

erase it and replace it with a fictional stopgap. He would confabulate, and in time believe it.

Twitch. Twitch.

I decided not to tell Stan and Peter what I knew about Graham. That he was a fence and a serial kidney-puncher. I liked having a secret. Besides, Stan made people who he wanted them to be: sharp or dull, heroes or pocket accessories. Sometimes I wondered, *If Graham was not a real person to Stan, an autonomous individual with a mind of his own, was I?*

It would be tempting to say that Stan underestimated Graham because Graham was disabled. Though his exact condition was never explained. But that would not be true. Stan also underestimated me, Peter, and Mother. Only Graham, unlike the rest of us, had nothing invested in the relationship, no fond memories of family Christmas mornings.

Twitch. Twitch.

My brother had *some* genuine concern about Graham — not as much as he should have — but he also believed this was on Stan. All of it. Peter believed that our father had cheated by relocating Graham. It had been Stan's time to experience loneliness, to pay for his careless neglect of Mother, who had done all the worrying and all the caring for all of us, and just when Peter was anticipating Stan's rightful purgatory, Stan came up with Graham. I understood where Peter was coming from — I could process his grievances — but I had issues of my own.

"Have you heard from Luke?" Stan decided to put Peter on the spot. It was a tough time with Suzanne and Luke, the family buffers, gone. Our interactions felt like metal on metal, bone on bone.

Suzanne was coming home for Christmas and then going back up North. The contracts paid well. She and Peter talked about building a family cottage that Luke could enjoy with them.

"Yeah," said Peter guardedly. "We text, his mother Skypes him."

"Very often?"

"Often enough."

"That's good," Stan said. "Tell him to stay in shape."

Twitch.

The last time I saw Luke he was with Molly, his golden Lab, which looked like a dog version of Luke. That photogenic and wholesome. Luke took Molly to Florida with him for training camp. He left her with his parents when he raced in Szeged, Hungary. Szeged, the paddling mecca, where big screens project the races like you are at a rock concert, and women in shimmering gowns carry out medals. When Luke was in Hungary, his parents had Molly FaceTime him.

To Peter, Luke had been proof that we could be normal.

I went to some of Luke's races. I took photos, which Peter mounted for a wall in his den. I was — and I don't want to sound as though I am bragging — the nice aunt who turned up for birthdays and Christmas, who brought cool gifts and saw nothing but the best in my nephew, who was clearly the best of *us.*

Stan was not satisfied with Peter's noncommittal answers. Stan liked sound bites, not vague generalities. So, he said — because he was in the habit of making Peter uncomfortable, because Peter had not given him the details he desired, because this reticence flew in the face of Stan's reputation as an interviewer — "I see that Allan Crowell was in the paper. Pretty important fellow."

"Whatever," replied Peter.

"Did they get that business cleared up, the business about his times?"

Not the Crowells again.

"There was no business to clear up."

Twitch.

"Well, the paper seems to think there was."

Peter did not reply, and then Stan asked a question no normal person, no decent person, would ask. "Do you ever see the mother?"

Twitch, twitch.

Peter left.

*

The main Halifax library is lavish by Nova Scotia standards. It has a vast open staircase, coffee shops, and rooms for performances. It is also an egalitarian building that provides a resting spot for unhomed people as well as computers for Kijiji surfers. It is predictably unpredictable.

I was at the library doing research for this memoir, and I went downstairs for a coffee. I was trying to forget that Stan had brought up the Crowells, but I could not any more than one can forget that the *Hindenburg* flew over Halifax in 1936. Two women were ahead of me. They were discussing a co-worker in Regina, although they could have been talking about chairs they had purchased online, their voices that impassive.

"He sent me an email and he only used my last name," one said.

"Maybe he doesn't remember your first name."

"No. No. We went on course together in Vancouver. *He* remembers it."

"Maybe he was trying to be formal."

I could tell that she was reaching.

"No. He just wrote, 'Hello, Beaver.'"

And then they went silent, as though there was nothing else to say. That is the thing about life—at times there is nothing else to say. I do not know what to say about the Crowells. I would have preferred to say nothing. But they *were* a part of our story, so I will try to explain them without sounding petty or moralistic.

There are four main types of people in Dartmouth: (a) the regular people (the vast majority) who enjoy the reasonable housing costs and the abundance of lakes; (b) the militants who are still mad about amalgamation; (c) the families who believe they are Dartmouth royalty due to historic nonsense nobody cares about; and (d) the *arrivistes* like Korey St. Clair Scudder and Graham who are *not* from Dartmouth but manage to cause much of the trouble. The Crowells, for no discernible reason, believed they were *c*.

We met the Crowells through paddling. Allan Crowell and Peter raced against each other in single boats and together in a two-man crew. They shared a room at a training camp. They hated the Germans, certain they were doping; they envied the Hungarians because they trained in a hidden sports centre where they did, it now seems established, systemically dope.

Peter and Allan raced canoes, not kayaks. The single boats are called C1s, the doubles C2s. C1 paddlers are a breed apart from the K1 paddlers, who sit upright and paddle on both sides. C1 looks like an eternal struggle. Canoeists kneel. One side of their body ends up larger than the other. When Peter raced, he lined up against giants from the USSR, Germany, or Czechoslovakia, men with gold teeth and bandanas on their bald heads. Men who looked like they could only ever be army officers or bodyguards, *Mad Max* villains. Men who pumped cold iron in a makeshift hut in a St. Petersburg cemetery.

There were five Crowell children. All had remarkably short legs and long upper bodies. They had the same cocky walk—with their chins jutted out so far that their heads titled back. A Crowell chin was like a fist coming at you. The Crowells were so aggressive that I wondered how they could have co-existed under one roof—there had once been an ugly fight over the last hot dog.

Allan Crowell was the mother's favourite. Mrs. Crowell, who considered herself a beauty, ran a ladies fashion shop. The father was a police sergeant. He had one bad eye. The story was that he had been hit in the eye with a cork while opening a bottle of champagne. That may have been a lie.

The whole family had too much invested in Allan's imagined paddling greatness. I was implicated in all this, this whole sinister Crowell subplot, because I had, a lifetime ago, been friends with Babs, the oldest girl.

Some people are put on the Earth only to test you. Your resilience, your belief in karma, the efficacy of turning the other cheek.

Those were the Crowells. The Crowells were the anti-Dandos, who lived in their own little orbit and never hurt anyone. The Crowells were in your face, screaming, "Look at us, we are the Crowells," and they would hurt you if they could. And they did. Peter had good reason to not want to hear about them. Stan had good reason not to bring them up, but he did, self-control being a lesson that Stan, accustomed to the impunity of minor celebrity, had not learned.

Allan Crowell had been in the newspaper for one reason. He had phoned the *Standard* to announce that he was competing in a masters paddling competition in Lithuania, and he needed to tell the world how amazing he was. Allan, who repeated the same fantasy he had been selling for decades. It went like this: Years ago, the legendary paddling coach Attila Szabó said that Allan might be the fastest C1 paddler in the world. Imagine, if you can, the Olympic medals, the halo of glory, the throngs of bleached blond Polish groupies at Allan's feet. While we are at it, let us imagine that your mail carrier is a Martian and that chocolate milk comes from brown cows.

First of all, no one heard the cold-eyed Hungarian say that. And if he did, he was smashed on pálinka and trying to sleep with Babs, who had been hanging around.

Babs had a smile that could be best described as excessive — it came at you with such intensity that you felt like you were being shouted at: *Look at how fun I am!* Your defences went up. But not everyone noticed it then. Any more than they noticed that she chased after men the way poor kids used to chase after an ice cream truck — "Hey, Mister" — yelling at the driver for something free. They just saw a short-legged woman who smiled too hard.

Second, this claim was based on one 1,000-metre time control with one coach's watch. Attila Szabó's. It ignored the fact that the time control took place, according to Peter, on a river with a current. It ignored the fact that Allan had a gale-force tailwind. It ignored the possibility that Attila Szabó might not have even started his watch because it was four p.m., and he was smashed. None of this mattered to the *Standard*, which ran a story and a photo of Allan. Allan, who had never been able to duplicate this time in an actual race with real timers.

✻

After I stole Jack, we drove to Tucumcari, New Mexico. We checked into the Blue Swallow Motel, a nostalgic slice of Americana wrapped in pink stucco. I admit it—we travelled thirty hours to bask in the glow of the motel's iconic swallow sign. Neon red, green, and blue. Kitschy and confident. We felt cool. We felt free and happy. There was never, in that time, a day that felt too long, a moment that felt wasted. Our life was a continuum of perpetual contentment and periodic bliss. On the drive down, Jack asked me if I thought our children would be blond like me or brown-eyed like him. They would, he promised, be beautiful.

The Blue Swallow owner smiled when she gave us our key. Nobody stumbled upon Route 66 anymore. You came here by choice. When we entered our room, it was like stepping back in time to an era when families drove station wagons and used rotary phones. Before an interstate highway made Route 66 redundant. Our room had a queen-sized bed covered with a white chenille bedspread with a blue swallow on it. Jack said his grandparents had a chenille bedspread when he was a boy. So did mine, I said, on my mother's side. It felt serendipitous that we had that tiny detail in common. Me and Jack, who came from such different places.

On our second night at the Blue Swallow, the owner lit a fire pit, and the guests sat outside on lawn chairs and looked at the New Mexico sky. It was the clearest, darkest sky I had ever seen; it was so clear that Jack and I saw Heaven.

15

The impetus for this memoir came from my first writing workshop. And so, while trying to figure out how to write my memoir, I signed up for another with Pamela, who told us that there are only two real plots: (a) someone goes on a journey and (b) a stranger comes to town. As it turned out, my story would have both. And I was the person on the journey.

It was winter now. My new group met around a long table. Ten of us, a disparate mix of ages and occupations, writing or attempting to write adult fiction, zombie stories, children's literature, and erotica. Four of us—me, Dorothy, Ingolf, and a woman named Bernice—had been in Pamela's previous workshop. Bernice had brought cookies, hoping Pamela would not be sad that she had stayed with her original idea of the underground stick people.

This workshop was for people who had taken an introductory workshop. This night's topic was plots. We would outline the plot of our work-in-progress and exchange feedback. I will not steal the plots, Pamela joked, and we laughed. Only the good ones, she joked again. *Ha, ha.* A man who never found anything funny frowned, as though Pamela might steal the plot of *Windy the Flatulent Windmill,* a children's picture book he was prepared to illustrate himself.

I went second. I told the group that my book was non-fiction. I told them about Graham and how Stan stole him. I told them about Shag Harbour and the UFO mystery. I told them I had discovered that Graham was musical. It sounded solid when I said it out loud, it sounded like it might work—the parallel search for Graham and the search for my family story. I mentioned the Crowells, but people's eyes drifted off.

Dorothy, a retired bookkeeper, went first. "It sounds lovely," she said. "People enjoy family stories, and everyone knows Stan Swim. It is too bad about Graham. I am sure that he was a nice person."

Maybe, I thought. *Maybe not.*

Ingolf went next. He said the Shag Harbour angle was strong. Aliens and the theory of anthropomorphic sovereignty were topical and that could contribute to the viability of the book.

"Ahhh, good to know," said Dorothy.

The room went quiet, and during that quiet I looked at the beige cape Dorothy was wearing. It had a Druid hood. As proof that it was handmade, it had embroidered images of puffins and a Newfoundland iceberg. Maybe she believed it made her look writerly. And maybe it did. Maybe that is how writers are supposed to look, oddly out of step, consumed by the tiny details nobody cares about.

I told myself I was off the hook with the Crowells. I had auditioned them and received no applause. And then one of the younger writers, a woman who was attempting a paranormal romance, said she sensed that I was hiding a secret involving the Crowells.

"Am I right?" asked Twyla in a paranormal voice.

"Well, yes," I admitted, "but it is a dark one, and that is the problem."

Dorothy chimed in: "To me, having a secret is like hiding candy from yourself so you won't eat it. At one point you really want that candy, and you can't find it because you have forgotten where it is. And when you do find it, it is mouldy and stale."

"That has happened to me so many times," Bernice claimed.

"Me too."

Twyla said, "Secrets are powerful so you might consider it. A few years ago, my parents had a big dust-up over a secret. It had to be big for *me* to know. My mother does not do confrontation. She won't open the door to strangers; she wears reflective sunglasses indoors and out so that people can't see her eyes. That is her *thing*."

Her father's thing, Twyla said, was the seventies. Every evening, Twyla recalled, when her mother was watching TV in sunglasses, her father sat in their bed strapped to earphones, listening to music from the seventies. Lynyrd Skynyrd. Pink Floyd. After a while it became clear: those were the best years of his life. For thirty years, her father had regaled her mother with stories of concerts and car camping. In those years *before* they met.

And one day he let it slip, a lie of omission he had kept for thirty years, Twyla told us. He had during those years — those golden years, when he had implied that he was as free as bad advice — lived with a woman named Cheryl.

"He said it didn't matter," Twyla explained, "that it wasn't really a secret. But my mother said it *was* a secret — it *was* a serious lie of omission — and she would not have listened to his stories if she had known another woman was in them."

"I agree with your mom," offered Dorothy.

"My mom said that the music he listened to every night was the soundtrack of life with Cheryl. At first, he wouldn't give my mom her full name."

"That is bad," tsked Dorothy.

"Eventually, he did. And the other woman was — and I don't want to sound terrible because I usually do not talk like this — a dogface. My mom looked her up on Facebook. At first, my father refused to look at her picture, which I thought was cheap. It was cheap that he wouldn't even give her that."

"He should have given your mother that, the dogface part," said Dorothy, who hand-painted rocks with images of her cats and left them on walking trails.

"You should write about it," Ingolf told Twyla.

"I might," she said, which meant she already had.

I told the group that I was not telling Stan the secret I had learned about Graham—that he was a crook in cahoots with my car thief. Everyone nodded as though that was fair, Stan being the subject of the book, and all of us wanting to get published, no matter who we sacrificed. And now I had an issue with the Crowell secret, which was deeply personal. Should I reveal it in my book or not? I asked the group.

Yes.

No.

It depends on how bad it is.

It *is* very bad.

Okay.

The group turned to Pamela for guidance, and she said, because she was wise and came, like most fiction writers, with the thinnest of enamels: "You will find your own truth; the story will lead you to it."

"Ahhh," I heard myself saying, "good to know."

✳

Shag Harbour. It had to be part of my story, I decided after the workshop. The Crowells could wait. To help me understand this enduring mystery, I watched a YouTube video made by a community college student. He teed it up with spooky music before he came on camera outside the Shag Harbour UFO Centre. I admired his flair, his bold use of hyperbole. The glowing alien on his T-shirt. His soliloquy went like this:

> Nova Scotians can be silly people. There are entire
> towns full of silly people, people who make too much of
> inconsequential things, claiming to be the first of this
> or that. The friendliest. People who wave at cars with
> out-of-province plates or see Jesus on a Tim's bagel.

Before the cannabis law was changed, Nova Scotians showed up in Statistics Canada surveys as the country's number one users of cannabis. More than British Columbia with its fragrant islands and organic farms? In my mind, as someone who has had the pleasure of visiting an undisclosed location outside Whistler, I would say: "debatable." Or were Nova Scotians too silly to realize they were confessing to an illegal activity, then punishable by prison, an activity that will still get you barred from the United States. They were confessing to a *government agency* controlled by the same people who control the RCMP.

Think about that.

Shag Harbour is not about those people. It is about people who understand the power of the mackerel sky, serious people who would not make up a story about a UFO because they have better things to do.

(A dramatic pause.)

Now let's go inside this great unsolved mystery. When you are a journalist, your default mode is cynical. UFO experiencers are thrown onto the junk heap of kooks, one level above flat earthers. But cynicism, at its most sneering, can create blind spots.

Shag Harbour had endured, a minor Roswell, New Mexico, for over fifty years. If I were to compare the two events, I would say that Shag Harbour was a CBC drama, earnest, with modestly dressed actors, all with their original teeth. Roswell was a Golden Globe–nominated production with Martin Sheen.

To get to Shag Harbour from Halifax, you take Highway 103, and you drive past the turn off to Lunenburg where the tableau is flawless. The eighteenth-century buildings, the fisheries museum, the *Bluenose*. You can spend days in Lunenburg learning about the architecture: Georgian, Colonial, and Victorian Gothic. Even if you are a *mondaine* Euro visitor with a pedigree, you will be impressed by Lunenburg, which offers a nuanced version of Nova Scotia.

After Lunenburg, you keep going on the 103, and you skip the turnoffs to Lockeport, which has a spectacular beach in the heart of town, and Shelburne, which flies the Union Jack in summer.

You take the turnoff to Barrington, and after that it gets real.

One day in Barrington, I found myself driving behind a canary-yellow Ram with a decal on the back window: *Zero Fucks Given*. And then, over the bumper in cursive, *Just Gonna Send It.*

*
*

The UFO museum did not open until June, so I waited months to visit.

By then, the landscape had changed like the set of a play replaced during intermission. Lupines now lined the main road as though it was a church aisle dressed up for a wedding, a flower-bedecked march to the altar. Rhododendrons were in bloom — one deep-pink bush covered an entire lawn. Wild roses added a nostalgic touch.

Lobster season was over, and in the air, you could smell relief.

A canteen was selling ice cream.

The summer cars had emerged. I saw a Camaro Z28 with racing stripes and a Mustang Mach 1, an automotive celebration after a long cold winter that could kill you. I heard the jarring whine of an after-market exhaust system attached to a twelve-year-old Honda Civic, and I could hear people saying, "Settle down, Mason, settle the fuck down."

"Your father's childhood was not easy," my mother told me. "No one even knew his birthday. Whether it was the first or the second. It wasn't easy down there."

It was a softer place this trip: a defused one, and it felt so natural, so easy, that you could wonder how there had once been room for all that fishing danger.

At the old Swim house, I saw the start of a vegetable garden.

Minutes later, I drove into tiny Shag Harbour. There was a dichotomy: a place this small involved in something this big, so epochal, so potentially world-altering that Ottawa and Washington had allegedly conspired to conceal it.

Even though the crash had happened mere kilometres from his home, Stan never discussed it. I assumed that the event had been eclipsed by the loss of Maynard that same day. Before I secretly drove to Shag Harbour, I brought up the UFO with Stan.

"One of those topics I never gave much thought to," my father replied haughtily. "Like cryptocurrency or anthropomorphic sex dolls."

"You only heard that word at the cop shop: cryptocurrency."

"Don't be ridiculous. I never gave it much thought. Someone else could figure it out. Someone from NASA or Project Blue Book. Not me. I'm a people person. That's how I made my living. Not looking for Little Green Men at the Superstore. 'Hello, Dawna. You seem to be having trouble with the scanner today. Are you actually an alien?'"

"I am surprised you didn't talk about it."

"I am surprised you aren't a private detective. Life is full of surprises."

Outside the low yellow museum were three flags, Canadian, American, and Acadian. Across the street a sign for the Guiding Light Baptist Church. The UFO Centre had a sign: *UFO Sighting, 1967, Shag Harbour Incident Centre* and a sketch of two people pointing at a spaceship. Other signs were shaped like Little Green Men.

The museum is as modest as the village it inhabits, but some things are timeless: those primeval concepts of deception and truth. There are people who have exhausted themselves trying to find the truth: writing books, unearthing military telexes. Stonewalled. All I had was a tourist's knowledge. I was not, and am still not, an expert, although I met a man who was.

I do know that around eleven p.m. the first call came in. There was a lit-up object in the sky travelling at unusual speed. The lights had a pattern, and they were losing altitude. When the object crashed in the ocean, it left a foamy slick described as a "giant snail trail" that smelled "like burnt sulphur."

A teenager made the first call to the RCMP on that clear, moonless night.

And then there was another call from another person.

And another.

And another.

By the time the RCMP arrived, a crowd had assembled. The object, witnesses testified, seemed to be making its way to the open sea. Lobster boats that had been called out reported bubbles.

But the official word, the only word anyone still has — after a series of searches, after navy divers went down, after a full government investigation — was nothing. No wreckage. No bodies. No answers. Open and unsolved, Canada's most investigated UFO case.

Parked in front of the museum were a car and two touring motorcycles, Honda Gold Wings with saddlebags and Union Jack stickers.

The man who took my two-dollar admission was Laurie Wickens. You cannot read an account of Shag Harbour and not read about Laurie Wickens. The teenager — the first person to make it to a payphone that night on his way home from a dance on Cape Sable Island.

Laurie and the Honda owners were the only people in the museum. Old enough to be retired, the couple looked like human sausages stuffed into a casing of black leather. The man seemed relaxed, the woman did not. When she crossed the room, her neck was tense, as though she could, at any time, be hit in the back of her head with a snowball.

The man reminded me of a copy editor at the *Standard*. A man who lived outside the city. Copy editors were, for the most part, a dry crowd. They would work in silence for hours, and then pop up from their screen for a brief discussion about a verb tense, a misplaced modifier, or an irksome word. One day, I heard the editor complain about a food story he was editing.

"Some expressions bother me," he said, "like 'piping hot.'"

"Is it the 'piping' part?" asked another editor.

"Sure. This guy also likes to use euphemisms: 'garment' instead of 'coat,' 'appendage' instead of 'arm.' And 'condiments.' He loves the word 'condiments,' which annoys the hell out of me. The restaurant had an ample supply of 'condiments.'"

"Is it because it sounds like 'condoms?'"

"Sure."

The couple—the woman was taking the lead—were discussing the Cold War era, which was the backdrop to the 1967 UFO. A time of subterfuge and spies, which started in 1945 and lasted until the Soviet Union collapsed in 1991. This, for some reason, had riled up the woman, who, like her companion, had a British accent.

"That filthy Philby, that Cambridge wanker," she said, decades after the infamous British spy betrayed his country to the Soviets.

"Should never have seen daylight after all the harm he did," the man agreed.

"He deserved the worst of it, didn't he? A cold dark cell or the end of a rope."

"Too good for him, I'd say."

"They made another film on the wanker. Showed him after he ran to Moscow like the gutter rat he was. God knows how many of ours he got killed. But there he was, a lush who abandoned his wife and children, not caring what mess he left behind, and one of his daughters looked at the camera and said, 'We loved him dearly.'"

"The brain of a cabbage."

I thought about Jeffrey Delisle, whose spy trial I had covered. He was nothing like Philby, an ideologue, a Communist who belonged to an elite club of spies named the Cambridge Five. Delisle was working class. He joined the navy as a reservist. Years later, he enrolled in the Royal Military College from which he graduated, and somewhere along the way, he decided that the best way to ruin his life was to sell information to the Russians.

The Brits did not seem to care that I could hear. They shuffled across the museum, stout as barrels, looking like people who had grown up on a diet of kidney pie.

"It is all quite fascinating," he said. "Isn't it?"

"Well, I suppose," she said.

The three of us watched the video that played on a loop. A primer. It used words such as "otherworldly, military divers, a cylinder, NORAD," and "British commandoes"—all part of the alleged conspiracy. The video mentioned Shelburne, once the site of "Canada's most secret base." The base was a joint operation of Canada and the US that claimed to be an oceanographic research centre when it was really a secret listening post for Soviet subs.

"Well, that's that," she concluded.

I milled about the museum. It only took so long—there was not that much to see, to be honest—but I had driven almost three hours, so I lingered. The couple decided to get their two dollars' worth by questioning Laurie Wickens. They marched to the counter. They seemed to know a fair bit about the story.

"What about the two women who were with you that night?" the woman asked, as though she had a right to know.

"They have passed," Laurie told her.

"What did you think it was at first?"

"An airplane," he said, and she continued to grill him.

She asked if he was retired—the answer was yes—and if he had ever been to England.

They chatted a bit longer, and then the woman, who was more aggressive than her partner, asked, "What do *you truly* think it was?"

Laurie, the president of the Shag Harbour UFO Society, the first person to make it to a payphone on that moonless night, a man who may have answered that vast question a thousand times, said, "Your guess is as good as mine."

"Very good," said the man. "Very good."

"I don't suppose you have traitors over here, do you?" the woman added. "Filthy ones willing to sell out their countrymen."

Laurie shrugged.

When I left the museum, I stood outside in the warm air enjoying the innocent smell of flowers, and then I saw something odd. A black F350 rumbled by pulling a military-grade Zodiac. The F350 turned down a side road and vanished. It was followed by a second black F350 filled with robust-looking men. And none of that seemed normal.

14

I was in no hurry to get home after the F350s passed the museum. I also had no firm opinion on the UFO. Was it simply a downed satellite or a meteorite? But it had floated on the surface and that was inconsistent with space debris. Was it a hoax? With those notorious jokers, the Mounties, involved? Not terribly likely. Was it a Soviet weapon, a disc-shaped one designed by German scientists captured during World War Two, or a "Secret War Machine from the US?"

Was it aliens? This was the most tantalizing theory. The one with legs. Supported by UFO expert Stanton Friedman at the University of New Brunswick, who was interviewed outside the centre. It was folly, he declared, for Earthlings to believe we were alone. And why would "they" reveal themselves to us? We are not nice guys bringing peace and joy. Friedman was famous as the first civilian to document Roswell, which was, believers claimed, the cover-up of cover-ups, comparable in scope to the JFK assassination.

I drove three minutes to the place where it had happened. The grassy knoll. Offshore is the area where the UFO floated for a few renowned minutes. The size, witnesses said, of a school bus. To commemorate it is a small park with a gazebo and a plaque. Two picnic tables and a bench. A sign: *Crash Site of the 1967 Shag Harbour UFO.*

I sat on the bench and looked out at the ocean. I could see infinity, either that or an imaginary island off the coast of Ireland. I could see a speck of a Cape Islander.

I was happy that day because jumpsuits seemed to be back in style, and I had bought one, and I felt good in a jumpsuit. I felt as though the whole issue of clothing had been taken care of in one shrewd move. I floated about in my jumpsuit, took photos, and then a vehicle pulled into the parking lot. The day was so lovely that I would speak to anyone. It was the pearl-white Range Rover I had seen at the McDonald's driven by the stranger with the bold green eyes, the stranger I had thought about longer than I should have. The SUV had Nova Scotia plates. It had a Thule cargo box on the roof.

*
*

The stranger—his name was Vincent—invited me to a house he had rented in Pollock Passage, and I went without thinking. He invited me for coffee.

I do not remember parts of our conversation. Did you ever feel like you were on autopilot, and you were doing things you had not planned to do? You didn't need to think because they were just happening, and you didn't need to feel guilty because they were just *happening*, and there was a freedom in that? An absolution.

Vincent's rental was near the old Swim home. It had a barn out back with a neon Habs sign. I have always liked the idea of barns in the same way that I like the idea of tree houses, although I would not know what to do with either. Sometimes, when you are on autopilot, that unplanned moment turns into the best moment of your life, and sometimes it is such a mistake that you mercifully allow yourself to forget it. Vincent was in the to-be-determined category.

"The owner," Vincent said, "runs her own business cleaning lobster boats. She has three employees. She rents this house and lives in another."

I was not working that night, so I could afford to linger in a stranger's house with a strange man, who had picked me up at a UFO memorial site. "Looks like her business is doing well," I said.

"She often gets calls when it is too rough for the boats to go out, so they work in nasty weather. She has a son who moved to Vancouver; he is a marine biologist who does research on orcas."

The living room told me nothing about Vincent. It was the owner's story and tastes. She had added a brown leather sofa and a matching chair, but otherwise, the décor had probably not changed in thirty years. There were paperbacks on a table for the entertainment of guests, and they looked like yard sale finds, a Maeve Binchy novel and Frederick Forsyth's *The Day of the Jackal*.

"Who knew I'd find such a place?" Vincent shrugged as a form of verbal punctuation. "Who knew?" He was referring to the view. Vincent had an accent that sounded European, not American as I had anticipated based on his clothes and his manners.

Over the fireplace mantle was a spooky monochromatic painting of a moor. And on the mantle a parade of china objects. A pair of Blue Mountain Pottery cats, both wearing bowties, at either end.

"I made a banana bread this morning. Would you like to try it?"

Vincent Caron was a professor from the University of Maine. He was on a one-year sabbatical. He was, he told me, writing a paper on how the 1967 UFO incident and the ensuing rumours developed against the backdrop of what he called the state's encroachment on a once *Gemeinschaft* society. He was not there to prove or disprove the crash. He was not a ufologist. He was an anthropologist.

I could imagine Vincent on a leafy East Coast campus. Sitting in a stern high-backed chair at a wooden table next to a *Plato's Cave* coffee mug. I could imagine that the air would smell like corduroy. I am ambivalent about PhDs. On one hand they know an infinite amount about one very specific thing, but on the other hand they know an infinite amount about one very specific thing.

Vincent thought that his introduction sounded dull, so he kept going. He said people invent rumours if they are easier than the truth. Rumours are the window into our uncertainties. And then he told me that some rumours become contemporary legend. And those have three things in common: a good storyline, a foundation in belief, and a moral.

"It doesn't take much to become a contemporary legend today," I noted.

"True."

"A man in Halifax started speaking with an Irish accent after he hit his head. He used expressions like 'It's a quare day.' Or 'I need a new car; me old one's banjaxed.' It was clearly fake, but he made *Daily Mail Online*." I paused. "And that's when I ask myself: 'How well do I understand the human condition?'"

"Are you a student of the human condition?" he asked.

I smiled and did not answer.

I told Vincent that I used to be a news photographer. I did not try to make it any more than it was. I always, I like to think, kept my old job in perspective. I was not the photographer who kept an action figure on his desk. Who slept with a scanner, racing to the scene of every car crash or murder. Who wore combat boots and a bulletproof vest purchased from a larcenous military private. Who travelled to hot spots. I was not *him*, addicted to the buzz of the byline. And then forced to the wilds of Serbia when the long buzz ended, reduced to taking in feral dogs. I was not, like the man I had once known, consumed by the business.

Because I am, like Stan, an occasional panic talker, I told Vincent that I had, for a brief time worked for the government, an admission that I now question, as it did nothing to make me seem glamorous. There was no need for me to bring this up.

"How did you like that?" he asked.

"So-so, I had a bad boss."

"Oh?"

"Her first name was Mackenzie; she went by Mac."

Why was I telling this stupid story?

Suddenly self-conscious, I wondered if jumpsuits really were back, or if I just thought they were. Maybe where Vincent came from, they never were in. Maybe I looked foolish, as odd as Dorothy in her Druid cape, never having been good with clothes.

"Makes sense."

I was usually better than this.

"She was over thirty but totally dependent on her mother. The mother was a prison guard who worked nights, and she came into our office every day. She wore square-toed biker boots. Her name was Tangeline. On her way to Mackenzie's office, Tangeline would check our pods as though we were on her rounds. She was fine with me at first. Pleasant enough. And then she changed. She started giving me that *I know what you did and you better watch your ass* look from *Orange Is the New Black*. And that's when I knew that Mackenzie was telling lies about me — to everyone, including her mother."

"You sound very observant," said Vincent, who should have hated my petty story.

"The mothers give it away," I said, "what is really going on."

"It is a good thing that you do not know my mother," Vincent joked, and the joke made me feel better. Vincent looked directly at me when he said it. His green eyes had voltage. When he was not looking at you, you might find yourself gazing around the room, taking an inventory, but when his eyes were on you, you stopped.

We chatted. We drank more coffee. The conversation righted itself. I stopped worrying about my jumpsuit. I did not mention the Lucky Lady, my first lie of omission. I told Vincent that I was there to look for Graham, which was barely true. "You may have seen the posters."

Nine months had passed. The immediate family had given up hope. I did not mention that Graham was a fence, a detail you do not volunteer when trying to make a reasonable first impression. The most optimistic rumour, I claimed, was that Graham was hiding in a hunting/drinking camp on a back road "for a reason." A man had written a book about the forgotten back roads of Nova Scotia, K-class roads, I told Vincent, trying to sound knowledgeable. There are 2,500 kilometres of them. While researching the forgotten roads, the author had found old foundations, rock walls, and remnants of bottles.

"Maybe we can look." He shrugged. Vincent made it sound like a question.

And then, in a move into the personal, an acknowledgement that we were alone for no good reason in a rented house in Pollock Passage, two strangers with nothing in common, two strangers who should have passed each other in the UFO park with a cursory "hello," he asked if I had ever been married.

What Should Have Happened

Mackenzie was no longer working for the government, where she and Tangeline had been free to abuse subordinates. Fired, she was now employed at Good Night, Sleep Tight. The bed retailer was in a mini-mall kilometres from the downtown, a location with no walk-in traffic. Next to a training operation for EMS technicians that had artificial limbs on display. When someone *did* walk through the Good Night, Sleep Tight door, it was as if a soldier had appeared in airport arrivals after a year-long deployment, and his family rushed forward sobbing. It was that much of an event.

The day I went there, I saw three hypervigilant, overanxious employees ready to pounce. At the cash was a bowl of candies set as bait. My throat tightened. There was only one other customer inside, a worn-out woman in her seventies in mismatched used clothing. I would have felt sorry for the employees if one of them had not been Mackenzie, who was wearing a name tag, *Mac*.

It was a foot race to see who could reach me first. A woman with the name tag *Cherry* won. She tried to hide her disappointment when I told her I was shopping for sheets, which cost a measly forty dollars. I felt bad.

Meanwhile, Mackenzie was following the seventy-ish woman around the room, trailing her from one $3,500 bed to another, stopping at a $5,200 king size, which the septuagenarian needed help to climb up on. Once on board, she stretched out her arms and closed her eyes. Yes, it did feel good, she said. And it might be the thing for my sciatic nerve, which has been hellish. Could you help me get back down? Could you rub my left foot? Mac said she would try with her good arm.

For the opening a few weeks back, the owner had rented a bouncy castle, and when no one showed up, he made employees use it to prove they were having fun. Mackenzie crashed into a co-worker on her first bounce, fracturing her arm, which was now in a sling.

The $5,200 would get you pocketed coils and *the soft, plush feel of a cloud*. The bed was worth more than any car parked outside. I glanced at the old woman. Her hair was thin and white with an artificial pink splash on one side, the pink of dyed Easter egg. She was wearing bike shorts and a purple fanny pack, and she would, never in this lifetime, purchase anything here.

Cherry went out back to find my forty-dollar sheets. She returned with a long face. They were out of the white.

"It's okay," I volunteered, desperate to escape, "the grey will be fine." Sheets in hand, I bolted, and not long after that, the other customer shuffled out. I saw her crossing the parking lot. I saw her throw a candy wrapper on the ground. I saw Tangeline lurking in her car.

15

This memoir started off as the story of Stan Swim, the celebrated broadcaster, so I must note at least one high point of his career. I must, before Graham, Vincent, et al. take over these pages, before you get the impression that Stan, depicted here in his declining years, was never a force. I must, before I veer too far off the path.

Other highlights can be found in the press release for his lifetime achievement award: Stan stayed on-air live for eight hours during a rescue at a coal mine. And he did a stand-up at the Great Wall of China. When Stan received his award in a ballroom, organizers played clips from his tougher interviews, sit-downs with people who had scant interest in the truth. Dictators. Cabinet ministers. The mastermind of a Ponzi scheme that wiped out thousands. I was in the audience with Mother.

"I knew an old prize fighter named Curly Top Moore," Stan told the assembled, "and he said there is that moment in a fight when you, *you just know*, you are better than the other guy. And you have to hide it. You have to play it cool. But *you know*. It is the same as with an interview. There is that moment that you *know* you are better. You smell confusion; he raises his voice when he shouldn't."

Pause.

And then Stan joked, because the crowd was expecting it, "I wish I had as many TKOs as Curly Top Moore."

The MC, a man who had once worked as a bingo caller, gushed, "Your record stands, Stan. It stands."

My father, despite his other weaknesses, was not one of those fatuous broadcast elites who used words like "chuffed" or "bunkie." Who blew into town in a cravat and would pretend, no matter how many times you had met, that he did not know you. "Harriett you say?" Or the Ottawa name dropper who let you know that he was uncomfortable with the "new people" attending concerts at the National Arts Centre. A ticket holder for sixteen years, he was seeing *parvenus*, and they were—horror upon horror—applauding between sections of a multi-part piece! Stan was not like that.

Stan was a groundbreaker, and more than once he did something important. He was capable of whipping up a hurricane of public outrage, culminating with real change. Before Stan, local anchors sat firmly in their chairs, their inertia adding *gravitas*. Stan did remotes. He conducted exclusives in places that anchors did not go, places like a desolate women's prison.

I remember the logistics around the prison piece. There were phone calls and meetings. Conditions. It went all the way to Ottawa. For the shoot, Stan requested his most dependable cameraman, Skippy, who made everyone feel at ease.

The prison piece is on a separate reel from the highlight reel. I watched it for my research. It opens with establishing shots of the prison. The interior was a stark white—everything looked painted over and over until it was bumpy and scarred. And in the air you could smell misery and disinfectant.

Wanda was Stan's first interview. She kept her hands folded in her lap. Her buzzed hair was spiked with gel. She was fifty. No makeup except for a hint of lip gloss. Wanda was wearing the regulation blue prison T-shirt and her arms were covered with ugly red scars. It was hard to take your eyes off those red scars—some fresh, some as old as tragedy. You were happy when Skippy focused on her eyes because then you could not see the scars.

"When I get out, I am going to help people," Wanda promised, as people do when seeking purpose for a life which had up to then had little.

"But let's go back in time," Stan suggested. "Let's go back so that we can help other people now."

Wanda said her parents were deemed unfit—she did not know why—and so she was placed in an orphanage. Orphanages have existed forever, but people do not think about them any more than they thought about the TB sanatoriums where people were quarantined for up to a decade. If you *did* think about them, it could be you inside. So people didn't.

"What was it like in the orphanage?" Stan asked, and it was as though Wanda had waited thirty years for that question. The interview felt important, I realized. You had to be in *that* time and *that* place to understand why. Women were rarely on the news, and never women like Wanda. Stan was doing something of value.

We were always hungry, Wanda told Stan unemotionally. Breakfast was a bowl of porridge, dinner a thin fish stew, mostly bones, and potatoes. Their nightdresses were made from old flour bags. If an inspector was coming in, the children were changed into proper clothes—a jumper and a top—which were immediately put back in a closet.

There were beatings with switches, and as further punishment, the children were forced to fight each other until one went down and could not get up. One boy was taken to hospital, unconscious, and never came back.

Have you peered into a well? It is dark and cold, and you *think* you can see the surface of the water, but you are not sure in the darkness. You thought you could see life in Wanda's eyes, but you were not sure.

"Did it get better?" asked Stan.

No. The nights were the worst, Wanda explained, because it was impossible to sleep when others were crying. It was impossible to sleep because that was when a predator would molest you. They were hiding in plain sight: like Reginald, a long-time employee who would take you off the grounds for ice cream and tell you that you were his favourite.

"Tell me about Reginald," Stan said.

When she was old enough, Reginald gave her drugs, he put her to work in the sex trade. After she got out of the orphanage, Reginald kept Wanda and four other women in a dump not far from the cop shop. There were sailors and salesmen. A judge.

After that, after the bar had been lowered as far as it could go, Wanda found trouble on her own. It was her third stint in prison, this time for helping a boyfriend hold up a gas station.

"I'm not the only one in here from that hell hole," she said.

And that led Stan to another cold white cell and another woman who had been in the same orphanage. He scheduled a second prison visit. Denise had stabbed a john. Before that she did time for stealing from a charity that had given her a chance. She had two children. She was a cancer survivor. Her hair was bleached blond, and she had a cross tattoo on her hand.

Her cell looked like the inside of the cheapest white fridge you have ever owned, an apartment fridge with one nasty light illuminating a loaf of Ben's bread.

"Goddamn Reginald," she cursed. "I'd cut his eyes."

Stan's interviews were, all of them, shocking. His followers, especially the older women who sent him fruitcake at Christmas, lost their collective minds. They phoned the TV station. They wrote letters to the premier and the police, so many letters that the government launched an inquiry into the orphanage, which was, as it should have been, shut down.

The justice minister instructed the police to investigate Reginald, who, like the cold-blooded snake he was, went underground. Reginald was never charged with anything, and maybe, Stan suggested on-air, he had the goods on someone. This story, Stan promised, was not over. But it was. It was as dead as Stan's Senate dream.

*
*

Stan continued to upgrade his downstairs after the pot lights. He was now building a recording studio. He was going to voice e-books *and* do interviews for a sponsored podcast. It almost made sense. Stan Swim and his distinctive voice added instant recognition to any project. Stan could make your grandmother, who had never been beyond Beaver Pond, sound like the most fascinating person on the face of the earth.

Besides, Stan could not go long without attention. One night, when he was still on TV, he told viewers that Baba, the imaginary husky, had a kidney infection and needed prayers to Saint Roch, the patron saint of dogs. Viewers sent Mass cards and fruitcake. Stan thanked them, and said Baba was doing better. Mother took the excess cake to a seniors' home.

Part of Stan's persona was being provocative. Near the end of his career, long after the prison piece, it was hard to tell when he was just pushing buttons. Messing with viewers and/or drinking. Like the time he debriefed a reporter who had done a piece on "foraging."

"In the old days, they would be called marauders, I suppose." Stan made it into a question. "Or plunderers."

The reporter stammered a reply.

"Not for me, I am afraid," Stan said. "I have a limited number of meals left in this lifetime, and I am not going to waste one on skunk roadkill. If someone else wants to forage, good on them. I am sure it is a lot of fun. You know what else is a lot of fun? Stealing underwear from clotheslines, but I am not going to do that either."

The reporter was speechless.

I *did* wonder how much the studio would cost. I expected that Stan would pay too much because he often did. Stan and money were problematic.

"Graham stole his six hundred dollars, right?" Peter asked me one day. "The money for the electrician."

The six hundred dollars, which could have been at the heart of everything. The reason Graham went to Pollock Passage. The reason he did not come back.

"I dunno," I replied and then conceded, "Yeah, probably. Sure. He was the only person in the house besides me, and I did not take it. Graham was always broke. He didn't pay rent with Rick."

"So, he needed money." Peter stated the obvious.

"Yeah. I thought that was why he took off, and that once things blew over, he'd come back."

"I don't think," said Peter, again stating the obvious, "that is going to happen."

$$*$$

One day when I was at the library, two young people were eating croissants at a table. The man was wearing a blue leopard-print jacket and a matching bucket hat, a bold look for Halifax. He had a perfectly shaded face; light struck it at all the right angles. He would have been easy to shoot.

He had graduated from art school, I picked up, and was pursuing a career as a rapper, a choice that his family was not supporting. The pair were talking in a serious tone, attempting to understand something, in the same way that I was trying to make sense of my current state of existence. The wannabe rapper had *Sons of the Saddle*, a Wild West adventure open on the table.

He said: "I told my parents that Drake listened to one of my tapes, and they said they had never heard of him." He shook his head and slowly repeated himself. "They said they *had never heard of* Drake."

Outside his jacket was a chrome chain as heavy as his mood.

"Or Kanye. My mother said she asked my brother, Josh, and he had never heard of Kanye either."

"That's a lie. You *know* that's a lie."

"Right. Even Josh is not that obtuse."

"He's the doctor? Yes?"

"Yes, a urologist. Look him up on Rate my Doctor. Patients hate him. They say his hands are always cold. I don't know why his hands are always cold, but don't tell me he has never heard of Kanye. That is not credible."

"My theory is that family is the ultimate bell curve. If someone in your family already scores high on something, you get a lower score. I had a friend who thought she was plain because her sister had been crowned the family beauty. And she was gorgeous. She had green eyes, like *real* green, like kryptonite, with double lashes."

"Ohhhhh, that sounds intense."

"She had a boyfriend, but he was a cheater. He was *too* good looking. You know the type, right? If you are born beautiful, if that is your advantage, why neutralize it by dating someone as beautiful as you?"

An interesting theory.

"Anyway, if Josh is successful in his career, maybe your parents think your score has to be low."

"Point."

She paused to let that argument defend itself—I could not tell if he was convinced or not—and then she added, "And you are spiritual, and that is hard for some people to grasp." At that, he nodded an absolute yes.

The man and the woman were not a couple. She was there to help him with his social media presence—she "knew influencers." I was skeptical, but then I thought: *What do I know?* It was all over my head, influencers and brand strategies, scarcity mindset versus abundance mindset. Exotic dogs. New ways of studying the Bible.

And then I wondered, because I could not get the idea out of my head: *Was every family a bell curve? What was left for me and Peter after Stan had given himself the top score in everything, when no one could be sicker or healthier, luckier or unluckier, taller, more handsome or more successful? What was left?*

And when did I start to care?

*
*

Stan enjoyed his old neighbour, Buck the spy. Sometimes Buck joined Stan for a Scotch or three, and like men of the world, they talked about the spy business in front of me and Mother. Ship surveillance. The monitoring of crews from Russia or China. Seafloor mapping. Routine observations that were worth something to the CIA and CSIS but clearly not *that* secret. Buck showed Stan an encrypted phone that looked like an old-school BlackBerry with the guts removed. "Makes an excellent paperweight," he winked.

You would expect a spy to be quiet and sneaky, but Buck was boisterous. Hiding, as the cliché goes, in plain sight. That, I assumed, was his cover.

There was scrutiny of local members of the Marxist-Leninist party, Buck volunteered, but it was not a priority. They were obsessed with dogma, not action, and spent most of their time celebrating obscure anniversaries and re-examining the battle of the Kerch Peninsula. Talkers they were, not players.

Buck *did* arrange to have a key logger installed on the laptop of the top local Marxist-Leninist. A postal worker. Buck's people sent the Marxist-Leninist a virus, and when he took his frozen laptop to a repair shop they installed the logger. It took seconds. It gave Buck's people access to passwords and everything the postie typed.

I can only assume that if Buck had *real* spy secrets, ones of import, he kept them to himself. Isn't that the point of being a spy?

I do know that Buck spent time at the covert intelligence facility on the Canadian Navy dockyard in Halifax. I was inside it once.

You surrender your phone. You go through an intricate entry process — through an air lock, a door within a door — but once you are inside, the employees look like they could be processing dog licences. It fools you.

Stan liked the subterfuge. He enjoyed being on the inside of something with scope. There will always be those people in society, the people Stan enjoyed, and when they die, someone will identify them as a spy or a war photographer or an ice climber, and one of them, or probably all of them, will have "died doing what he loved."

Conversely, Stan could not stand his other neighbour. Shrum or "Cement Head" was one of those men who spent every moment of every day on his personal strip of asphalt. A Driveway Dweller, Stan called him. Stan swore that Shrum was in that driveway on Christmas Day, and would yell, as soon as you opened your door, "Hot enough for you?" or "Cold enough for you?" depending on the weather. "He had a cat," Stan claimed, "and it died of boredom."

Shrum, a tiny man, had retired after winning a lottery. That freed him to do nothing beyond his driveway. His only child, the actor, dropped in on occasion. Always high.

Stan had no trees on his front lawn, only the hydrangea. Shrum had four massive maples, and every fall the four trees shed their leaves. And every fall the leaves blew across the street onto Stan's yard, bag after bag. In winter, it was the same with snow. Shrum did not *will* the leaves and the snow to land in Stan's yard — that was a bizarre combination of roof lines and wind — but it was a reason for Stan to hate him.

I heard about Shrum more times than I care to remember.

Shrum set up a circular saw in his driveway. He changed tires. From eight a.m. to dusk. Sometimes dressed in coveralls. His stooped wife would come to the door and gesture for him to turn off his high-decibel rotary sander. Do you want me to wash your white socks? she would shout, no banality too banal for a public airing. And he would shout back, Yes. I told you that already.

His wife looked like that dotty woman who steals chocolate from the bulk food section and eats it in plain sight. Once, Stan swore he heard her shouting, "Help me, help me," from the garage, but my mother said that was a lie.

Shrum built shelves in his driveway. *Bam bam bam.* He hammered metal. *Ping.*

"What does he do out there all day?" Stan snapped one morning.

"He's bored," my mother told him. "That's all. He's bored."

"If I get that bored," said Stan, "smother me with a pillow, and then have me stuffed and mounted as an example of a Man Without a Brain."

Mother told me the following story in horrifying detail because she was horrified. And because the doctor told her that she should share it with family. Our support, he said, would be helpful.

On Remembrance Day, that day when people honour the dead and their sacrifices with a moment of silence, Shrum decided to use a pneumatic impact wrench to change the tires on his car. On the eleventh hour of the eleventh day. Usually, Stan and my mother went to the cenotaph, but this year they were watching the ceremony on TV because Mother was ill. Stan had a soft spot for veterans, having gone to Bosnia with Canadian troops. Stan had been too young for the Second World War, but he had a friend who was torpedoed and kept awake for the next forty years by the sight of shipmates drowning.

Stan had also, around this time, not been sleeping.

There had been changes at the station. Eva had gone to Toronto.

Whrrrrrrrrrrrrrrrrrrr went the drill.

Whrrrrrrrrrrrrrrrrrr.

Stan later claimed that Shrum was playing Wagner's *Die Walküre* at high volume, but Mother told the doctor that was a lie.

"Ignore him," she told Stan, pointing to the TV.

Whrrrrrrrrrrrrrrrrrr.

Mother said it again—ignore him—but that did not calm Stan

down; it agitated him. It agitated him so much that his heart raced as he ripped open the front door and shouted, on behalf, he later said, of the men and women who had given their lives, including the nine hundred sixteen who died at Dieppe, "You bored, ignorant bastard. Turn that thing off, or I will kill you." Brandishing a fireplace poker.

When the ambulance arrived, Stan was having difficulty breathing. He had chest pains. A paramedic said his blood pressure was 210/120, a hypertensive crisis that could cause a stroke or organ damage. It was important to stabilize him, he said, as they took him away.

Mother said that the ER doctor questioned Stan in front of her, and Stan told him that it was not just the noise of the drill. Or the disrespect. It was the smallness of it all. Stan Swim, lover of all that was outsized and bold and outlandish, could not exist, thinking that the world, the only one we get to live in, was that bloody small. Two hours later, Stan saw a psychiatrist.

After that, Stan did not go to work for a month. The police did not pursue the threat against Shrum. Stan's station told viewers that he had had a hip replacement. Some knew the truth. The breakdown was moderate. The psychiatrist said it was the result of stress; the good news was that Stan did not have a brain tumour. The crisis was exacerbated by "his psychiatric condition," which contributed to his feelings of grandiosity and frustration.

Therapy could help Stan understand "his condition." It could increase his ability to recognize his feelings and to relate better with others. It could teach him to recognize when he was being manipulative or deflective, the psychiatrist believed.

Stan later *did* see a therapist, which he saw mainly as an opportunity to revisit his grievances against his neighbour. Stan recounted one visit to Mother. He said he told the therapist that Shrum, whom he later described as too lazy to die, was *too stupid* to be mentally ill, *too stupid* to know what was happening in the world. Some of that was true.

After that, Stan rarely saw a doctor. I think he was afraid of what one might tell him.

"Why would I participate in a system that treats patients like grifters and bums?" he demanded of Mother.

"Because you *have* to," she replied.

"I *have* to end up like Skippy, sent home from the ER when he was having a stroke? When his head was about to explode like a purple water balloon tossed out a second-storey window?"

"That *was* unfortunate."

"Do you know what else was unfortunate — Napoleon invading Russia."

If I had to guess, I would guess that the psychiatrist diagnosed Stan with a narcissistic personality disorder.[13] Good news, one could argue, for anyone who might find themselves in the same rocky boat. Stan's life was successful compared to most. But only my father met with the psychiatrist, and only my father was in control of his full medical information, and he was not about to share it with me.

I would have liked to have known what the psychiatrist said, other than the good part about the brain tumour. A diagnosis gives you a framework. It gives you parameters. It gives you an explanation for all the things that were, up to then, unexplainable. It tells you if you might be next in line. A diagnosis would have made my story more credible — is it even a condition, you might ask, if it does not have a name?

Mother did tell me that Stan claimed he had a frank talk with the therapist about how he had become the celebrated interviewer he was. He had the ability, he told the therapist, to read minds. Really? Mother replied.

---

13 *The Diagnostic and Statistical Manual of Mental Disorders* (DSM) is a guidebook used by mental health professionals. It defines narcissistic personality disorder as a pervasive pattern of grandiosity (in fantasy or behaviour), a constant need for admiration, and a lack of empathy.

"That," she told me, as though it needed to be said, "is not normal."

The ER doctor spoke to Mother directly. He told her that mental illness can have a ripple effect on families, creating tension, uncertainty, and changes in how other members live their lives. Different people react differently, he noted. Some become fearful. Some run away. But you, he said—with the detachment of a professional who would never see her again—seem to be doing well.

It was the first time anyone had said the words "mental illness" out loud about Stan. The ER doctor did not seem to know that. He spoke as though it was a given. He assumed that Mother would not flinch from the initial sting of those two words when most people do. He assumed she knew why the psychiatrist was needed.

Months after his breakdown, long after he had returned to work, Stan brought up the ER doctor to me and Mother. We had been having a chat about gardens when he brought him up. Stan called him "that lunatic who suggested there was something wrong with ME! The man was wearing red-and-yellow sneakers, for God's sake. You are going to listen to a man in clown shoes?"

"He *was* a doctor," I noted as tactfully as I could.

"He was A CLOWN!"

"Okay." I really did not want to discuss this.

"Would I be where I am today if there was something wrong with Me?" And then, because I was there, *just there*, not causing the least bit of trouble, Stan turned on me. "Imagine what he would say if he saw YOU."

"Stan," my mother snapped, "stop that."

Normal was not Stan's comfort zone; normal made Stan uneasy. It made him feel as though he was not trying hard enough or not forcing *someone else* to try hard enough. At one point, he gave Graham a used Fitbit and instructed him to perform ten thousand steps a day, even though Graham had a bad leg and was painfully thin.

Some of my father's bad decisions—like moving Graham to

The City—took place during "normal" times. Some happened during those intermittent times when he was intractable. Mad, one could argue. Proof can be found in interviews that did *not* make the highlight reel. Such as the debacle involving ParticipACTION, a government program that was supposed to encourage Canadians to be active.

Stan was interviewing a young filmmaker who had made a documentary on Sable Island, (not to be confused with Cape Sable). Stan was fascinated by the sandy island, which is one hundred sixty kilometres offshore. He had visited it and seen its fabled wild horses, which became a temporary obsession. Stan was so obsessed that he bought the $4,000 watercolour that hangs over his sofa.

Not long after the interview began, Stan took the conversation off on a wild tangent that left both the floor director and viewers confused. No one knew how to stop him. This was live.

"Canadians have been brainwashed to believe that we are genetically inferior to Scandinavians. *Correct?*" announced Stan when no one had mentioned Scandinavia or brainwashing. "Would you, as a filmmaker, not agree?" He did not give the man time to respond. "I trace it all back to that idiotic ParticipACTION ad from the seventies. The one with the thirty-year-old Canadian out jogging with the sixty-year-old Swede, barely able to keep up. The one that played to our self-flagellating inferiority complex."[14]

The filmmaker cleared his throat nervously in an attempt to change the subject.

Stan continued: "According to ParticipACTION, we are all lazy mixed-breed mongrels: *Untermenschen*. While they are lean and blond and alluring, blindly fetishized down to their bikini lines."

Pause.

---

14 The ad ran six times during Canadian Football League games in 1973. A ParticipACTION official later admitted that the agency had no statistical evidence to back the commercial's storyline about the slovenly Canadian and the superior Swede.

"I'm not sure how influential those ads are in terms of today's thinking," said the filmmaker, not knowing where to go with this. He was there to talk about Sable Island, referred to as the Graveyard of the Atlantic because of the historic shipwrecks on its sands. Sable Island, which was forty-two kilometres long and home to up to five hundred wild horses. He was not even alive when the ParticipACTION ad was made.

"They didn't even have the decency to hire a Swedish actor," charged Stan before he let out a sharp manic laugh. "I think that is the part that bothered me most, the terrible casting. *Terrible.* The man looked like someone's sad-sack uncle. Someone named Wally who has gout. Not Lars. And this whole they-are-better-than-you-are message. Do you really think that a poor devil who goes to sea for ten days— and I know about this, as my father and brother fished—a poor devil who is lucky to make it back alive, needs to be gene-shamed by his own government?"

"Ah, no," managed the filmmaker. "I don't."

And then Stan took on two voices, one male and one female, for an imaginary back and forth.

Male: "No, I won't have a beer, Jade. I'm going to go for a jog instead because that's what they do in Sweden."

Female: "Aren't the people all beautiful, there, Craig?"

Male: "Oh yes, Jade, not like us. They are all blond, blue-eyed, and lean."

Female: *Sigh.* "I wish I could look like that."

Male: "I know, but you can't. You are Canadian."

It was a debacle. With other gratuitous nonsense from Stan.

What if the things that made us bright and shiny, special and abnormal, I wondered, *were all the same?*

‡

When we were in Montréal, Jack and I moved into a stone town-house, next door to a Lebanese restaurant. We had the main floor, spacious enough for a light-filled studio for Jack and a darkroom for me. Outside was a fountain that turned different colours at night. Things were happening around us all the time. I was used to seeing work crews at six a.m. with coolers of food that would last them all day. I saw waitresses, and I could imagine them, after a long day, going home to wine, a cigarette, and friends who read poetry out loud.

Our upstairs neighbour was a doorman at a massage parlour. He lived alone. If you walked by his place of employment, you could see him at the bottom of a stairwell that led to the second-floor business. His name was Seb. He dated a tattoo artist, who could draw better than anyone I ever knew; she could draw anything from her head. I found Seb confusing. He told Jack that he was planning to train his own police dog, which could sniff out drugs and explosives. It seemed like a weird plan, since Seb worked in a place filled with drugs.

Jack had to go find Seb one night, when Seb's apartment flooded, and the water was pouring through the ceiling into our bedroom. It was a ten-minute walk. When Jack got there, he climbed the stair-well and was greeted by two women wearing bras. There was a charge to get in, they told him, which covered entry, a private room, a free beer, and your choice of dancer. Jack said thank you, but he was there to see Seb.

Jack and Seb walked back to our building together. I helped mop up the water, and the next day Jack took up running, and I never understood why the two events were connected. But they were. And then, after everything happened, the bad stuff, it did not stop. The running. It escalated. It became abnormal. It went from incidental to all-consuming. Jack cut his long hair. He lost weight. Jack ran so hard, so far, that he started to vanish, until he was stripped down, hollow-eyed, and humbled. He ran as though he could outrun tragedy; he ran as though he was already paying for his sins.

16

Before I was laid off, I covered the sentencing of a Mountie caught stealing and distributing cocaine. His family was there *en force*, insisting that despite a multi-year investigation and two snitches, he was innocent. His supporters stood outside the courtroom waiting for it to open, and they kept talking about what a stellar person he was, separating him from the common criminals who wore track suits. They kept talking until they convinced themselves. One woman gave me a scowl. I heard the words "vultures" and "media assholes" as though it was *our* fault that he had stolen cocaine from an exhibit locker and bought a $17,000 Harley.

The outrage was absurd, of course. The Mountie had more choices and more chances than the "common criminal." This was clearly on him. In Halifax, if you are in a very big mess, you hire one of three lawyers, and if the media sees one attached to a case, they know it will be juicy. The oldest of the trio was there.

"Who is over there laughing?" the scowling woman demanded as though she was the laughter police. "Assholes, vultures." Focusing, as people often do, on the peripheral because the real problem was too unmanageable.

And then I heard a menacing voice behind me. "You're going to fucking jail." And again, "You're doing the time, yardbird."

When I turned, I saw a burly man chirping the Mountie, who was carrying a smart shoulder bag. You see that at court — the shoulder bag, meant again to separate you from the more common criminals, to suggest you have documents inside that can *totally* prove your innocence. When, in fact, you do not. This bag was antique brown leather. It had a buckle on the front. It looked like a bag that an English professor who specialized in *fin de siècle* popular fiction might carry.

"You got a toothbrush in that bag?" the chirper chirped.

If the accused elects to carry a shoulder bag to court, you will probably also see him vigorously taking notes during his trial, the suggestion being that he is (a) more educated than the common criminal and (b) intelligent enough to be an active part of his defence. It is theatre.

As quickly as the chirping started, an equally burly man from the Mounties' entourage was in the chirper's face. They stood there for five minutes like wrestlers at the start of a match. They stood there, eye to eye, until the door opened, and the Mountie and his entourage shuffled inside.

Photographers cannot shoot inside the courtroom, so I stayed outside. The chirper approached me because he wanted someone to know that he had been arrested twice by the Mountie, both times, he alleged, unjustly. I did not know if the chirper deserved to be arrested. He might have; he seemed erratic. He told me a convoluted story about how he had epilepsy and a lying ex-wife, and all I knew was that he wanted payback.

He got it, I suppose. The Mountie was sentenced to ten years for what the judge called a "fall from grace." And his followers still believed him.

There is who you are and who you *pretend* to be to your family, and that is necessary for your survival and for the survival of the entire human race. I get that.

When you see people like the Mountie, you wonder: *How did they get to that place?* But it is not a straight line from A to an Epic Bad Decision. It is a meandering path of gambles and self-delusion, of risks and flying fucks, and sometimes you find yourself on a dimly lit path and you know you should not be there, but you *are* there, and it doesn't feel that bad. Have you not done things that you would today—humbled by life, levelled by its brutality—not do? But you did do them, didn't you?

*

The first few times I was at Vincent's house, we talked about the UFO sighting. It was an easy thing to talk about—it revealed nothing about who we were and where we had been. We could pretend that nothing was happening, when it was.

I was old, so my choices were limited. If I were young, I would have fancied a man who looked like the lead in a Swedish crime drama. He would dress in skinny-legged black jeans, an olive V-neck T-shirt, and a black leather bomber jacket. And his face would be gaunt, as though he was too distracted or too intense to eat, his focus on self-punishment or shots of vodka. After a while, I would solve all my issues with clothes and I would dress like him, and it would be grim and romantic. But I was old. And Vincent, despite his outstanding green eyes, was not so beautiful as to be either Swedish or dangerous.

A while back, I saw a photo of one of the Montréal playboys. One of the men I had tried to resist. And he was wearing his sins on his face. All the careless in-the-moment transgressions that had once seemed outré—he wore them now as liver spots, jowls, and a turkey neck. He wore them like a best-before sticker. If Vincent had sins, they had not yet come back to mark him.

Vincent had interviewed people with knowledge of the UFO. Some had turned to religion, some were committed to denial. One witness did not talk about the incident for forty years because he feared people would call him a kook. Vincent made "kook" into two syllables with a shrug in the middle. Ahhhh. I encouraged him. Another shrug. And then there were the rumours.

Vincent carried no extra weight and no superfluous belongings, and that reminded me of the tortured Swedish lead. Nothing in the rental, other than a computer and some clothes, belonged to him, and that gave the feeling that he could come and go at any time; he could disappear as mysteriously as a UFO.

Over the next few weeks, as the wall of superficiality came down, Vincent and I talked about more important things, and eventually, as we became used to each other, Vincent introduced me to a couple he had befriended in Pollock Passage, the owners of the stilt house, and that was curious.

*
*

There was a time when I kept up with old photo-school classmates who went on to do big things. One shot for the *LA Times*. Another went to Benghazi and won a Pulitzer. He moved to Tel Aviv and gave up contact with his past, crossing over into a world of conflict. At times, I asked myself, *What have you done?* And I had replied, *I am happy*, and that was as important as anything anyone had done. Then, it was no longer true, so what *had* I done?

Vincent had encouraged me to take black-and-white photos with my Leica. Like I did in Montréal, when I was a street photographer, shooting for myself. I used a light meter on a lanyard. I set the shutter speed and aperture. I used a 35mm lens. And a 90mm. I started to make real photos, not app fantasies of spectacular clouds that were never there, furious ocean froth, or sunsets so intensely luminous that people were no longer satisfied with real ones.

After years of working with Canons — a noisy camera that announces your presence — I enjoyed the company of my Leica. Because it is a rangefinder, the Leica is quiet. It looks like any point-and-shoot, and the lenses are sublimely small. It has a viewfinder on the left side of the body, not the centre. You can see around you.

When I was in the city, I made black-and-white prints at an artists' co-op. Colour distracts me. Colour tricks me. Colour obscures my truth. Black and white is poetic. Canadian photo icon Ted Grant said: "When you photograph people in colour, you photograph their clothes. But when you photograph people in black and white, you photograph their souls." Jack the painter lived his life suffused in mad colour, and I don't know what that says about us.

"May I see?" Vincent asked after I edited frames from a pancake breakfast in Lockeport. "That is good," he said. The thick gnarled hands of a skipper juxtaposed with a frail paper plate. "So good."

It was foggy that day. Light falls off by the inverse square of the distance, but in the fog, it just falls off. It is tricky, as tricky as the most dangerous man you have ever known.

"Do you know what else I saw that day when I saw you in the parking lot?" Vincent asked.

"No," I replied.

"Nothing," he said. "I saw nothing."

*

I am trying to be as truthful as I can, but memory is selective. People lie to themselves. I get that. After I met Dante, the failed comic I dated for three tragic months, he told me that his parents were old-fashioned squares. Straitlaced religious squares who lived outside the city so that they could garden and hike. It made him seem like a free spirit, I suppose; made them seem quaint.

I did not understand why Dante's parents would not visit him when he fell off a stage and broke his arm. Or attend Easter dinner when invited. And yet, he felt compelled to go there on their birthdays, to an inland house that smelled stale and miserable, where they kept a photo of his old girlfriend, Chevonne, on a table.

They started smoking weed at eight a.m., I discovered, and they had not been inside a church in thirty years. There was no garden—just weed plants. They did not hike. At a cousin's wedding, Dante's father groped the senior citizen handing out cake. When I pointed this out to Dante, he looked at me as though I was mad. I get that.

I told Dante that Stan was a good person.

I told him that my parents were devoted to each other.

I told him that my husband had a rare undetected heart condition, and he died in his sleep.

I told none of those lies to Vincent. I am not sure why.

Jack was not dead, as you may have guessed. That was someone else. Years after we moved to Nova Scotia, Jack *did*, however, as a delayed and indirect result of that death, attend a week-long retreat at a monastery in the woods. It was something he needed, we agreed, with the way things were going. I drove and left him two hours from our home. The air smelled like pine needles and decomposing moss. Isn't it curious how you remember those things? Those trivial things.

You may think my story is vague about time, the months and the years. How long were Jack and I in Montréal? How long we were here before it fell apart?

My memory has deliberately made it unclear—it has lengthened the good parts and shortened the bad to the point of being unreliable, and I cannot, would not, change that.

Jack's running had become dangerous sometime after Montréal. He tore an ACL. He suffered a concussion when he fell on ice. When someone is harming themselves, you are constantly on edge, you are *running running running* in another dimension, and you can't slow down, and you can't be exhausted because that state does not exist in your altered world. Your world is too dangerous. Maybe exhaustion exists in the next world, one without jagged cliffs and screaming sirens. But not here and now.

Jack had never been interested in running before he started in Montréal. He did not even own a pair of running shoes. He came tall and lean, and yes, he loved baseball, but baseball was a game. It had camaraderie and scorecards, a uniform and highlight reels you could play over and over again. Running was lonely.

While Jack was at the monastery, he wore a lanyard with a card that said, *Please respect my silence.* After days of respected silence, a retired banker spoke to Jack. "Does it give you pleasure, the running, or does it obliterate your pain?"

"Does it matter?" asked Jack.

"Why, yes," the banker said.

The banker suggested that Jack join a Bible group that met once a week. It was a mix of young and old, folks from different faith groups. They studied the Bible, he said, but they came at it from an alternate angle. Jack said he would think it over, Jack who had been raised by wealthy agnostics in Montréal and had never been slightly religious.

✻

I had been coming to Pollock Passage on my days off. When I made that turnoff, the air changed. All the rules were lifted, the rules about owning the right dog and having two perfect kids and never being seen in a chain restaurant. I felt free. Free to fix myself.

I was starting to see myself in black and white. It felt like therapy, which I clearly needed. Have you ever known anyone to go to therapy because life is going too well? And they need to figure out why they are so rich and happy. Or why everyone loves them. It doesn't happen, does it? People go to therapy to sort things out, their issues and the issues of the people who hurt them.

On this trip down, I noticed cars, because cars are one of the things I like. Cars I understand. People I am not so good with, but cars I understand. When the boats are out in Pollock Passage, all you will see on the roads are compact vehicles such as Toyota Corollas, and they are all driven by women or men too old to fish. Old men who ritualistically drive to the government wharf. When the old men are at the wharf, talking to each other, the parking lot is three deep with Rams and F-150s, the rides of the younger men at sea. Most trucks are local. Some have New Brunswick or PEI plates.

When I was on the shore, I thought about Shag Harbour, the curiosity that had brought Vincent into my life. We were dating, I should acknowledge. It's not a word I like to use about people my age, even though I admitted dating Dante, but that was to punish myself. To remind myself what rock bottom felt like. Why I didn't want to return there.

One day, Vincent and I watched the Shag Harbour video made by the community college student. The one I had viewed. It was fascinatingly bad, melodramatic with shaky camera work that gave it a seventies porn vibe.

Midway, the narrator introduces Americans Barney and Betty Hill, who were, during a turbulent time in the UFO movement, the mom-and-pop faces of alien abduction. A biracial couple from Portsmouth, New Hampshire, they had, the story went, been taken aboard an alien spaceship where their memories were erased. Their tale was the prototype for those that followed. Here is what the narrator said:

> The Hills engaged in the civil rights movement. In photos I have viewed, they look like sensible people. Shortly before midnight on September 19, 1961, their lives changed forever. The Hills were driving home from Canada when they saw a light in the sky. They pulled over and spotted an odd-shaped craft with flashing lights. They were followed. They got out binoculars. To their shock, they saw humanoid figures in black uniforms. Yes, humanoid figures. The cat and mouse game continued, and then the Hills heard unusual sounds, they felt a tingling sensation, and they lost consciousness.

They had no idea how they ended up thirty-five miles away. They felt dirty. Their watches were no longer working. Under hypnosis, the couple remembered being taken onto the spaceship. The alien abductors were grey beings with large eyes. Grey, not green. The aliens were fascinated by the fact that Barney wore dentures because this was not a known thing in their world. Did they themselves have perfect teeth? That we do not know. To protect their identity, the aliens erased the Hills' memories.

So here is the question we must ask ourselves as we go inside the mystery of Shag Harbour. Is there a Betty or Barney Hill among us? Were they brainwashed?

*
*

From Vincent's, I could see the old Swim house. Some days there was laundry on the line. Some days I saw a man mowing the grass. Some days I saw Stan and Maynard tossing a ball back and forth, the wind changing the ball's course as though it was my future. Or so I imagined.

"Do you remember the hole in their kitchen ceiling?" Peter once asked. Being older, he could remember more. "It was by the wood stove, and it let warm air up into the bedrooms?"

"No," I honestly replied.

"Do you remember when their neighbour died of a ruptured spleen?"

"No."

I never saw Vincent write a word, and I was beginning, despite my fondness for him, to think that sabbaticals were a scam. Not that I cared. Vincent *did* spend many hours in Shag Harbour, even going out on fishing boats. He did attend the annual international

UFO symposium in Shag Harbour, a multi-day event that draws experts, eyewitnesses, and "experiencers." But I never saw him write a word. His laptop, a Librem 13 with a Linux operating system, was always off. Was all this a ruse? Could Vincent be as duplicitous as the Mountie whose family believed him?

When I was young, I took a train to Montréal. A woman struck up a conversation with me — she was carrying a deck of Tarot cards inside a black velvet bag. The woman paused too long at some words, giving her story an uneasy cadence. "It *is* a shock," she said, hanging on the word "is," "when you discover someone is far more invested in part of their life than you know. A part you think is incidental. Or silly. But is really the *essence* of who they are. It might be a job you consider dreary. It may be a strange — to you — church. And then you go to your brother's funeral, and he is laid out in a Star Wars stormtrooper costume, and there is an honour guard of *Star Wars* characters, and you know you totally misread the situation."

"Maybe," I sighed, "that is my problem. I am bad at reading situations."

"Maybe," she said, as though she knew me better than I knew myself, "you *want* to misread them."

"Maybe."

How did she know?

Now and then, Vincent did give me updates from his research. One man, he said, had left the church after the UFO incident because his beliefs had been challenged. A fisherman became obsessed with a sea monster shaped like a gigantic crocodile that was, according to rumour, capable of swallowing a boat. Vincent made it sound as though his work was progressing as it should.

On this day, he was at the counter making coffee, and he turned too slowly to face me. He turned the way a person turns when they are exaggerating their nonchalance, when they are trying to bring it down — the mood, the intensity — because they are going to ask for a divorce. They want you slack and subdued. Have you been there?

And then he asked, and I am sure he knew the answer, "Is Pelly Swim the same person as Maynard?"

"Yes. Graham's father. Stan's brother."

I know I told him this. Why is he pretending to not remember?

"I see."

"He was nicknamed Pelly because he spotted a white pelican that had appeared out of its natural habitat. My grandfather's nickname was Lark. Many people had bird nicknames down here, I was told. Ruff and Tern."

"Ahhh." Vincent shrugged. "And you know the rumour about Pelly?"

I looked at Vincent, and I noticed his hair had receded like William Hurt's, when he was in *Gorky Park* playing the Soviet militsiya officer. I noticed his glasses were bifocals. I wondered if he knew that he had a brown spot on his forehead that he probably should get looked at.

"Yes. No."

Vincent decided to stall, to further bring down the mood.

"Usually when outrageous rumours are spread, they at least seem plausible. But, in periods of intense anxiety, such as war or a plague, plausibility is thrown out the window like the family cat in a fire." Shrug. "But that all sounds rather dry, doesn't it?" A shrug. "Except for the cat."

I wanted to believe the rumour he was about to tell me, plausible or not. In the same way I wanted to believe that life is fair, and that forgiveness is afforded based on a formula that factors in what you have endured and where you now are. I noticed a Helly Hansen flotation jacket on a hook and wondered when he had bought it.

"What," I asked, "about Pelly?"

The rumour had been circulating for decades, he said. In the rumour, Pelly, or Maynard—people called him both—an experienced fisherman, had not fallen out of his boat on a still day and vanished. There was no logic to that. He had—like the Americans

Barney and Betty Hill—been abducted, only not returned to Earth. On the day of the UFO sighting.

"Well, that is quite a rumour," I replied. "That would make Pelly a contemporary legend, I suppose."

If this rumour had been around for years, why had Stan not heard it? Stan who loved nothing more than the outlandish. This was a far better story than a circus trunk washed up on a shore. It was as good as the one about Lady, the Appaloosa reportedly mutilated and killed by aliens in 1967 in Colorado. A story still discussed.

I wondered how long Vincent had been sitting on this. Why now? This was the first time that I did not quite believe Vincent. It made me question who he was. I had grown up in a household of lies and this was, I was convinced, a lie. Was I subconsciously attracted to liars? Dante, the failed comedian, had told me that he was set to inherit a valuable piece of real estate in the Bahamas when his degenerate parents died. The ones who liked living in the basement of a burned-out house.

"That is the rumour," Vincent said too firmly. At that moment, Vincent's electric green eyes looked like a cheap trick.

I took a slow sip of my coffee and then another, exaggerating my nonchalance in the same way that Vincent had. *Did Vincent need one spectacular rumour to validate his work, the work I never saw him doing? Or was this a test? Was he evaluating me? To see what I would believe.*

There were other murmurs about Pelly, what *could* have happened, I reminded myself. Ones I had heard. Grim ones with outcomes that turned on a confluence of bad luck and bad timing, one abject moment of fog-induced hopelessness. Rumours that scared me more than this one.

"Do people believe this?" I asked.

Was this the inflection point?

"Some. Particularly those who assume that aliens are malevolent and hostile, capable of destroying humanity. A fear-filled belief that feeds into rumours."

"Ahh. Will this be in your paper?"

"Possibly."

What, I wondered, *do you want me to say?*

*
*

You notice the trivial during the surreal moments of life, those *How did I find myself here?* moments, the ones you never signed up for. One day, Jack and I were in Emergency. He had fractured his ankle while running on gravel. The waiting area was filled with people bleeding or on oxygen, half-conscious and on stretchers. A man was talking to himself. A television was broadcasting messages telling you what "triage" was and how many patients were being looked at, asking you to see your family doctor instead of coming *here*, a place that held your life unsteadily in its hands.

I went to the washroom, and I saw a poster taped at four points to a door. A colour poster of six stock photo faces, smiling as though they did not care if they were ever treated.

Did you know? the poster asked over an image of a fox-faced blond who was supposed to be from Siberia. *That Russians consume vodka and sugar to treat a cough.*

Did you know? it asked over a man with a black ponytail. *That Native Canadians leave the window open so the soul can depart at death.*

Did you know? it asked four more times, and I wondered: *Why are you telling me this? Isn't this information your doctors and nurses should know? And if they don't know, why is this "information" posted on a washroom door, imploring me, of all people, to do something?*

Why?

At the time, a volunteer in a smock and running shoes kept moving people around the room. She told a man on oxygen to move from chair A to chair B, and a woman who was bleeding to move from chair C to chair D. Nobody was getting any closer to where they needed to be. But they moved because she told them to. They moved because they were afraid that if they didn't, they might be disqualified, found dead in chair A. Or sent home like Skippy while having a stroke.

I looked at the man who was talking to himself. He was a millennial who had forgotten how to sleep. He was alone, but the chairs were so close together that the stranger next to him joined him in conversation. The stranger was wearing canvas work coveralls and safety boots.

"I will tell you what is going to happen here," said the millennial, nodding at a closed door. "They'll eventually—in about six hours—let me see a doctor, and he'll have one question for me, just one: 'Are you thinking of killing yourself?' And that's a shitty, loaded question, doc, because that's a place where I try not to go. I try not to put that on my shopping list, but he already knows that. And if I say no, he will show me the street."

"He *will* ask you," said the stranger, who could have been a carpenter. "I can *guarantee* that. He will. So, think about what you want to say."

And when the sleepless man, who may have been in university before this, stood up to leave, I noticed his jeans were in danger of falling off. I noticed he was wearing a scuffed pair of eight-hundred-dollar yellow Yeezys that had once felt special.

At some point in your life, you will feel powerless, and the system will make you feel insignificant. And you may be the first, but you are *not* the latter. The stranger tapped the young man's arm, as if to say, *Take care of yourself, buddy.*

One day, I found myself driving to Vincent's early, and I parked down the road. I saw a man coming out of the barn, the barn that was always locked. He did not look like he was from here. He did not look like a fisherman or a handyman. He was followed by Vincent, who locked the door behind them, and then double-checked it. The man was wearing rust-coloured cowboy boots. That is what I noticed. The most trivial thing.

11

Back in the city, I attended a funeral with Peter. It was for his old paddling coach Zoltan Tóth, who had years ago defected from Hungary. I had gone to school with Zoltan's daughter Elena—their house had a chin-up bar and tubs of brewer's yeast—and so I went.

Zoltan was hard-core. He had raced on the Hungarian national team for fifteen years—he had the scars and mentality to prove it. In the old country, he said, you were hit with a wooden stick if you had a bad practice. You had your hair pulled. One day, Zoltan dropped Peter and two others off thirty kilometres from the club and told them to paddle back in a storm. Zoltan's idea of normal was Hungarian C1 star György Zala, whom you can find on YouTube knocking off more than five hundred pull-ups in thirty minutes.

In his later years, Zoltan had, and this was news to me and undoubtedly to György Zala, joined the Church of Jesus Christ of Latter-day Saints, which was surprising and yet not, because Zoltan never did anything in half measures. You could not be a Mormon and be cavalier about it.

Zoltan's funeral was in a building adjacent to the grand temple, which was off limits to us. We filed into a utilitarian room with a food table at the back. The program had a photo of Zoltan in a Hungarian team track suit and sideburns. The crowd consisted of three groups: church members, former paddlers, and family. Zoltan's widow, children, and spouses were up front with the grandchildren.

I had the feeling that nothing was being revealed here, in this unadorned room outside the temple. No rituals, no secret to peace and salvation. No guidance on how one must behave if one wants to dwell with God in a state of eternal joy. Was that what I had come here for? Guidance? Or the chance sighting of a once-handsome face from the old days.

The funeral started with words from the bishop, who kept breaking down in sobs. It seemed odd for a bishop. Two speakers then delivered eulogies. Zoltan's daughter Elena went first, and I thought she did well. Elena was followed by an old Polish coach who had a dense accent after twenty years in Canada. He began by recounting Zoltan's 1,000-metre gold medal race at worlds, breaking it down by quarters. The first two-fifty. The second. It was a raging headwind, he said, which Zoltan liked. "A headwind separate the men from the boys. A tailwind blows the shit to the front." (He pronounced the word "shee-yit.") The Pole was straying; the use of the word "shit" was beyond the parameters of acceptability, and then it got worse. He started giving shout-outs to old paddlers in the room as though he was at a pep rally.

"And there is Peter Swim, one of Zoltan's best."

Peter nodded, trying not to draw attention to himself.

And then louder, sounding unhinged: "And Allan Crowell, still a competitor to this day." He paused. "Zoltan say, 'Crowell die like a pig at the three hundred' but still a competitor. I used to say, 'Make a man of him, Zoltan, not a pig,' but he could not. Not even Zoltan could do it." He shook his head in regret.

After the service, the crowd migrated to the back. The old Pole did not recognize one man at first. And then when he did, he said: "You look like you ate your boat. Is that what you did? Did you eat your boat?" Two ex-paddlers were trashing another ex-paddler, who was absent. One was wearing a long-sleeved paisley shirt. "Have you seen Joe Hollywood lately?" he asked too zealously. And then added, "Nothing changed. Still Joe Hollywood, still the same. Still one eye on the mirror."

The family was in two clusters, a few speaking Hungarian. Peter and I stood at the edge of one, near the food table. I wondered how long we would have to stay.

"There they are," Peter murmured. "Not heading this way, I hope."

"Who?"

"The Crowells."

The Crowells. Must we deal with them for the rest of our lives, chasing us around corners, reminding us of things we did not want to be reminded of?

I heard Babs before I saw her, Babs who had, years ago, adopted the trademark Crowell conversational technique. As soon as a person started to talk, and she sensed they were about to disagree, she would drown them out with *N-n-n-n-n-n-n-no*. And so, I heard it. "N-n-n-n-n-n-n-no."

I turned for a look. Babs had a death grip on a man, trying to convince him of something. Babs wore her hair in a brittle orange pageboy. It was clear that whatever it was that had once made her attractive — an opportune combination of a boyish figure and a too-eager smile — was long gone. Her face, which had once had cheekbones, was formless. Only Babs's lips, painted pink, managed to make a mark. A thin line across her ashen face, as she roared, "N-n-n-n-n-n-n-no."

Babs and I had been friends in high school. Babs had sleepovers at our house. We lent each other clothes. We hung around paddling because of our brothers. Babs had a desperate side, but I was not exactly an angel.

At an international regatta in Dartmouth, Babs "dated" an entire Soviet C-4 and told everyone about it. Aleksei, Sergei, Nikolai, and Maksim — she recited their names as though they were a boy band: the cute one, the quiet one, the funny one, the smart one. Maksim

Morozov, who weighed 225 pounds in his Soviet short shorts, was the quiet one, and according to Babs, "a doll."

Babs was laughing, the exaggerated *look at me; we are the Crowells* laugh. She said something about the Supreme Court and mandatory retirement. Babs was a lawyer, and when she was admitted to the bar, Stan said it was like putting a flamethrower in the hands of a deranged chimpanzee, which proved prophetic.

Babs was married to a navy officer. Rarely seen together, they had one son named Max. For years, she had volunteered her services to the national canoe/kayak team, which was only too happy to get something for free. Peter bumped into her at trials, where she gushed, "Give my love to darling Harriett." She attended meetings in Ottawa. She represented the team in legal disputes, her proximity to the sport all part of her need to stay in the same sub-world as Maksim Morozov, two-time Olympic gold medallist.

Morozov had a lengthy and heralded career, all the while eating staggering amounts of red meat. He raced in three Olympics in C1 and made his last international appearance at Worlds in a C2 that was stripped of its medals after his partner failed a doping test. Morozov moved into coaching.

Morozov, like many elite Soviet paddlers, had trained himself to drop into the splits during gym workouts. *Bam.* It was an impressive move for a man his size. Knowing that, Morozov often, while under the influence of vodka and the glow of an international regatta, dropped into the splits at after-parties. *Bam.* Down he went. A 225-pound behemoth in a tank top. Babs saw him do it in Dartmouth and was hypnotized.

A man who volunteered as an official—and once was the starter for a race with Morozov in Lane 4—approached Peter, whom he had known for years. He reached him before the Crowells could.

"How is Luke doing?" he asked. His tone was sadder than the tone most were using for Zoltan, who was *dead.*

"Doing all right."

"Good to hear. I loved to watch him race; he made it exciting. I know I'm not supposed to say that, but..."

If you haven't done it—if you haven't channelled every thought and every penny into a dream, if you haven't willingly set your alarm for five a.m. for years, if you haven't hung your heart on a hook of fair play and hard work with a little luck when you needed it— you can't understand. The official had seen it all. He had seen boats dock after races skewed by bad starts or freak winds; he had witnessed the tears.

"Yeah," smiled Peter, "Mister Come-from-Behind. I used to say, 'Could you spare your dad's heart and get off the line a little quicker?'"

"He did great." Patting Peter on the shoulder, as though he needed it. "He did great."

There is an expression that Maritimers like to use, and it is mean and small. *Where did all that get him?* You hear it when a dreamer's dream falls short, when all the heart and all the passion were not enough. That misses the whole point, doesn't it? The point is the doing.

Allan Crowell was getting closer. He was wearing a salmon-coloured blazer. He looked like the guy who microwaves fish in the office lunchroom because he is "eating healthy." In real life, he sold Kia cars.

"Time to go." A nudge from Peter.

We almost made it to our car when Peter was ambushed by an ex-paddler who had been making a phone call. "I am doing dragon-boat," he told Peter with an unnatural intensity. "Man, we could use you. You should consider it. We went to nationals in BC. We are going to worlds in France. We get ice cream after workouts." There was no shutting him up.

"Look, Dale," interrupted Peter, sounding like an engineer with a bridge to build. "All this sounds interesting, but I *have* to go."

*
*

Stan found out that Peter and I had been at Zoltan's funeral. I do not know who told him; I had only mentioned it to Vincent. I had told him in a phone call, during which he said he had a small gift for me. He hoped I would like it. I am sure, I said, that I would.

I wanted to like the gift. I *wanted* to like Vincent, despite the dubious story about Maynard that he had told me. The awkward one that made me question who he was. A liar? A fraud? And yet, the last night that I was in Pollock Passage, the windows were open, and the wind was flapping the blinds, and I could have been anywhere. I heard wheelers ripping by, wide-open, and the monotone roar sounded like freedom; it sounded like someone doing exactly what they wanted to at that moment because they might not get another.

"Who was there?" asked Stan of the funeral.

"The usual crowd," replied Peter.

"Surprised they didn't ask me to say a few words," said Stan.

A few words?

Peter, the person who had been close to Zoltan, dropped his eyes. Paddling was Peter's world, not Stan's. If you look at old photos, it was where Peter bloomed. He grew his hair the way he wanted to, he wore cool racing clothes. I remember being at the canoe club when a twelve-year-old girl stepped on a nail, and Peter carried her to a car, and all her twelve-year-old friends almost fainted.

When Peter was in high school, he came home and discovered that Stan had given his room to the Romanian stowaway he had befriended. When my mother objected, Stan said Peter did not care about people the way he did. It was exam week. When Peter was forty, his appendix ruptured, and Stan snorted, "If he had half the health problems I did." If Peter tried to assert himself, Stan retaliated with the predictable: After all I did for you. When he had never done anything extraordinary at all.

I could have felt guilty about the fact that Stan could not let Peter have anything. But my guilt would have been insincere because every child—no matter how unworthy the distinction—covets the position of Favourite. Was I being easy on Stan because he was old? Or was my situation, the one I had created for myself, Convenient—Convenient being the safe house for apaths, quislings, and individuals unable to face the truth about themselves?

"I suppose Allan Crowell was there, acting important after being in the newspaper," said Stan. "Is he that special?"

Twitch.

I knew that Stan was drinking. I knew, or I thought I knew, many things, but I elected to keep them to myself.

"He sells cars, doesn't he? Kias? At least Babs was smart enough to get through law school. You have to give her that."

Peter and I did not have to give Babs anything.

Twitch. Twitch.

"She had to have some brains." Stan doubled down. He was now goading me. I was the person who had not been good at school. Peter found school easy. I was the one who brought home report cards that said, "Harriett must make better use of her time." Or "Harriet must try harder to be organized." In grade 8, I had a shrew of a math teacher who told me I would grow up to be a messy old woman. She wore tight skirts and clingy sweaters, and she pranced down the halls like a baneful little beast. My father was being mean to me because he had not been informed about a funeral he had no business attending.

"Law school is not easy," he noted.

How would YOU know? You didn't even finish high school.

Every time Stan was mean, his meanness shocked me. No matter how many times I experienced it, I was shocked. It was as though this new act of meanness awakened memories of past meanness, and they joined together in a mob of cheap shots and petulance.

"Graham was a crook, you know." In my state of shock, I blurted the secret I had been harbouring. "He was fencing stolen goods at the pawn shop with his gnome."

Silence.

And then, "Are you saying Graham fenced his gnome?" asked Stan.

"No."

"Because he *loved* that gnome. That is why I saved it."

I then told Stan (and Peter) the convoluted story about my lens and the hipster pawnshop. I spared no details. I told them about Korey St. Clair Scudder and how the truth about Graham had been found between a Royal Doulton Dick Turpin Toby mug and a red electric Walden guitar. I mentioned the kidney punch. It took a while.

Peter nodded, vindicated. Stan had two diametrically opposed standards: one for Peter, who *had* done something in life, and one for Graham, who did not even try. I half expected Stan to be shocked. I half expected him to apologize for bringing Graham into The City, but instead, he slapped his leg. "I wondered where he was getting that casino money." And then he laughed. "He was over there three or four times a week."

"Well, he *did* steal your six hundred dollars," Peter muttered half under his breath.

"You don't know what you are talking about."

"I know he stole your money."

"You know everything, don't you? I guess that's what happens when you fall out a window and land on your head."

Twitch.

And then I said, because I was the person who had broken the news, "It was *my* lens."

"You got it back, didn't you?" demanded Stan. "Don't ask me why it was in your car in the first place. The only person who lost anything was that fireman, and he knew the lens was stolen."

"Graham was involved in crime," said Peter, sounding stiff after the head-injury dig.

"Half the cops on the force are involved in crime," Stan stated with no proof. "One got charged with pointing a loaded service revolver at another one. Part of a gay sex triangle. Oh yes. Do not talk to me about crime."

And then, because I was frustrated with his illogical response, I said, "Nobody thinks any of this is amusing except for you."

"I suppose *you* think a gay sex triangle on the police force is amusing. I can't compete with You People. You are too much for me."

I left Stan's with Peter, and we talked outside. Peter was upset, not about Graham, who had, after all, punched him. No, he was upset about Luke, whom he had not heard from in weeks. Luke was working nights at a warehouse. He and his Swedish girlfriend had broken up. She was now dating a beastly C1 paddler from Kazakhstan, who wore ill-fitting unitards and told Luke that he would beat him up if he saw him. Luke, who used to be our proof that we could be normal.

Here is the problem with normal. There are positions in society that require such enormous egos, such feelings of potency and infallibility—the willingness, for example, to determine if another individual should live or die—that you should not be surprised if those people, while celebrated, are not exactly *normal*. What normal person becomes a US Supreme Court justice? Or volunteers for a one-way mission to Mars? Who becomes an Olympic multi-medallist like Maksim Morozov? Normal people? No.

"He needs to get over this paddling business," Peter said. "It's not the end of the world. This shit happens."

"He put a lot into it," I said, "but you're right, it's not the end of the world."

"He blames me because of the Crowells. He says they were supposed to be my friends."

"The Crowells aren't anyone's friends."

"He told his mother he never should have gotten into a bullshit sport. But I *made* him."

"Well, he's said that before."

"Don't tell him," Peter nodded toward Stan's house, "any of this."

"Of course not. How is Molly?" I asked to lighten the mood.

"Molly is great. He let Suzanne Skype her."

"Well, there's that, anyway. He's good as long as he has Molly."

✻

Let me explain the whole catastrophe with Luke, the one that broke him. It is all connected to another part of our family story. A tawdry part. It is connected to the Crowells. When I think about Luke's sketchy sports arbitration, I think about something the *Standard* court reporter told me.

"The courts are built for career criminals and sociopaths. If you are a normal person, you can't handle it. The Hell's Angels have the top lawyers. And the sociopaths roll the dice every day. I covered a Coast Guard cook who had five wives. Remember him? No. Okay. Regular-looking dude. Hard to say how he got five wives, but he did, which proves a theory I have: *anyone* can get married if they want to. When he got charged, he was cool. Wife Number Three showed up dressed like an Irish traveller in a poufy yellow dress, trying to look like 'the best' of the wives. He waved."

Luke was twenty-two when he found himself before an arbitration body named the Fair Sports Resolution Board (FSRB). He was not an Irish traveller or a sociopath. He was too normal for the process that Peter explained to me in excruciating detail. He was a naïf.

I tried to understand the arbitration process by comparing it to the courts I covered, the ones with Hell's Angels, sociopaths, and low-level car thieves like Korey St. Clair Scudder.

The first difference between Luke and Korey is that Korey stole at least one Audi to land himself in court, while Luke did nothing. He did not break a rule or take a banned substance. He was what they call "an affected party," which means that someone else—a paddler named Anatoly from Trois-Rivières, Quebec—had appealed a team decision, and Luke was the human domino.

The second difference is that Korey had a Legal Aid lawyer.

He may have looked like a rural undertaker who lives above the family funeral home. His last name may have been Swindells. But he *was a* lawyer. Luke did *not* have a lawyer. He had been assured by the FSRB that he did not need one because "this is a friendly mediation-based process that you can navigate on your own," which is like telling you that you *can* stick your hand into the cage of a bear. But *should* you?

The third difference was that Korey could, if someone got it wrong, appeal his decision. Luke could not. Let us imagine that Korey's case was heard by a cocaine-happy judge appointed to the bench *only* because he had blackmailed a federal cabinet minister, a married bon vivant known for his unusually attractive executive assistants named Jason. If the judge's decision was ridiculous, Korey could appeal. If Luke's case was heard by an isolated disrupter intent on upending the patriarchy, and *her* decision was ridiculous, he could not. Her decision was binding.

The fourth difference — and this is the critical one, the one that caused the most damage, the one that made Luke abandon the sport, his family, and all he believed about fair play — was that Korey was wired for this. He was used to being treated like a criminal because he *was* one. Luke was not.

Other than that, the process was similar. It was harsh and cold and devious, and some of the people involved told unbelievable lies.

You can find the results of Luke's case online. I did.

Luke's file will tell you that the appeal, a seat selection for a pre-Olympic crew, was heard by a single FSRB arbitrator. The arbitrator who decides your fate at these hearings will have absolutely *no knowledge* of your sport. The equipment, the impact of variables such as crosswind or current. The average horizontal velocity over two consecutive strokes at race pace ($r=-0.83$, $p<0.05$). People can lie, and they will *not* know. They can feed them gibberish like this:

V " P L2 3 = P3 # L $ 2 3.

Thus, the hull speed is proportional to the cube root of the applied power.

And the arbitrator will have no idea if they are lying.

The arbitrators are lawyers, not sports scientists. They come from a pool, and most know each other. Luke drew Keitha J. Armstrong, QC, from Whitehorse, Yukon. Armstrong was an isolated disrupter, who had never seen a sprint kayak in her life but had, according to her CV, been "active in orienteering." Orienteering is, from what I can tell, an activity that involves a map and a compass and appeals to individuals who might have enjoyed the Boy Scouts. People who embrace haphazard rules, and may have, at another time in history, felt at home in the *Hitler-Jugend, Bund deutscher Arbeiterjugend.*

The FSRB hearing was conducted by emails and conference calls from Ottawa. The calls were hard to hear, and the bilingual individual in charge kept introducing Luke as Duke. Duke Swim.

Anatoly, who was in Trois-Rivières, barely spoke. He had only been in Canada for two years—he had previously attended the Belarusian State University of Physical Culture in Minsk. His English was weak, and he had limited knowledge of how anything here worked. His coach Igor had filed the appeal.

Luke had not been worried, Peter told me, because the selection had been by the book. Proper. Unbeknownst to Luke, the case was about to take an unexpected twist. By the time Anatoly came on the line, he had submitted a twenty-page legal argument complete with precedents and graphs that looked convincing *only* to a person outside the sport.

There was nonsense about how a one-degree difference in shoulder rotation produces a .05 second speed differential over two hundred metres. Previously unseen emails. Most critically, there was a time control of Anatoly recorded on an iPhone. It had no reference points and no running clock at the bottom, *nothing* to prove that it had not been sped up or altered to Anatoly's advantage, but none of that occurred to Keitha J. Armstrong, QC.

Anatoly's argument was fantastical. It was laughable, and it had been drafted *pro bono* by Barbara Crowell, QC, who up until this point, was considered a family friend. Babs, who had attended a two-day Women and Law and Sport seminar in Ottawa with Keitha and become "fierce" female allies.

In her first and last FSRB decision, Keitha J. Armstrong ruled in favour of Anatoly, citing the fake time-control video. I scoured the FSRB database, and I never found another decision by Keitha J. Armstrong, who was, I can only assume, excluded by the patriarchy because she had undermined the credibility of the entire patriarchal organization.

It was two weeks before we learned of Babs's role. Anatoly, who was as surprised as anyone by both the decision and Babs's unsolicited largesse, told a paddler named Dominic, who told Luke, who then told Peter.

Any time anything unfortunate happens, my father asks one of his unanswerable questions, the one meant to paint you into a corner of culpability and shame. When Peter was hit by lighting in his C1, an event so unusual that he made the news — "Paddler Struck by Lightning, Remembers Nothing" — my father demanded, "Were you wearing rubber gloves?"

Why no.

In the aftermath of Babs's betrayal, I found myself falling into that same warped pattern of victim blaming. I thought about asking Peter, *Should you have hired a lawyer anyway? Did you know that Babs and Keitha had attended a seminar in Ottawa where they bonded over litres of Campari? Did you know that Anatoly's Russian coach, Igor, raced with Maksim Morozov?* And then I told myself, *That is madness.*

There is a sting to gratuitous meanness, a long-lasting burn. It stays with you. It is one thing for people to act badly when they are backed into a corner of desperation, when they are fighting, with every resource they have, to survive. But Babs was doing quite well.

If it had not been for Babs, Luke would not have quit the sport and fled to BC, Suzanne would not have escaped to the higher ground of a prefab fourplex in Tuktoyaktuk, and I would not have been left with Peter and Stan, pondering how much of the Crowell story I should reveal.

18

It was a hectic night at the Lucky Lady. I had spent two days on the shore, where Vincent and I had visited the old NORAD station and taken photos. On the shore, the air contained more oxygen. The houses had more space. In the morning, I could look out a window, knowing that people were doing the work that needed to be done. And so on this night, in this pointless place, everything felt off kilter.

At nine p.m., a senior collapsed. When this happens, the casino's prime objective is to contain and *conceal* the victim. You do not want a personal injury lawyer to see an iPhone photo of Grandma upside down. Security has a device for this: a three-sided white privacy screen on wheels. The Gawker Blocker went up.

Thirty minutes later, a scary dude was at the blackjack table. He looked like the mover who drinks an entire bottle of Lemon Hart Overproof Rum on the job and adds five hours to your bill. When you object, he returns and slashes your tires. Security was hovering.

Around ten p.m., back-to-back jackpot winners. The first was a woman with 163 spins in the buffalo bonus. She looked like a woman who spent every summer, for thirty years, in her semi-permanent trailer at the Enchanted Forest Campground.

There is a protocol when a player wins a jackpot. The VLT locks up and an employee goes to the station. They say congratulations, take the person's name, and wait for a supervisor, who goes through more procedure and hands over the cash. There is protocol for note taking in the event of incidents: (a) write in pen, (b) do not double space, (c) initial any changes you make, (d) do not rip pages out of your report book, and (e) cross out empty lines at the bottom of your report so again you can't be accused of adding lies. All this is necessary in case your notes end up in court.

It took a while for the supervisor to arrive. The buffalo woman tipped me twenty dollars on her twenty-five-hundred-dollar win. I later discovered that her name was on a list of compulsive gamblers who had asked to be banned.

The second winner was sour for someone who had won $620. After she gave me her name, she asked for mine.

"My name is Harriett."

No one asks your name; it is none of their business. It is *not* protocol.

"In my business, the public relations business, we give our full names. Mine is Doris Hahn Crowell. The Hahns were very important people in Dartmouth. They owned a sawmill."

I already knew who she was. I knew that Mrs. Crowell had never worked in public relations. I had been inside Mrs. Crowell's house, when it had a pole lamp and a faux brass room divider. I had visited her "fashion" store when it sold pink Ultrasuede suits. How did she not remember me?

"Where do you live?" she asked.

You aren't supposed to ask me that.

"Near Lake Banook."

"Well, you must know my son, Allan Crowell, the paddler. Allan should have been at the Olympics, but they had the times wrong."

"Okay."

I was not going to tell her that I knew Allan, and for that matter all her children, and that I had seen two of them at a funeral. On the floor next to her chair was an enormous brown purse. I sensed the purse had been expensive twenty years ago, and she was proud to be its owner.

"For my birthday Allan gave me a whistle; it cost him $14.99."

Mrs. Crowell's hair was dyed a severe black that made her skin look sallow. She was wearing a leather maxi skirt and a paisley scarf that came from her store, closed years ago. It was unnerving that she did not know me. I had seen her at the casino before. Always alone. Sergeant Crowell, the retired cop with the bad eye, was never with her.

"That is nice."

And then, barely listening: "My daughter Barbara could have been a judge, but she didn't have the time."

"It's hard to find time."

"Not everyone can do what she does. You might not be capable. You might not have the drive or the intelligence like my children, or you would not be working here."

My supervisor arrived. We counted out Mrs. Crowell's $620, and she did not tip.

What Could Have Happened

I saw a man wearing a Rasta slouch beanie. He had a white handle-bar moustache, and he was shuffling toward the ZZ Top VLTs. Rasta Man was wearing a faded T-shirt with *Reggae One Love* over a lion's head. He smelled like a flea market. He was part of that group that comes in from the county on Thursdays wearing no-name jeans with studded belts. They drive to Costco where they stack their carts with jumbo packs of the eighteen-ounce plastic Big Red Cup. Then they hit the casino.

It did not take me long to recognize that chin, those stunted legs. It was Jamie, the Crowell at the bottom of the pecking order, the mother's least favourite.

Jamie found an empty ZZ Top game next to Little Red Riding Hood.

You just got paid, it announced when things went well.

Jamie looked transformed. As soon as he was in that chair, his body changed. He could have been driving a snowmobile across a moonlit field, all his senses focused on the task at hand. He could have been ripping up the roads on a dirt bike. I had heard that Jamie had moved to a rural no man's land not far from Dante's parents, and that he worked part-time as an airport commissionaire.

An hour later, Jamie came to my wicket to cash in an eighty-dollar win. Jamie, the anti-Crowell, looked antsy. Then excited.

"Harriett," he said, knowing me at once. "Does your father still have that monkey?"

"No," I admitted. "They took him away."

"Too bad. What was his name?" His face looked strained trying to pull this from his memory.

"Mikey."

"I thought it was Bobby."

"No, that was the squirrel. Bobby was the 'tame' squirrel."

"I asked your father if Mikey bit and he said, 'just for fun.' I thought that was pretty funny."

"They're both dead, Bobby and Mikey."

"Your father's dead?"

"No, the monkey."

"Ah, okay." His face relaxed, his memory off the hook. "He took him on TV, didn't he?"

"Yes. That is why they took him away. He bit the soundman. He bit my brother, too. "

"Peter?"

"Yep."

"The funny thing is, I don't have any bad feelings about your father. Not me. *I* don't. People are just people, the way I see it."

There was no one behind Jamie in the lineup, and Jamie, who had been wounded by a shard of life, could not stop talking. He reminded me of the man I had seen at the Mountie's sentencing, the man who needed to tell someone.

"Do you see Barbara?" he asked, using Babs's given name.

"No," I said.

"You two were friends, right?"

"Yep."

"They lead separate lives, you know, her and her husband."

"Happens."

Jamie kept going, releasing what seemed like a lifetime of resentment.

"You know she went to Russia, don't you?" he said, "To stalk that juiced-up Russian paddler. Thirty years she's been stalking him. She found out that he worked in a gym in Moscow, and she went there. He had a hot twenty-five-year-old wife, turns out. He didn't know what was going on when Barbara found him; he thought she wanted to give him money."

"Awkward," I conceded.

"I would call it pathetic."

I shrugged.

"Barbara's husband has his own apartment," said Jamie. "Allan is gay. Did you know that? I don't care, I got plenty of gay friends. Real friends, not fake friends. They are my family, my chosen family, including the gay ones. But I didn't know if you knew that —"

"No."

"Well, like I said, I don't care."

"Okay." I had nothing to say.

"I was always surprised you guys were still nice to us." He paused. "After all the shit that went down, your father, the paddle, and everything."

*

When I was eight, Stan started collecting cats. He did not describe it that way, but that's what it was. He found a ratty old stray he named Napoleon, and he brought him home in a shopping bag. Napoleon had been through the wars: half of one ear was missing and one eye permanently wept. Within a week, Stan found another "lost" cat, a black one, and he brought her home too. He named her Smokey, and she had six kittens. And that would have been fine, except that Stan kept bringing home cats, more and more, and there was nothing, it seemed, that Mother could do about it, and soon it stopped being normal. Stan was *stealing* cats in the same way he stole Graham. Then he adopted Bobby the tame squirrel. And a monkey named Mikey. Stan picked Mikey up at the Mission to Seafarers on the Halifax waterfront—the monkey came off a Venezuelan oil tanker. Mikey was originally named Changuito, Spanish for "little monkey," but Stan renamed him Mikey because he looked, he claimed, like the actor Michael Douglas. Stan took Mikey into the station to show everyone how much he looked like Michael Douglas, but Mikey bit Gary the soundman. Mikey was a terrible monkey. He tried to bite me. After he bit Gary, Stan told viewers that Mikey would not be back—he was in a program that would send him into space. Mikey the Space Monkey became a thing, and then people forgot about it. Stan forgot about it for a while, although he did keep a photo of Mikey in a straw hat as well as his cremated remains.

When you grow up in chaos, all this makes me wonder, do you then seek chaos because that is what you know? Are you caught in a permanent trauma loop?

*

Mrs. Crowell, despite her diminished capacity, or maybe because of it, was a regular at the Lucky Lady, always dressed in leather or Ultrasuede. I managed to avoid her. The casino had no problem taking money from people like her. It was easy. Mrs. Crowell arrived at seven p.m. She could have come in at ten a.m. and left during daylight, but she preferred the heightened atmosphere at night.

At night you see the high rollers: the businessman who owns an office tower, the Hell's Angel pretending not to be a Hell's Angel, the oil patch worker visiting from out West. They are all the same. They are deluding themselves, suspending all doubt, blocking out the realities of life and *going there*—night after night—in a vintage red Spitfire of wishful thinking, with the top down and the sun in their eyes.

I looked at Mrs. Crowell's player card online. One week she lost $1,035. One night $750. There were a couple of wins, but she was deep in the red and getting deeper. I was good with that.

Mrs. Crowell travelled by bus both ways. I took the same bus once, and a passenger was shouting that the cops were looking for him, but he was armed with a piece. A woman was asleep in the back.

I cannot imagine taking the bus at one a.m., but Mrs. Crowell, old and under the care of no one, did. Mrs. Crowell, in fact, took two buses, transferring in a neighbourhood of drug deals. After she got off the second bus, she shuffled up a short hill to a McDonald's, where she bought herself a meal, surrounded by the type of people you might find in a McDonald's at 1:30 a.m. The whole exercise, from the casino to home, was like a video game and she was a character who had ducked elimination at five junctures. All this came out later.

19

I did not tell anyone about Mrs. Crowell. For weeks, I had wrestled with another dilemma. Did I mention Vincent's rumour about Maynard and the aliens to Stan or Peter? First off, it was preposterous. Secondly, how could I without admitting that I was going to Pollock Passage to see a mysterious man who told me stories I may not have believed? A man I, nonetheless, wanted to keep seeing.

I liked inhabiting two worlds, with one knowing nothing about the other. I liked being secretive, duplicitous even, after years of people keeping secrets from me. Stan. Jack. Managers at the *Standard*. In Pollock Passage, I could see the stars at night, and in the morning, saturated sunrises that make you believe the sky was on fire.

Vincent was fifty-four. There were no wives, no catamaran. He had gone to school on a military scholarship and become an academic. There were other details, but they did not matter. Some of his story may have been true.

I wasn't *there yet*, I told myself. I wasn't one of *them*. The amnesiacs who forgot there was any such thing as romance or adventure. They wore a habit of sensible shoes and MEC hats, preaching a puritanical sermon of yarn and homemade jam. They demonstrated their virtue with photos of pickled beets and wild honeysuckle. They took torturous hikes. I was not there yet.

Vincent and I were going to explore the back roads—the shadowy inland—where there were camps and stills and grow-ops. I was going to take notes. We were going to do all kinds of things.

When I was dating Dante, we drove to his parent's house, a blip on the map that compelled me to wonder, *Why does anyone live here? Were they all born here, or sent here as a form of religious exile?* There were bends in a road unchanged in forty years. A lone horse. An *actual* van down on the river. I saw, near a business that sold sod, the tiniest of convenience stores, and it had one illuminated sign that screamed:

SHOE POLISH
SOLD HERE

It seemed so out of place that I wondered if SHOE POLISH was code for something sinister. Heroin. Meth. Moonshine. I wondered, *Who, in a landscape of wood piles and wood ticks, was so enthused about shoe polish?*

"That's weird, isn't it?" I said to Dante because *it was*.

"You see things," said Dante the gaslighter, "that are not there."

Vincent could not have been more different than Dante. He knew how to eat in a restaurant. He did not steal from weddings. When I was in The City, we talked by phone. Vincent saw things and described them in detail, and I liked that.

Vincent had visited a new lobster export company in Shag Harbour run by investors from mainland China. It was, he said, creating a buzz. This intrigued Vincent because his field of study included the sociological theory of *Gemeinschaft* versus *Gesellschaft*, the shift from a community-based society to a more profit-driven, impersonal model. Was this evidence of the shift?

The premier was there for the opening, said Vincent. The premier had been on eight trade missions to China, sometimes accompanied by the fisheries minister. The public had been invited to the opening, along with the press.

A young executive from China had flown in for the event, Vincent said, and he could have stepped off a fashion runway. His hair was swept across his forehead early Justin Bieber. He wore pricey half-rim glasses and an elegant suit.

The business had a real name but it had quickly become known locally as Rainbow Lobsters because the manager, a shorter and less fashionable man, was fond of rainbow metaphors. "If we work with honour," he told the press, "we will find our rainbow." Vincent's story included a Chinese woman, who was an efficiency expert and dressed as well as the executive.

I told Vincent that it all sounded intriguing. And then he said, "Maybe we will have Rainbow lobsters when you come down." And that, I said, would be nice.

Vincent bought Rainbow lobsters for my next visit, and we ate them in his kitchen with the view. After dinner, Vincent gave me a gift: a gold charm bracelet. How did Vincent know that I—a person who did not seem the least bit sentimental, a person who understood nothing about clothes—liked charm bracelets? I liked the fact that they were no more in fashion than I was, that stylish people found them kitschy. I liked being able to say, with the certainty of a gold charm, *I like this, I like that, and all of these very things make me happy.*

*

Instead of telling Stan and Peter about the Pelly/Maynard rumour, I went online to a Facebook page for Barrington. I went looking for any mention of Maynard or alien abduction and, of course, there was none. Maynard was ancient history, and Vincent's story sounded flimsy to me. Instead, I saw posts about current events, some ribald, most trivial.

An innocuous post about Tim Hortons: Can't they get an order right?

The comeback: Quit bitching and being a skid.

An insulting post: Men from Woods Harbour has small pens.

The comeback: Small pens write big cheques.

There was a discussion about a fisherman in West Pubnico and how his community had rallied behind him after his boat sank at the start of the season. The community found him another boat, rope, and gear. Most people sounded impressed.

One man was bitter: Why the fuck did he need rope?

And someone snapped: That is why people in Pubnico has nice things. They help each other out. And they don't complain about someone getting rope.

In another thread, a man alleged that Rainbow Lobsters was up to something shady: That place ain't right. You mark my words.

There was a back and forth with another man, who said he worked there.

Man 2: Well, you'd know about anything shady, buddy.

Man 1: Are youse in on it too? Enjoy your time in prison. Maybe Jackie Chan can break you out.

Man 2: You'll delete this shit when you sobers up. You always do.

The only thing stranger than reading about your family in a newspaper is seeing it discussed online by people who assume you are a non-person who cannot read or might not be offended by what they write. Tracking back months, I found a thread about Graham.

Man 1: I would see him walking Chief and he would give you a wave.

Man 2: You mean Damien the devil child?

Followed by a copied quote about heterochromia:

Heterochromia is a sign of Witchery. It occurs at birth or through an injury. In Eastern European pagan cultures, heterochromia is a sign that a newborn's eye has been swapped out with a Witch's.

Man 1: Is there a difference between a witch and a devil?

The posters seemed to know Graham. Another man, whose profile photo showed him with a snake coiled around his neck, went off on a tangent about cheating spouses, but then admitted that none of that had anything to do with Graham.

Someone wrote: I hear he got his self into trouble in the city, which is too bad if you heard him play the harmonica. Thats why he has them devil eyes because he made a deal with the devil. I seen him play Blue Bijou after hearing it once and he done the whole thing right through. Never missed a note.

Someone else: Graham should never have given Jesse Fancy the time of day. That Fancy Pants, his fucken head better be on a swivel. I hope he is reading this. If you is, Fancy Pants your fucken head better be on a swivel.

Someone else: When you lives that handy to Satan's Kingdom.

I left this page and found a Facebook page for *Fancy Pants*, legally known as Jesse Fancy. Like Graham, he looked minor enough to be blown away by the wind. Jesse Fancy wore an oversized custom ball cap with *Fancy Pants* in gigantic cursive font. His face was covered with wispy red hair that he tried to make look like a moustache and/ or a beard. He seemed to be half Graham's age. Jesse Fancy did not look capable of causing the trouble people said he was causing, but what did I know?

Fancy Pants had one older brother, according to his page. Known by the nickname Fresh, he was killed when his Harley hit a deer. "Some walk through the Pearly Gates, some ride."

Since I was already on Facebook, I clicked on the page for Korey St. Clair Scudder who now self-identified as "Scotia soldja."

I would have clicked on Vincent's page to see who he really was, but he did not have one.

*

One week later, Vincent and I decided to go visit *Fancy Pants*, who lived with his mother, not in Satan's Kingdom but in a mobile home park. Vincent, like people from the newspaper business, had no problem showing up, uninvited, on the doorsteps of strangers, and that worked for me. The park was off the main road, tucked away so that you would not see it if you were a tourist. It would not spoil the coastal view.

"People don't like *Fancy Pants*," I told Vincent. "The Mounties don't like him either."

"Understandable." Vincent shrugged. "He is an arsonist, the most pointless of criminals."

"He's in court next month. He set himself on fire the last time he torched something. That's how they caught him — he was on fire."

The trailer park was well kept. It looked like a community where residents owned rather than rented their property. The Fancy home was easy to spot. Light green, it had a sign outside: *Fancy* in colourful font. In the front yard were five ceramic creatures of varying sizes: a husky, a cherub, a frog, a jockey, and an eagle that was four times as big as the husky.

Jesse's mother did not seem seemed surprised to see us. "I always had time for Graham. Some people didn't. I did. We took him in now and then."

She led us into the tight living room, where Jesse was sitting on a plaid couch with a black cat on his lap. To one side was an old Silvertone guitar that he had decorated with stick-on metallic letters: **Fancy**. The strap had *Fender* written on it in gold cursive lettering, fooling no one. His guitar was a cheap Sears knock-off.

Jesse was playing a video game, and he was sporting his custom *Fancy Pants* ball cap. He was also wearing a spectacular blinding hoodie with duelling wolves on the front. One a fluorescent green and the other a fluorescent pink. The wolves were eye to eye, and underneath them, dwarfed by their ferocity, was a white Planet Earth.

The vibe in the room was overwhelmingly DIY. The main wall art was a jigsaw puzzle of Niagara Falls glued to a board and coated with wax. On a card table was another puzzle in progress—it looked like outer space. One chair was a nylon lawn chair.

As Vincent and I were taking a seat, Jesse's phone went off and the ringtone was the hillbilly anthem "Cotton Eye Joe." After the call, he patted the black cat.

"I see you like cats." I was used to warming people up for photos.

"This here guy is the one with the brains," *Fancy Pants* informed me. "That other guy over there"—he gestured at a fluffy grey-and-white cat that was carrying a few extra pounds—"he's just for show." He tapped the side of his head so hard that I could hear it. "No brains."

"How much brains does a cat need?" I joked, hoping to lighten the mood.

"How much brains does it take to ruin a person's life? To accuse him of setting a hunting camp on fire? When he never done it."

I nodded to show that I was listening. "Good question."

"Jesse." His mother came back in the room. "The lawyer told you not to talk about that. The fires."

"Just online," he replied.

"Okay." She seemed used to deferring to her son, which may have been the problem. "I can't keep up with that stuff."

"I can," he said, and she seemed to believe him.

Up to this point, Vincent had been quiet. But then, not caring that Jesse would not look at him, and did not seem to like him, he went straight to the point. "Were you and Graham involved in something that may have endangered him?"

"Me? You are looking in the wrong direction, Amigo."

"Okay. What is the right direction?"

"Look, Amigo—I don't remember what your name is—I don't know where Graham is or what he done. For all I know he could be working for Donald F. Trump."

Another phone call, another rendition of "Cotton Eye Joe."

The call ended. ("Later. I got pedestrians here.")

"Do you remember anything Graham said?" asked Vincent.

"No, I don't. Doctors say that people with the fast brains has to get rid of unimportant stuff to make more room. That's me. If I had one of them slow brains, I could remember more."

"Ahhh," said Vincent.

"But I got the fast brain so" — he waved a hand in the air — "gone."

"Jesse." His mother was back in the room. "Didn't the lawyer tell you not to talk about that? Your brain."

"Only online."

"Okay."

Jesse stopped, rubbed the cat's back. He looked at me, not Vincent. *Fancy Pants* was wearing a hospital bracelet.

"Graham had a lot of big ideas. He said he was going to go to Boston and meet Chára like I would care. That Balkan freak. I told him I got a career to run."

"In music?" I asked to encourage him.

"That's right."

"Ahh."

"Graham said he seen where Marchand played in Dartmouth, and I said, 'Big fucken deal.' I am a Leafs fan one hundred per cent. If I seen that rat-faced King Rat up around these parts, I would run him over. I'd pave him."

"Jesse," his mother shouted, "don't go saying that!!"

After we left the Fancy trailer, Vincent and I sorted out our thoughts about *Fancy Pants*. Under one leg of his sweatpants, I had seen a bandage. The burn, maybe? Vincent suggested that the mother was part of the problem. When we were leaving, she had followed us outside. "He's very talented, you know." And then lowering the limbo bar of self-delusion as low as it could go. "If the music don't work out, he will probably become an astronaut. That is his other interest, astronaut."

"I see," replied Vincent.

"I don't like to speak ill of people — I am not one of them — but I think Graham was a bad influence. I'm almost sorry I let him stay here."

Vincent and I elected not to talk about the Fancys anymore. They were a depressing whorl of dysfunction. We decided instead to finally explore the back roads: those inland tracks with stills and hunting camps. Nova Scotia is primarily coastline, 7,500 kilometres of rock and sand, and then there is the inland, which is hard to understand, its energy or place.

*
*

Twenty minutes from the trailer park, we turned off the main road. There were no signs. We kept driving, and the air changed the further inland we went — it smelled like mosquitoes, muggy and dense. Thick enough to stifle conversation.

We reached the end of a dirt road with a bad work ethic and one decrepit house. The windows were covered with condensation. You could have drawn a peace sign or a swastika on them, depending on your inclination. The smell changed to a toxic mix of rotting cabbage and fabric softener. I saw the *Beware of Dog* sign; I heard humming fans.

"What do you think?" I asked Vincent.

If something bad happens in a place like this, it is all over by the time the Mounties arrive — all they will find are the smouldering building and the bodies.

As Vincent and I were considering leaving this *nothing good ever happens here* place, two motorcycles roared up the road, spitting dirt. All-black Harleys with high handlebars. Instead of speeding to the highway as I would have, Vincent casually pulled away. He pulled away so casually that I had time to see the gang colours. Time to see the words *COPS LIE* painted on one half helmet. Time to read the writing on a huge denim vest:

I COME
I fuck shit up
I LEAVE

While I was wondering how this was going to work out, and if I was going to end up in a crime story in the *Standard*, Vincent reached under the steering wheel and pulled out a black handgun, which he kept on his lap until we reached the highway.

20

The interior of the house on stilts was as you would imagine. One week after Vincent produced the gun from under his steering wheel, he took me there. It was like stepping into a glossy magazine. The house was surrounded by surf and slippery grey rocks. There was the sense that you could, at any moment, be swept away. Or you could be lifted into the sky, where you could observe the kingdom beneath — the boats, the people, the blue-grey water — and you could hover like an entitled angel.

Vincent introduced the owners, whom he had known since he moved here. They were dressed simply in jeans and plain T-shirts, his short-sleeved, hers long. This, I assumed, was to minimize their role in all this. To keep the opulence down to a dull acceptable roar.

"Vincent says you are a photographer," said the man, who moved like a rich person might, a human Roomba. "I have a Hasselblad. Those Zeiss lenses are amazing. The way they handle contrast."

"For sure," I replied.

The man's name was Klaus. He was wearing flip-flops, and he looked as though he was channelling a yoga guru with narrowed, all-seeing eyes.

Klaus poured Vincent a Scotch and me an Evian, while the woman had white wine. Her name was Margaret. They were

Americans. Their last name was Bittenbender. She had sleek grey hair pulled back from her face, and blue eyes you would pay good money for. She did not need makeup, not with those eyes, that hair, and a straight proper nose that had the confidence of privilege.

"Did Margaret tell you about Urban Newell's decoy?" Klaus's question was for Vincent. They all seemed to know Urban Newell, a local fisherman.

"Yes, it was from an island, wasn't it? Made by a lighthouse keeper."

"Yes, an extremely rare—I would say one-of-a-kind—hooded merganser drake. It has the most detailed feather paint and a lovely patina. Been in Urban's family for years. A huckster from Toronto offered him a hundred bucks. Margaret told Urban no. It is worth far more."

They talked, the both of them, the way rich Americans talk, although Vincent had, he had told me, grown up fatherless, as poor as Stan and Maynard in the little white house I could see from a window. Maybe that was true.

"Urban is a lovely man," Margaret added. "He pulled me out of a snowbank when my car was stuck."

"Does Urban's son drive for Rainbow Lobsters?" asked Klaus. "A reefer truck?"

Klaus had an eerie rich-person massage-parlour glow. Margaret was less obvious—she had that *cedar-shingled cottage on a windswept beach in Maine* look. Margaret could afford to be austere; she could pretend that she was not trying. After decades of enjoying exceptional beauty, she could pretend to renounce her beauty with plain T-shirts and loose jeans while still enjoying it.

"Yes," replied Margaret. "It is steady work. Urban was afraid the son would have to move out West. He won't fish anymore. Not since he almost died. He was rescued by another crew after his boat caught fire offshore. Urban told me that when his son came in, he was ashen and he said, 'I seen angels, Dad, and they was aboard the *Jenny Marie.*'"

"Well, ahem," said Klaus, "glad to hear, glad to hear."

There is an adage: everyone you meet, you meet for a reason. They are part of your destiny. Or sent to teach you a lesson about tolerance or how not to live. First, I had met Vincent and now the Bittenbenders. Margaret, I think, was there to open my eyes to truths, but they were truths I did not want to see, and by the time I did want to see them, it was too late for me to change direction. I was not sure why I met Vincent, who carried a handgun.

The Bittenbenders were from Williamsburg in New York, I learned that first day. They had built the stilt house three years ago. I would know the architect's name if I heard it, they said. The room we were seated in had soaring ceilings and wood the intense orange of marbles. The white walls were alive with art. I soaked up the paintings — two metres square — abstract and chaotic with colour.

We were having a pleasant enough time. Klaus produced a charcuterie board, smoked duck and spicy venison sausage. I cannot imagine where he got it. The men talked about a sailing trip Klaus had taken. They talked about two islands purchased by an unknown buyer. I was wearing my bracelet, which had its first charm — a Leica camera Vincent had ordered from Germany — and I instinctively touched it.

When you are with people who do not have the worry of money, the air is lighter. The house cleans itself. The bills pay themselves. If there are rain boots in the hallway, they are for fun. Words are entitled to do what they please.

Klaus was a semi-retired plastic surgeon. Margaret an artist. They had one daughter, Inge, a choreographer who lived with her wife in Copenhagen. Margaret missed Inge — I could tell by the way she kept bringing up her name — but she also knew that her daughter adored her. She had that and countless tomorrows in her back pocket.

After two glasses of wine, Margaret's demeanour changed as suddenly as a cloud blocks out the sun.

"Have you noticed that when people reveal something negative, something dark, about themselves, others are delighted?" Margaret paused for an awkward smile that she directed at me. She was the type of woman who had never had to smile to please people, so it was awkward. "They say, 'Good for you, good for you,' if it's 'I had an eating disorder,' or 'I grew up in foster homes.' No one says, 'Good for you,' when it is, 'I was a piano prodigy.'"

"Ahh, yes," I said.

Klaus, in an obvious attempt to leaven the mood, turned to me and asked, "Do you play?" It was clear what he was doing, and he would do it again.

"I'm afraid not," I replied.

"You are too pretty to have spent your youth hunched over a piano," Margaret declared. "Leave that to the hunchbacks."

We both smiled past the word "hunchback," and she picked up her thoughts.

"It's the same as when people reveal that they had a major medical procedure and managed to survive. Everyone goes, 'Good for you. You are so brave.' And the people who are the most enthusiastic are the people who are most happy it was *not* them. And when they say, 'Good *for* you,' they really mean, 'Good *it is* you.'"

"That's harsh," scolded her husband.

"Life is harsh, or we would all own angora rabbits."

"It's not too late," Vincent joked. Shrug. "Is it? For the rabbits?"

I offered a vague smile of support.

"Have you ever had a major medical procedure," Margaret asked me, "that changes who you are?" When Margaret began a story, her blue eyes would be elsewhere, and then, just as she reached the good part, they would land.

"No," I said truthfully, "I've been lucky." *Not a medical procedure. Other trauma.*

"Margaret," Klaus, who was more accustomed to smiling, flashed a *let's all be pleasant* smile, "had a heart transplant two years ago. It is a major procedure, but it went very well."

"Did it?" she demanded.

"I would say so, yes."

"You would say that the Civil War went well."

I was starting to suspect that something was amiss, so I glanced at Vincent, who acted as though this was normal.

"There are *always* issues with major procedures," explained Klaus. "Psychological adaptation —"

"If by *issues*, you mean that you are no longer yourself, that you suddenly like things you never liked before, such as Ram trucks. You want to go hunting — *hunting!* — and think you must have a hunting dog."

"We *do* have a dog," Klaus pointed out.

"Yes! *We*" —she emphasized the word "we"— "have a hunting dog. His name is Tracker. I want you to think about that, Klaus. Think about that: *you and I* have a dog bred to hunt wild boar."

"It wasn't me." Barely audible.

"Of course, it wasn't *you*. You still have your own heart, the one you were born with. It wasn't replaced with one that belonged to a hunter who lived his entire life in Lewiston, Maine."

The conversation had become complicated — a hunter, a foreign heart — but I was used to being in complicated places, and so I volunteered, "These paintings," to change the subject, "are any of them yours?"

"Yes." Margaret softened. "All of them."

And at that moment, a bloodhound came into the room, a white pashmina shawl in his mouth, and the attention shifted. Tracker — that was the bloodhound's name — did not match the art or the minimalist Scandinavian décor. He was not the least bit photogenic. He was the epitome of obvious. The dog easily weighed 150 pounds. He had a stiff red coat. Tracker had jowls and wrinkled skin that gave him a sad yet comical look. Droopy ears. Tracker settled onto a spot on the wooden floor and created a puddle of drool.

"The poor thing is prone to gastrointestinal ailments," said Margaret. "They all are."

The big dog started to whine and then bay. If his eyes had not been open, I would have thought that he was having a bad dream in which he was chasing a wild boar or a missing person he would never find.

"So, what kind of photography did you do?" Klaus asked me, keen to change direction.

"*News* photography." I wanted to make that distinction: *news*, not art. "I covered courts. Chased some ambulances but mainly courts."

"Murders?"

"Yes."

"My brother is a defence lawyer in New York."

"Ahhh. Busy, I am sure."

"Oh yes. What kind of camera did you use?"

"I used a Canon on the job. It's sturdy."

I was not an artist like Margaret or Jack, I wanted to establish. Jack, who has up to now been little more than an overwrought diary entry. I was not one of them: a photographer who dealt in the aesthetic, who used arcane techniques like the collodion process and employed large format cameras. That was not what I did.

Vincent thought I was selling myself short.

"Harriett has an excellent eye," he said, and the Bittenbenders seemed to like that. "She has shot some striking photos down here with her Leica — spontaneous with nuances I never would see."

When we left the stilt house, Tracker was on his feet, sniffing.

What Could Have Happened

Margaret showed me her scar, which ran from her collarbone to just above her navel. It was raised and red, and she seemed to like it. A woman like her could afford to have an exotic scar. The surgery *had* "gone well," she told me. She was able to paint with a degree of sincerity after three months. It was another three before she was fully recovered. And, of course, she was grateful to the donor, a truck driver from Lewiston.

"He hit a moose, you know, on the highway." But now there was this hunting business and some days.... "It is possible," she explained, to inherit the donor's traits—and of course, she was grateful...*She kept saying that.* "But...Me?" she said, aghast. "This is ME!"

When rich people talk about problems, it is as though they are talking about someone else. Their stories are never weighted down by the helplessness of the poor, the likelihood that there will *not* be a solution. They can be both alarming and entertaining.

"The donor was a member of the NRA," she said.

"I see," I replied.

"And Lewiston," Margaret stated, "Lewiston was fine until they closed the mill—now all they have is that dreadful balloon festival where poor people squander a week's pay on the carny games."

I told Margaret that Vincent had a gun in his car, held in place by a powerful magnet, and she said, "Well, of course, he does. It is a SIG P226. But it is not for hunting." And we left it at that. Sometimes in life you know what is going on, but you pretend you do not because it is easier that way, easier on everyone. Have I said that before?

I told her that my husband was a painter. He was beautiful and his art was beautiful, and one bounced off the other: an echo chamber of beauty.

"He's not with me anymore," I explained.

"Okay," she said, "I assumed that. *En plein air?*"

"No. His studio was in our home."

"Was he okay there?" she asked.

"At the start, but no, not later. But what do you know," I asked, "about a person who has no time clock, no office, no boss, a person who never sleeps when normal people sleep and sees things that aren't there but could be?"

"Nothing," said Margaret. "You know nothing, and they *want* it that way."

"At one point," I explained, "Jack could not paint with Quinacridone Rose because the colour was too vulnerable."

Margaret had understood all of that—she had understood it perfectly, she said, until they cut out her heart.

"Was it trustworthy?" she asked. "His art?"

What an odd question.

"Was *he* trustworthy?"

Why would you ask?

21

I went back to visit Margaret the next time I was in Pollock Passage. We got along well, it turned out. Margaret liked the fact I had once been as pretty as she had. She liked the fact that we could talk about difficult things. Klaus, she informed me, wanted to brush off her transplant, to maintain the patina of perfection because that was his profession: perfection.

Margaret and I were alone at first. Klaus, the plastic surgeon, was off buying groceries. Vincent had gone to interview a woman about the Shag Harbour UFO. Both men would be back soon. "It is good that you and Vincent are doing things down here," she said. "You work well together."

"Thank you."

Would Margaret have liked me before she received her proletarian heart, the Lewiston, Maine, heart with an affinity for hunting dogs and rifles? Or would I have been too common? As common as Graham or the Dandos.

"Vincent can be good company," Margaret said. "He is dry and occasionally pedantic. Imagine a dissertation on rumours. Why not a dissertation on vowels? It seems a waste for a man of his intellect. Klaus says Vincent speaks perfect Mandarin and German. Of course, Klaus speaks German himself, as you might imagine..."

I had imagined no such thing, but Margaret was still talking.

"Klaus says Vincent had his nose done, but Klaus looks at everyone as though they are in a consultation. I told him, 'You are becoming tiresome, dear. If you deal in illusions, and they keep you comfortable, you must let people enjoy theirs.' You cannot be a rat *and* live in the Land of Illusions."

"I never thought about his nose," I muttered.

Margaret left to make us tea. While she was in the kitchen, I wondered if she was feeling me out. Seeing if I cared for Vincent. Or not. Deciding if she should tell me things. And then, after an absence longer than it should have taken to make tea, she was back.

"Well, I shouldn't have brought up Vincent's nose." Regretful. "I am now as bad as Klaus." Rushing forward. "Did you show Vincent around when he was in Halifax?"

Vincent was in Halifax?

"Ah no," I lied. "I was working."

I like to think that I am good at vague smiles that commit to nothing, so I flashed one.

And then Margaret, sensing that she had made a miscalculation *and* that I was lying, changed direction abruptly. "I think what we *should* do is figure out what happened to your cousin — Graham is his name, isn't it? I think we should do that. You know that the Mounties don't give a flying fuck."

Since her transplant, Margaret swore too often for Klaus. He winced when she swore.

"Well, one of them was nice," I said, "the one who called my father."

"The fellow from Saskatchewan? Have you ever met a normal person from Saskatchewan?"

"No."

"It is like meeting a normal person from Oklahoma or a normal person named Adolph or Lucifer or Lolita. There are names you should talk to your parents about. Isn't your Mountie's name Officer Numchuck?"

"No," I corrected her, "it's Constable Ostapchuk, but people here call him Officer Numchuck after the fighting sticks."

"Ahhh, well. What do you know?"

"His first name is Maverick, though."

"*That* was a choice."

"People down here call Graham 'Damien the Devil Child.'"

"As in the Antichrist, who discovers the number of the Beast birthmark on his scalp?"

"Yes."

"Well, let's ignore that."

"Okay."

Margaret asked me if Graham had a companion. The question caught me off guard. No one in my family had ever considered the idea of Graham and a companion, his *Fast Cars Hot Women* T-shirt an empty boast. I did not think I could explain that to Margaret, who Graham was and how he lived—their realities too far apart—so I answered, "No, but he had friends."

On the drive down, I had seen a man walking along the highway with a bag of takeout food, kilometres from any restaurant. An air of aloneness around him. He looked like that person who donates a kidney to his sister. He gets an infection, the donated kidney fails, and his sister takes him to Small Claims Court over a beagle named Buddy that she gave him. He is a seasonal worker. A person who never, in his life, had anything go right for him, a person whose existence was so doomed that you could barely look at him.

Margaret, who had never known anyone like the man on the highway, decided I should bring her "an article of Graham's clothing." She would give it to Tracker. It sounded like a line from an old movie, "an article of Graham's clothing," and a dog that tracked deer and wild boar. A sleuthhound. It sounded as improbable as me sitting there in the first place, suspended over the ocean, suspended between my fourteen-dollar hourly wage at the Lucky Lady and the real space that real money buys.

"Bloodhounds have been doing this forever," Margaret noted. "Imagine every day waking up and feeling like you have to find something. No wonder they look sad. If I lose something, I am out of sorts all day. But they do *do* it. They do it for the police and for people who have misplaced their grandmother or their angora goat."

"That's good, I guess," I offered.

"And they *like* it. They have been bred to like it in the same way that I was bred to like white gold and the irony of gingham."

I heard myself saying, "Good to know."

*
*

Klaus returned from the grocery store. He strolled into the room with a question he should not have asked. "What do you think of the Wildes coming for a visit?" I had never heard of the Wildes before, but I would hear of them again. They were, it seemed, a metaphor for the Bittenbenders' prior existence, all that was bad about it.

"The Wildes?" Margaret asked pointedly. "You know how tiresome they are."

"Who isn't tiresome *these* days, Margaret?" He added a smile to make the question less sarcastic.

Margaret turned her expensive blue eyes on me, not Klaus, making it clear that I was involved in adjudicating. And then she said, "People who do not play music from the twenties incessantly because they think it makes them 'special'—that is who. Do you know how many times I have heard 'Lena from Palesteena'?"

"Maybe they like music from the twenties," Klaus said.

"Maybe I like firing a gun in a crowded mall."

"Not the best comparison." Klaus exaggerated a frown for the benefit of me and Vincent, who had arrived and pretended he had not heard mention of the gun.

Klaus had a signal he gave to company when Margaret was not sounding herself. He tapped his heart, making sure she could not see him. Margaret got up, went into the kitchen, and returned with a bowl of grapes, which she placed on a table without the slightest interest. The Wildes had taken away her appetite.

"The Wildes had a tragedy, and after that, you could not talk to them," she explained to me. "They couldn't see anyone else's problems because theirs was so huge, and it *was*. Everyone else's seemed trite. You did not have a problem unless someone was dead, unless you had a cold stiff body. Well, my heart *was gone!*"

"You got a new one, dear," Klaus noted from across the room.

"That," Margaret enunciated clearly, "is not the point."

Vincent settled into a chair.

"How was your interview?" I asked as the Bittenbenders conversed.

"Very good," he replied. "Another sea monster, this one with the face of the devil and a vertical tail. I will tell you about it later."

Vincent and I got up to leave. Klaus and Margaret continued to debate a visit from the Wildes.

"Nobody just *happens* to be passing through Pollock Passage," Margaret declared.

"You used to like the Wildes," said Klaus.

"I used to like a lot of things," said Margaret. "They talk down to people," she added, "and they are cheap with wait staff and tradespeople. I don't know why they are so cheap when he works on Wall Street."

No one in Pollock Passage seemed to have a problem with the Bittenbenders or Vincent, who were all technically come from aways, because they were *not* cheap. A CFA, when used in the *pejorative* sense, the *judgmental* sense, the *resentful* sense, is defined by attitude, not birthplace. That CFA Knows Better Than You. He knows better because he went to a better school—Upper Canada College or Cushing—and he was raised by people who wore red pants and claimed an association with the Kennedys, people with three generations of privilege. And he was always looking for a deal. That was the rub. That rare decoy, the farm a family lost in a tax sale. The Bittenbenders and Vincent paid a fair price for everything, while the Wildes sounded problematic.

When we left the stilt house, I felt overwhelmed. I liked the fact that so much was happening that I could forget what I was looking for. Or escaping from. The Wildes. Tracker. A foreign heart. So much to process. I liked the fact that Margaret, like me, did not know who she was anymore.

I am not that person who is good at everything: the gourmand who makes cilantro ice cream and speaks three languages, the intellectual who studied behavioural finance. I am not the fashionista who glides through life in stunning clothes at a stunning weight and is still not a bitch. I am far more specific. I am good with people and street photography. That might be it.

Vincent and I walked down the driveway past a Mercedes-Benz wagon. In its elegant shadow was a Jeep Rubicon customized in a brown/green hunter's camo. I looked at Vincent's nose and decided that I did not care if it had been fixed. Why would I? Who was exactly who they said they were, and what was a new nose compared to some of the lies I had heard?

I decided, as we walked down the path, that I was starting to like many things about Vincent. I liked his predictable shrug. I liked the fact that he knew things. When I dated Dante, his parents did not know that anyone had died in the 1917 Halifax Explosion, which had a death toll of almost 2,000 with 9,000 maimed and injured.

"Was Margaret off on one of her tangents before I arrived?" Vincent asked, a joke in his voice.

"No," I lied, "she was lovely."

Klaus and Margaret were the first people we knew together and that was something, wasn't it, shared friends? Maybe we would have them to dinner. Margaret clearly liked us better than the Wildes. Vincent did not seem like a man at the mercy his emotions. He did not seem prone to sadness, and I liked that too.

"Do you think this thing with Tracker can work?" I asked. "I told Margaret that I would bring a sock of Graham's. There is one in Peter's room."

"There is a chance." Vincent shrugged.

*
*

Jack and Dicky could talk baseball for hours. One day, after they had exhausted the topic of baseball, Dicky told Jack a story about his parents. His mother died in her sixties, his father twenty years later. I do not know why Dicky told this story at this particular time; you would have to ask him that. Dicky's father, he told Jack, was a bombastic little man who had risen through the ranks of government until he retired with a better-than-he-deserved pension. He somehow "missed" Dicky's wedding to Pierre. He never watched Dicky play a single game of baseball. After Dicky's mother died, his father spent his money as though it had been accidentally deposited in his bank account and he needed to get rid of it before someone discovered the mistake. He took junkets to Vegas. He got a girlfriend named Sandra. He sold the family home, all the while assuring Dicky, whom he relied on for favours, that his inheritance was secure in a priceless violin collection that Dicky's grandfather, a concert violinist, had passed down.

Dicky would have driven him to doctor's appointments anyway, he told Jack. But he often thought about the violins. He researched similar instruments online. He scanned auctions. He imagined that one day he might be comfortable enough to grandly donate the violins to a prestigious music school. He thought about how Pierre would admire him for being so cultured and so benevolent.

And when his father *did* die—flat broke by then—Dicky took the fabled violins to an expert, who told him they were worthless. And that, Dicky told Jack, was pretty fucken funny, wasn't it? A lame-assed deception that lasted *that* many years.

Instead of laughing, Jack looked disturbed—the story lying in front of him like a body on the street—and as soon as Dicky left, he went for a run.

*
*

Vincent phoned to tell me that he had to go away for a while. A colleague had died while doing research in South America, the details imprecise. This is terrible, Vincent muttered, terrible. He left Pollock Passage and was gone for two weeks, during which time I occupied myself in the city and wondered, *Who are you really, Vincent? Should I trust you?*

In Vincent's absence, I visited Stan, who was bored without Graham to boss around. That day, to stave off the boredom and remind himself of the good old days, he visited his old cameraman Skippy, who lived in a facility optimistically named Sunrise Manor. Back in the day, Skippy had worked in international hot spots where he picked up malaria and some in-the-field habits. Skippy was in the habit, for example, of putting out smokes with the heel of his boot. It was fine when he was in a tent on a war-ravaged desert with bombs exploding; it was an issue when he was at the station.

Stan's visit coincided with the Sunrise Manor Summer Jubilee, a three-hour talent show/extravaganza put on by community volunteers, who recited poetry, performed Irish dances, and sang "The Whiffenpoof Song" in the Social Room.

"Do you know the best thing about seniors' homes?" Stan asked after he had returned from the spectacle. I sensed that it was not a sincere question. I sensed that by the way he widened his eyes.

"No," I said anyway.

"Seniors' homes give the most hopelessly untalented people in society a free place to perform. The people you used to see in church variety shows dressed up as leprechauns. And no matter how bad they might be—how corny, off-key, or out of tune—the chairs will be filled, and those unable to sit in chairs will be wheeled in against their will."

"So, it's a good thing then?"

"Of course, in the same way that losing your hearing and sense of smell is a good thing. Or being incontinent."

Sigh.

"How was Skippy anyway?"

"He was great."

"Was he?"

"Yes! He said he liked to remember the old days, like the time we did a remote at the mine cave-in. Before he found himself surrounded by lunatics wearing homemade cowgirl costumes and banging on guitars. Before Gary got railroaded for that cocaine business."

"Gary did have a lot of cocaine," I noted, but Stan was not listening.

"So, I told him we were having a station reunion, and that Gary would be there. He was all gung-ho."

"Are you?

"Of course not."

Stan did not mention Graham that day. In fact, if anyone brought up Graham, he acted bothered. One day Peter asked if there was any news about Graham. Stan responded with a *let me tell you something about life* speech.

"I saw a *National Geographic* piece from China about a family that adopted a dog," Stan told Peter. "The seller said the pup was a Tibetan mastiff. The new family named him Little Black. The dog was always hungry. He grew too fast. And the owners became alarmed by the size of his teeth. The dog's face changed, he roared, and he was, a veterinarian told them two years after the fact, an Asiatic black bear. My point is, you don't know who anyone is these days."

"I think I would know the difference between a dog and a bear," replied Peter.

"Would you? I guess you are just smarter than all the people in China."

22

Two weeks passed. Vincent returned from his colleague's funeral, and I went back down the shore.

"We don't need to go," I told Vincent.

"No, I want to," he insisted. "We can't ignore *this*." When, of course, we could.

We were going to drive to Cape Sable Island, that low untamed place with a past because of Tracker. Margaret had taken the hunting dog for a walk on a CSI beach. When they were there, he had, she swore, become so excited that she knew, she *just knew*, that he had picked up the scent of Graham, presumed by most sensible people to be dead. The same scent that had been on a sock.

Who were we kidding? And did we want to find a body?

"Where?" I had asked Vincent.

"The south side of the island, but it was foggy so —"

As we crossed the causeway to CSI, I wound down my window. The ocean was naked that day; it was naked and throwing itself against the shoreline like it was smashed on moonshine. I saw a gull run for cover amid the whitecaps, I saw waves of confusion. There were capricious forces at play, trying to tell me something; I just didn't know what that was.

Vincent's Range Rover displayed the outside temperature on its dash. The same dash that harboured the concealed weapon we did not talk about. The further we drove onto CSI, the lower the number — down one degree, and then another, the ocean air enveloping us, chilling us, until it was six degrees cooler than the mainland.

Vincent had bought me an osprey charm for my bracelet, Vincent who was turning out to be deft with small thoughtful gifts. He had suggested that I set up a darkroom in his rented house — there was no space in my austere condo. Vincent's house had a second bathroom. It had room for an enlarger, chemicals, and a line to hang prints to dry. I would not have to go to the artists' co-op in the city. That would work, I said.

The houses, the fish plants, the bait shops — they all blend together in my memory. There is nothing easy about Cape Sable Island; you can taste the grit in the air; you can feel people digging down deep. I saw a graveyard of weather-beaten headstones. In one section, the headstones were white and adorned with ornamental lambs: lambs, which signify purity and innocence.

"This is not going to work, is it?" I said after thirty minutes.

"The island's bigger than I thought," Vincent conceded. "More roads."

"I don't trust Margaret on some of these things. She is not that experienced with hunting dogs."

The island was about four kilometres long, but there were side roads everywhere — Stoney Island Road, Centreville South Side Road — spokes we would never have the time to cover, spokes with dead ends or potential mysteries.

The north side of CSI is the working side, the south side is the enigmatic one with beaches and bird people. We drove to a glorious beach named The Hawk, where Margaret had taken Tracker. Named after a shipwreck, it is home to a dreamlike sight, a fifteen-hundred-year-old drowned forest: petrified stumps exposed at low tide. The wind was blowing hard enough to wake the stumps. Overlooking the beach, all by itself, was a show house built with grey cedar shingles and windows that afforded a view you could not put a price on.

Vincent and I made our way back to the main road. Suddenly in front of us was a white goat. And it was running stupidly because it had no plan. Behind the goat was a teenager trying to catch it, panting, and wondering what he had done to deserve this. He was wearing Helly Hansen fleece long johns that had stared to pile. They were tucked into rubber boots. The goat was beating him.

Without a word, Vincent stopped his Range Rover and, with an agility I had not anticipated, leapt out, and corralled the goat. I was impressed. The teen caught his breath. Vincent handed off the goat, and when he got back behind the wheel, we laughed.

Have you been in a place and felt as though you had experienced it before? I felt as though I had been on that road before, and I could anticipate everything that was about to happen. The air smelled the same; the boy looked the same; the goat moved in the same stupid way. I felt that a person was with me, standing at a distance, but when I looked around, there was no one.

We drove away. It was one of those days when we were both saying things we did not mean. Me and Vincent. Maybe it was the drunken ocean or the wind pushing against us so hard that we felt off balance. Maybe we were ignoring something we should not have been ignoring because that is what people do.

"What do you think," I asked after the buzz of the goat abated, "about collecting sea glass? A woman on PEI found a red piece worth five hundred dollars—it was from the brake light of an old car."

"Ahh, I see."

"The reds are very rare."

We drove by an empty ball field. And we knew, as surely as I knew that I would never collect sea glass, that we were not going to find Graham. Maybe Tracker had become excited by a coyote or the wind. *Should we start knocking on doors? Excuse me have you seen a tall thin man in a Chára ball cap, a man with devil eyes?*

There is a rock on CSI known as Ghost Rock, named after an apparition in a trailing white dress. Many have seen her, the story goes, but none have dared to ask her story. I was certain that her story involved heartbreak—why else would she be so lost? I thought that maybe we had passed that rock, but without a marker I was not sure.

We came to the end of a road where there was a breakwater.

"Let's stretch our legs," Vincent suggested, despite the frantic air.

All around the breakwater were gulls, dozens of them, floating down low and back up again; they were touching down on rocks and then floating up again like kites. If you did not know better, you would think there was a giant air blower beneath them. In their midst was a cormorant drying its feathers. Maybe the gulls were nesting. Was there food there? Maybe the ocean had riled them up? And then one gull broke free from the group and flew straight at me, heading for my face, so close that I could see the silvery fish in its mouth. Before I had a chance to lower my Leica, Vincent raised his hand.

Jack had never, I thought, *saved me from anything, had he?*

*

What Could Have Happened

I met the ghost in the long white dress by a shallow inlet. The water behind her was four colours—green, pale blue, tan, and navy—all separate and yet overlapping like paint on a palette. Nearby was a cemetery with graves adorned with artificial flowers—hot pink and yellow—as resilient as the island itself. On the gravestones were surnames that repeated themselves over and over, a roll call unchanged for decades.

The ghost's name was Rose, and she had large sorrowful eyes. All that you really saw of her were her eyes; they belonged on another creature, one with the power to erase memories or trick men into doing things they might regret. The rest of her face could have been Photoshopped because you only saw her eyes.

Rose told me she been murdered by a jealous boyfriend, a fisherman who wanted to keep her but could not. I told her I was sorry. She said, thank you, Harriett. She knew my name. I told her that she looked like someone I had once known or could have known, someone who would have been important to me.

Rose knew all about my people, she told me. They were good people, she said, and you should never judge a person by a single act. Unless, of course, that act was murder.

I told Rose that she deserved better than her jealous boyfriend, and she said I deserved better than the men I had known. You should, she said, take care of yourself. And with that, she floated away like the spores from a dandelion before I could ask her what she knew or if she understood what it was that had wounded me. Because I was wounded, wasn't I?

25

When I lived in Montréal, I worked with a graphic designer named Madeleine at the newspaper. She looked like my idea of a ballerina. She was petite and graceful, and she walked with an unusually upright gait. With short black hair and soulful eyes, she could have been a modern Audrey Hepburn.

Some people come with an innate style, a look that they have never had to think about; unlike me, they just come that way. I was tall and dirty blond. I never knew what to do with my hair or my clothes. I was all over the place in big clumsy feet. When Peter and I were children, my mother bought our shoes at one store.

The owner invariably made the same joke: "Maybe we should give her the boxes," and my mother invariably laughed.

Madeleine could wear things I could not think of wearing: vintage polka-dot dresses with belts. Fake fur coats from the seventies. Madeleine kept fresh white flowers on her desk. Lilies, roses, tulips. She lived in a red-brick building as charming as she was. It was easy to spot her bedroom window — outside she had flowerpots and a birdhouse. Next to the house was a glass shelf she stocked with birdfeed, turning it into a year-round chickadee social.

Madeleine married a towering wild man, a rowdy character five years her junior, handsome in a Jason Momoa type of way. She was sublimely perfect in white silk. He looked as though he had been plucked from a logging camp. He was studying to be an architect, he drove a big-ass Harley, and everyone noted how different and how happy they were.

Two years later he got cancer, and he died.

And Madeleine retreated and never came back. She retreated into a life of pulled blinds and steeped tea; she retreated to a place where life's cruelty could no longer find her. I saw her in a bookstore years later, heavy and grey, unable to fit into her vintage dresses, and she told me: "There are worse things than a quiet life."

Are there?

One night, after I started all this, this story, I asked myself, *What are you looking for?* Does it exist? If I were to unspool my truth, would it consist of uneven threads of deception and heartbreak? And how sacred is the truth? More sacred than survival?

I found a support group online for people who had suffered loss. Here are the things you should not say to someone like Madeleine if you find yourself in that situation.

I know how you feel.

My uncle had the same disease, but he was a fighter.

You are so brave.

It is a good thing that your mortgage will be paid off.

There are shocks that your body never recovers from. After that you may jump if approached from behind, you may involuntarily shout. You are the defective smoke alarm that goes off when someone showers. Or you may be impotent, your battery removed. People hit by the cruellest of tragedies may tuck into a cocoon of grief, unable to deal with the din of the outside world. And all the mundane grievances that do reach them — complaints over bad coffee or a rude salesperson — feel unbearably petty.

Grief counsellors use a ranking system to assess your misery.

They award points based on the age of the deceased, their position in a family, the years they had been in your life, their physical proximity, and none of that helps.

And what if there are two of you, and you are grieving differently? Who can help you with that?

I photographed a military widow once who was channelling all of her pain, all of her trauma, into a cause, counselling the families of disabled veterans dealing with the obdurate Department of Veterans Affairs. At the time, she was running on fervour. She met with politicians, she appeared before committees, she filed access to information requests. And I wondered how long that would last, if the opioid of service would soon wear off, if its efficacy would diminish, and her mind would clear, and she would find herself standing alone in a war-torn field of grief.

✳

Jack had two modes: either locked down in his studio or in extreme motion. For years, after he started in Montréal, Jack ran. He ran for an hour, then two, then three; he ran through the streets like he had discovered this thing called freedom, and he would lose it if he slowed down. He ran too fast, too far. Jack ran as though every step, every stride, was pumping up the dopamine levels in his brain, until one day that was not enough.

So, he got a bike after we moved East. And he rode too far, too fast.

It was a black fixed gear. Sometimes Jack was gone for five hours on his fixie, and sometimes he "forgot" to tell me he was going. And people like Jack are always *gone*, out the door, before their mind catches up with their actions. They are in motion before they know they are fleeing something that is, at that moment, getting close.

When Jack returned from his rides, soaked with mud or sweat, he seemed able to handle it all again: life. Jack drove a fixie, he claimed, because nobody stole them. I was suspicious of Jack's bike. It was too stripped, too unforgiving, the nihilist of bikes. If you stopped pedalling, it bucked you. Kamikaze bike messengers drive fixed gears through Manhattan. They drive them for the thrill, they drive them to say, "Fuck you." With one gear and no brakes, Jack's bike belonged in NYC or on a velodrome with padded walls. It had no place on a narrow highway.

One night, when Jack took off on his bicycle and forgot to say goodbye, I trailed him. For two hours, I stayed five car lengths behind him. I pulled off onto side roads, I pulled back on again, and only when his ride was almost over, did I drive back home and act like I had never left. I could never say what I was afraid of when he went on those interminable rides. You cannot say those things out loud, because if you *do* say them, they could happen. So, you don't. I am not sure what happened to Jack's brain, if he felt agony or elation. One night, he crashed crossing a railway track and broke his collarbone. I took him to Emergency. We waited six hours, and they patched him up.

Jack had not sold me a bill of goods. I knew from the start that he was beautiful and spoiled and prone to running away. I knew the protective coating on his heart was thin.

When Jack became sad, he did things that made him sadder. He was sad when he missed my birthday. He was sad when he crashed his bike outside Dartmouth. He was sad that time he left home in Montréal without telling me. He hitchhiked through Alberta and got picked up by a Rock Machine biker named Serge. They shared a room in Brandon, Manitoba, and Serge showed him a picture of a stripper named Roxanne, who had broken his heart, and Jack told him she was beautiful, and she was.

And beautiful people are like *that*, aren't they? People like Jack and Roxanne. They do not see *you*. They see your reaction to *them*. They see you falling under their spell; they see you toppling into something you have no business toppling into. And the harder you fall, the more wondrous they seem.

*

Dicky and I met at the same sports bar as the last time. We ordered the same thing: Dicky, fish and chips, me, a chicken wrap. But things were different this day. Dicky and I were each on a highway, and there were turnoffs up ahead. Beyond them could be anything, but none of that was clear yet, and so, we followed our template.

Dicky told me he had unjoined a Facebook group for alumni from the *Standard*. A wannabe author had self-published his "memoirs" and was bombarding the group with "reviews," which were in reality emails from his relatives. "So pleased to get this incredible review from [Uncle] Barry."

"He is calling an email from his uncle a review," scoffed Dicky, who was wearing his standard uniform of shorts and a golf shirt. "A man who was in the news business for thirty years."

"Are you in the memoir?" I asked.

"Page one hundred and sixty-three. He says he sold me a Gouda wheel when he was running the office cheese club."

"Am I in it?"

"No."

"Okay."

"Did you ever notice that he smelled like dust?" asked Dicky. "I imagined that his apartment window was filled with dusty macramé plant holders covered with ceramic beads. And that is where he sits with his collection of *Archie* comic books and writes bullshit while wearing an Australian stockman's hat."

"I *did* notice the dust smell."

There were two happy endings from the paper, Dicky revealed. A former reporter had learned to code and was now well employed. A female editor had met a man online and moved to Ireland, where they lived in a centuries-old cottage with an actual thatched roof and actual sheep. The man had never been outside the village. "It's a very peat-moss-and-fairy-bower-type vibe," said Dicky, "but she likes it."

And then Dicky asked, "Are you still doing *your* book?"

"Yeah," I said, self-conscious. "Just research at this point. I'll start writing eventually."

"Well, write what you want about me. Say that I left my passport on a plane and spent four days stuck in the Prague airport, say that I went to Vegas and got arrested for jumping into a fountain. Say I was stuck with a four-hundred-dollar bar bill at The Extra End when the Scottish curlers stiffed me. I like the attention."

"All those things happened, right?"

"Yes."

Moving on from old colleagues, Dicky stopped clutching his beer like it was a can of mace. He mentioned a championship boxing bout in the US involving Nova Scotia's Custio Clayton,[15] whom he had, of course, "discovered." And then he turned grim. "According to Pierre, I am supposed to be getting our dishwasher fixed today." Sarcasm. "*That* won't be happening."

"Obviously."

I was not that fond of Pierre, to be truthful. He was one of those people who could be counted on to deliver the furtive blow that people had no reason to expect: *You still have TV?*—as though you owned a boa constrictor; *I think it's* grand *that your mother loves* Pokémon Go. The truth was that Pierre could barely see Dicky through his purple progressive eyeglasses anymore. Dicky was in that blurry spot where the insignificant and the inconsequential live, an area that grew, in Pierre's field of vision, larger each day.

"I did my thirty years of nights," Dicky said. "Paid my dues. Nights will kill you; they will suck the life out of you."

The only good thing about nights, Dicky said, was that you were able to get to the mail first. So, if, *just if,* you had ordered a rare Sandy Koufax baseball card, you could hide it before someone else arrived home, someone who might disapprove of your "investment."

---

15 Custio Clayton represented Canada at the 2012 Olympics. Clayton began training at his great-uncle's City of Lakes Boxing Club in Dartmouth, and fought his first bout at the age of eleven. His ring name is/was War Machine.

Thirty years of nights had not done Dicky any favours. Dicky was attractive when he met Pierre; now he was stout and permanently flushed. Like Jack, he had, in his day, been an exceptional baseball player. Jack was a first baseman, and Dicky was a catcher. People liked the look of Dicky back then. They liked his confidence; they liked the way he took control of home plate as though he were standing between them and every danger in the world. And then he became someone else.

"Hey, we're that age," I shrugged.

"Sometimes it takes a giant setback to figure out who you are," Dicky said. "I am *not* a fighter—that is what I figured out. I've had friends for forty years and never had a fight. I quit ball teams that were toxic. I grew up in a house where fighting was the norm—I think my parents fought every single day—and maybe that's why I have no appetite for it. Pierre is a lawyer. His entire existence is fighting."

"Right." *How could I argue?*

"Sometimes," Dicky said, "you have to face the truth."

I considered telling Dicky my story about Pollock Passage and Vincent. I contemplated bringing up the Pelly rumour. Except that our template did not have a line for an armed American professor and alien abductions. Besides, Dicky had a secret as considerable as mine.

"Are you thinking of doing any freelancing?" I asked, because that was better than talking about Pierre. "Besides the blog?"

"There's no market. There is a bigger market for fire jugglers."

It was all over for Dicky, wasn't it? And what had it amounted to: his hard-nosed take on minor sports, his slavish devotion to stars? Dicky had aspired to be part of that travelling road show of Sports columnists, men who believed they were bigger than the athletes. Dicky had wanted to be one of them, men with a belly full of free food and hyperbole, men who became, as the news business became more marginal, more hyperbolic. The proverbial ship had sailed, and Dicky was deplatformed.

"That is why I have a plan."

"Plans are good."

"No. I have a real one. If I tell you, you can't say a word."

"You know me."

Dicky and I had an unusual degree of trust.

"I am getting the hell out of Dodge."

"Is Pierre going to retire?"

"Pierre can do whatever he wants. I'm moving to Sarasota, Florida, baby—Grapefruit League. I am going to start living with a capital *L*. When I am down there, I can watch baseball—I mean *real* baseball—instead of freezing my ass in the dark. If I drive one hour, I am in Tampa, I am in Clearwater, I am in Fort Myers. I am watching the Yankees, the Blue Jays, and the Red Sox. I have a tattoo on my ass that says *I Love Baseball.*"

Dicky's surprise was so big, so consequential, that we did not mention Jack, and that was a first, Jack being the last item on our template. We always ended with Jack. Dicky still saw Jack. I should have mentioned that earlier. A lie, I suppose, of omission. We both knew that was the reason that we met: so that Dicky would tell me what Jack was doing, and I would listen to how he had discovered famous athletes. We were good with our arrangement, me and Dicky. But on this day, we did, for once, not talk about Jack. Jack, who trampled over people with the immunity that the beautiful possess. And now Dicky, my conduit, my spy, was leaving, and maybe that was best for both of us.

What Could Have Happened

"Did Jack ever tell you about my father?" Dicky asked.

"Yes. The violins."

The violins. Dicky let it sit there, the false promise held over his head.

"I shot a parolee once," I told Dicky, because it seemed like a good time to tell this story, as good a time as any. "He murdered his mother during one of those interminable winters that felt like Hell. She had, he told the court, tormented him every day of his life. When he had a crucial job interview, his last desperate chance to stay clean, she phoned him. 'The weather is going to be terrible on Friday, just terrible,' she said. 'A blizzard. You won't get there.' The same call the next day: 'You won't get there.' And then the night before, 'The buses won't be running in that storm. You won't get there.' Until he couldn't sleep, her threat stuck in his irrational, tortured, fucked-up junkie head, *'You won't get there.'*"

"Okay."

"And so, he killed her. With a flashlight."

"How big a flashlight?" asked Dicky.

"Big enough."

Dicky stared out the window while processing the story. At an intersection were three cars, a Ferrari, a BMW, and a Porsche, all with massive Pikachu stickers. One vehicle had the graphic of a company from the *Resident Evil* movies/video games, and all were driven by young men.

"Why," I asked Dicky, "were you good to your father when he was so mean to you?"

"Sometimes," he said, "you overlook the fucked-up parts of your family because you don't want to seem fucked-up yourself. So you tell yourself it was fine, and you show up for Christmas dinner with a pie to prove it was fine. And you save mementoes from your childhood as evidence it was fine, when it wasn't."

And then Dicky looked at me and asked, because it seemed like a good time to ask, as good a time as any: "Who do you think he *really* he is, this friend of yours? This Vincent? A Hells Angel, a cocaine and diamond smuggler from Brazil? You know he is not a goddamn American anthropology professor living in Pollock Passage studying the quaint customs of the inhabitants, their crude tools and weapons. Right? You *know* that."

"No. I think he is who he says he is."

"That would be a first."

24

I returned to Pollock Passage. Margaret was disappointed that Tracker had not led us to Graham, or at least a body. "He doesn't normally make mistakes," she said. I shrugged. And then to make her feel better I told her that I was working on a family memoir while looking for Graham.

"You have the discipline," Margaret announced, without knowing if that was true. "Do you remember the Wildes? I do not think they are coming, by the way. There are some minor blessings. Well, years ago, she started a family memoir, and she did *not* have the discipline for it. All she really wanted to do was make herself into a character in a Tennessee Williams play, tragic and broken by her past."

Margaret was flattering me, but I did not need it.

"I won't do that," I told her.

"The past is the past. It is not a living, breathing thing like a bear."

"That's true."

"She never finished the memoir, of course, but then she decided that she would only wear black. That was to be her signature. And when they had their tragedy —I am not sure if it is a tragedy if it is of your own making—she stabbed her doorman with a black Pasotti umbrella."

Ahhh, the problems of the rich.

"It was in the *New York Post*. All of it, the umbrella."

"Oh, I see."

"You can't be a nasty old thing and stab a doorman with an umbrella and expect people to be there when you need them. After your husband killed two people in a boating accident. I know that. I knew that when I was begging for a heart like a panhandler with an *I Need Food* sign."

Just then Klaus entered the room. "You never begged, Margaret. Those people who donated your heart were good people, that is all. I thank them daily." Klaus tapped his heart.

"I know, I know." Margaret started to tear up. "But my life has become so confusing." She looked at me with those expensive blue eyes and said, "I think it is wonderful that you are writing a memoir. Yours will be grand. I should not have brought up the Wildes. He was driving that boat too fast *and* drinking. Klaus's brother Heiner got him off, and that is why they keep bothering us. They think we are on their side because of Heiner. Well, *I* am not."

"Nobody said you have to be on their side," chided Klaus.

"It is inferred." Pause. "Because of Heiner."

And then facing me, "They have a son, and he cannot stop talking about Burning Man, as though he discovered it, which is their precise problem. They think they discovered *everything*: pain, suffering, killing people with speed boats. Tom Ford dinner jackets. Music from the twenties . . ."

Having exhausted both herself and the Wildes, Margaret caught her breath, "Do you think that we could be in it, the memoir?"

"Why," I said, "yes."

"Lovely."

✳

Two days later, I received a message from Margaret.

Tracker is onto something new. There could be hope for Graham. There could be hope for us all.

✳

When I was at the *Standard*, I was run down by a moped while covering a climate change protest hijacked by anarchists. The driver's face was concealed by a balaclava, and he hit me from behind. The anarchists were doing that for a while, ruining demonstrations organized by sincere people espousing good causes. My right pectoral muscle was torn, an injury so debilitating that I could not lift a camera. My side was a violent purple bruise.

Because it was a work-related injury, I was required to go to the Workers' Compensation Board, where my injury would, I was told, be assessed. I went to the office, and twenty minutes after my appointment time, the doctor walked in covered with sweat. He was wearing a backwards Blue Jays ball cap.

The lone staff member on duty said, "It's just you today, doc," and he gave her a thumbs up and kept walking.

Eventually, I was sent into the inner office.

"So, we are examining your shoulder," the doctor said.

"Actually, it is my pectoral."

"We call that the shoulder."

The doctor had a paper that contained eight statements of fact, which he appeared obligated to read out loud, starting with:

"I am a doctor."

"I am following the standards in this book." (He had a book that looked at least twenty years old.)

"The rules of doctor-patient confidentiality *do not* apply."

Really?

The doctor had an odd demeanour. He looked like a man with

a head full of childhood grievances. A man whose mother had told him year after year that she would put his birthday money from Grandma in her savings account, where it would be safe. And when he asked for it one day, it was gone. He had *that* look.

After asking generic questions, he performed a five-minute examination, using tools that seemed to be from 1960: an ancient protractor device that measured my arm movement, a reflex hammer, and a wheel-like apparatus that would determine if my arm was numb. I had assumed that he would have more modern diagnostic tools, like an ultrasound, but apparently not.

After all that, he washed his hands, slicked back his hair with his still-wet hands, and said, "Okay. That's the examination. A case worker will contact you." It never happened.

I admired the doctor and his bold indifference, I told Vincent one day when we were telling each other stories. "This doctor," I said, "was more forgiving than the doctors who held patients up to the mirror of their own perfection and found them lacking: anxious, alcoholic, inarticulate, abandoned, overweight/underweight, to blame for their condition. I liked the fact that this doctor barely saw me."

"How could anyone," Vincent asked, "not see you?"

✲

One day, three years ago, I saw Jack with a woman in a coffee shop. I was parked across the street. The woman looked edgy and off-key, like an indie actress. She was not as pretty as the red-lipped woman I later saw with Dicky. But she had *a look*. She had dark straight hair cut into bangs and a wry, too-big mouth. A woman with weaker bones could not have carried off those bangs, any more than she could have carried off the baggy white pants and Converse sneakers she was wearing. Or the leather cadet cap, which would have looked ridiculous on me.

I did not know how Jack knew her, but she was young. I could tell that she had, like Jack, grown up on a cushion of money. She had that air.

She looked like she listened to sad music because *she could.* Ray LaMontagne, Gretchen Peters. "On a Bus to St. Cloud." Oh, to be that unscathed, I thought, your enamel that thick, able to immerse yourself in a sea of pathos and melancholy without drowning.

Jack had never stopped being beautiful. He got too thin. His face said something terrible had happened once, but that only made him look poetic. Deep. It made women think that he would be sensitive to whatever heartbreak or trauma they had endured, when that was not the case.

The strange woman and Jack were sitting across from each other. And they were just talking, calmly, peacefully. And I could tell that she was not a marathon runner or a long-distance cyclist. She was not one of those people who could not slow down long enough to have a single intelligent thought in their head. Later, I found out that she was from his Bible study group.

The woman had a dog tied outside. An Australian shepherd with merle colouring that reminded me of butterscotch ripple ice cream. The dog had a penetrating gaze. If I had been shooting the dog, I would have lain down on the pavement and shot him at eye level.

I thought, no, I *knew*, the whole thing was troubling. At one point, Jack and the woman walked outside to check on the merle dog. Jack, who had never liked dogs.

25

Have you ever eavesdropped on a parent and heard a single thing that made you happy? It doesn't happen, does it? Instead, you learn that one of them is having an affair. Or that the family is losing the house. Nothing good ever comes of it.

I was downstairs at Stan's and I heard an ambulance passing. It felt unnaturally quiet after the sirens faded. There was the void of unfinished drama, and then through the void, I heard Stan and a visitor talking, and it was *that* loud agitated tone I had learned to dread. I stood at the bottom of the stairs. The visitor had come to the house, I determined, because he wanted to nominate Stan for a hall of fame, and Stan, being in several already, said he did not believe in them.

"Are you sure, Stan?" asked the man.

"One hundred per cent. I'm not like *that*," declared Stan, when he unequivocally was.

"I know you aren't, Stan, but —"

The visitor was hanging on Stan's every word, and so my father boldly claimed, "When some people see time running out, they panic, they become desperate to leave a mark on this Earth. Not *me*."

"Of course not."

This was a familiar theme of Stan's: the attention he *did not need*.

"The people"—he pronounced the word "people" as though it was his kingdom—"know what I have done. I do not have to donate my 'family story' to a museum that can't be bothered to check which side of the Second World War we were on. Did you see that? The family *donated* Papa's story. And the man was in the Austrian Gendarmerie, working with the Nazis, for God's sake. The museum sent out a tweet celebrating the fact that he fought the Communists. They were on *our goddamn side!*"

I had heard this story numerous times, the one about Nazis and the museum. Stan had a grudge against someone at the museum. I don't know exactly who. My father kept an ongoing list of enemies, people who had, in his mind, crossed him or wronged him. We were all supposed to abide by the list, even though it changed from week to week, and we had no dealings, good or bad, with anyone on it. They could have been fine. They could have been the devil.

"That is crazy," snorted the visitor, who had no idea what Stan was talking about but went along with it anyway. "Crazy."

"Did they miss that whole business with the Red Army and the Battle of Kursk? The siege of Leningrad."

An unnatural laugh.

I had by now figured out who the stranger was. It was Robert Dooley, the recycle-plant worker affiliated with the Boy Scouts and the Dartmouth separatists, Robert the fanboy who was obsessed with Stan and Facebook quizzes, Robert who had taken a data-trolling quiz that told him: *I am single because no one truly deserves me.*

Robert had been in trouble recently—he had approached a small boy outside a school—and the boy threw a rock at him. And then told the school principal.

Emboldened by Robert's obsequiousness, Stan switched to his *I am going to tell you a secret* tone. "My daughter is downstairs," he confided, as though he and Robert were in on something together. Robert, who should have been locked up for stalking children. "She has problems."

"Don't they all?"

Problems? Are you really talking about Me to a man who frightens small children?

"I got her a job with the government, and she quit. Quit! How hard could that be? I know a man who worked there for thirty years and was off on sick leave for fifteen. He said he was allergic to dust. When he retired, they gave him a medal as though he had been to war."

I can hear you!

I climbed the stairs. I sat on the top step with my ear cocked, just as I had done when I was a child and Stan and Mother were having an adult party with brash people who wore fox fur coats. Before the varnish on the top stair was scuffed.

"Harriett was always a challenge, making foolish decisions. Today they would say she had ADHD. Back then they didn't have a name for it. One year, on her mother's birthday, she showed up an hour late because she saw people picking wildflowers on the side of the road and thought that was a good idea."

It was a good idea.

"Is that right?"

"And then the husband left her. An artist, so I don't know what she expected. Even though she likes that art stuff herself. She drives like a maniac too. She did not get that from me, I can tell you. Picked it up in Montréal, where they all think they are Mario Andretti."

"The Montréal drivers are crazy, aren't they?" asked Robert, who had never been to Montréal and did not drive a car.

"I am sure that is part of the reason that Kaye declined so quickly." Stan paused long enough for the lie to take shape in his head, the lie that exonerated him of his sins and painted him in a heroic light. "Harriett and her problems."

Really!

"Kids never appreciate nothin' you do for them, Stan."

Stan ignored the reply; this was not a conversation. It was a monologue. He was telling a dubious story to a dubious individual, a person who was too confused to question any of it, a person to whom he owed nothing, especially the truth.

"Harriett and the husband should have stayed in Montréal; it suited them. You know the French: *joie de vivre* and terrible comics, which seems to be a weakness of hers by the way. Terrible comics. But the husband got mixed up in a shooting, and he couldn't handle it anymore."

Mixed up in a shooting?

"His friend got shot. Gideon or Dideon or whatever the hell his foolish name was. It made the news. Around the time of one of the gang wars. After that, Harriett's husband fell apart like a cheap pair of pants. I knew a tank driver who did three tours of duty in Afghanistan, and he didn't fall apart like that."

Thump thump. I felt a thumping beat in my chest — as urgent as a bird trapped in a chimney. *Thump thump thump.* I steadied myself on the stairs.

"Sounds like a marshmallow, Stan."

Marshmallow? Didier was shot to death. And Jack was there.

"They came back here," said Stan, "Harriett and the husband, but it all went to hell."

Why do you keeping calling him "the husband" when you know his name?

"The husband turned into one of those running nuts. Never had kids after that. He said he couldn't handle it. You would have thought he was Kipchoge Keino outracing a buffalo on the plains of Kenya, barefoot. Not some flakey artist."

You weren't supposed to tell this. It is not your story. It is my story, remembered the way I have to remember it.

"Anyway, it was hard on Kaye. There were nights she was in her room crying because of it."

A lie. You are being horrible. You ARE horrible. No wonder Peter hates you.

"Well, it is good you were there for her, Stan."

It sounded like madness, the untruth bumping against the truth.

Some of what Stan said was true: the shooting, me picking wild-flowers for Mother. But there were so many lies, mean ones. I was *not* the person who made Mother cry—that was him, him and the odious rabbit-faced Eva.

But yes, Didier was shot, and yes, he *did* die, and yes, Jack *was* there. And yes, that did ruin everything.

Some people remember a traumatic event as though they have a photograph of it on their night table. A photograph that shows the stairs, the blood, and the leg at an angle that a leg would never naturally assume.

All I can tell you is that it happened.

Jack and Didier had gone to the massage parlour to find Seb because there was water leaking from his upstairs unit again. It was the same day that the dead mouse fell on my head. The one I photographed.

When they were about to enter the building, shots were fired from a car. Jack and Didier were, the police said, bystanders, in the wrong place at the wrong time. How many times have you heard that, and how many times does it sound like a meaningless cliché? And sometimes I think it was yesterday; sometimes I think it was forty years ago.

∗
∗

The obituary page can be a fantasy of half-truths and wishful think-ing. Unless you are being libellous, you can say anything you want in a paid obituary. You can say that your nana was a world-renowned trainer of big circus cats. You can say that Captain Ken slipped the lines one last time and glided out into the sea of the great unknown.

I saw an obituary once and the name sounded familiar. In the obituary, the family talked about the man's wonderful smile. He had a heart of gold and a twinkle in his eyes. He teased those who knew him well. I googled his name and there he was, convicted ten years ago of killing a man with a baseball bat.

Didier's obituary was mostly true.

It did state that Didier died unexpectedly.

It did say that he was deeply loved.

It said that he was an artist with an interest in geodes.

It did *not* say that Camille's heart also stopped, and that Jack could not bear to be around her anymore, and so we fled, leaving her as broken as Madeleine who had once worn beautiful clothes. We packed a U-Haul and fled. Jack's idea, not mine.

And it did not, it *could not*, work out for me and Jack after that. It sputtered and stalled, we made plans and we abandoned them. Jack ran; I worked. I put away my Leica—street photos felt frivolous. I only shot pictures for work, criminals and their victims. Jack announced that he could never have a child because the fear of losing one was unbearable. When he said it, he was crying. He would not, he could not, he said, survive a loss that great. Didier's death convinced him of that.

If you are part of something tragic, how much do you owe the other survivors? Are you forever bound, shackled by heartbreak and duty? Or are you free to forget, to pretend you never were there?

Jack disappeared from time to time, saying he was sad. People said things such as: "Well, surely he must be over it by now." Or "My father was a police officer, and he saw shootings all the time." Or "There must have been something wrong with your relationship to begin with." Some of that was true.

*

I photographed two old men once for a flashback on the VE day riots in Halifax,[16] when the sailors went mad at the end of World War Two. After authorities decided to close the liquor stores and bars at

---

16 Over five hundred businesses were damaged and/or looted on May 7–8, 1945, during the poorly planned Victory in Europe celebrations. Three rioters died. Some were sentenced to prison. It was, history will attest, a collective failure on all sides.

a time when the servicemen, might, just *might*, want to celebrate the end of six years of hell.

The first man was a shopkeeper whose windows were smashed in the mayhem. He said the looters took a dozen suits, a display table, and two mannequins. Merchant seamen and opportunistic civilians joined in the rampage. It took days to clean up the mess.

The second man was one of the sailors. Sixteen when he enlisted. Close to ninety when I spoke to him. He couldn't explain why he got caught up in the madness. He didn't even drink.

The sailor — a man who had been handsome in his youth — said he never lost any sleep over the fact that he stole a lamp. He gave it to his mother. I asked him why. Because she was a good mother, he said. And that was that. From a man who lost all of youth and much of his goodness in a nightmare he did not ask for.

If you don't go looking for something untenable, something horrific, if it comes looking for you, then the rules do not apply. The rules of comportment and niceness that exist in another space, a less violent and fucked-up space. In this space, your immediate and awful space, there are no rules.

*
*

Jack had ridden his bike for four hours that night, and when he came home, he went to bed, and he was spent. His heart, he said, was worn out, or life had broken it. He was done. With everything. And I knew it would happen. I just did not know when. His memories and my memories were too much together; my atoms of lifelessness were colliding with his atoms of anguish, and the fallout was so toxic, so radioactive, that he left. And maybe the spoiled woman who looked like an indie actress thinks she stole him from me, but that was not our story. That was not our story at all.

26

I finally went to see my cousin Rick. Vincent offered to join me, but I went alone. Angry at Stan for lying about me, I expected Rick to also be angry at Stan for stealing Graham. Our like anger would validate us — it would merge into a force field of virtuous indignation — but Rick was fine when he answered his door. Just fine.

My cousin was wearing a George Strait T-shirt. In person, he was as dark as Graham but not as thin. He was clean-shaven, but his eyebrows were as wild as rockweed. Rick gestured to a leather armchair. The wall above the chair was covered with photos, in interlocking frames, of people who looked nothing like me or Peter.

"I should have called first," I said.

"Nah, good to see you, good to see you."

Rick sat across from me. More than anything, he looked like a man who enjoyed his home: the stability of the hardwood under his feet, the heat from the wood stove. Outside, Rick's house had all the rural accoutrements: a work shed, two wheelers, a duck pond, and a Ram pickup. A cement jockey in a perky red cap.

Against one wall was a piano with sheet music for "Let it Go."

"So, you live in town, right?" Rick asked.

"Yes."

"We get into town now and then." He mentioned a popular tavern.

"It is good there. Great steaks."

"Do you have any kids?"

"No."

"Your brother does, right?"

"Yes, one boy named Luke."

Rick and Rhonda had two grandchildren, he told me, although I knew that. He gave me their names. Ten and twelve, the kids were. I knew that too. "The grandchildren liked Graham," Rick said. "The girl—she plays the piano. She is musical like Graham. They would play together sometimes." He looked at the door, as though he was waiting for help. "My wife, she'll be back soon."

I studied an acrylic painting of a yellow Cape Islander on one wall—it was the yellow of optimism and sunshine. I asked Rick if that was his boat, although I already knew the answer. It was the *Rosie & Rhonda*.

"A man in Digby did the painting. I'm gonna get my new boat done."

"What's her name?"

"*Second Chance*," he said, but I already knew that too. The all-black Darth Vader boat, the eight ball on the snooker table. If I had had any doubts, there was a windbreaker on a hook in the hallway. On the back was the embroidered image of a black Cape Islander with the words *Second Chance*. On the sleeve, *Captain*.

"Ahhhh, that's a good name."

I had expected Rick to show the scars of his near-death experience, but he looked okay. His hair was not even grey. Rick, I realized, represented things that Stan did not like—stability and dependability. As the captain of his own boat, $1M+ when geared up and licensed, Rick was someone in Pollock Passage, and Stan did not like that either. Stan, the self-appointed family alpha.

Rick kept looking at the door, and then Rhonda arrived. After a couple of minutes, she cut through the impasse, and without making anyone feel the least bit uncomfortable, got to the heart of the matter.

"We enjoyed having Graham with us," said Rhonda, who seemed like she could do practical things like keep the books and drive a truck. "He was family. Him and Chief"—she gestured at a golden Lab asleep in the kitchen—"they was buds. After Graham left, Chief waited by the door for a week for him to come back. The whole thing is sad."

This was the first time anyone had seemed genuinely sad about Graham.

"Yes, it is sad," agreed Rick. "But there was no need for any of it."

"He was family," Rhonda repeated.

"There was no need for Graham to start running the roads with Jesse Fancy, but he done that too."

"I grew up near the Fancys," said Rhonda. "The grandfather, he loved his ham radio. One man came all the way from Georgia to have a look at his system. There must have been something unusual about it, he come all the way from Georgia. They was good people except for Jesse."

"When you has balls the size of Skittles," scoffed Rick.

Rhonda, who seemed used to filling in the details, added, "Jesse set three fires. Two were abandoned buildings and one was a hunting camp. He and his mother let Graham stay there when he come down. I'm surprised they didn't have him setting fires."

"Nothing surprises me with Jesse," said Rick.

There was a longer pause, and it felt as though we were still feeling each other out. No one wanted to say the wrong thing. Rhonda said that it was good to meet me. Stan used to phone here all the time, she said. It didn't matter what hour of the day, she added with a *you know what I mean* smile.

"He would phone for *Graham*," emphasized Rick. "Not us," he said, letting out a gush of air. "They both liked to enlarge on things."

Rick asked if Stan was on TV anymore. I said no. He asked about my mother. I told him that she had been in a wheelchair for twenty years before she died.

"Sorry to hear that," he said. "Everyone said she was a nice woman."

"Yes, she was," I replied, "she was the nice one in the family."

Rhonda smiled, knowing what I meant.

I told Rick and Rhonda that I had been to Maynard's funeral, but I had been too young to remember it.

"That is okay," Rhonda said. "It is nice that you were there. It was nice that Stan never held a grudge against Maynard after what Maynard done to him when they was kids. I guess the family owed him one."

"What did Maynard do?"

"Besides chopping off Stan's toe with an axe?"

"Okay." I did not know, I admitted, how Stan had lost his toe. Rhonda said she was surprised. It was never a secret.

"That's what everyone down here called him: Nine-Toed Stan. Everyone knew Maynard done it," she said. "They knew he was mean to Stan."

"They was just little kids," added Rick. "Dad was chopping up a spruce tree, and Stan would not shut up, so he axed him. That is how they told it anyway: *Stan would not shut up.* You would have to have one frightful temper to do that. Their mother wrapped the foot in a sheet."

Rhonda nodded.

"They never seen a doctor," Rick said. "They was lucky he never bled to death."

"Your grandfather," recalled Rhonda, "said Stan had it coming."

"That was only because he favoured Dad."

"Well, you know why," said Rhonda without explaining.

"Yes. But it shouldn't have been that way. None of it. I was told that there were never two men so much alike. My father and his father. People said they looked the same and acted the same. Both were not right, I'd say. Nobody should have their toe chopped off because they talked too much. As a child!" Rick shook his head. "Nowadays, they'd have you taken away."

"Children's Aid," said Rhonda.

"There are days I wonder if this whole family is not right," sighed Rick. "Well, I know that my father was not right, but I wonder about the rest of us, I do. And that includes Graham, God bless his soul. Graham was never right."

When I left, Rhonda told me to be sure to come back again. I could meet the grandchildren—the girl was visiting a friend; the boy was out on his scooter.

"Don't get me started on those bloody scooters," griped Rick.

And Rhonda replied, "It is better than sitting in a room playing *Call of Duty* and smoking weed."

*
*

I am afraid to say too much about my father, or you may hate him. Or maybe I want you to hate him. Maybe I am *that* angry even after hearing how he lost his toe.

My mother had multiple sclerosis, and in her last year, she needed home care. Stan hired a lovely woman from Newfoundland named Stella. The caretaker came in during the week, and she made blueberry muffins, and they talked. Mother showed her photos.

Stan would pop in during the day; he would pop in and Stella, for my mother's sake, would act like she was delighted to be in his company. When he left, the two women went back to their own conversations. About family. Life. Heartache.

I do not think anyone changes when they are old. Their dominant trait becomes more obvious. The sweet people become sweeter, the mean people meaner, and the duplicitous finally overplay a hand, exposing the pattern of duplicity that defined them. Stan's lying became as obvious as a terrible dye job, and my mother made her decline easy on us, as easy as she had made everything in life.

My mother could have left Stan after Eva from Oslo, but she did not. Eva, in case you are wondering, was not beautiful like my mother. She had mousey hair and a red nose. She looked like a woman who might win a local Excellence in Teaching award or be mistaken for a rabbit. If my mother was as beautiful as Michael Corleone, Eva was Fredo, who got his revenge by betraying the beautiful don.

After a parent "normalizes" behaviour, you are forced to go along with it. Cowed into silence. It is as though you unwittingly signed a contract, waiving your right to anger or hurt or humiliation. One year, Eva showed up at our house on Christmas Eve in a leather mini skirt. She brought a can of Quality Street chocolates, and everyone acted as though it was normal. The things families cannot talk about—the things that are woven into the fabric of their life—can consume an inordinate amount of energy.

You can say that Mother should have left after Eva, who was always introduced as a "producer." I would have. But I was relieved that Mother stayed because I was, at the time, a teenager, who wasn't doing great at school. And then I left for photo school, where I was for the first time, free from Stan's madness. And I never saw Eva again.

*
*

At my writing workshop, Ingolf, the organic chemistry professor, told us that the villain in his novel, a character who meets a grim end, was based on his late father. It was the first time that Ingolf had told a story with literary potential.

"My father was the paradigmatic head of the household," he said. "He took his job very seriously, when in fact it was a minor one. We could not speak to him before his morning coffee or before he had his dinner. He resented any attention that was diverted from him to us, so our mother had to be covert about it. If she bought me a winter coat, she did it in secret. If she helped me with my homework, it was done before he came home. It created a sense of shame around the very act of being loved, and that confused me for years."

And then he paused, as though a seemingly infallible hypothesis had not been supported. "We had a relationship of needless secrets and subversive affection, me and my mother. I am not sure why it had to be like that."

"So, you kill him in the book?" Dorothy asked.

"Yes."

"But it's funny, right?"

"Yes."

"That is good," the group agreed.

Before my mother died, she told me, "You and Peter made me so happy. There was never a day that I was not happy." I told her that I did not think I had done enough or been enough, and so she said it again, "There was never a day that I was not happy." And I believed her.

Stan was not jealous of my mother's affection for us; he *liked* it. It was one of the many things he liked, no loved, about her. He loved the fact that she was good, and she was steady and indefatigably loyal. When my mother was in a room, the air was lighter, the food tasted better. Mother had the discipline to stick with it when life was hard and our hearts were broken. She was the centreboard that kept us upright, and when she was gone it was all fucked-up. It would always be all fucked-up.

And isn't that the story of every family?

At some point, it will be totally, irrevocably fucked-up.

What Should Have Happened

Stella, the caregiver, was at the funeral home, and she was carrying a prayer book and a purse. At first, I wasn't sure it was her—she was wearing a black pantsuit, and I had never seen her in black. Only florals. When Stella saw me, she crossed the room. "It's about your mother," she whispered.

Well clearly, I thought, *since she is the person who just left us.*

"She would have wanted it," said Stella. She was one of those people who could sell you anything—a sad story or a terrible joke. She could sell it.

"Wanted what?"

Stella opened her purse and produced a black-and-white photo from another time and place. "Look at that face and tell me there is no such thing as love at first sight."

Joseph—that was his name—did look handsome and achingly young in the photo, in a way that Stan had never looked young with his lollipop head. You could imagine Joseph scrambling up a mast or chopping down a tree. Able, he looked. The picture appeared to be taken on a farm—there was a workhorse in the background. Joseph was wearing a white sleeveless undershirt and a small black beret you might see in an old French movie, and he had Al Pacino eyes.

Before Stella produced the photo, the day was already surreal. Across the street from the funeral home was a towering, inflatable King Kong. The gorilla was an advertisement for a party business. It was windy, and the gorilla was swaying, dipping down so low that I thought he might topple. His arms were extended above his head, and his mouth was open, showing garish blood-red gums.

The gorilla added to the strangeness of the day, a day I only remember parts of. I had taken a sedative to make it through the viewing, and I was having trouble forming words. *So, this is what it feels like,* I thought, *to be that person who cannot keep up in conversations.*

This is what it feels like. I tried to remember the word for "inflatable," but I could not.

Someone at the viewing—I may or may not have known him—mentioned King Kong. "It could be worse," he noted. "One day, the party business erected a jail, on another day a disgusting 'pile of poo.' They have no sense of decency, do they?" the near stranger said.

Ahh, decency, I thought, *a forgotten trait, as quaint as a handwritten thank-you card.* Among the flowers in the room was an arrangement from "Your old colleague Eva," now retired in Toronto. I tried to remember the words "swamp rabbit."

Stan was talking to someone more "important" across the room, when Stella pulled out the photo of Joseph. Only I saw her tuck it under Mother's arm, hidden from sight. Poor handsome Joseph, killed in a logging accident.

If Joseph had not perished, I wondered, as King Kong dipped and swayed like an inflatable force of evil, *would Peter and I have been raised in an orderly home without a violent monkey? Would life have been normal? Would Joseph have taken Peter into the woods and shown him how to do useful things that Peter might have enjoyed? Would Peter's left eye not twitch?*

Do you have a list you go through at night, and is there one person you pause at, and do you wonder what would have happened if they had been different and you had been different—if the stars had been aligned or the gods kinder?

It did not matter if Stella had embellished the story of Joseph, or if he was the last person Mother thought of each night. What Stella did, in that surreal place on that surreal day, felt right.

"Your father's childhood was different," Mother told me once. I never knew what she meant, "different" being a vague meaningless modifier that tells you nothing. "And some people are different because that is who they are. Sylvester Stallone tried out for every part in *The Godfather*, and they turned him down every time. Four years later, he was Rocky. Stallone was *different*, so they could not see him as the no-name assassin who blows up Michael's wife in the old country. Your father was always going to be different."

Why was he different? I wondered, as I turned on my headlights and drove through the fog. *Why do we make excuses for people we love?* I parked outside a small community archives in Pollock Passage, sensing I would return.

The outer room had pineapple-patterned wallpaper. It felt like a parlour, where you sit in your good clothes after church, a room too fancy for the old Swim house.

The second room contained items related to the fishery. Wooden compasses. Model ships under glass. A display on Cape Island boats. In one corner was a table devoted to local folklore with fantastical drawings. I read a newspaper story about a fisherman challenged by a sea monster. He could, he said, feel the hair stand up on the back of his neck. The monster kept coming at his boat, and then it reared up and opened its mouth, exposing rows of teeth that looked like tusks.

The third room had a computer that visitors could use. It was the room in which they stored the records of Births, Deaths, Marriages. The records I had come for.

There was a noisy clock on the wall, and I could hear it.

Tick. Tock. Tick. Tock.

What did I want to find?

Tick. Tock.

What was so different about Stan's childhood?

Tick. Tock.

On the computer, I started with Stan's mother. With no trouble, I found her death certificate and the official cause of death: *Septicaemia.*

Septicaemia. Also known as blood poisoning, treatable today with antibiotics.

Her certificate led me backwards to her parents, and I saw the causes of their deaths laid out for anyone to see.

Her father: *Brain tumour, cystic glioma left cerebral hemisphere.*

Her mother: *Ruptured uterus.*

Tick. Tock.

I turned to the paternal side of the family, Swim. The name was a recurring one. The Swim surname was historically found in the German state of Saxony; variations included Schwimin, Zwemen, and Schwehmann. I went looking for people I knew were related to us, and I found Stan's grandfather, Ebenezer.

Cause of death: *Severe haemoptysis. Antecedent causes: pulmonary tuberculosis, rheumatoid arthritis, and coronary insufficiency.*

Severe haemoptysis. Defined as a "spitting of blood that originated in the lungs or bronchial tubes," the cause of which was varied, including cancer. I looked up Ebenezer's antecedent causes: *tuberculosis, rheumatoid arthritis, and coronary insufficiency.* I saw the notation on his death certificate: *Query from doctor states that TBC was inactive.* His death sounded like a poor person's death. Ebenezer had lived a working man's life, it appeared on Cape Sable Island, not Pollock Passage as I had believed. *Did Stan know this?*

This is where it became disturbing—where I began to question what I knew and what I thought I knew about the Swims. Ebenezer had *four children*—not one, as I had believed. Stan's father, Clarence aka Lark, was not an only child. My grandfather had three siblings I had never heard of before.

A brother Clyde.

The cause of death: *tuberculosis.* Clyde died on Christmas Eve, twelve days after his third birthday.

Certificate of Death

Place: County Shelburne

In the City or Town of Clark's Harbour

Length of Stay (years, months, days) in City, Town where death occurred: life

In Province: life

Name of Deceased: Clyde Ebenezer Swim

Residence: Clark's Harbour, Cape Sable Island

Province: Nova Scotia

Sex: M   Nationality: CDN   Racial Origin: English

Single/Married/Widowed/Divorced: single

Birthplace: Clark's Harbour

Date of Birth: December 12, 1900

Age: 3   3   0   12
              Years Months Days

Trade, Profession, or Kind of Work: child

Kind of Industry or Business: home

Date Deceased Had Last Worked in this Industry: _____

If Married, Give Name of Wife or Husband of Deceased:

Father's Name: Ebenezer   Birthplace: Clark's Harbour

Mother's Name: Jane   Birthplace: Clark's Harbour

Date of Death: <u>December 24, 1903</u>
I <u>Alfred Nickerson</u> hereby certify that I attended the
deceased who was last seen alive on _____
Cause of Death: <u>Tuberculosis</u>

A sister, June, whom I looked up with trepidation. Death from
appendicitis. She would have been seven the following day.
Tick. Tock.
I was not sure that I liked all these deaths laid out so coldly, so
clinically, and yet I kept going. And there it was: the third deceased
child, the second uncle whom Stan had never spoken of. He had not
died in childhood like the other two. Vernon James Swim, nineteen,
had been murdered.

Certificate of Death

Place: County <u>Shelburne</u>
In the City or Town of <u>Clark's Harbour</u>
Length of Stay (years, months, days) in City, Town where
death occurred: <u>life</u>
In Province: <u>life</u>
Name of Deceased: <u>Vernon James</u>
Residence: <u>Clark's Harbour, Cape Sable Island</u>
Province: <u>Nova Scotia</u>
Sex: <u>M</u>   Nationality: <u>CDN</u>   Racial Origin: <u>English</u>
Single/Married/Widowed/Divorced: <u>single</u>
Birthplace: <u>Clark's Harbour</u>
Date of Birth: <u>December 3, 1902</u>
Age: <u>19</u>   <u>19</u>   <u>9</u>   <u>0</u>
                    Years Months Days

Trade, Profession, or Kind of Work: <u>fisherman</u>
Kind of Industry or Business: <u>fishery</u>

Date Deceased Had Last Worked in this Industry:
September 1, 1921
If Married, Give Name of Wife or Husband of Deceased:
Father's Name: _Ebenezer_ Birthplace: _Clark's Harbour_
Mother's Name: _Jane_ Birthplace: _Clark's Harbour_
Date of Death: _September 3, 1921_
I _Alfred Nickerson_ hereby certify that I attended the
deceased who was last seen alive on _____
Cause of Death: _chest wound_
If death was caused by external causes (violence) fill in the
following:
Accident, Suicide, or Homicide, state which: _homicide_
Date of Injury: _September 3, 1921_
Nature of Injury: _gunshot_
Specify if injury occurred in Industry, Home or Public
Place: _hunting camp_

Vernon, a fisherman, had been shot three months before his
twentieth birthday at a hunting camp in the woods. I could feel my
breath coming in and out, unnaturally aware of it happening. In.
Out. It gave me something to focus on besides the screen before me.
In. Out. In. Out. *Tick. Tock. Tick. Tock.*

Vernon had been murdered—I had no idea by whom—and
Stan's best stories were about an imaginary captain and a washed-up
circus trunk? What else had Stan neglected to tell us?

And then, I searched for Maynard. The outcome was as I had
feared. It was not the improbable rumour that Vincent had told me
about aliens, the one that buried the truth under a cover of intrigue,
but something far worse. It did not align with the family story of
the missing body. There it was in black and white. Suicide. Had the
family lied out of shock and shame? Did Stan know the truth?

*

The next day, I went to Stan's house with a purpose. I was going to ask about my discoveries — Maynard's suicide, and the three unspoken-of relations — but before I could get to any of that, I noticed an orange cat, the one that had been hanging around outside, and it was sleeping in the white velveteen visitor's chair.

"What is he doing here?" I asked.

"Chico?" Stan feigned confusion at my question. "He lives here."

"So that's his name, Chico?"

"Yes. I am surprised you didn't know that."

Stan, who once claimed he could read minds, sensed that I was there for something. And so, without missing a beat, he informed me that he had run into an old colleague.

"You remember Aubrey?"

A distraction.

"Barely. I remember he wore an ascot."

"Correct. He liked to tell people that he 'was a storyteller.' 'Who are you,' I asked him once, 'a journalist or Hans Christian Andersen?' 'I like a good yarn,' he mused while puffing on a corncob pipe, and I said, 'I like a good set of facts, one that does not involve talking frogs or a little mermaid.'"

Stan offered me a liqueur-filled chocolate from the bowl on his coffee table. He allowed himself one a week. Guests were offered the sweets, which had seemed sophisticated when Stan could first afford them but were by now unnecessary proof that he had arrived. They were flavoured with rum or whisky. I nodded no.

"I was in Pollock Passage," I said, "and I went to the local archives."

Surprisingly, Stan did not seem surprised. "Loose use of the word 'archives' if it is the place I am thinking of."

"Well, it —"

"I can't imagine you being interested in the gleanings of amateur historians."

I told Stan that I had looked up the Swims' records. "I did not know," I said, "that the family lived on Cape Sable Island, not Pollock Passage."

"Of course," he replied as though it was public knowledge, "Clark's Harbour."

"When did they move?"

"How," he replied, "would I know? Am I the moving police?"

I did not know, I told him, that there were three prior-to-now unmentioned aunts and uncles, one of whom had been murdered, Vernon, the fisherman.

"Who knows what that bunch was up to," he scoffed.

"That *bunch?*"

"Yes, that bunch. The Swims. I take after my mother's side, all sensible people, the Nickersons. She was a schoolteacher, you know. I don't know anything about the CSI bunch. I went there with Maynard for a dance, and they accused us of stealing their girls and I never went back."

"Okay, but it could explain —"

"Just a minute, will you."

Stan still had a landline, and he left the room to answer it.

Five minutes later, back.

"That was Skippy. He said he just got back from a fishing lodge in Sherbrooke."

"Did he?"

"Of course. He is part of that new trend, virtual vacations. Saving the environment. Skippy said the assisted-suicide ghouls were in the manor trying to make him feel guilty for still being alive. One ghoul handed him a brochure and whispered, 'You have options, you know.' It reminded him, he said, of a stinking hot day in Manhattan when a man was on a ledge and underneath a craven mob had gathered, and they were yelling, with blood in their eyes, 'Jump.' It reminded him of that."

"Really?"

"Why would I make that up?"

"The archives —" I tried to resume the conversation.

"Skippy knows a bloodthirsty mob when he sees one."

"The archives —"

"If you want to believe nonsense you found scribbled in an *archives* — and please don't use that word around intelligent people — that is up to you. Were these official documents next to the section on sea monsters with red saucer eyes? Or the one on ghost stories. The woman who stood looking out to sea for eternity waiting for her son to return?"

"There was some of that, but —"

"And did you read about Twinkle Corner, and how a Mr. Twinkle killed himself and was buried at a crossroads with a stake through his heart? And it is best to avoid Twinkle Corner at night."

"Yes."

"And what does that tell you? Maybe it wasn't just Graham who was born short and left over."

28

I knew that I would return to the archives. But first, before I tell you more about that place and its secrets, I need to settle some matters, both slight and consequential.

I *can* confirm—for what it is worth—that Slim's brother Corky exists. I found him in a police report in Cape Breton. Garett (Corky) Devoe volunteered to guard the house of a senior during the man's funeral. The widow accepted his offer. Corky then robbed the house himself, stealing oxycodone and moose meat from the freezer. Corky is of no consequence. Hughie the Twin is also of no consequence—both were red herrings introduced by people with something to hide. Jesse Fancy led nowhere. Kenny the Twin was irrelevant.

Aksel Andersson, with whom my father had been secretly meeting while I wrote this memoir, died as enigmatically as he had lived. It made the news. Acting on an anonymous tip, a TV news crew went to a remote graveyard that personified loneliness. They found a headstone inscribed with his name, but the ground where he was supposed to be resting had not yet been disturbed.

Stan insisted that the jewel thief was *not* dead—he had returned to Russia with his hidden treasures. "Where is his plane?" he demanded. "Where?" Aksel's estranged girlfriend told the TV station that his parents were not from Denmark. His real name, she said, was Reid MacLean, and his family was local, as common as fish cakes.

None of that matters.

Graham was never found. That is what matters. The person at the opening of this story, a person also known as Slick, Damien the Devil Child, and the Missing Link, does not have a satisfactory ending because I cannot with certainty tell you what happened.

If you like, you can imagine that Graham made his way to Boston, where he met Zdeno Chára, his six-foot-nine hockey hero, who autographed his hat.[17] If I were writing a novel, that is the ending I would write. If you like, you can also imagine that Graham joined a band, and every night he plays "Tom Dooley" on his harmonica. That, too, is a good ending.

Who was Graham? you might rightfully ask, this individual who associated with criminals and made friends too easily, a man who could play the harmonica so hauntingly that he made hard men cry. Was he a villain or a victim, a survivor of tough times or a casualty of an ableist system that believed he was broken and less? I wish I knew.

When I was at Rick's, my cousin, the person who understood Graham best, said their mother had "babied" Graham. "He coulda done more than he done, but she babied him. After our father disappeared, she never let him out of her sight, him being the oldest and a little bit different. Now he liked music and he was good at that. But she never let him do nothing else. I'd have taken him on as a bander, I would. I think that the way she raised him made him do stupid stuff just to show people he could. I blame her, I do."

"Easy to blame the mother," sighed Rhonda.

"Yes, it is," agreed Rick. "I told my mother—and you remember this, Rhonda—I told her: 'Satan was an angel once too.'"

---

17 On December 30, 2020, Chára signed a one-year, $795,000 contract with the Washington Capitals. In 2022, he retired after signing a one-day contract with Boston, allowing him to end his career as a Bruin.

There was no further mention of Graham online, and that was easy to understand. Lobster catches were down, the weather was rotten, and one night, while the three-man crew of a fishing boat was asleep in their bunks, the captain went overboard. This was real time, this was tangible, this was urgent enough for the call to go out online:

> *If you want to take part in the search for the missing fisherman that fell overboard, the location is West of Seal Island. You MUST call JRCC at 1-902-427-XXXX to be given a search area. This is from JRCC directly.*
>
> *43.4104° N, 66.0137° W (Seal Island)*
> *Let's bring him home.*
> Followed by: ⚓⚓⚓

*

One day I talked to the old Black man who said he had been a sparring partner for Muhammad Ali. He was jogging around Lake Banook. I listened to his story, which probably was not true. But it didn't matter, you see, because he was going there, he was going to a higher place where the brutality of life could not crush him; he was going there in a pair of work boots and an eight-dollar Value Village Adidas hoodie. He was telling his story the way it should have been because no one was going to do it for him. His truth and your truth and my truth may all be different. And they may all be real. And how could any of us survive if there was only one truth: an absolute truth that did not allow for fairness, mercy, or redemption?

29

I am getting near the end, and it is time for some hard truths. Here is the real reason that Peter could not forgive Stan. It had nothing to do with Stan giving away his room to a stowaway or letting him fall out a window as a baby.

Stan did something rotten. To Mother, but also to Peter. Eva the swamp rabbit was one thing, but this was indefensibly, stupidly worse. Stan had a sordid little thing with Mrs. Crowell during the anything-goes days of the sexual revolution — the one that hit Nova Scotia in a late-breaking wave of bell-bottom pants and platform shoes — back when Peter was paddling with Allan. When people thought Hugh Hefner was hip, and not an abusive pervert. It never occurred to Stan that this might be a problem for Peter.

Naturally, as is the case with all sordid little things, the story was more of a murmur than a statement. And naturally, Stan carried on as though no one had a right to challenge anything he did, Stan Swim being Stan Swim.

The details were not talked about. When. Where. But *something* happened, and Mother, who had dealt with this sort of thing before, coped. Mother who believed that there was "something wrong" with Stan in the same way that there was something medically wrong with her. Stan "was not right," she said, a euphemism for whatever the medical diagnosis should have been. "His whole family was not right. Look at Maynard."

Peter saw Stan's actions — all of them — as selfish rotten *choices* that Stan should be held accountable for in perpetuity. Peter had stored the Mrs. Crowell betrayal in his head, a tumour of resentment. My brother saw Stan's "condition" as nothing like Mother's, a definable neurological disease that started in her forties and progressed until she was in a wheelchair. Stan was, Peter believed, just a bad person.

✻

One night, a Lucky Lady co-worker thought she was having a heart attack. Ramona did not own a car, and so I volunteered to drive her to Emergency, saving her the $146.55 ambulance charge. "This is good of you," said Ramona, who then went quiet, too frightened or overwhelmed to speak.

I decided to not leave Ramona alone. The ER is a horror show. Once inside, you feel that you are drunk, or you *should* be drunk because your surroundings are that aberrant. There is no predictable outcome, there is no blanket of humanity. You might as well be lying on your back, hammered on low-grade tequila, slurring jusssstgimmeaaminute as your bed spins. It is that messed up.

Ramona and I took seats in a waiting room with people who had been there for eight hours and had exhausted all sensible conversation. Two men were across from us — one had a gaping hole in his forehead. He had been hit with a hockey puck.

In the time that we were there, the men talked about the game, they talked about a dog named Charger, and then, after running out of topics, they talked about a story in the *Globe and Mail*. The story had reported on a study that said humans, over time, physically change in response to their climate. The study had focused on the

Maasai in Africa who, according to researchers, grew longer limbs to help lose body heat. Conversely, people who lived in the Arctic became proficient at storing body fat.

"I think that whole thing is potentially racist," said the man with the hole in his forehead.

Both Ramona and I were listening, which was easier than making conversation. She had barely spoken since we left the Lucky Lady; she had not even looked at her phone.

It was clear that the man felt good about his injury. He was flaunting it as proof that he had a right to be here, unlike the people like Ramona with invisible ailments who risked being branded a hypochondriac, a grifter, or a bum. The people who go to the ER, if you believe the fallacy, because it is Fun. More Fun than *FarmVille* or Tinder.

"I think you are right," the friend agreed.

"If that was true, we would all have fog-resistant hair. It would be made of Dacron. Everyone in Nova Scotia would have Dacron hair."

"What do you think we'd look like if we lived in a place without fog?"

"I would be taller with better hair."

"My eyes would be properly aligned."

"Why?"

"I dunno, I just think they would."

As interesting as their conversation was, the men went silent when a commotion broke out at one a.m. Suddenly, there were cops and paramedics and a burst of cold air as the automatic doors opened and chaos came inside. The paramedics were tending to a man on a gurney. I could see a pair of red-and-black forester boots sticking out from under a blanket.

"I'd say," said Ramona, speaking for the first time in hours, "that guy got shot."

The cops were escorting an elderly woman. They clutched her arm the way they do when a person requires medical attention but has been involved in a crime or a suicide attempt. A female cop held the woman's enormous purse.

"And," said Ramona, as surprised as I was, "look who it is."

We both knew who the woman was before we saw her face. We recognized the purse, the Ultrasuede skirt, and the paisley scarf of Mrs. Crowell. We had seen her hours earlier at the Lucky Lady. She had been making angry confused faces because the man next to her was wearing leaky iPod headphones, and she could not tell where the sound was coming from. She now looked uncommonly passive.

Before long, all of them — the cops, the paramedics, and Mrs. Crowell — vanished inside, into the area with doctors, the area where everyone wanted to be.

The man with the hole in his head knew the security guard. After the commotion subsided, he ambled over, and while pretending to talk hockey, asked what had happened. He ambled back. It took him a while because he was wearing hockey pants and shin pads.

"What's the deal?" his friend asked half under his breath.

"The old lady," he whispered loud enough for me and Ramona to hear, "shot the dude on the gurney at a McDonald's. She had a gun in her purse. She claimed he cut in front of her in the line, so she super-sized him."

"Where did she get a gun?"

"Her husband used to be a cop. It was his old service revolver."

"Woooaaaaahhhhh."

"Yep."

The friend repeated the news because it was such a good story, "So the old lady shot him."

"Yep."

"Woooaaaaahhhhh."

The victim, it later emerged, was a thirty-five-year-old arborist who owned his own business. Married with two children, he had never been in trouble with the law. Fortunately, his injuries were not life-threatening. The McDonald's night manager told the *Standard* that Mrs. Crowell made no attempt to leave after she shot the arborist; she said she wanted her Big Mac meal. When the paramedics arrived, she complained of chest pains.

Man Gunned Down in Dartmouth Mickey D's
Shooter, 85, Says She Was Hungry

Mrs. Crowell was charged with attempted murder, illegal possession of a handgun, and improper storage of a firearm. Given her age, mental state, and Babs's connections, prison seems unlikely. But the Crowells would have to hire one of the city's three go-to lawyers, and that would be expensive.

The courts move slowly, and at the time of this writing, Doris Bernice Crowell (Hahn was her maiden name) had not had a preliminary hearing or a psychiatric evaluation. A gossip rag printed a story noting that her husband was a retired cop and that her daughter, pictured at a charity event with a wine glass in her hand, was Barbara G. Crowell, QC.

Peter told Suzanne about the shooting, and she told Luke, who then said he was coming home for Christmas. It may have been connected; it may have just been time. Suzanne's contract up North was ending. Molly missed everyone. Luke said that the three of them could go to that windswept park on the ocean with Molly. They could let her get wet. It would be nice. For everyone.

And then, Luke signed off the way he used to when he was in Szeged, racing on the big screen, while coaches on bicycles raced down the course, shouting, *Arrive arrive.*

Love you
Luke
xoxo

*

If Luke's paddling dream ended in a shoddily constructed arbitration process, Peter's ended on a windy racecourse that felt, that day, like a bad dream.

Someone stole Peter's paddle before his race. Mother, Stan, and I were in the stands in Montréal. We had no idea what was happening in the boat bays, which were populated by paddlers, coaches, and the odd hanger-on. All we saw was Peter paddling up to the line, paddling back down in fourth place, and collapsing on the wharf. Gutted.

We did not know that forty minutes before the race, the one for all the marbles, the one that mattered as much as anything in his young life had, Peter's paddle went missing. It should have been in his C1, where he had left it, but it was not. It was gone. The paddle was customized, cut for his height and weight. It was taped at specific points. Peter knew what it felt like in his hands; he knew precisely how it responded to the water. It was a variable he could control.

Sports psychologists say that over fifty per cent of performance is mental, and so when Peter's paddle went missing, there was panic. A blinding panic as he searched the boat bays. A heart-pumping panic as he looked under tarps in boat trailers. And finally, a *this can't be happening* panic as he borrowed a paddle he had never used before, and unsteadily made his way to the line.

It was already a nasty day. It was raining. There was a tricky crosswind that helped canoeists who paddled on the right, and all the gods, it seemed, had conspired against Peter, the race favourite, who paddled on the left.

The race was one of those events that Mother and I never spoke of again. It was too awful.

But Stan, the blamer and shamer, *did* ask one of his unanswerable questions of Peter, the one intended to paint him into a corner of culpability and shame: "Did you have someone watching your paddle when you went to the washroom?" When no one did. You left your paddle in your boat, and it was there when you returned. No one stole it or tampered with it. There was that much honour in the sport, or so you thought.

I always believed that one of the Crowells, the same feral family that fought over the last hot dog, stole Peter's paddle. Two of them had been in the boat bay. I believed it for decades, but I had no proof. I still believed it on the day that Mrs. Crowell shot an innocent arborist.

30

I returned to the Pollock Passage archives. A white-haired woman was that day's caretaker of birth and loss, the kind of loss that sobers a community and keeps it from ever being silly. She was wearing a cardigan as faded as her eyes. She was one of those strangers I immediately trusted. Rightly or wrongly, I believe that they have no game. They have no artifice because they are beyond that — they have reached that time and place when all the good and all the bad have already happened.

If I were shooting the woman, I would shoot her walking through a doorway. Backlit and half in silhouette.

We were the only people there, and so I said, "It's a nice day."

And the woman — her name was Loretta — responded, "Yes, we could use it." We both knew she was going to tell me something important. Only she knew what it was.

I busied myself with old newspapers, while Loretta adjusted a display on Cape Islanders, which are so ubiquitous that it is hard to believe they were only invented in 1905, with two builders from Clark's Harbour given credit, Ephraim Atkinson and William A. Kenney.

The death files were across the room, and I could feel myself drawn in that direction. There was a humming, buzzing energy coming from the computer, and the buzz was the reason I had come back.

"Is there anything I can do?" Loretta asked.

"I am not sure," I said.

She could see that I was stuck on a sandbar of trouble.

"We have old land grants," she offered. "Lists of settlers who came from New England in the 1760s on shallop boats. You can see what they brought. Furniture, fishing gear, and boards for houses. There were no buoys for navigation, so at night they kept together by sending signals from torches. It is all quite interesting. Yes, it is."

"Actually, I've been looking at the records of my family, the Swims."

"So, which of the Swims are you?"

I believe — no, I know — that she already knew my answer, "Stan Swim's daughter, Maynard's niece."

I hoped she was going to tell me that my people were good at something clever like carving decoys or building boats, but she didn't.

"My husband fished near of Maynard. He said he'd be on the water before anyone could dress their feet. My husband was always hunting, too. He was foolish for it, and so was Maynard."

"I found Maynard's records the last time I was here. But I can't find Stan's."

"Everyone knows Nine-Toed Stan."

Hmm.

Loretta may have hesitated — that part is unclear right now. She was, as it turns out, not going to tell me a story about clever ancestors. She was going to tell me a story about Stan, and it would change both the ending and the title of my memoir.

"Did your father tell you how he grew up?"

"Not really. I *did* hear the story of his toe."

"There were many children like your father back then. People did what had to be done."

They chopped off toes? "Of course."

"Those were different times."

"For sure."

"So, you know about the gift children?"

"Of course," I said. She knew that I was lying; we both knew that I was lying in the same way that Vincent and I lied to each other.

Gift children were a fact of life, Loretta started to explain, because this needed explaining. Life was different then, she said. Loretta was being matter of fact, not unkind, the way that people can be when you are vulnerable. Once, when Jack was being released from the ER, and I was hurriedly gathering his belongings, a nurse homed in on me. And maybe I had a glimmer of hope in my eyes, or maybe I was just that exposed. But she sidled up, so close that no one else could hear, and she hissed, "He won't last long." Her cruelty was so sharp, so sudden, that I cried. Loretta was telling me things but not using them as a weapon, not exorcizing a demon of spite. She was just telling.

It was not uncommon for a child to show up at a home where people would raise him as their own, she said. Neighbours did not ask. It was life. The new family found the child a place in a bed with the other children and that was that. Her voice was measured, as though she was showing me an old topographical map. *Look here and here and here.* Leading me to our destination.

It happened for different reasons, she said. Sometimes a family had too many children and sent one to live with a relative who did not. Sometimes, an unwed girl could not take care of a baby. Or a mother died. A child was sent as comfort for a family that had lost a baby. Or a ten-year-old girl was dispatched to help an older sister with her children and never returned.

"Nobody talked about your father." Loretta let the story expand, to douse the room with ramifications." Pause. "He was two maybe."

"That is young."

"I'd say two. Maybe three."

The typical reaction to such a story so large, a story told without permission, would have been, *I don't believe you*, but I *did*. *Was the life of a liar a confluence of lies?*

"So, you don't know where he came from?" I asked.

"That I could not say." And then she whispered, as though she was not supposed to tell, "Not family. Close family anyway."

Not family.

Did Rick know this? Had Graham known this? Did they care?

And then she added, because she knew I deserved more: "I always heard he was from here. My husband heard in or around Boston. He had people there himself. There were different stories."

"I see."

I contemplated the scenario:

> Stan was not the son of Clarence (Lark) and Minnie (Nickerson) Swim.
> He was not the brother of Maynard (Pelly) or the uncle of Graham and Rick.
> He was not the nephew of the murdered Vernon Swim.

I was not genetically linked to a single one of the above individuals, except for Stan. Not the ones who were fine, and not the ones who were "not right."

Who was I?

I could speculate that my father was the biological son of the fabled Captain Ruff Comeau, a headstrong man who shot a pedophile and thieves. A man Stan admired more than the man who raised him.

I could imagine that Stan came up from buttoned-down Boston, where Nova Scotians settled during a mass out-migration from 1860 to 1900. They took jobs in textile factories. Or as housekeepers. They found work as carpenters, using their boatbuilding skills. They clustered in East Boston and continued to build wooden ships; they lived in Dorchester and built houses. They sent gifts back home. Possibly children.

Or maybe Stan was from untamed Cape Sable Island, where people knew the meaning of hard work. Where I may have seen a ghost. Where I had seen stickers. *Freedom not Fear. Salt Life.* I could be anyone, couldn't I? "It was not uncommon." And then again. "It was not uncommon."

That was all she would tell me. And so, in an archives filled with folklore about two-headed sea monsters, I had reached either a dead end or the open highway. I had no Swim DNA to foretell my future. No dead relations. No entitlements or excuses. All that I had was a genetic connection to Peter, Stan, and Mother, and one of them was not normal.

*
*

That night, after I developed prints in my Pollock Passage darkroom, I told Vincent what I had discovered: the story of the gift children. He did not seem that surprised. I liked that about Vincent—nothing surprised him.

Dante, my tragic comic date, was surprised when I told him that Frankenstein and Zorro were not real, and I let that pass. You can lie to yourself about anything, you know. You can convince yourself that someone else is the cause of your problems. You can convince yourself that you are an exemplary judge of character. I have.

After Vincent heard my gift child story, he turned his attention to my prints. He seemed to know more about photography than an amateur would. Maybe he was a quick learner. Maybe he was studying up. Two weeks earlier, Vincent had suggested that I have a show in Yarmouth, and now he was helping to plan it. It would take work.

"These are excellent," he said. "Such details in the shadows. And so many tones."

"Thanks," I replied. "I like them."

Vincent had bought me twenty 16 × 20 inch photo frames, ordered from New York. They were multi-mat metal frames in a black powder-coated finish. They were, I knew, upon seeing them, perfect.

"Should I come into the city with you?" he asked, knowing I was going to see my father. I was going to ask about the gift children.

"No," I told him. "You don't need to meet Stan."

A shrug.

We were both good with that.

*
*

Stan had a tired trick—he would go off on a riff if he wanted to distract you. How many times had he tricked me before his tricks became apparent?

I went to my father's house, and Stan, the gift child, pretended to be reading the newspaper. The question—the one that hung in the air like a foil birthday balloon—was this: Did he *know*? Did his reality surface in moments of stress? On birthdays, when he could be forgiven for wondering who his real relatives were and if they resembled him.

What *do* you remember from the time you were three? Do you remember being dropped off at a house by the ocean? Many scientists say our earliest memories date back to when we were three and a half. Others say further. The earliest childhood memories are always of emotional events, and those events may be good or bad but are always detailed. The earliest moment I recall is being driven to a roadside ice cream stand where the owner kept two black bears in cages. Stan was behind the wheel, and I may have been four.

As children, we were used to Stan not giving us his undivided attention. For a man who made his living staring into the faces of strangers, he was uncomfortable face to face with us. And so, he had a habit of acting busy when we were in his company—he would watch TV or check a pot of spaghetti sauce on the stove.

"I was back in Pollock Passage," I said.

Stan turned a page of the newspaper. Maybe he *knew* that I knew something.

"Clearly you have too much time on your hands. Have you considered a hobby? Pickleball?"

Stan began reading the obituaries for funerals he might attend. When you are a self-made man like Stan, your own creation, do you abandon the tricks that made you? Do you turn your back on the qualities that allowed you to rise above your ordained station in life, a station that may have worked fine for others but not for you?

Stan had moved the bronze sculpture into the living room. The one made by a viewer. The one that looked like Lucille Ball. It was on top of the china cabinet. Next to an urn containing Mother's ashes and another containing those of Mikey the Space Monkey.

After a theatrical pause, Stan put down the paper and looked at me with that *I can't even bear it* look. "What is wrong with people?"

A rather loaded question, I thought, *from you in particular. On this particular day.*

Some things are so absurd, so farcical, that they can, with the proper perspective, be funny. *Was Stan Swim not really Stan Swim?*

When Stan was trying to trick people, he lost the naturalness that had made him a name—he took on the mannerisms of a politician or a dinner theatre performer, the gestures too obvious, too grand.

"There is an obituary for Helen Smiley, a friend of your mother's." He peered over the top of his glasses for emphasis. "The family submitted the most hideous photo they could find. In it, the poor woman is near death with filthy hair and those—what are those things?—oxygen thingies, in her nose."

"Maybe she was on oxygen," I said.

"Maybe I had chicken pox once, and I was covered with sores and calamine lotion. Is that the photo you would put in the paper?" Stan asked.

"It is still *you*."

"And I never, for a single day in my life, looked better than that? Than when I was covered with sores?"

Stan crossed his arms on his chest, and it seemed forced; it seemed like he had watched a tough guy do it in a vintage movie. While he waited, arms crossed, for his last sentence to sink in, I wondered how long this would go on.

What will your obituary say? Stan Swim, the son of Unknown Parents from Parts Unknown, the brother of Persons Unknown? A Gift Child.

"The woman had a good career as a banker," Stan continued. "Do you think she would have had a good career as a banker if she always looked like that? Like a char woman from Dickens."

"Helen Smiley was an attractive woman." I felt a need to defend my mother's friend even though this was ridiculous. "She never looked like a char woman from Dickens."

"She does here."

"Now you sound sexist."

"Sexist? IIIIIIIIII—" he stretched out the word—"am on the poor woman's side."

As Stan sat there with his arms crossed, I thought about blind-siding him, but I did not. This was his life, not mine. I could, at that moment, see a white-haired boy left with strangers in a house with drafty windows and a kerosene heater that smoked. Put to bed next to a mercurial child who one day, in a fit of rage, chopped off the interloper's toe, a mercurial child who was the father's favourite because he resembled him.

I looked at my father who was acting engrossed by the obituaries. Memory is neither true nor objective; it has bias and filters. Who knows what Stan remembered?

Was there a smoke-spewing textile factory where Stan was born?

Were there boys who fished using a wooden square with twine wrapped around it?

Was there a daybed near the wood stove? And was it covered with a worn quilt that felt like cotton batting?

Is this why Stan was "different"? Some people are born sad, the trauma of poverty embedded in their genes; some angry, primed to fight the injustices of the past. Stan was born tricky and a talker. Maybe he understood early on that he needed to ingratiate himself with strangers to survive. Maybe he needed to reinvent himself a second time and a third time, until he became the person he admired. A name.

*
*

Stan's obituary was an issue before this. He had already written it. He had delivered it to me and Peter, with the warning, "It is not to be changed." The obituary did not mention his parents, known or unknown. It did not mention me, Peter, or Mother either, which felt mean. Especially to Mother. It consisted of two words only: "I'm out." It was Stan's final on-air sign-off directed at his most loyal and devoted viewers, Beatrice, Andy, and Georgina, his "family." The people who believed in Baba and sent him Mass cards when the imaginary husky was ill. The people who lined up for sheet cake on Canada Day.

My father lifted his eyes, raising his brows as though he had come across something interesting.

"Ahh, I see that Senator Billy Bow Tie died." Pause. "Just as well."

It was clear that Stan was not going to have a sensible conversation with me. Not about where he came from or who we were. Maybe Stan did not want to think about the people who gave him away because they did not matter to him. Maybe I did not matter. Maybe he did consider Beatrice, Andy, and Georgina his true family. That realization stung, and yet it didn't.

*
*

And maybe, if I am being honest, this story, all of it, was never just about Stan. It was an elaborate exercise — a forensic self-audit — to figure out *Me* and why Jack was so easily stolen from *Me*, with Stan as the central and distracting character. The Name. The trellis to support my own prickly story, the story of *Me* and Jack and what could have been.

Jack had a baby with the woman who stole him—the indie actress/millennial who now has a tiny, framed handprint on her wall. A girl. As beautiful as you might imagine. Jack who said he was too damaged, too afraid of more loss, to have a baby with me. So there it is: My Truth. My heartbreak.

We had "an understanding" about family after Didier was shot, and Jack decided that we should leave Montréal where I was happy. We had an understanding for years—when Jack disappeared on his bike, when he went to the silent retreat in the woods, when I worked at the paper shooting court scenes and cadavers—and what was it worth, that "understanding"? That agreement I thought we had signed off on. That he and I would have to be enough.

When I found out about the baby, I cried and cried. Dicky told me that her name was Scarlett Rose and she weighed eight pounds. She had dark hair. And I cried some more.

Jack bought a running stroller, and he ran through the streets with Scarlett Rose, his beautiful baby, and they never got tired. He had her name tattooed on his arm.

I had miscalculated. I had, through no fault of my own, been tripped up and sprawled on the indoor-outdoor green polypropylene carpet of humiliation and regrets.

My epic fall was far worse than anything I discovered about Stan.

And maybe—and I realize there are too many "maybes" here, too many "ands,"—maybe after rattling my family tree until the frail branches snapped, I have determined what is wrong with me. I am just bad at picking men. I *am* good at other things, meritorious or mundane, but bad at picking men.

31

A Lie of Omission

I promised that this memoir would be truthful. I must confess that I omitted one story, one that *could* connect the dots between Graham's disappearance and his empty apartment. Without this, my story is incomplete, some might say worthless. I had my reasons, but they were, I have now decided, all versions of denial.

The day that Stan and I went to Graham's apartment, something odd happened, besides the odd things I already noted. Mary, the Superstore cake decorator, was in the lobby collecting her mail. She gave us a surreptitious *come see me later* nod.

When Mary opened her apartment door, Stan and I stepped into a space filled with trinkets. It could have been the Bradford Exchange. The wall above the couch featured eight Marilyn Monroe collector plates, all showing Marilyn at her most alluring, one with her white dress blown up, another of Marilyn saucily looking over her shoulder.

Mary's apartment had a La-Z-Boy recliner reserved for her sixty-year-old boyfriend who drove heavy equipment in Fort Mac and came home twice a year. Mary gestured for us to take a seat under Marilyn. We did.

Mary had heard the super talking about Hughie the Twin. Hughie had never, she stressed, stayed in the building. "I don't know who he was trying to fool."

Mary was one of those women who had found her look twenty years ago and stayed with it because it made her happy. It made her as happy as three-layered wedding cake with fondant figurines. Mary's hair was bright blond. She loved the colour pink, and her nails were flawless.

Mary and I were *not there yet*, at that age when you grouse about "young people" being unable to make change in stores. When you join a mad geriatric bike gang clad in matching spandex, and careen through a park screaming at teenagers for "not following the rules." Have you seen them? Grey, bald, flubby. Charging by, blindly, desperately heading for a turnaround with ice cream. And it is the ice cream that seems so aberrant, the way they fetishize it, that common mixture of fat and sugar associated with children's birthday parties and jilted women in rom-coms. Mary and I were *not there yet.*

Mary crossed the room and retrieved the laptop she used to Skype her boyfriend in Alberta. Melvin was his name. She opened it gently; she had a light touch with everything, it seemed. She clicked on an Airbnb page to an ad. "Look at this," she said.

> 14 Cavalier Drive. Clean one bedroom in established building. $100 a day. Fully furnished. Top floor. Good tenants in other units. Privacy guaranteed.

"Well, that is interesting," said Stan.

We hadn't been to the top floor, had we? Graham's apartment was on the first. Slim's the second.

"This Airbnb business had been going on for some time."

"I see."

"This is the gentleman they rented to." Mary clicked on an Instagram page. "He lives—I guess that is the right word for it—in that halfway house up in the industrial park. The modern one. You might have seen it. They had a big opening. During the day he is allowed to go to the gym, and he rents Airbnbs where he can *socialize*." She stretched the word.

The Instagram account belonged to Darren Dodds, who was originally from Newfoundland. Dodds was in his mid-thirties. He had prison-gym bulk and prison-gang tattoos and status-symbol gold chains around his neck. A top bun.

"Convicted murderer. Manslaughter, same thing where I come from. They made him wear an ankle bracelet at first. You could see it under his pants."

A man one crime away from dangerous-offender status.

Occasionally, you shoot a Name Criminal in court, someone who spent his life in and out of prison, and he relishes his bad reputation because that is all he has. He shows up in a shiny suit and flashy alligator shoes, making sure photographers get a clear shot of him. He has a grade 4 education; his mother is a drug-addicted armed robber; and the person he killed was his best friend. That was Darren Dodds. The man I had seen outside 14 Cavalier with the black Chevy Malibu. The man in the topknot. I was sure of it now.

"Ahhh," said Stan, who had suspected the super was up to something. But not this.

"He pays the super in cash. Carries a roll."

On the bell curve of criminality, Darren Dodds would get a top score. He was leagues above Korey St. Clair Scudder and Jesse Fancy, a different breed than the arguably elegant Aksel Andersson. He was a very dangerous man.

Most of Dodd's crimes took place in Newfoundland, so I only shot him once. If you look at his record, there is barely a crime he has missed. Kidnapping. Murder. Armed Robbery. Extortion. Drug Trafficking. Human Trafficking. Weapons charges, including possession of a weapon for a dangerous purpose and carrying a concealed weapon. For starters.

Dodds, whom I did not find the least bit attractive, apparently appealed to others with more liberal tastes. Once when he was being arrested, cops found him inside the home of his lawyer with whom he was "involved." A woman who *must* have had choices. A woman who was clearly worse at picking men than I was.

"I hope, Mary, that he never bothered you," said Stan.

"Oh no," replied Mary. "I stay clear of his type."

Is that why Nightingale and the short detective went to Graham's building? Did they know that Darren Dodds hung out there? Did they go to the fourth floor after seeing off me and Stan with a cheery goodbye? You never know with cops—you think you know where it is going... and then... boom.

"Some of his friends from Renous would spend the day with him," Mary told us. "But he has gone uptown now, Mister Dodds and his Chevy Malibu. He puts it all on the Instagram. You can see for yourself. He rents an Airbnb on the waterfront in one of them towers where the millionaires live. They have a sushi restaurant on the ground floor. A pool."

"Platinum Place?" asked Stan.

Mary clicked on a newer Instagram photo of Darren Dodds posing in front of a floor-to-ceiling window with a harbour view. His arms spread like he was on the bow of the *Titanic*. Dodds was wearing a long-sleeved Jordan T-shirt, black pants, and white high-tops.

She clicked on a second photo of him crouching on the hood of a cop car.

"Yes," Mary said. "So those millionaires is keeping good company. Oh yes, they are. You can see he's got the ankle bracelet off here."

"I know a retired judge in that building," noted Stan. "Lovely man. He has Parkinson's now. I ran into him at the market, and he was so happy to see me. He said 'Stan, you should be back on the air. That new fellow can't hold a candle to you.'"

Mary ignored Stan's aside. "So, what I am trying to say is, I *did* see Graham talking to Mister Dodds here more than once. It worried me at the time. Graham and his little friend Korey."

"Graham had too much sense to get mixed up with the likes of Dodds," stated Stan, when that was not true.

"I felt a need to tell somebody."

"It is good that you did."

"He still comes around from time to time. Mister Dodds. Knows the super."

I had no doubt now that the detectives were interested in Dodds.

"I see."

"I always felt bad for Graham," said Mary. "He told me he used to have a dog. He said he'd like to get another one when he got the money."

"Ah yes," said Stan uncomfortably.

"I think Mister Dodds had a beef with Graham over money. Everything is money."

We thanked Mary for her disclosure, and we left. And we never, and this may be hard to believe, discussed Darren Dodds again, me and Stan.

Stan was in the habit of erasing anything that could show him in a less than flattering light, information that challenged his grandiose self-perception. I had not wanted to think about Dodds because the conclusion was too grim. I did not want to entertain the likelihood that Graham had gone to Pollock Passage to escape Darren Dodds, his "associate," for all the reasons that arise around people like that. And that Dodds had found him. I did not want to be part of that story.

The witness who thought she saw a black Chevy Malibu with smoked windows probably did see a black Chevy Malibu with smoked windows and 20-inch chrome wheels. And Darren Dodds was no doubt inside. That, if I had to guess, is what happened to Graham. He had not hidden in an inland camp, as I had fantasized. He was one of "the 8% of victims killed by someone with whom they had a criminal relationship."

Scientists have done studies on homicide, the micro-environmental and situational dynamics. They try to determine what cognitive and emotional factors lead someone to kill and what factors inhibit them. I do not think that Darren Dodds had any inhibitors. Dodds, who was slick enough to seduce his lawyer, cold enough to kill his best friend.

Pamela told our workshop that a character must be complex — they cannot be all good or all bad because that is unrealistic and boring. I kept that in mind when writing about Stan and Jack. But Darren Dodds was, despite what his delusional lawyer told herself, all bad. That is precisely who he was. The bad man who kills a person as minor as Graham — a person who had six hundred dollars in his pocket for the first time in his life.

I guess — and this is another guess — that the shady super emptied Graham's apartment and pawned the Bruins gnome. He knew that Graham was not coming back. He knew Dodds had killed him. And yes, my fantasy of Graham going to Boston to meet Chára was garbage.

I found an old TV clip of Darren Dodds during one of his court appearances. He had removed his suit jacket, exposing a matching vest over a dark-red shirt that could barely contain his biceps. He had a neck tattoo and a star on his cheek, and his mother sobbed after he was sentenced, telling reporters, "You got to know him — he is very kind-hearted. He got a bigger heart than he is himself."

Not mentioning Darren Dodds earlier was a lie of omission, and that makes me an unreliable narrator, doesn't it? And so, you may wonder what else I have omitted, obfuscated, or glossed over. You may wonder if you can believe a single word I have written. I get that.

The Dream

This is the dream I had one night, the one I willed myself to have:

Jack and I are in a dense woods — I cannot tell where it
is because parts of the dream are vague. He is wearing
running shoes, and I am wearing boots, and we come
across a wedding in a clearing, and it is the strangest
thing. It is like a fairy tale. The bride is a wood nymph,
as beautiful as Jack or my mother, and everything
is surreal. The trees glow with white lights, and the
moss on the ground is not moss but plush green velvet.
Warm to the touch. I cannot see the groom at first and
when I do, it is Didier. The bride is Camille, and she
has a full bouquet and a half veil. There is a softness to
the scene, an unnatural gauze-like softness. The foliage
reminds me of green tissue paper stuffed in a gift bag,
enveloping everything, including us.

From a cloud of velvet and chiffon, Camille says,
"Welcome." And then I ask myself, *Why are we late?*
Why are we not better dressed? I am missing things because
I am too busy being anxious, anxious about a lifetime
of bad decisions. I start to panic because I am ruining everything, and surely Camille must hate me for
running away.

But she smiles. And she says, "Welcome, friends,
to our perfect day in this perfect place." She throws a
flower into the air, and I catch it, and no one is sad or
angry anymore, no one is broken. Jack takes my hand,
and we walk home. And I wake up believing that it all
makes sense, me and Jack, this train wreck they call
Life. I wake up happy.

32

Vincent had made paella, and the Bittenbenders were coming for dinner.

When they arrived, Margaret was excited. Inge and her wife were expecting a baby. Such news. Such news.

"Maybe," Margaret said, "I will go there."

"Well, of course you will," replied Klaus, "your heart is safe to fly. We will put Tracker in a kennel. He is a sociable dog."

Margaret pulled up a new photo of Inge. Her daughter had a blunt nose, flat cheekbones, and Klaus's eyes. Inge's skin was flawless, as though she was shot in a defused light. Otherwise, she was defiantly unadornedly plain, and she stared at life head-on with a take-it-or-leave-it gaze, and that made her beautiful, and that made Margaret, who had too often counted on her conventional beauty, happy. She was happy that Inge was both like her, and not. Inge who redefined the notion of beautiful.

If everything had worked out for me and Jack — if we had stayed in Montréal, if we had had *our* beautiful baby, I would not have given a flying fuck about Stan or Graham or Mrs. Crowell. I *would* have been happy. I would have lived on Serendipity Street, as self-satisfied as I was that night in the desert when Jack and I saw Heaven. But this is where I am.

It was a cool October evening, and I was wearing a maroon velvet dress soft to the touch. As soft as the first time I put it on in Montréal, when life was grand and heightened and less real. Vincent had given me a pair of black open-toed pumps imprinted with tiny flowers. Red, green, and blue. Like the ones I had imagined for a character in a novel. When I crossed the floor, the heels clicked like castanets. *Where*, I wondered, *had he found them?*

"I didn't think I could wear them," I had confessed.

"You can wear anything you want," Vincent had replied. "You can *be* anything you want."

We—the four of us—had plans for the following day. We were going to go to The Hawk, the long unknowable beach on Cape Sable Island, the one with the black petrified forest you can see at low tide. I was going to take photos and, if the wind was not blowing too hard and the fog was not too wet, sit on the sand.

After talk of the beach, Vincent served drinks. He had interviewed a woman, he told us, who lived in Yarmouth.

"Part of your paper?" asked Klaus.

"Yes. At the time of the UFO crash, she was dating a navy diver from the Shelburne base. He was sent to Shag Harbour to search the waters, and he saw things. Not only a spaceship but *actual aliens.*"

Margaret looked skeptical; Klaus narrowed his eyes.

"She had not talked about it before," explained Vincent, "because she was fourteen, and he was in his twenties. It could have been a scandal."

"What isn't a scandal?" scoffed Margaret.

"The diver gave her a vivid description of what he saw—the aliens."

"Ahh," said Klaus, "I am sure that will be good for your paper." And then he proceeded to drink far too much.

*
*

That night I told Vincent what it was that had happened to Didier and Jack in Montréal, and how I tried to keep it a secret from everyone. And Vincent nodded as though he might have had a story just like mine. A story that had scorched the fear from his soul. When I went home the next day, I opened a dresser drawer. Under a pile of street photos was a leather bracelet. It was thin and brown and tied at one end. The oil on the leather, the oil that had darkened it in places, had come from Jack's wrist. I picked up the bracelet and for a moment, it felt warm. And I am not sure if I imagined that or not. Any more than I imagined us in a pub where college students came for burgers, a shabby pub where the waitresses were unflappable, and Jack and I talked as though we knew nothing about each other and everything about each other at the very same time. I put the bracelet in a locked box under my bed, a box that I never opened. I felt a sense of order. The order you feel when you have cleared the air of chaos.

*
*

What Could Have Happened

It was nine p.m., and Vincent and I had been drinking. He wanted to take me to the barn behind the house. On the way there, I saw the red Habs sign, and it was glowing like the lights of a spaceship.

I do things at times like this. I fell in love with a Quebecois paddler I met at Lake Banook when Peter was paddling. I had a fling with my college photo instructor. I got involved with one of the photo playboys, the one with the indecent eyes and the necklace of press passes, the one I vowed to never fall for. Who now lives in a shack in Serbia. But you may have already guessed that.

"The sunsets here are brilliant, aren't they?" said Vincent as he produced a key. "It's the big sky. I feel free in a place with a big sky."

I looked at the sky, and it was big. It was red and pink and purple; it was the colours of a neon road sign at a cheap motel on a nostalgic New Mexico highway where Jack and I stayed after I stole him.

Vincent unlocked the barn door, and the night was quiet. It was that dark rural silence, obscuring the fact that things were happening all around. Important things like men laying out boots, wives already counting the days. Mothers praying. The quiet that makes room in the universe for major things to happen. For Graham and Maynard to disappear without a trace, for a UFO to come and go without a goodbye.

The barn was bigger than I had envisioned. Taking up much of the space was a Model T Ford. It would have been something that I normally paid attention to. I might have touched the black canvas roof. I might have tried the Klaxon horn. I might have wondered how fast it could go on the highway, but I was tipsy, and Vincent was climbing up a ladder and climbing back down with a box in his hand.

Vincent unlocked a metal box inside the locked metal box. Now that the chaos was cleared from the air, there was room for other things. There was a void. Like the one that Stan filled with Graham because he was accustomed to having a degree of turmoil, a vortex of weirdness and disorder, in his life. As was I.

"Tell me what you think of this," said Vincent as he showed me an RPG-7, a shoulder-mounted grenade launcher.

"It's intense," I admitted.

They have been in use since Vietnam and weighed fifteen pounds, Vincent explained after giving me the weapon's name, as though I would possibly know it. He had picked it up in the Congo after he worked as a private security contractor at a diamond mine in South Africa. Before that, he was Special Forces, which is how he met the handlers.

Maybe I should have figured that out. Or maybe I had.

"Why don't you put your glass down?" Vincent suggested. He handed me the weapon, the first firearm I have ever in my insular life touched. Its wood-wrapped tube felt like one of Jack's prized baseball bats, solid and warm. The Model T added a wholesomeness to the scene. It belonged in a Canada Day parade with baton twirlers. It took the edge off the grenade launcher.

"You take it on a bus, and it looks like a keyboard," he said. Vincent put the RPG-7 inside a flat black case to prove his point. "That's the beauty of it. It looks like a keyboard."

I went over things in my mind, wondering what I missed, what I could have/should have put together. Vincent's trips to Halifax, the boat rides off Shag Harbour with a retired fisherman, the strange man I had seen leaving this barn in rust cowboy boots. The *other* gun.

Sometimes you know what is going on, but you pretend you do not because it is better that way.

"But *you* won't have to use it."

"Good to know," I replied, and again, "good to know."

"It's a tool of the trade, that's all."

"Good to know."

And then, as though he was reading my mind, Vincent said, "intelligence" and "Rainbow Lobsters" and "cyberwarfare" and the words sounded, through the filter of wine, reasonable. Vincent looked at me to gauge my reaction, to see if I were in or out, and all I could think of was the woman Dorothy had talked about, the one with the fifty-five-pound canoe on her head: *How many choices did I have left?*

Vincent gave me a smile of reassurance—the wine made it feel more sincere than it was. He knew when he met me, he said, that I was looking for more than Graham. I had gifts. I was that lucky individual whom no one is guarded around.

"Look," he said, "how quickly Margaret came to like you, and she is a terrible snob." Vincent mentioned a ridiculous amount of money, and it sounded like the answer to one of my problems. *Maybe there are rebirths and recalibrations. Maybe this is where I need to go, into an unknown so radical that it overshadows the past, it obliterates everything with an epic degree of strangeness.*

Vincent smiled again, and I thought: *It's never a straight line from A to an Epic Bad Decision.* In the dim light of the windowless barn, he did not look like William Hurt anymore; he did not look like Buck or Jeffrey Delisle. But spies come in many disguises, some better, more subtle, than others.

"And of course," Vincent added, "you *must* take pictures."

"Yes."

"Your show will be amazing."

"Yes."

I believed that it would.

All of a sudden it was not quiet anymore. The night sounded like the booming blasting track of *T2 Trainspotting*. It sounded like that. And how many times did I watch that film? Twenty years after Jack and Didier played the original soundtrack over and over again, thinking they would be spared. And how many times did I smile when Ewan McGregor aka Renton ends up in his childhood bedroom with the weird wallpaper and he dances, all by himself, to Iggy Pop. And I do not know what made me happier: Ewan McGregor dancing, or the fact that he was saved.

Postscript

Darren Dodds, the career criminal I believe killed Graham, was arrested in Dartmouth for breaching a probation order and breaching a recognizance order. At the time of this writing, Dodds was behind bars and was being represented by a Toronto lawyer.

Acknowledgements

I want to thank the amazing team at Goose Lane Editions for bringing this book to life. GLE's brilliant fiction editor Bethany Gibson immediately understood *The Gift Child*. And then made everything infinitely better. Bethany was able to appreciate the characters and their actions, and then ask, because it needed to be asked, "But why?" In numerous places, that query led me one layer deeper, to a place of hurts and hard truths, the stuff of life and fiction. Paula Sarson copy edited this book, ensuring that it was letter perfect. The talented Julie Scriver was responsible for the stunning cover and design. Production editor Alan Sheppard kept all the moving parts moving. Susanne Alexander, Goose Lane's eminent publisher, oversaw everything, and I owe a big thanks to her for her vision.

I would like to acknowledge my family for continuing on this writing journey with me. This is our seventh such adventure. In the past, I have drawn on them for details and feedback. For this book, my husband, Andrew Vaughan, provided technical expertise on cameras, angles, and light. This was invaluable because my narrator is a photographer, and Andrew was an award-winning photojournalist for decades. Parts of this book involve the world of sprint canoe/kayak, which I inhabited when I was young. My children, Hannah and Paddy, as well as my son-in-law, Marc, excelled in this sport and were the athletes I could only hope to be.

Thanks to Dartmouth for being Dartmouth and Shag Harbour for preserving one of Canada's most enduring mysteries.

Elaine McCluskey writes about the aggrieved and the unlucky, people stuck in the margins of life. A "vigorous, colourful and often humorous writer, with a sharp and sometimes wicked eye" (*Globe and Mail*), McCluskey uses humour and Maritime resilience to neutralize the blows of loss, betrayal, and regret that might otherwise destroy us. A former Atlantic Canada bureau chief with the Canadian Press, McCluskey has also worked as a book editor, a writing coach, and a journalism instructor at the University of King's College.

The Gift Child is McCluskey's seventh book of fiction. She has published two previous novels, *Going Fast*, winner of the H.R. (Bill) Percy Award, and *The Most Heartless Town in Canada,* plus four short-story collections, including *Rafael Has Pretty Eyes*, winner of the Alistair MacLeod Prize for Short Fiction. McCluskey's stories have won the Other Voices short story contest and been chosen as finalists for the Journey Prize in Canada and the Fish Short Story Prize in Ireland. They have also appeared in numerous anthologies and journals, including *Room*, the *Antigonish Review*, and the *Fiddlehead*. McCluskey lives in Dartmouth, Nova Scotia.